LUKE

LUKE

Jennifer Blake

This first world hardcover edition published 2011
in Great Britain and in the USA by
SEVERN HOUSE PUBLISHERS LTD of
9–15 High Street, Sutton, Surrey, England, SM1 1DF,
by arrangement with Harlequin Books.
First published 1999 in the USA in mass market format only.

British Library Cataloguing in Publication Data

Blake, Jennifer, 1942-
  Luke.
  1. Women novelists--Protection--Fiction. 2. Louisiana--
  Fiction. 3. Romantic suspense novels.
  I. Title
  813.5'4-dc22

  ISBN-13: 978-0-7278-8008-6   (cased)

All Severn House titles are printed on acid-free paper.

Printed and bound in Great Britain by
MPG Books Ltd., Bodmin, Cornwall.

LUKE

1

April Halstead gripped the phone so hard her knuckles ached. She stared at the book-lined walls of her office with her cane syrup brown eyes wide in disbelief. The words pouring into her ear were crude and vulgar. The radio control booth through which they were being funneled amplified the obscene threat they contained.

This wasn't supposed to happen, not on a live talk radio interview via phone with hundreds of thousands of people listening in. It was like a public assault.

April's heart beat with sickening jolts as she fought the urge to slam down the receiver. She couldn't do it. She was the featured guest on this early morning radio show that reached most of south central Louisiana. She should say something, anything, to stop the tirade, but her mind was blank.

A sharp click sounded as the radio host in his studio miles away broke the caller's connection. "I apologize for that incident, Ms. Halstead," he said in well-rounded, professional tones. "It takes a determined caller to get past our screening, but some crank manages it now and then—one of the perils of a live show. I was taken by surprise, I'll admit.

That reaction is not what you'd expect during a show about love and romance with one of Louisiana's best-known romance novelists. Certainly, it's not the kind of thing a reader would look for in your books. Am I right about that?''

"Absolutely right," April answered. For a split second, she allowed herself to wonder if the show host had let the caller rant those few extra moments just to create a lead for that question. The idea sent a spurt of annoyance through her that helped settle her jangled nerves. "I prefer to concentrate on the dynamics of the male-female relationship—the most important relationship that exists among human beings."

The host wasn't about to touch that claim. "Interesting," he commented. Then he went on quickly, "So, just how do you go about constructing a romance novel? Where do you get your ideas?"

"They come from everywhere, newspaper clippings, magazine articles, sometimes just a comment overheard at the grocery store." April reeled off the rest of the response she'd given a thousand times during more than nine years of interviews since her first book had hit the bestseller lists. Her usual feeling about such stock questions was resignation, but now she was happy to be able to supply an answer that didn't require fast thinking. The talk session continued with the host's semiembarrassed jocularity for the intimate nature of romance writing and reluctant admiration for someone who had managed to sell several million books. There were, thankfully, no more surprises.

Minutes later, April said her routine thanks for

the radio host's interest and hung up the phone. She clasped her hands tightly together on her desktop to still their shaking. Squeezing her eyes shut, she breathed deep in an effort at composure. The interview was a jumble in her mind other than the first one or two questions. She had no idea whether it had gone well or been a complete flop.

The pressure inside her brain made her feel sick. The urge to jump up and pace while cursing and screaming was so strong she barely subdued it. What held her back was the fear that once she started, she might not be able to stop.

She didn't like phone interviews, even if they could be done from the comfort of her own home while wearing her scruffiest jeans and sweatshirt. They were much too impersonal and it was hard to judge the purpose and direction of questions without visual clues. The call-in radio shows were the worst since it was impossible to guess what people were like or what they might say. Still, she'd never before fielded an obscene call while on the air. That kind of cheap shot was upsetting in the privacy of her home, much less with half the state listening.

Book promotion in general tore her nerves to shreds. Why writers were expected to excel at it was a great mystery. Most were natural introverts; April had begun writing years ago at least in part because putting words on paper was easier than speaking them aloud. She'd learned to do media interviews because they were part of the job, but getting psyched up for them was always a major effort. It amazed her when someone told her she was good at the promo business since she couldn't see it herself.

She'd been expecting to be revealed as a fraud for some time. Maybe that day had come. It would be about right. Nothing else in her life was going as it should just now.

The doorbell shrilled. April jumped and inhaled with a sharp sound. Before she could force herself to move, it pealed again, an impatient summons from the antique brass pull at the front door of the old Louisiana mansion. She slid from her desk chair and went to see who was visiting at this early hour.

A man stood on her front porch with his hands on his hips and a frown on his face. As she peered through the lace curtain over the door's sidelights, she could see his hair shining with blue-black luster, his eyes like rain-wet obsidian. His copper-tinged features might have been taken from a painting of some noble Native American. Tall in a rangy fashion, he was as handsome as the devil incarnate and as careless of that fact as he was of nearly everything else that had a name.

Luke Benedict.

Luke-de-la-Nuit, some called him, or Nighttime Luke. Easily the most irritating man in the town of Turn-Coupe—or in all of Tunica Parish for that matter—he had a positive genius for showing up when he wasn't wanted. Such as now.

April leaned her head against the thick oak of the old door and closed her eyes. This was too much. She had a phone nut on her hands and Martin, her ex-husband, was trying to worm his way back into her good graces. Her newest book had received a devastating review, and that had led to writer's block over her work in progress. On top of all this, her white elephant of a house needed repair work. The absolute last thing she needed was to deal with Luke Benedict.

Luke's knuckles thudded on the opposite side of the wood directly above her head. April sighed and raked her fingers back through the golden brown length of her hair. Then she jerked the door open.

"Are you all right?" Luke demanded. "I was listening to the interview on the Jeep radio when that creep came on."

Of course he'd been listening, she thought with exasperation. It could have happened no other way. "I'm fine," she said with a dismissive gesture. "You can go on about your business."

He ignored the suggestion as if she hadn't spoken. "You know the guy? He sound familiar?"

"No to both questions." That was not the exact truth, but she wasn't about to give Luke anything he might use as a lever to pry into her affairs. Someone with a similar voice had called a week ago, waking her at three in the morning. At least she thought the voice was similar, though the caller had said little that time. Still, it was accepted wisdom that heavy breathers weren't usually dangerous, wasn't it?

"What set him off? Any idea?"

"I expect he's just a few bricks shy of a load. Really, it's no big deal."

Luke's gaze moved over the oval of her face as if noting her paleness and the fine lines of strain around her wide-set eyes. "Right. I know radio stations have a second or two of time delay built into the broadcast so they can cut off a caller like that before he goes too far. You probably heard more than the listeners did. Was there no clue where he might have called from?"

"I think it was a cell phone. Look—"

"You should call Roan."

Roan was the sheriff of Tunica Parish as well as a member of the huge and far-reaching Benedict clan that formed a tight enclave around Horseshoe Lake where April's house was set. Everyone always called Roan.

"What is he supposed to do, tell me that? I have no name to give him, no description, no motive, nothing."

"The radio station must have gotten some kind of information from the guy before they let him on."

"No doubt, but what do you the think the chances are that it's accurate?"

Luke was silent a moment, watching her while a muscle clenched in his jaw. When he spoke again, his voice was rough. "He threatened you—I got that much, even if I didn't catch all the words. It should be a matter of record. Call Roan."

"I don't have time to waste complaining about something that can't be fixed! I have a book to write, a deadline to meet. Besides, you're blowing this all out of proportion. Whoever the guy may have been, he was just getting his kicks out of the situation. If it doesn't bother me, I don't see why it should bother you."

"You're not bothered, huh?"

She shook back her hair as she gave him a stiff smile. "Not in the least."

"Just one of those things, right? No sweat."

"Exactly," she agreed, refusing to back down in spite of the sarcasm in his voice.

"Then why," he said as he stepped over the threshold and snatched her hands in his own, "are your fingers like ice and your lips so blue you look like you ought to be in bed?"

"With someone to warm me up, I suppose?" She tugged at her fingers, trying to free herself. The heat of his hands, the strength of his grasp and the sense of power that radiated from him through it, made her feel weak in the knees. She had to fight off the urge to lean into his bountiful protection and the safety he represented, if only for an instant.

"I didn't say that," he answered with a slow smile curling a corner of his mouth. "But if you're looking for a volunteer..."

"No!"

He released her abruptly, his humor vanishing. "I didn't think so. But don't try to con me by telling me you're not afraid, either. You're scared spitless, so why not admit it."

The description touched her on the raw, perhaps because it was so true. She reached instinctively for her ultimate defensive weapon: words, sharp-edged and lethal words. "Shall I wring my hands and cry prettily while begging you to save me? That may be feminine as all get-out, but it's also useless and old-fashioned. Rescue, I seem to remember, was never your strong suit."

"*God, April.*"

The disbelief that laced his whisper was as vivid as the pain in his eyes. He fell back a half step while dusky red stained his skin.

Regret touched April for the blow she'd dealt with her quick tongue. She hadn't realized he could be hurt quite so deeply by that slanting reference to past events. At the same time, she'd opened a shared wound that was never mentioned between them, had not been in thirteen long years. To acknowledge the error, however, would give that long-ago incident more power than it deserved. She stared at him without reply.

His face tightened. "Right. But if you'll remember, honey, I didn't offer to ride to the rescue. That's Roan's job."

It was also the only real suggestion Luke had made. Rattled by the earlier call as well as the man in front of her, she had turned it into something else, something personal. That was a major mistake. Though they went back a long way together, she and Luke, there was nothing personal whatsoever between them, not any more.

For the briefest of seconds, she recalled a velvety summer twilight with the lavender-rose of sunset spilling in a watercolor wash across the stillness of the lake. The whisper of a breeze coming over the water. Two young bodies entwined, hot and breathless in discovery, on a crumpled quilt beside the remains of a picnic. A portable tape player pouring out the strains of *Afternoon of a Faun*.

To this day, she couldn't stand to listen to Debussy. Nor could she stand to think of it now.

She grasped the door's edge, preparing to close

it in defiance of all the tenets of hospitality instilled in childhood, hospitality that insisted that a person offering aid and comfort should at least be invited inside. "I don't need anyone's help," she said, her voice as steady as she could make it.

He put out his hand to hold the door open. "Oh, we're clear on that. You'd rather be raped by some weirdo than let me set foot in your house, much less in your life. Got it. You don't need me, or anyone else. Only what the hell are you going to do all alone in this huge old place if somebody comes after you? A whole army could march in the back way and you'd never hear. Do you have even a pistol in the house?"

"For what, target practice at a stray roach? I prefer less noisy pest control."

He stared at her an instant, then his face changed as comprehension rose in his eyes. "A gun is just a weapon," he said quietly. "It doesn't kill by itself."

Not many people could follow her serpentine thought processes or catch her more oblique references. That Luke could when he made the effort had been one of the strong points of their relationship years ago. She'd forgotten that. The meeting of minds left a disturbing feeling of intimacy. Her voice carried acid rejection of that sensation when she spoke. "I'll remember you said so next time I put flowers on my mother's grave."

"And what will you remember when somebody puts a knife to your throat?"

She lifted a hand to her neck, then let it drop

again in an abrupt movement. "What would you like me to think about? That you warned me?"

"What I'd like," he said deliberately, "is to know you're safe. I'd like to know that nothing I did a thousand years ago turned you into the kind of recluse who winds up alone in a decrepit mansion, dying in a pool of her own blood because she's too afraid of living to let anybody get near enough to help."

The words were like blows and she felt every one. With a grim smile, she said, "You give yourself too much credit. My ex-husband deserves the major part. Not to mention an ex-publisher and a critic or two."

"At least you admit the possibility. That's something."

"Is it? Avoiding pain can be an intelligent decision."

"It's a cop-out," he declared. "Being alive is a painful business, but the alternative isn't very exciting."

"I don't need excitement."

Unholy amusement shone in the dark depths of his eyes. "You don't know what you're missing."

Oh, but she did, and it was all there in the wicked curl of his firm lips, the latent strength of his square, competent hands. She said with disdain, "Is that what you call living? A new woman every week, laughing, drinking and copping a few minutes in a strange bed? From where I stand, it looks like another way of avoiding the real business of living."

"Which you, a sensitive, artistic type living

solely in your mind and your scribbled fantasies, know all about?''

''I know,'' she said in stark admission.

''Then why don't you have a permanent man and a house full of kids passing out hugs and heaven?''

His answer proved that he knew, too. She inhaled sharply against the sudden stab of that understanding. Or perhaps it was the prick of old dreams, since she'd once thought her children would look like the man in front of her.

''I did try for that,'' she said evenly. ''Can you say the same?''

''All but the legal step.''

''I can imagine,'' she said in ironic reference to his swinging image. At the same time she remembered hearing that Luke had been serious about some girl from out of town a few years back. When it had come to nothing, she'd figured it had been just a rumor.

''I doubt you have the full picture,'' he said. ''The lady hated country life in general and Turn-Coupe in particular. She expected me to sell Chemin-a-Haut and move to New Orleans.''

''Sell a place that's been in your family for nearly two hundred years? And she really thought you might? What a jewel!''

His smile was brief. ''Shiny bright and about as hard. I'd have let her keep the engagement ring except she threw it at my head.''

''You got as far as planning a wedding with no idea of what she liked or really wanted?''

He shoved his hands a few inches into the pockets of his jeans as he looked away to follow the flight of a mockingbird. "I was distracted by other things."

"Were you really?" The drawled comment was supposed to be in recognition of the driving force behind most of his recent relationships, that of pure sexual attraction. Instead, it sounded sour.

"She reminded me of you." He swung back to meet her gaze as he spoke. His face was expressionless, but something dark and disturbing lay in the liquid depths of his eyes.

"I expect you had a lucky escape then." The fast retreat from that personal comment was instinctive. How had they gotten onto the subject of his love life? It was not something she wanted to hear about in detail—or at all.

"Is that how you think of your divorce, an escape?"

"My divorce is something I prefer not to talk about."

"I've noticed. That bad, huh?"

"That far behind me. Luke—"

"Yeah, yeah, you want me gone. Fine." He half turned away before swinging back again. "But if you hear from the nut on the phone again, let me or Roan know, will you? It may be nothing, but it could turn out to be something else again."

Agreeing seemed a small concession if it would send him on his way. "I'll keep it in mind."

He moved off the porch and into the morning sunshine. The swing of his long legs was free and natural, with the athletic fluidity provided by excellent muscle conditioning. His shoulders were wide and straight before they tapered into the lean lines of his waist and hips. Like some male animal of the deep woods, he was at ease with his body and sublimely unconscious of its innate power and grace.

Why was it, April wondered, that some men looked as good walking away as they did face-to-face? It was as disturbing as it was unfair. She was paying attention strictly for research purposes, of course. She needed to make mental notes for the next time she described the way the hero walked in her work in progress.

Abruptly Luke turned around. He backed up a couple of quick steps as he stared up at the roof of her house. A frown drew his brows together before he called to her, "You lost a few roof slates in the storm the other night. I noticed when I drove up since I've been replacing the casualties at Chemin-a-Haut. You have any leaks?"

She had a small one in the stair hall and a more drastic one in the back bedroom upstairs. They were none of Luke Benedict's business, however, like the rest of her life. With precision, she said, "Nothing I can't handle."

"I could take care of it for you. Roofers charge an arm and a leg for patching these big old houses, you know. They get nervous climbing around on anything higher off the ground than a story and a half."

"You don't, I suppose," she said dryly.

"I'm used to it after crawling around on top of Chemin-a-Haut all my life."

The temptation to take him up on his offer was strong. She'd stayed awake for several nights worrying over who to call for the repair job and how she was going to manage to pay them. Regardless, becoming involved with him in any way wouldn't be smart. In polite rejection, she said, "I'm sure you have better things to do."

"Doesn't matter. We're neighbors, and out here on the lake neighbors help each other. It's been that way since the days when it was twenty miles into town over rough wagon roads so you learned to count on the man next door."

"These aren't olden times," she said shortly. "I can manage."

He grunted before a frown of dissatisfaction drew his thick brows together. "You should have whoever comes out check the windows, too, make sure the sashes aren't loose in the frames. Your heating and cooling system will work better, not to mention your latches."

"You see a security problem?" She stepped out onto the porch then moved to join him on the walk. Facing the house, she scanned its wide, graceful facade, her gaze running over its spreading bungalow roof, the massive columns that supported the upper gallery, the mellow peach color of the plastered walls and the graceful arched insets that held the windows and doors.

"I doubt half your window locks would keep out a two-year-old," he answered.

The glance she gave him was scathing. "You're just saying that to scare me."

"Think so? You want to go back inside and lock up, then see how long it takes me to get to you?"

"No, thank you!" She couldn't prevent the gooseflesh that pebbled the surface of her skin.

Some of the locks could use a few new screws, now that she thought about it.

He glanced down at her, his gaze measuring. "You're afraid, admit it."

She shook her head but couldn't quite manage a complete denial.

"I could stick around a while, at least until you're sure your caller isn't going to pay a visit. I wouldn't even have to come inside since I see plenty to do out here. You could forget I was on the place."

Forget he was there? Not likely. She parted her lips to answer, then stopped as she caught a soft sound. It was a stealthy rustling coming from around the corner of the house. Abruptly, it stopped.

Luke moved at lightning speed to catch her arm and draw her behind him. He faced in the direction of the noise. For long seconds, nothing moved. The only sound was the sigh of a lake breeze through the great mulberry tree that gave Mulberry Point its name and the calls of birds enjoying the warm summer morning.

The dry scratching came again, closer this time. Luke tensed.

Then from around the end of the house stepped a sleek black cat. Its coat shone in the sun like silk and its ears were cocked forward inquiringly. In its mouth, carried like a kitten, was a wriggling peridot green chameleon.

A short, winded laugh escaped April; she couldn't help it. Luke said something under his breath that maligned all felines. The cat gave him a look of disdain before moving forward to deposit his prize at April's feet. The chameleon made a wild dash for freedom and the cat leaped after it, catching it with a quick pounce. April sprang forward and scooped her pet up in her arms before he could inflict further damage. The heavy swath of her hair slid forward to lie like dark gold silk against the satin of the cat's pelt before she flung it back out of the way behind her shoulders.

"Good boy, Midnight," she crooned as she cradled him against her chest and rubbed behind his ears. "You're a fine cat and mighty dragon slayer. I'm proud of you."

"He's a damn nuisance," Luke said in disgust as he eyed the animal in her arms.

She hid a smile as she brushed the big cat's fur with her cheek. "That's right, you're not a cat lover, are you?"

"Give me a dog any time."

"It's all right, isn't it, Midnight," she murmured. "He just doesn't know you. He has no idea what a fine watch cat you are."

"Watch cat," Luke repeated in pained accents.

"He sleeps on the foot of my bed and gives an earsplitting howl whenever anything disturbs him."

An arrested look appeared in Luke's dark eyes. "Does he now? How does he feel about sharing the covers with a third party?"

"Since the situation hasn't come up, I have no idea." Her voice cooled by several degrees as she added, "Anyway, he's all the protection I need."

"Sure," Luke replied, setting his hands on his hips. "I can see you're nice and safe—if it's a lizard that shows up in the middle of the night. I'd point out that a cat's no substitute for a man in your bed, but I'm sure I'd be wasting my breath.''

''And my time.'' Common sense might have told her to leave it at that but she wasn't listening. ''Though I guess preoccupation with what's going on in bed should be expected from a man who has been in and out of every female's in Tunica Parish.''

''Except yours—but who's keeping score? And why should you notice, sweetheart, much less care?''

''Why indeed?'' she asked with a twist to her smooth, beautifully formed lips. ''I just think it's juvenile, egotistical and far more dangerous these days than my getting a call from a heavy breather.''

A dark scowl drew his brows together. ''So it might be, if I deserved half the credit people gave me.''

''Poor, misunderstood Luke-de-la-Nuit. I guess all the women who claim you're hotter than Cajun spice are building up your reputation to make themselves look good.''

''Could be,'' he answered, the words scathing. ''Don't you wish you knew?''

She inhaled in sharp outrage as she searched for the perfect annihilating remark as a comeback. Before she could find it, Luke turned and stalked toward his Jeep that sat on the circle drive.

''I do know,'' she called after him finally. ''Or have you forgotten?''

With his hand on the vehicle door, he faced her again. His eyes burned and there was dark color under the deep olive of his skin. ''That was a long time ago,'' he said with precision. ''Things change. So do people.''

He climbed in the Jeep and turned the key, then pulled away down the drive. He didn't look back.

April stared after him while anger swelled inside her. What an arrogant, presumptuous, stiff-necked know-it-all! She'd die before she'd let him touch a single board or pane of glass at Mulberry Point. She didn't need Luke Benedict, didn't want him, and didn't care beans about his well-earned reputation. How good he might be in bed never crossed her mind.

Well, she might think about it when she wrote a love scene, but that was different. It was a part of her job.

No, she neither wanted nor needed his services, thank you very much. All she required was to be left alone in her house with her cat and her stories. To the devil with the man.

Regardless, she'd gained one bit of information from his visit. It was something she'd wondered about for a long time. The answer was interesting and, as much as she hated to admit it, even satisfying.

Luke *did* remember.

2

Luke was several miles away from Mulberry Point before his temper began to cool. He shouldn't let the things April said bother him, but he couldn't help it. She had a positive genius for getting to him. Some of her barbs were like snake bites; he felt the sting when they struck but only minutes afterward did the real poison reach the heart.

Not that she intended it to happen that way, he thought. She didn't realize how thin his skin was these days. Nobody did, and that's the way he liked it.

He hadn't seen a lot of April in the year that she'd been back in the area after buying the old Tully place. Her showing up for his Memorial Day open house earlier in the summer had been a fluke, he'd thought. She'd come with his cousin Kane for moral support when Kane had been in trouble with his red-haired Yankee lady, Regina. Kane and Regina had finally straightened out their problems. Luke wondered how April felt about that, since she and Kane had been thick for a while back in high school and still had a mellow kind of friendship. April would be attending the wedding, he knew, since Regina had asked her to be maid of honor. That might get interesting since he was Kane's best man.

Jeez, but he'd nearly lost it when he'd heard that jerk on the phone mouthing off to April. He hated that kind of low-down junk anyway. To think of her being subjected to it set his teeth on edge. April hadn't been too happy with him for showing up on her doorstep because of the call, but he was glad he'd gone. He knew now just how upset she'd been about it.

Maybe he could get a tape of the show from the radio station. Roan had some fancy equipment that he might be able to use to analyze the caller's voice or isolate any background noise enough to identify it. As the sheriff, Roan really needed to know about the incident anyway, and Luke intended to see that he did. April might not thank him for looking into the mess for her, but he'd manage to live with that. He'd given up expecting anything from her long ago.

He was passing Chemin-a-Haut again, since April's place was a few miles down the road from his own. He'd been heading to town when her interview came on the radio, and had turned around to check on her. He wouldn't stop at home now, but go on into town.

The sight of his neat green fields stretching row after row toward the distant tree line never failed to lift his heart—even when he frowned over a weed-clogged drainage ditch. He liked farming, enjoyed the smell and feel of the earth. The backbreaking labor in sun and rain and the intrinsic uncertainty didn't bother him; the constant challenge kept him on his toes. There was no place on earth he'd rather live than on this modern plantation with the lake at the back door of his big, old West Indies style house, and the swamp beyond that crowded right up to the levee of the Mississippi River. Turn-Coupe was right down his alley as well. A sleepy little town dating back to before the Civil War, it was big enough to supply his needs, but not so big that people didn't nod and speak when they met. He fully intended to live out his life here. It still surprised him, however, that April had apparently decided the same thing.

She'd mentioned the wreck. That was amazing. Not that she'd spoken the words, but the subject had been there between them all the same. The twisted metal, the fire, the screams had hovered close, so close that he'd thought for a second that he saw them reflected in her eyes. He wished he knew what it meant after all these years. Understanding that much might make having it thrown up to him again worthwhile.

The need to ask her had been so strong he could taste it. What kept him from it was the same thing that had held him silent back then: pride, sheer stubborn masculine pride. He clung to it now as a last refuge, he thought, since it was all he had left.

April certainly hadn't forgiven him any more than he'd forgiven himself, that much was for damn sure.

A short time later, Luke pulled his truck into a parking place in front of the courthouse. The sheriff's office was located on the lower floor of the old antebellum era building with its graying marble walls and white columns. There had been some attempt to modernize the place with safety rails on the granite steps and a wheelchair ramp, but it hadn't helped a lot. It was a relic from the past with an air of solid strength, heavy responsibility, and not a lot to offer in the way of comfort. It was, Luke had often thought, a lot like Turn-Coupe's sheriff himself.

Luke found his cousin in his office. Roan's hair looked like he'd been combing it with a John Deere and a cultivator, and a harassed frown drew his brows together over the bridge of his nose. Seeing Luke, he stacked the papers he'd been reading and laid them aside on one of several neat piles. His lean face creased into smile lines.

"Morning, cousin. Coffee?"

"Black, strong, sweet as an angel and hot as hell."

"What other kind is there?" Roan pushed to his feet with a lithe movement and sauntered over to the coffee machine that was always going in one corner of the big corner room. Speaking over his shoulder as he reached for cups and sugar packets, he made some comment about the big River Pirate Revel, the town festival coming up at the end of the month. They exchanged views, plans and a couple of funny stories about the arrangements for that shindig. They talked about the price of cotton futures, a concern for Luke since he made his living raising cotton and soybeans, then segued into another passion they shared: bass fishing. Roan glanced at Luke a couple of times as if he suspected something was up, but he didn't press it at once.

Finally, when they were both on their second

cups of coffee, the sheriff leaned back in his chair and crossed one booted ankle over his knee. "So," he said, "are you just visiting, or you got something on your mind?"

"Both," Luke replied with a rueful grin.

Roan studied him, his gray eyes alert. "So shoot."

Luke told him the story of April's radio caller, including his own quick trip by her house to check on her. For the hell of it, he even added his own suspicion that she might have heard from the person before. When he was done, he sipped his coffee and waited.

"April say she'd had other calls?"

"Not in so many words. It was more what she didn't say, if you know what I mean."

"Did she tell you what she thought it was about? If there was a reason beyond the usual jerk-off session?"

"She doesn't have much to say to me at the best of times. You might get more out of her if you drove out there."

Roan gave a judicious nod, though his gaze was on the brew in his cup.

"So, what will you ask her? Got any ideas?" The question was abrupt, but Luke made no attempt to soften it.

"A few." Roan leaned back in his chair as he rattled them off. "What about her ex? Where is he, and what was he doing this morning? Has she made any enemies? Has she had any contact with strange men in the past few weeks such as dates, repairmen, deliverymen, and salesmen? Any new men in her life and how did she meet them? Have any unusual calls been made to her home that are unconnected to the radio incident? Has she had any visitors out of the ordinary or noticed any activity around her house that strikes her as strange? Things like that.''

Luke signaled his understanding. He wasn't sure how much good any of it would do, but getting the answers would be a start.

''What I was really wondering about is this book she's supposed to be working on,'' Roan said with a thoughtful twist to his lips. ''The local angle, you know?''

''What book? What local angle?''

''About the Benedicts. She's using the family background for a story or series of stories, according to the tale going around. Seems she talked to Kane's Aunt Vivian last week—which is about like broadcasting the news to the countryside. Don't tell me you haven't heard.''

''I'm not in the thick of things like you.'' Luke grimaced. ''But why in the world would she want to write about us?''

''Not us, but our great-granddaddies. They were a pretty colorful bunch back in the old days.''

''No more than most around here. Why not pick on her own kin?''

''Too close to see the attraction, I expect.'' Roan looked at him over the rim of his coffee cup. ''Besides, she might stir up that business about her parents, and that's the last thing she'd want.''

Luke stared at his thumb as he smoothed the handle of his coffee mug. His voice carefully neutral, he said, ''Have you ever looked into all that, since you were elected, I mean? I know it was a long time ago and there's no reason to go into it, but I've always wondered if it happened the way everybody said. Did her dad really shoot her mother while April watched?''

"And then turned the gun on himself. At least that's the gist of it that I got the one time I glanced at the file. You can go through it closer if you want."

Luke nodded his appreciation for the offer. It was the sort of quiet accommodation often made among relatives and friends in small towns, but it meant a lot. "She was all of what? Five years old, six?"

"Five. She didn't testify at the trial, didn't say a word of any kind for nearly six months—mental trauma, according to the doctor's report. It's all in the file."

Sick pity flooded Luke, along with rage that no one had been there for her back then and there was nothing he could do about it now. He said tightly, "I think it still bothers her."

"I wouldn't be surprised. The doctor theorized that she'd retreated into a fantasy world where everything was safe and rosy. Could be she still lives there."

Luke made a scoffing sound. "I didn't mean that she can't function as a normal person, or anything like that. She's fine on the surface—only it seems as if it still affects her and the things she does. It gives her a different slant on people."

"You're thinking of that business with the wreck, when that girl was killed," Roan suggested, his voice deep.

"Yeah."

"It wasn't the same."

Luke looked up. "Wasn't it? Mary Ellen Randall ceased to exist one fine summer night thirteen years ago, and I'm to blame."

"You didn't kill her."

"She was riding in my car when she shouldn't have been. It ran off the road. She died, screaming, while I stood and did nothing."

Roan set his cup down and leaned forward in his chair with his hands clasped loosely together on his desk. "There was nothing you could have done. Let it go."

"Yeah." Arguing wasn't going to help, Luke knew that only too well. Some things couldn't be understood without having been there. Nor could they be shared. After a moment, he said, "To get back to what you were saying, there are Benedicts who might not want their family trees shook all that hard, either."

"Such as?" Relief for the return to a neutral topic flashed across the other man's face.

"Granny May, for one. I may think it's a hoot that her granddad earned the money for his first Model T by peddling bootleg booze to half the politicians in town, but she still turns as red as a beet when anybody mentions it. She'd like to forget about the Indian woman in our family tree, too, not to mention the great aunt who ran off from her husband and three kids to become a—what is it Granny May calls her, a floozy?—in the gold camps of Colorado."

Roan grinned at him as he said, "You should

have a circuit riding preacher in your bloodlines, an upstanding, hell-and-brimstone, hard-shelled Baptist saver of souls who just happened to have three wives in as many states. Your Granny wouldn't know whether to be embarrassed or proud as punch.''

A preacher in the family was usually a big deal in the Bible Belt. One with scandal attached to his coattails was a little hard to place in the normal scheme of things. Luke shook his head as he said, ''Your great granddad, wasn't he? I'd about forgotten.''

''Right—and he was a saint compared to some of the other outlaws. But I was wondering if maybe some of the crowd out on the lake might not be getting back at April.''

Luke shook his head. ''They're a wild bunch, some of them. But that just means they're even less likely than tamer types to give a damn for how they might appear in a novel. Hell, most of the guys would probably get a kick out of it.''

''Doesn't have to be a guy.''

''No? I didn't know women were big on obscene phone calls.''

''It happens.''

''In a male voice?''

''Ever hear of phones that disguise voices? A lot of women living alone have them to make it sound as if there's a man in the house.''

Luke gave him a look of dry reproach. ''Are you suggesting my dear old Granny knows anything about the kind of suggestions that were made to April on the phone?''

"You've got a point," Roan answered on a dutiful laugh. "I'll look into the situation, but there's not much else I can do without April's cooperation. Even if we manage to run down the perp, a warning is about as far as we can go until he does something besides talk."

"You could warn him clear out of the country." Luke meant that exactly as it sounded.

"Suppose I might, depending."

"On what?"

"Who he is, whether he has a record, how much of a threat he appears to be. In the meantime…"

"In the meantime?" Luke repeated as his cousin paused.

"Somebody should keep an eye on April. I don't like the sound of this guy going public. It's a flag, behavior out of the norm."

"I already offered. She turned me down flat."

"So, don't let her know."

"Fine idea. And who's going to vouch for me when she has me picked up for loitering with intent and assorted other offenses?"

"I will—so long as the offenses don't get committed."

"Roan, son," Luke said, "you wound me. Would I do anything like that?"

"In a heartbeat, given provocation."

"Then we'll have to hope April doesn't get to feeling provocative, won't we?" The corners of Luke's mouth tilted upward as he leaned back in his chair and stretched his long legs out in front of him. "So, where do I volunteer?"

"I'm not joking," Roan warned.

"Neither am I," Luke said, his black gaze level as he stared across the desk.

"As long as we have an understanding. If that's settled, what about New Orleans?"

Luke tried to make the connection, but there was none as far as he could see. "New Orleans?"

Roan reached to lift a piece of cream-colored stationery from the top of a two-drawer file cabinet. With a flip of his wrist, he spun the open page across his desk.

Luke caught it by reflex action, then held Roan's serious gray gaze an instant before he looked down. The letter in his hand was from April. A photo of her in an oval frame stared up at him from the page. For a second, his whole attention centered on the secretive depths of her eyes, the intriguing shadows under her cheekbones, the sensuous yet sensitive curves of her mouth and her neat tip-tilted nose. He swallowed hard before he looked up again.

"What's this?"

"April's newsletter. She sends one out every quarter. Don't tell me you didn't know."

"How come you get one when I don't?"

"Not me, my secretary. Glenda's a big fan." Roan twitched a shoulder. "I glance over it when I have the time. This is the summer version, came last week. It says April will be down in New Orleans this weekend to speak at some conference."

Luke frowned. "Is that good or bad?"

"Hard to say. If her problem is local, it's good. If not—"

"Then there's no telling how many people know about it, if not from her newsletter then from the literature sent out about the conference. If she's really in any kind of danger, she'll be an easy target.''

''Exactly.'' Roan paused, then said deliberately, ''Her ex, Martin Tinsley, still lives in New Orleans.''

Luke cursed in a quiet monotone. After a moment, he asked, ''What kind of security do they have at these conferences?''

''Not much, I'd imagine. She's an author, not a rock star. The people she'll be talking to are writers and would-be writers, most of them women. In the normal course of things, problems should be nil.''

''But are things normal or not?'' Luke asked, speaking almost to himself as he stared down at the details of the New Orleans meeting. The thing started early Saturday morning. April would probably be driving down this evening.

''Who knows?'' Roan answered in grim tones. ''The only thing you have to go by is gut instinct. So, what does yours say?''

''That I'd better pack a duffel bag and gas up the Jeep.'' Luke stood up, put his coffee cup on Roan's desk, and started toward the door.

''Cuz?''

He turned back, though something in Roan's voice told him he might be better off if he kept going.

Roan got up, dug a file out of the beat-up cabinet behind him, then handed it across his desk. As Luke took the folder marked Halstead, Roan held on to it. With his brows almost meeting in a frown, he asked finally, ''Why?''

"Why what?" Luke had to ask, though he thought he knew.

"Why this sudden interest in April?"

"What's sudden about it? I've always been interested in April—I've known her all my life. We both have."

"You know what I'm getting at, so don't play dumb. Are you going down to New Orleans because you care about what happens to her, or because it could be a way, at long last, to get to her?"

"That's a hell of a thing to say!" He let his anger come through loud and strong.

"It's a hell of a thing to do, if it's a fact. But you and April have been at loggerheads for years, have hardly spoken two civil words to each other since she came back here. Why am I suddenly supposed to believe you're going out of your way to look out for her from no more than the goodness of your heart?"

Luke narrowed his eyes. "You don't believe I'm serious about keeping her safe?"

"Oh, I believe that. But is it because something inside you says this world wouldn't be worth two cents without her in it? Or is she just the one who got away, the one woman in Turn-Coupe who has no trouble resisting Luke-de-la-Nuit?"

Luke gave a short, hard laugh and shook his head as he lifted his gaze to the yellowed ceiling tiles above Roan's desk. "You, of all people, ought to know what a load of manure that is—since not much goes on in Turn-Coupe you don't hear about one way or another. Anyway, if I'd slept with half the women everybody likes to think I have, I'd be too bandy-legged to walk.''

''No doubt. But I also know that there's some fire to go with all the smoke. You've had a few more than a fair share.''

He returned his gaze to the sheriff. His voice bleak, he said, ''And vice versa. It wasn't exactly one-sided.''

Roan tipped his head in brief acknowledgment. ''That still doesn't answer the question.''

Luke thought his cousin might have been willing to allow that women had chased him because he'd been pursued a few times himself. The idea led to an unwelcome thought. ''Just why are you so all-fired interested in my motives? It wouldn't be because you've got an eye for April?''

''She's special, and not just because she's a writer. She sees things others miss, feels what others don't. I don't want to see her get hurt.''

Roan didn't pass out many accolades, Luke knew. He wondered what was behind this tribute to April. He also wondered how long his cousin had been noticing things about her. He said shortly, ''You really think I'd hurt her?''

''I don't know, that's why I'm asking.'' There was no compromise in Roan's gray eyes.

Luke drew air deep into his lungs and let it out again in a long sigh as he stared at the worn marble floor underfoot. At last he looked up. ''I don't know what to tell you. Watching out for her right now is just something I have to do because I'd never be able to live with myself if anything happened to her. Okay?''

Roan watched him a long moment before he gave a slow nod. Luke returned it with one of his own, then he spun around and went out the door. He strode through the marble-lined walls of the old courthouse with a scowl on his face. At the exit, he hit the swinging glass door with his hand and walked out into the heat and bright sunshine. There he stopped. He liked open air and space around him; he could just think better in natural surroundings.

Almost immediately, he knew what was bothering him. Neither he nor his cousin had really answered the question about each other's interest in April. He wondered if Roan knew that.

When he reached Chemin-a-Haut a short while later, Granny May was busy in the kitchen. She didn't live with him, but had a small place of her own down the road that she'd inherited from her parents. She'd moved back there after Luke's grandfather had died, making way, so she said, for Luke's future wife. Still, she liked to come in and check on him a couple of days a week, and usually cooked a big pot of red beans and rice or something similar for him.

She didn't like being disturbed in her kitchen, so he left her alone while he climbed the stairs to his bedroom, dug out a duffel bag from his closet, and began to stuff things into it. He'd almost finished packing when he heard a scuffling step outside in the hall. As his grandmother appeared in the doorway, he gave her an automatic smile but kept on with what he was doing.

"Going somewhere in particular?" she asked.

He told her in a few brief sentences. Walking to

his sock drawer, he pulled out a couple of pairs and threw them into his bag.

"Don't sound too smart to me," she said in querulous displeasure. "That girl like to have killed you last time."

He turned back to the drawer, staring at a pair of argyle socks that were the last thing he'd dream of taking with him. "It wasn't that bad."

"Humph. Could've fooled me." The old woman hunched her shoulders.

"You're just mad at her because she's writing about the family." It was no hardship to move into the connecting bathroom away from his grandmother's sharp eyes while he gathered his shaving supplies.

"So, what if I am? She's got no right."

"Not much way we can keep her from it," he answered as he returned.

"We could sue."

He tossed the things he carried into the bag and zipped it up before he turned to her. "I thought you were against nuisance suits."

"This goes beyond that, way beyond." She crossed her arms over her chest. "We ought to be able to charge her with slander or something."

"Libel, maybe, since it would be written instead of spoken. But why does it matter so much? What's got you so stirred up?"

She stared at him a moment, her fine old eyes unfathomable. Then she looked away. "That's my business. You just take my word—you don't want her messing around in our family background any more than I do. You're the Benedict, after all. I only

married into the family—though it's been so long
that I feel more a Benedict than I do a Seton like I
was born.''

''Granny—''

''Anyway, you don't wash your dirty linen in
public.''

''What dirty linen?''

She folded her lips, staring at him.

''If you can't supply a good reason,'' he warned,
''then I'm out of here and on my way to New Orleans.''

It was a war of wills as they stared at each other.
She hunched a shoulder. He stood perfectly still,
watching her. She turned her head.

''Fine. I guess you want me to leave then.''

''Oh, all right!'' she exclaimed in waspish tones
as she shifted to face him again. ''It goes way back,
way back, to when the four Benedict brothers first
came here. There was a woman with them, you
know, one they all hankered after. Some say she led
the way, but others used to whisper that it was on
account of her that they came at all, that otherwise
she'd have been taken from them.''

''So, she was a Native American. What's so bad
about that?''

''Nothing. If that's what's behind the story.''

Luke stared at her, noting the doubt in her face.
Abruptly, something clicked in his mind. ''You
don't think it is. You think—''

''I don't know, but I don't aim to have anybody
poking around trying to find out exactly how it all
went.''

''That's crazy. There's no reason to believe such

a thing, especially since nobody ever bothered to check out the story.''

''They won't, either, not if I can help it. The only time it will happen is after I'm dead and gone.''

''I could pay somebody to check the records. We could find out once and for all. Wouldn't that be better than living in fear that somebody's going to stumble across it when you least expect it?''

''No, no, no,'' she said, her voice rising with every repeat of the word. ''Didn't I raise you, boy? Haven't I always known what was best? Didn't I show you how to go on in the swamps, what plants to pick, how to fish and trap and take your boat where nobody else can go? You mind me, now. Stay away from that girl.''

''She's not a girl any more, Granny May. She's a woman.''

''All the more reason. She knows what she wants, or will as soon as she figures it out. She'll wring everything you ever heard about the family from you, turn you inside out, and hang you up to dry. When she's through, she'll know all there is to know about you and me and the whole lot of us. Then you'll see it plastered all over the country.''

That was inarguable, since he had reason to suspect she was right. ''I'm not a boy anymore, either. Our sweet April may not find it quite that easy.''

Granny May cocked her head as if listening to what he hadn't said instead of the words he'd spoken. ''What are you up to now?''

''Could be,'' he mocked her gently, ''that she'll have more to think about than writing stories.''

''You think you can keep her from doing it?''

"I can try."

She stared at him as if assessing him for something more than normal ability. "Maybe so, maybe so. But you'll have to be careful."

"I will be."

"You don't want to get caught again."

"No. That's the last thing I want."

"You got something else up your sleeve, don't you? There's something you want from her that's got nothing to do with me. I wonder now..."

He picked up his bag and walked to the door, so she had to step back to let him out of the room. In the hall, he said, "We have some unfinished business, April and I."

"That's so," she said with a slow nod. "But you be sure, this time, that it don't finish you."

"It won't," he said with more confidence than he felt. As he passed her, he gave her a quick hug, then moved on down the hall.

"Knock on wood," she called after him, and reached to tap the wall in the superstitious gesture meant to ward off danger.

He didn't answer. Still, as he went quickly down the wide staircase of the old house, he rapped twice with his knuckles on the thick wooden railing.

3

April checked into her suite at the Windsor Court Hotel in mid-afternoon. She'd tried to work after the phone call, but not much came of it. Her present state of mind, added to the distraction of the weekend conference, was too much to combat. Besides, she was anxious to reach New Orleans. She enjoyed the city, and felt so comfortable in it that she often wondered if she might have lived there in another life. Only the fact that she loved Turn-Coupe more had kept her from remaining in the city after her divorce.

The Windsor Court, with its sheltered courtyard entrance centered by a rose granite fountain, and trademark enormous bouquet of fresh pink roses in the lobby, was one of her favorite hotels. She appreciated the quiet elegance and river view of her usual corner suite, and always settled into it as if coming home. Afternoon tea in the salon off the lobby was a tradition for her. Because she'd skipped lunch, she headed in that direction at once.

She leaned back in her tapestry-covered chair, feeling herself relax under the influence of discreet service, fine linen, delicate china, and the soft strains of Mozart played by a harpist near the front windows. With her favorite Earl Grey tea in front of her, along with a silver server holding crisp cucumber sandwiches, warm scones with clotted cream and jam, chocolate-dipped strawberries and truffles, she began to think that the weekend might not turn out half bad.

Afterward, April placed a call to a friend whom she always visited when she came to the city. Julianne Cazenave was home and longing to have a good gossip, or so she said. She'd have the mint juleps ready on the patio by the time April reached her apartment.

The sound of a jazz band could be heard as April crossed Canal Street and entered the French Quarter. It seemed to be coming from the dark, alcohol-scented depths of a bar with its antique French doors flung open to the street. The song, a catchy rendition of a tune she associated with Satchmo Armstrong, followed her as she walked. April matched her pace to its rhythm. She felt anonymous there among the tourist crowd and the locals who were so used to being invaded by strangers that they paid no attention to one more. Few people knew where she was and what she was doing at the moment, including her radio caller with the overactive hormones. The knowledge lifted her spirits a notch higher.

There was one person who might have a good idea of her location. Luke had called just before she left and told her, in his usual high-handed way, that she should stay at home where he could keep an eye on her. Naturally, she'd refused. Living her life to suit his convenience was not high on her list of priorities. She'd informed him that security at the

Windsor Court was second to none. They were accustomed to keeping heads of state safe, so she was sure they would do the same for her. She couldn't live her life in fear. And if she was all the more determined to keep to her schedule because Luke Benedict thought she shouldn't, that was her secret.

Julianne's apartment was on Saint Louis just down from one of the Quarter's more famous restaurants. The scents of brewing coffee, baking bread, browning onions and caramelizing sugar drifted to April as she pressed the buzzer beside the door then stood waiting. With these smells came the sweet, lemony fragrance of butterfly lilies from some nearby courtyard. An appreciative smile curved her lips. If she were led blindfolded to this spot, she would still know she was in New Orleans.

The door lock clicked and she entered, stepping into the long, stone-lined corridor that stretched under the building. Once part of a porte cochere, it led toward the mellow light and tropical greenery of an interior courtyard.

"Up here, *chère!*"

The call came from overhead. April turned to search the balcony that rose on the front wall of the building above her. Catching the bright splash of color that was Julianne's usual caftan, she waved to her friend then turned to climb the stairs that led to the upper level apartment.

"It's just too hot to sit in the courtyard. I hope you don't mind," Julianne said as she let her inside.

"Not at all." April took the mint julep that Julianne thrust into her hand and drank deep. The heat on the streets had really been ferocious; she only realized how hot as she felt the air-conditioned cool of the apartment.

"It's so fantastic to see you," Julianne continued. "Come into the parlor and tell me why you're in town."

"It's the conference, of course, as you should know. Don't you belong to the local romance writers' chapter?"

"Oh, I never go to meetings. They always want me to run for office, and I'm not organized enough to know what to do for me, much less for other people."

April's smile was sympathetic but skeptical. "Is this the same woman who always has three writing projects going at one time? Your problem is that you have no sense of obligation to your fellow writers."

"I was publishing books before RWA was a gleam in the eyes of the ladies in Texas who started it. Besides, I don't notice you on anybody's board of directors."

"Touché—though there's the small matter of deadlines to be considered."

"The whole world has deadlines," Julianne returned. "You're just as selfish as I am. So, what have you been up to lately?"

"Are you sure you want to know?" April asked in dry warning.

Her friend laughed, a rich contralto sound laced with delight. "That bad, huh? In that case, I'm positive that I do! Details, give me details."

April followed her hostess into a dim room furnished with an antique parlor set covered in a wildly unlikely tropical print. The room was scattered with tables, most of which were extremely valuable except for one that looked like a miniature butler in a tailcoat. The setting was just like Julianne, she thought, half traditional, half quirkily artistic. How old her friend was, April had never thought to ask. With her long, narrow face crinkled in a constant smile, clear sea blue eyes, silver-streaked black hair in a braid down her back, and gently padded shape, she could have been any age from forty to seventy. She was warm and genuine, a woman of some experience who had learned her lessons well. That she was also one of the most revered of romance authors, with many *New York Times* bestsellers to her credit, was only incidental.

Julianne didn't rest until she had every crumb of information from April about what had happened with the radio caller. Afterward, she sat without speaking while she stared into her julep glass as if fascinated by the sight of ice melting.

"So, what do you think?" April asked finally. "Have you ever run into anything like this before?"

"Not personally, though I heard about an author who was attacked in her hotel room. It's possible she was singled out because she was attractive and traveling alone rather than because of who she was or what she wrote. No one can say that about what happened to you."

April nodded. "I think the worst thing about it was that he called me by name. He also seemed to have a pretty good grasp of my work since he mentioned a couple of book titles when he first came on the line."

"You think he reads your books?"

"Maybe. I suppose he could also be married to a fan."

Julianne made a sound of agreement. "So, tell me about this Galahad of yours who came riding up to protect you. Where does he fit into the picture?"

"He doesn't," April answered shortly. "He's just an interfering busybody."

"I seem to have heard his name before. Isn't he the same guy—"

"Yes, he is," April said in hasty acknowledgment as she remembered one night some years back, before she'd learned not to stay too late in the lounge at writers' conferences. She'd had too many champagne cocktails and wound up telling Julianne everything there was to know about her teenage affair with Luke Benedict.

"Sounds as if he's still interested."

"He feels responsible, a different thing altogether."

"And not a bad trait under the circumstances. Couldn't you let him hang around a while?"

"I don't think so."

"Why not? I mean, if he means nothing to you, what's wrong with using his macho muscles for protective cover?"

"You don't know Luke. Give him an inch and he'll take a mile—or more likely, have his boots parked under a woman's bed in record time."

"My kind of guy," Julianne declared as a grin tilted her mouth. "If you're sure you don't want him, could you send him my way?"

"You don't send Luke anywhere. He's a law unto

himself, goes exactly where he pleases." As she realized the truth of that statement, April felt a small disquiet shift through her. She banished it firmly as she took another sip of her julep.

"And there's no one else you're in love with just now?"

"Love," April said on a laconic laugh. "I'm not certain I know what that is any more."

Julianne reached out to lay her fingers on her arm. "Oh, *chère*."

"Truth to tell, I'm not sure I ever did know. Do you ever feel that way?"

"Not really. I was married for thirty years to a wonderful man, so I guess you'd say I write from memory. How are you managing it?"

"Who knows? Maybe out of my fantasies of what love should be. I try not to analyze the process too much for fear it will go away. Anyhow, my current book isn't going that well. My deadline is just two months off, and I don't think I'm going to make it."

"There's a lot of deadline angst going around. Some of us are just plain tired after years of deadlines. Some have other problems. What is it with you, I mean really? The divorce? Trouble with your ex? Or just this business with the caller?"

"All of the above," April answered with a wry smile. "I've been thinking about the past a lot as well, since moving back to Turn-Coupe."

"The past meaning Luke?"

"He's a large part of it," she admitted with a sigh. "That girl should never have been in his car that night. We were all but engaged, Luke and I.

We'd been to the movies and he'd taken me home. Why did he pick up another girl? He never said, not then or later. Of course, I don't suppose he had to have a reason. It's just a man thing, like my dad and his women.''

''Not all men are womanizing heels like your father, *chère*.''

''No, some of them are controlling heels who like to manipulate— Never mind.'' She shook back her hair as she looked away.

''Like your ex? You've been unlucky with the men in your life, haven't you? But that doesn't mean there aren't good ones out there. You just have to sift through them.''

''I think I've lost my taste for it. Just like I've lost all real idea of what romance is about. It's affecting my writing—and my reviews.''

''I saw the review you got in the local paper. I was livid, I can tell you, just couldn't imagine who would write such drivel about your work. I called up and asked for the name of the reviewer, and I couldn't believe it when they told me. Muriel Potts, of all people.''

April met Julianne's gaze a long moment. They both knew why Muriel might have written a less than positive review. ''It was nice of you to bother,'' April said, trying to smile, ''but it doesn't matter. I know myself that the book wasn't as strong as some of my others.''

''It was a wonderful book! Never believe your press, April. That's always fatal whether what they're saying is good or bad, biased or unbiased.''

''I don't know, Julianne. I just feel so numb. I

think I've lost it, lost all ability to make a reader believe in anything, much less mad, passionate sexual attraction to a noble hero. How can I, when I don't believe it myself?''

''Oh, right,'' Julianne said dryly. ''Tell me you felt nothing for this Adonis of the swamp who came pounding on your door. Tell me he didn't bring your blood to a simmer, if not to a boil.''

April gave her a scathing look. ''That's different. I was furious with him.''

''Yes, but you felt *something*. And you might feel more, given half the chance.''

''I don't think so,'' she said with finality.

''Now why not? What's wrong with a nice affair with a willing man, especially one with a moniker like Luke-de-la-Nuit? Might do you a world of good.''

''And it might be a disaster!''

''How? If you fall in love with him, you'll know what love is about again. Heartbreak is an emotion you need to have felt in order to write convincingly about it. At least you won't be numb any more.''

''No, I'll be devastated.''

''Will you now?'' Julianne said with speculation in her dark blue eyes.

April's lips tightened before she said, ''I don't mean that way. If I have an affair and still feel nothing, it will just prove that I've lost it. Sex as the glue for an affair or a marriage doesn't last long. I found that out with Martin.''

''He was a clod with all the sensitivity of mud. Forget Martin.''

''I'd like to, but I think he wants to come back.''

"You don't intend to let him!" Incredulity strained Julianne's voice.

"Not a chance. Not if he got down on his knees and begged."

"Good. Is he begging?"

"The same thing as. Also promising he'll be faithful forever and that we'll be good together, whatever that means." April gave a short laugh. "Actually, I think he's running short of cash and wants to dip into my royalties again."

"You didn't have to pay him alimony?"

"No, though he got half my pension plan. He did like being able to write checks on my bank account, though—almost as much as he likes his toys such as boats and cars. What's more, he always had the odd idea that the advances I got for the books were my payment while royalties were lagniappe, something I got for doing nothing. He convinced himself without too much trouble that he deserved that money as much as I did."

"For what?" The words held shocked amazement.

"All his promotional efforts, of course. Talking up my books in the bars at conferences. He was good at that. I just hope he doesn't show up at the conference this weekend to take up where he left off."

Julianne muttered something extremely uncomplimentary about the mental powers and antecedents of ex-husbands in general and Martin in particular. Then she added, "So, have the affair. It will convince Martin you're not interested. Besides, with any luck, you might get some nice research out of it. What do you have to lose?''

April stared at the woman across from her a frowning moment. Then as she saw the glint in Julianne's eyes, a laugh shook her. ''You're impossible. People don't have affairs just to improve their writing.''

''And a darned shame, too. Inspiration for the love scenes might be so much easier that way.''

''There's more to romance than love scenes,'' April said with some asperity.

''Too true,'' Julianne agreed, her voice softening. ''I wondered if you'd forgotten.''

''Not—quite.''

''On the other hand,'' her friend continued with a flashing grin, ''there's a lot to be said for sex. Some mighty hot affairs have begun with physical attraction that turned into something more.''

''That's the way it happens in our books, at least,'' April said in dry disparagement.

The afternoon turned into evening as they talked. Beyond the windows, the lavender-rose light of sunset gave the Quarter rooftops a melancholy air. Shadows filled the courtyard below, sliding over the ancient bricks with their coating of green moss and niches filled with tiny ferns. A breeze from the direction of Lake Pontchartrain stirred the banana trees in a corner to a slow, tropical rhythm. Suddenly the light was gone and it was night.

Julianne insisted April stay for dinner, saying it would be no trouble since she would just whip up an omelet. The two of them puttered in the kitchen, chopping green onions and mushrooms, mincing ham and grating cheese. The result, served with fresh crusty French bread and a marvelous Chardonnay, was light, golden brown and delicious, but it was the banter between the two friends that made the meal memorable.

April didn't linger afterward, since she needed to look over her notes for the keynote speech she'd be giving in the morning. To walk back to her hotel at night was not a good idea, even if she wanted to risk it. Julianne called a cab, then came downstairs to put her in it with a hug and a promise to show up at the conference. By the time April reached the Windsor Court she was yawning, almost done in by mint juleps and wine, good food, good conversation and the release of the last of her tension.

An hour later, she'd had a bath and wrapped herself in the thick terry bathrobe provided by the hotel. It was only then that she noticed the message light flashing on her bedside telephone and picked up the receiver to check it out. A floral arrangement had been left for her with the concierge. It would be delivered whenever convenient.

The flowers were a nice gesture from the organizers of the writers' conference, April thought. She asked that they be brought up immediately so she would know what to say when she saw the conference chairperson in the morning. She considered slipping into a pair of jeans and a knit shirt, but was afraid she'd be caught half dressed. Besides, the robe she wore was perfectly respectable.

The bouquet was lovely when it arrived, an elegant arrangement of peach roses amid spikes of blue Russian sage. April tipped the bellman and closed the door behind him, then carried the flowers into the bedroom where she put them on a table. She was still searching among the foliage for a card when the suite's door chime rang again.

It was more flowers, this time a large arrangement of gladiola and daisies that obscured the bellman's face when she looked through the fish eye viewer of the peephole.

"I think you've made a mistake," she called through the door. "You just delivered my flowers."

"Sorry to disturb you again, Ms. Halstead," the bellman said in muffled reply. "I didn't notice this second arrangement for you on the cart."

It was a natural enough mistake. She unfastened the safety catch and opened the door. As the man stepped inside, she turned and moved ahead of him, intending to retrieve an additional tip.

The bellman set the flowers on the marble-topped console table against the opposite wall. Then he turned and slammed the door shut.

April spun around with her heart crowding into her throat. The bellman, tall and dark-haired, totally unlike the first deliveryman, stood watching her with a cocky grin on his face and satisfaction in his eyes.

Rage flared through her. "Damn you, Luke Benedict! You nearly gave me a heart attack."

He put his wide shoulders against the door and leaned against it as he crossed his arms over his chest. "I'm glad to see you have sense enough to be scared."

"Are you? You may not be so glad before it's over. What do you think you're doing?"

His smile and the look in his black eyes were both grim. "Showing you how easy it is to get to you, wherever you are."

"What you're showing me is how big of an a—"

"Careful," he mocked. "Romance heroines shouldn't cuss."

She narrowed her eyes. "I'm the author, not the heroine, and some situations call for a curse word or two."

"Fire away, then. I can take it."

"On second thought, I'd rather not waste the breath or the time. Don't let the door hit you on your way out."

"I'm not going anywhere," he said with a slow shake of his head.

"Wrong," she snapped.

"Can't do it."

"Of course you can. Just put one foot in front of the other."

"Then who will protect you from the next yo-yo who comes along?"

"I don't need protecting. What I need is peace and quiet—and your absence."

He shook his head. "Funny, but seems as if I've heard all this before."

"Exactly," she answered with ice in her voice. "I could call hotel security and have you thrown out. How about that?"

"You wouldn't."

She swung around so fast that the heavy robe flared open to expose her legs well past the knee. Luke noticed, she thought, but she was too incensed to care. Striding to the phone on an end table, she picked up the receiver.

"All right," he said hastily. "I guess this means I don't get to stay the night?"

The look she gave him should have turned him to a block of ice where he stood. "Don't even think about it."

"Can't help it. The sofa looks fairly comfortable. I could bed down there."

It looked too short to her, as if his long legs would hang over the edge. It would almost be worth it to watch him try to get comfortable enough to sleep. "I don't think so."

"You're offering to share your king-size mattress?" He rubbed the edge of his square jaw. "I don't know, it could be dangerous."

"I'm not offering anything, as you know very well!"

"Be reasonable, April." His voice deepened to a more serious tone as he went on. "I'm here now. Why not let me stay?"

She looked at him in amazement. "How can you ask such a thing?"

"This isn't about me and you or any kind of attraction between us," he said with a frown of exasperation. "I just want you to be safe."

"And I will be, the minute you leave."

"Oh, for crying out loud! I'm not going to attack you. It's not my style, thank you very much. I prefer my women willing, even eager."

Color rose in her face and she lifted her chin. "I imagine you do."

"Right. Imagine all you want. You ought to be

good at it. In the meantime, we're both adults and nobody's watching. Who's going to be taking pictures if we come out of this room together in the morning?''

''Is that what worries you when you spend the night with a woman, who'll be taking pictures? Funny, but I'd have thought you'd have other things on your mind.''

''What I have on my mind when I spend the night with a woman is not—'' He stopped, took a deep breath. ''Hell, April. Why do you have to be so damned prickly? This is no big deal. Believe me.''

''It's a big deal to me,'' she said evenly. ''I don't want you here. I don't want you anywhere near me.''

''That's something you've made abundantly clear, both now and thirteen years ago. What I want to know is, just what are you afraid of? Is it me, or is it yourself?''

She stared at him, unable to form an answer for the dangerous boil of emotions inside her. He watched her, his black gaze intense. The moment stretched interminably. In the strained quiet, she could hear the distant wail of an ambulance siren.

Abruptly, a firm knock came on the outer door. April started, then clenched her hands into fists. Luke turned quickly and looked through the peephole viewer. A flash of anger followed by resignation crossed his strong features. He motioned to her to answer the knock and she moved forward.

''Yes?'' she said.

''Security, Ms. Halstead. We had a report of

unauthorized personnel seen outside your room. Just checking to be sure that you're all right.''

She reached for the doorknob and pulled the door open. To the man who stood outside, she said, ''Thank you very much for your concern. It was just a joke, someone I know impersonating a bellman. He'll be leaving now.''

''Yes, ma'am,'' the man said with a nod, then looked at Luke. ''Coming, sir?''

The suppressed anger in Luke Benedict's eyes made April's heart constrict in her chest, but she only stepped back out of his way. He brushed past her, but turned as he reached the hall. ''I think your conference is at a hotel off Veteran's Drive, isn't it? I'll pick you up early in the morning.''

How did he know that? And why had he been troubled enough to find out? She couldn't imagine, nor did she have time to figure it out just now. She said with a dismissive gesture, ''Don't bother, I can manage.''

''No bother,'' Luke said. ''I'm going anyway. Eight be about right?''

To argue further in front of the security officer would be suspicious as well as embarrassing. Besides, with any luck at all she'd be gone by the time Luke got there. In something less than gracious acceptance, she answered, ''All right then.''

Luke gave her a hard nod and a smile. Then he said good-night and walked away with the other man.

That smile remained with April as she shut the door. There was something in it she didn't like. She didn't like it at all.

4

Luke made sure he was outside the Windsor Court, leaning on the hood of his Jeep, when April came out of the hotel. She was smiling as she returned a greeting from the doorman. Then she glanced toward Luke's Jeep.

The hostility that surfaced in her eyes was like a blow to the stomach. Luke didn't let it deter him. Walking forward with calm assurance, he took her elbow.

"This is the lady I was telling you about," he said to the uniformed attendant. "I can handle it from here."

The doorman appeared undecided about interfering, which was hardly surprising considering that one of the hotel's star guests was doing her best to snatch her arm from Luke's grasp. Leaning toward April in a pose of loving greeting, he brushed her cheek with his lips. At the same time, he said, "You can come quietly, or I'll pick you up and cart you off right here in front of God and everybody."

Resentment and a promise of retribution seethed in the look she gave him. After a bare second of scanning his face, however, she allowed herself to be handed into the vehicle. Luke heaved a sigh of relief as he closed her door and moved around to the driver's side.

"What did you say to that doorman?" she demanded the minute he was in his seat.

Luke started the Jeep and pulled out of the brick-paved courtyard onto the street. It seemed like a sensible precaution since he didn't want her trying to jump out when he decided to answer. "I told him I was your live-in lover, but we'd had words— you'd told me to buy the ring or get out. I'd decided this morning to go for the ring."

"You didn't!"

"Seemed better than telling him you were cracking up under deadline strain and I was your therapist about to sign you into a nice rest home."

"As if he'd believe that," she said with contempt.

He sent her crooked smile. "You don't think I look professional enough?"

Her gaze flickered over him, taking in his dark, conservative dress slacks and light gray oxford cloth shirt with a discreetly monogrammed pocket and the sleeves rolled to his elbows. It did wonders for his ego to watch her expression take on a modicum of respect. That lasted about two seconds.

"So, where are you going?" she inquired sweetly. "To a funeral?"

"I'm going with you."

He braced himself for an explosion. It didn't come. Instead, she stared at him while swift consideration flickered in the golden depths of her eyes.

"You do know what kind of meeting I'm attending?" she asked at last.

"Along with half the population of New Orleans," he said with a nod, "since it was in the morning paper."

"But that's not where you found out about it."

Annoyance for the disdain in her voice rose inside him. "No, I saw it in your newsletter."

"I didn't know you cared about anything that happened outside of Tunica Parish, especially anything so strictly female."

The look he gave her was straight. "There are a lot of things you don't know about me."

She returned his gaze a long moment before she said in abrupt tones, "Why? Why are you doing this?"

"For the fun of it." That much was true, even if it wasn't the only reason.

"You're really going with me to this conference where you'll be one of the few men among dozens of romance-minded women?"

"My kind of get-together." He arched a brow at her.

"You don't know what you're getting yourself into."

Luke didn't care for the grim anticipation in her eyes but did his best to conceal his uneasiness. "I'll find out, won't I?"

"You certainly will," she answered. "You most certainly will."

The conference appeared well attended, at least from Luke's point of view. There were females everywhere. Females unloaded cars in the hotel parking lot, females stood in line at the desk. There were females sitting in the lobby with purses and book bags with the conference logo at their feet, females laughing and talking and calling to each other as they waited for the elevators. Most of them seemed to know April. Those who didn't give her a big hug or a wave watched her with faint smiles of recognition and interest in their eyes. She took it in stride, he thought, though he wasn't sure half the time whether she actually remembered the women who came up to her or only pretended for the sake of politeness.

Luke was both fascinated by the glimpse of April's other life and nervous of it. She looked so polished in a suit of periwinkle blue and with her hair in a smooth and regal coil on top of her head, had such an aura of success, that she was like another person. She was treated with what seemed to be genuine warmth, yet beneath it was a degree of admiration that made him stop and think. In a strange sort of way, it seemed everyone knew her better than he did. He wondered if it might be because everyone seemed to have read her books.

April allowed him to carry her briefcase and remain at her side, but she didn't introduce him. That the individuals who came up to her were curious about him was plain enough. Speculation gleamed in their eyes as they glanced from April to him and then back again. She paid no attention, just as she ignored him. It roused the devil in him, made him want to do something outrageous to make her acknowledge his presence. A plump little lady with white hair and a twinkle in her eyes saved him from it.

"Don't keep us in suspense any longer, my dear

April. Tell us about this good-looking man you've brought with you," she urged. "You haven't gone and got married without telling anybody, now have you?"

"Heaven's no," April answered without turning a hair. "This is Luke, and he's the cover model for my next book. Don't you think he's just the perfect dark and handsome, devil-may-care hero?"

Luke turned his head sharply to stare at her. She held his gaze, her own limpid with innocence. She meant to get his goat, he thought, maybe even embarrass him enough so he'd turn tail and run.

"Oh, my," the white-haired lady said, reaching out to touch his arm as she took a deep breath that swelled her bosom to notable proportions. "I most certainly *do* think so! He's got Fabio and the Topaz man beat all to pieces."

Luke had no idea who those guys were, but the worshipful look on the woman's face suddenly tickled his funny bone. At the same time, he saw that playing up to the image April had given him just might be the best way to turn the tables on her.

Taking the white-haired lady's hand, he raised it to his lips. In the sultriest tones he could conjure up on short notice, he said, "Thank you, ma'am. You're too kind."

She leaned forward, eyes sparkling, to whisper, "Not half as kind as I might have been once upon a time."

He laughed; he just couldn't help it. Suddenly he felt a little more in control. He was going to be harder to dislodge than April might think. With a little luck everything might yet turn out all right.

Leaning closer to the audacious older woman, he said, "If I'd been around then I might have been extremely grateful for the—favor."

"Favors, you mean—or at least I hope you did," she returned, her face crinkled in a thousand lines of enjoyment as she tipped her head coquettishly.

"Certainly I did. What else?" He sketched a bow that he devoutly hoped wasn't an insult to his gentlemen ancestors.

The elderly charmer giggled; there was no other word for it. Heads turned in their direction and people smiled. April didn't appear to think it was funny at all. Luke, watching her turn and stride away, felt his lips twitch in a barely controlled grin.

Later, however, as April mounted to the podium to give her keynote speech, his mood turned more somber. She was fantastic, speaking straight from the shoulder, telling it the way she saw it. At the same time she was self-deprecating and touchingly frank about her problems and insecurities. Her remarks drew applause several times. When she said her final thank you and stepped back from the microphone, the standing ovation she received seemed to surprise her as much as it delighted her.

Luke rose with the others, giving April Halstead the applause that was her due. She was a special lady, he thought; Roan had been right about that. He could still hear her voice reverberating in his mind as it had echoed through the room from the loudspeaker. Its soft yet clear timbre lingered deep inside him. It ignited a slow fire in his blood, yes, but there was more to it than that. Watching her, listening to her, made him incredibly glad they were both alive here and now.

It also made him feel fiercely protective.

Standing there with his gaze on the glowing planes of her face, Luke took a solemn vow. Nothing ugly or painful must touch her, not now, not ever. He would see to that, no matter what he had to do to prevent it.

The conference agenda included a series of workshops. One of them, taught by April, was on career planning. Luke tagged along. The subject was apparently popular since the room was filled to capacity. By the time the session ended, Luke had a much better idea of how April spent her time, also of the dedication it had taken to get to her present position and the hard work she put in to stay there.

A number of attendees approached her with different comments and questions. She answered them with patience and humor, even those from a desperate-looking young woman with long black hair straggling down to her waist, skeletal hands, and a manuscript in her arms that was the size of a feather bed. She kept thrusting the bundle of paper at April as if she expected her to take it and read it before the end of the day, then send it off with a glowing recommendation for publication.

Luke was thinking of stepping in when April, glancing beyond the importuning would-be author, suddenly touched the young woman's arm. "Here is someone who can help you," she said kindly. "She's a freelance editor for a local publishing house who enjoys helping writers who are just starting out.'' April raised her voice a bit. ''Oh, Muriel, here's someone in need of your services.''

The person April was addressing turned slowly to face her. A cornered expression hovered in the woman's hazel eyes and her movements were jerky, as if she had to force her angular, big-boned body to answer her commands. Pushing flyaway blond hair back from her face with one hand in a nervous gesture, she inquired, ''Are you talking to me?''

As Luke watched, April explained the would-be author's situation to Muriel. The freelance editor did not look happy to have a prospective new client. With a shrill edge in her voice, she said, ''Darling April should have told you that I conduct how-to-write seminars as well. Perhaps you'd care to sign up for one?''

''Oh, I don't need that,'' the woman said as she reached out and caught the editor's arm as if grasping a lifeline. ''But if you would only give me a few minutes, I'm sure I can convince you to take a chance on my book.''

''The publishing house I work with doesn't do romance novels.'' The tone was as blunt as the words.

''I can write anything you want!''

''Local history?''

''Of course.''

The answer was given so blithely that it was obvious even to Luke that the unpublished author would have replied the same if the editor had asked for a treatise on the flora and fauna of the Amazon basin. Without pausing, she launched into a spirited description of her romantic opus interspersed with questions that indicated she suspected Muriel of having New York publishing connections that she hadn't divulged.

Glancing at April to see what she thought of it all, Luke caught sight of a crooked smile she was trying to hide. The minute she saw that he'd noticed, color stained her cheekbones and she turned sharply away. A second later she was out of the room as if she were being chased, stopping for nothing and no one.

Luke was still staring after her when he heard a throaty chuckle at his elbow. As he glanced down, the woman beside him gave him a friendly nod. "Sneaky," she said quietly, "but effective, wouldn't you say?"

"Excuse me?"

"Oh, my mistake. Something about your expression—well, I thought you knew what was going on."

"I don't, but I'd like to," he said frankly. "If you'd be kind enough to enlighten me."

The woman, in a purple dress like some kind of bedsheet, searched his face a long moment. Then she took his arm. "Walk with me to the next workshop?"

Luke went willingly enough, compelled by his own curiosity as much as the grip on his biceps. She led him toward the door through which April had disappeared, then into the carpeted hallway beyond it.

"You don't know who I am, do you?" his captor said. "I'm Julianne Cazenave, another of these 'damned scribbling women,' as Dickens is supposed to have called our kind in his day. And I suspect you're the man who's been causing April to lose sleep.''

''I doubt that,'' he said dryly. ''I'm just looking after her for today.''

''I know that, *cher*. Everybody knows that, I assure you, and have from the moment you stepped through the door. You are a very large blip on the radar screen of this conference. I'm sure April regrets bringing you with her or will before the day is out. Why did she, by the way?''

''Because I wanted to come and she couldn't figure out how to stop me.''

Her eyes narrowed a fraction. ''Really? I was right. You are Luke Benedict, aren't you?''

''How did you—?''

''I've known April a long time,'' she answered obliquely without taking her eyes off his face. ''How...intriguing.''

He wasn't about to fall into the conversational trap set by the tell-me-more note in her voice. Instead, he said, ''You were going to explain why you thought April was being sneaky?''

''Because she was, *cher*. Muriel Potts is not only a freelance editor but picks up a few dollars by doing reviews for the city paper. She panned April's last book unmercifully.''

''Panned it?''

''Called it flowery and unrealistic, said that it lacked psychological depth, that the plot was derivative and that the action scenes were without expertise from the viewpoint of an ex-military officer—which is what Muriel was before she left the service to take up writing. That was just the beginning.''

''None of it was true?''

''By no means.''

''Good grief.''

''Exactly. Oh, April's style might seem a little lush if you're a Hemingway fan, but Papa Hemingway was about as macho as they come. That's fine since he wrote for a primarily male literary audience. However, his minimalist style would be all wrong for a romance novel. The books have a language of their own, one much more sensual and emotional, for the tastes of women.''

Luke grinned as he said, ''I'll take your word for it.''

''Yes, well, you'll have to forgive me for getting on my hobby horse.''

''No problem.'' He waited a second for the sake of politeness before he asked, ''So, you think April was getting back at this Muriel by throwing her to the overeager author back there?''

''That's my guess.'' Julianne lifted a rounded shoulder under the flowing fabric of her dress. ''April's human. She has a temper and she strikes out when she's hurt. But she's never vindictive or petty, and she hasn't a mean bone in her body.''

''You do know her well,'' he commented.

''As I said, we go back a long way together, have weathered a lot of changes in the romance industry. It counts.''

Abruptly, Luke had a flashing mental image of the name Julianne Cazenave as he'd seen it last on book covers in multiple pockets at New Orleans International Airport. He also remembered a television movie he'd sat through a couple of years back. Without preamble, he said, "You're famous, aren't you?"

Julianne chuckled. "Instantly recognizable, a household name, in fact. I can tell you're honored as all get-out."

"Truthfully," he said with a quizzical smile, "I think I am."

She stared up at him a long moment, then she sighed. "Such a charmer, and it's all natural, too. I believe darling April may be in trouble."

He studied her through his lashes as he tried to decide if she was putting him on. She returned his gaze without evasion. After a moment, he asked, "You really think so, do you?"

"It's possible. Depends on how much finesse you can muster."

"Finesse," he repeated, his voice flat.

"Don't push too hard. She can be led, but not shoved." Julianne paused, then went on. "You and April were a real item at one time, weren't you?"

"She told you about that?"

"Among other things. So what happened to spoil it? I mean, from your point of view."

"I let her down," he said starkly, then wondered what it was about the writer beside him that prompted him to answer such a personal question. There was something, he didn't doubt. He didn't go around baring his soul to just anybody.

"There was an accident, I think. April thought you cared about her, but discovered differently when you had a wreck and the girl with you was killed.''

"It wasn't the way it sounds.'' The words had more force behind them than Luke intended.

"How was it?'' Julianne asked quietly.

They had stopped outside another meeting room. The sign beside the door said that Julianne Cazenave would be giving a workshop inside. The time listed for the start had passed five minutes ago. This was not the place to go into details, then, even if he was so inclined.

"It was a mistake,'' he said, "one I'll regret all my life. For a lot of reasons.''

Julianne nodded before glancing inside the room where her audience was waiting. Giving him her hand, she said with a slight smile, "I'd like to hear more. In case I don't get the chance today, won't you come see me next time you're in New Orleans?''

"My pleasure,'' he said, and meant it.

The rest of the day passed quickly. There was a luncheon that he skipped for a burger in the hotel coffee shop. Afterward, he sat in on a session called How To Turn Up the Heat In Love Scenes. He was so intimidated by the lively discussion of exactly how to describe the male anatomy, however, that he left after ten minutes.

He roamed the halls looking for April, but she wasn't in any of the meeting rooms, nor was she in the lobby or lounge. A woman with an official-looking badge hung on her chest noticed his lost expression and informed him that she was in an executive meeting of some kind. He retreated to a seating area near the door of the room where April's meeting was taking place.

He was soon joined by a bevy of talented females, writers who seemed as fun loving as they were savvy about their business. As he listened to their conversation, he learned quite a bit more about the writing life and picked up a few pointers for future conversations with April. However, he excused himself as he saw her finally emerge with Julianne Cazenave and four other women.

They were in the middle of a discussion about an impromptu group dinner at a restaurant in the Quarter later in the evening when he walked up behind them. He quickly included himself before April could find a way to stop him. When the decision of where to go stalled and someone asked his choice of food, he suggested Italian at Bacco's on Chartres Street. The suggestion was adopted forthwith.

Bacco's, named for the god of wine and merriment, was owned by Ralph Brennan, a member of New Orleans's premier restaurant family. It was known for its great Italian food with Creole-Cajun influence served with a judicious mixture of comfort and sophistication. The place was beginning to fill when they arrived, but Luke had called ahead to reserve a table in the back. They were greeted promptly, then led past the front dining room with its Italian earth tones that glowed in the mellow light from antique Venetian silk chandeliers, up stone steps to the bar backed by Gothic arches, and through to the patio dining room. The area was nicely atmospheric, with wide windows through which could be seen a pool surrounded by palm trees and illuminated by flickering gaslights. Watching over them was a trompe l'oeil painting of a castle doorway topped by the watchful face of old Bacchus himself.

They ordered two bottles of wine, a white and a red, then selected calamari and cannelloni for appetizers. After that substantial beginning, the ladies seemed in no mood for anything heavy. Bypassing the more elite menu items, they settled for something they could all share, the house specialty of wood-fired pizzas topped with grilled shrimp and andouille, Louisiana crawfish tails and Calabrese hot salami.

By the time the wine made its second round, the romance authors were feeling no pain. They flirted with the waiter, traded suggestive innuendoes with the wine steward, and told bawdy jokes with gusto. Luke might have suspected them of testing him as the only man in the group, except that none of them seemed in the least self-conscious. He thought, rather, that as a group they had lost most of their inhibitions during the process of writing about love and physical attraction—or it might have been that they wrote about these things simply because they had so little embarrassment about them. Whichever it was, they had an open and natural appreciation for the dynamics of sex combined with unusual tolerance toward most subjects. It was a combination of attitudes he could get used to without much effort, he thought. He couldn't remember when he'd had more fun with a bunch of women.

April joined in, though she wasn't quite as boisterous. He was seated across from her in the center of the long table, so had plenty of opportunity to hear whatever she said in her low, musical tones. He wondered briefly about her more intimate inhibitions, or lack of them, now. She'd once been a little shy, yet had responded to the right encouragement with a naturalness that it hurt him to remember.

As his thoughts drifted, he watched the candlelight gleam across the crown of her hair when she turned her head, noted the softness of her mouth in repose and the warmth that rose in her eyes for everyone except him. Slowly there grew inside him an errant need to be alone with her there in that semisecluded back dining room, just the two of them. It was so strong that he felt almost feverish with it.

Perhaps the table of women picked up on that mental defection. Shortly afterward, they turned on him.

"So, you're the hero of April's next book," a cute little redhead with traces of white at her temples said. "How did you wind up with the role?"

"Lord, what a question," another one said before he could answer. "I mean, look at him! Those shoulders, and the long legs, the dark hair, the bedroom eyes…"

"I know," the first said with a sigh. "Even the white teeth in the tanned face." She turned to April. "Where on earth did you find him?"

"I just looked around and there he was," April answered dryly.

"Nobody like that is ever lying around when I need him." That droll comment came from an attractive silver-haired woman with a smoke-roughened voice.

"I never said he was lying around," April replied in laughing protest. "I just needed dark and devilish and there he was next door."

"How convenient!" the redhead drawled.

"Wasn't it?" April acted as if she hadn't caught the sly insinuation.

Luke leaned back in his chair and crossed his arms over his chest. He thought of answering for himself, but decided not to risk it. Of course, he could put a stop to the teasing whenever he chose, but he wanted to see how far April would go.

"Does he fit the rest of the mold? Does he have all the qualities you usually put into your heroes?" Julianne sent a bland glance in his direction as she spoke.

"Most of them," April allowed thoughtfully. "He's strong, obviously. He has intelligence, humor and charm. He moves with the typical athletic ease…"

The one with the smoky voice threw up her hands. "He's perfect, in fact."

"Not quite."

"Gad, April, what could he be missing?"

"Self-sacrifice, dedication to a cause," she answered thoughtfully. "Oh, and one thing more."

Luke felt his stomach muscles tighten in instinctive preparation for the blow he knew had to be coming. April would never say such things for any other reason except to set him up. The moment stretched, becoming so unendurable that it was a relief when Julianne asked, "And what might that be?"

April met his gaze over the linen cloth. Her lips barely moved as she answered quietly, "He's missing the most important quality of all in a hero. He has no honor."

The pain that sliced through Luke was so vicious that he set his teeth against it. He'd thought he had long ago given up caring about April Halstead's opinion of him. This wasn't a good time to find out that he'd been wrong.

At the same time, he saw what she was doing; she wanted to tick him off so he'd leave before the time came to go back to the hotel. Of course, that didn't prevent her from meaning every word she'd spoken.

"Well, now," the redhead said on an uncertain laugh, "I think maybe I could do without something so measly for the sake of the rest."

That comment was an apparent attempt to smooth over the slight to his male ego. It was nice of her, but Luke didn't much care to be an object of pity.

That April had no such inclination was proven as she spoke again. "I'm glad you think he fits the role. I was afraid he might be too sure of himself."

"Now, wait a minute," Luke exclaimed, annoyed into protest.

"For myself, I like a man who knows what he wants," the redhead said with a quick glance in his direction.

"Luke certainly is that," April answered with a cool smile. "What's more, he comes with a ready-made nickname, just like a character. I don't even have to make one up.''

He closed his eyes as she rolled the nickname off her tongue with gusto. He despised it, and she knew it. Still, he wouldn't let her get to him again. Running him off was going to be harder than she dreamed.

''Luke-of-the-Night,'' Julianne translated as a couple of the women looked puzzled. Looking at April, she continued, ''Is he, by any chance, going to appear in the book you're doing about that family out on the lake where you live? What was the title?''

''Not likely,'' April said a shade louder than necessary to cut off her friend, then gave an infinitesimal shake of her head. Luke felt his need to learn more about that book solidify, but now was not the time to go into it.

''Nighttime Luke,'' the gravely voiced one drawled in the small silence. ''Now I wonder what he did to deserve such a moniker.''

''The question is more what he hasn't done,'' April answered. ''And the answer is, there isn't much.''

''Is it now?'' he muttered, scowling. Julianne had said that April struck out at people when she was hurt. He couldn't help wondering if this was an example of it. Still, a person couldn't be hurt unless they cared, could they?

She ignored him as she smiled around the table. ''Our Luke is a man of vast experience. Unlike poor old Freud, he knows exactly what women want.''

Luke tucked his arms tighter across his chest

since he was afraid he might strangle her otherwise. "And just how would you know that?"

"Common gossip," she quipped, but the light from the table candle revealed a trace of trepidation in her eyes.

"And is that really how you see me?"

She tipped her head as if trying to bring him into focus. "Not exactly. To me you're a pirate taking what you want and sailing away with no concern for the poor females left in your wake."

"I thought pirates sailed off with their helpless captives instead of away from them," he objected before glancing around the table with what he hoped was a piratical grin.

"Not you. You're a river pirate, a regular Mike Fink who takes no prisoners."

Luke was not thrilled with the comparison, even if the River Pirate Revel was in recognition of Fink's exploits. Mike Fink had been the terror of the lower Mississippi River during the early antebellum period. From his hideout in a river cave, he'd wreaked havoc on river shipping and all boat travelers unfortunate enough to fall into his clutches.

"That depends on the prisoner," he said, arching a brow. "And where she wants to be taken."

"Whoa!" the redhead said, pretending to fan herself with her hand.

"He has a point, *chère*," Julianne said to April without bothering to hide her smile.

"What he has is a fine opinion of himself," April declared with a dark look in their direction. "And you two aren't helping any."

Luke agreed, not that he needed help. "A person

has to take credit where it's due,'' he said. ''I may not be much in the way of a hero, April, sweetheart, but I'm sure the reason you're a romance author.''

''You're what?'' The look she gave him was blank with surprise.

''Admit it,'' he said. ''If I'd been different, where would you be now? A married woman with nothing to show for the past decade and more except a run-down barn of a house and a half dozen kids clinging to your skirts.''

The redhead pushed her pizza away as she eyed them both with frank curiosity. ''Hey, I thought you two had just got together recently. You really go back that far?''

''Farther,'' Luke said, and smiled into April's eyes.

She drew a swift, uneven breath. ''What a poignant picture, especially with a loving husband at my side. Failing one beautiful dream, however, I turned to another. It was a matter of survival, not of choice.''

The triumph Luke had felt vanished as if it had never been. He thought he just might need all the help he could get, after all.

5

The group dinner finally wound to an end. The goodbyes were said, the promises to get together again were made, and April's friends and colleagues went their separate ways. She walked beside Luke toward the parking lot where he'd left his Jeep. Only a few more minutes, she told herself, and she would be back in the blessed privacy of her hotel suite.

Though she was more than ready to call it a night, it was the shank of the evening in the Quarter. Cars eased through the narrow, one-way streets in company with tour buses, cabs, mule-drawn carriages and the occasional black and white of the city police. People looking for a good time in the Big Easy filled the sidewalks and moved in and out of the open doors of the restaurants and bars. The strident sounds of jazz and zydeco spilled out into the night along with wasteful currents of air-conditioned coolness. The tart scent of mustard from the hot dog-shaped pushcart on the corner hung in the warm, moist air. Blending with it was the ubiquitous smell of alcohol. It was a typical Saturday night in New Orleans.

The day hadn't been quite the disaster April expected. Luke had behaved himself for the most part, neither intruding on what she had to do nor trying to prevent her from doing it. His presence had actually been helpful once or twice. Still, her relief that she would soon be free of his company was so strong she felt almost euphoric. That or the wine she'd had with dinner had to be the reason for the bubbling sensation in her veins. It could hardly be the man at her side.

"Not a bad day, all things being equal," Luke said in meditative tones.

For a brief moment, it felt as if he'd read her mind. She sent him a quick glance where he strolled with his hands in his pockets, matching his long strides to her shorter ones. He appeared relaxed, oblivious of any undercurrents between them. It struck her as unfair.

"Speaking for yourself, I suppose?" she said without expression.

"You carried it off in fine style, I thought. The lady of the hour, very cool and collected." He gave her a quick glance. "You didn't even attack the woman who'd low-rated your book."

Her eyes widened a fraction as she asked, "How did you know about that?"

"Heard it around."

"I'll bet you did." The comment was a pained acknowledgment of the well-oiled gears of the romance writers' gossip machine.

"You shouldn't let things like that get to you. The opinion of one person doesn't matter."

"Not if it's honest."

He studied her for a second. "Meaning?"

"I'm not exactly Muriel Potts's favorite person."

"I suppose there's a reason?"

She lifted a shoulder. "She sent me a manuscript of her first book when she sold it a few years back and requested a quote."

"A quote?"

"A few sentences describing the book in glowing terms—sentences designed to be printed on the book's cover when it's published."

"An endorsement, in other words," he said with a nod of understanding. "So, did you give her a bad one or something?"

"Not quite, but close. Her story was trite and unrealistic. I didn't see how I could praise it and still have any credibility left with readers. Since I was in a deadline crunch at the time, I shelved the manuscript while I tried to think what to tell her. Somehow I forgot about it until after the book went to print. She's wasn't happy." The last was an understatement of gigantic proportions. Muriel had made no direct reply to the letter of explanation April sent later, but statements she'd made to others showed that she'd been enraged.

"It mattered that much, did it?"

"To her mind. Sales figures for the book were terrible, so her publisher didn't exercise the option to buy her next. Muriel has published nothing since then, which of course is entirely my fault."

"She made you the scapegoat. You could take that as a salute to your power in the industry."

A group of college boys were coming toward them. Since they seemed to be taking up most of sidewalk, Luke put an arm around her waist to steer her closer until they'd passed by. April registered each contact point of his long fingers as a spot of glowing heat. She stepped away as soon as she could, answering his comment almost at random. "I don't know about that. Publishers seem to think cover quotes help, but I've never bought a book based on what some other author said about it."

"You have a different perspective," he said with an ironic look for the distance she'd placed between them. "Celebrity endorsement apparently works wonders with average folks. It must, or there wouldn't be so many famous faces out there hawking everything from credit cards to salad dressing."

He was so reasonable and so right that he left her with no rational objection. April hated that. Reverting to his previous remark, she said, "Anyway, it makes sense for writers to be upset by criticism, whatever its source. It takes a supersensitive person to be a writer in the first place, so why shouldn't negative comments be felt as intensely as everything else?"

"Sticks and stones?" he suggested, though there seemed a trace of sympathy in his smile.

"The pen is mightier," she said, returning quote for quote.

"A thousand angels swearing on the Bible can't make it the truth if it isn't so."

Her glance was jaundiced. "What do you know about it? You've never read my books."

"No," he agreed, his gaze steady, "but maybe I should."

Funny, but coming from Luke, that almost sounded like a threat.

Just ahead of them, the owner of one of the picturesque Quarter shops was hosing down the sidewalk in front of his store. Though he deflected the spray of water at their approach, the uneven paving was slick underfoot. April stepped ahead of Luke, veering toward the street as much as possible. He moved with her, taking her arm. Since April was wearing heels, she accepted his support without pulling away.

Just beyond the wet stretch was one of the Quarter's landmark nightspots. The amplified tinkling of twin pianos blared from inside, mingling with the voices of entertainers and also the low hum of satisfied customers. Out front, a crowd of people straggled in an uneven line, taking up most of the sidewalk as they waited to be admitted. Many of them had mixed drinks in plastic go-cups in their hands, though a few appeared to be having a better time than the others. This last group staggered against each other in drunken cheerfulness, oblivious to the frowns from those around them.

April kept near the sidewalk's edge, murmuring politely as she moved around an older couple near the middle of the customer line. She'd taken another couple of steps when she caught a flash of movement on the edge of her vision as if someone had thrown their drink.

Luke cursed. He dragged her backward, then spun her to face the street. His arms clamped around her in a sheltering hold. In the same instant, something wet splattered around her feet with an acrid, sulfurous stench and sizzling wisps of vapor.

Luke's grasp tightened. April heard him draw a

hissing breath of pain. For an instant, they stood in frozen immobility.

Then someone screamed. Pandemonium broke loose as people scattered in every direction. April and Luke were left in isolation on the sidewalk.

"What happened?" she cried as she broke free of Luke's hold then whirled to face him.

"Acid," he said through clenched teeth. "Are you all right?"

"Yes, fine," she answered in spite of a burning sting on one ankle and across the top of her other foot. "But you're not. Where are you hurt?"

He didn't answer, but swung away from her to stride back the way they'd come. As he reached the shop they'd just passed, he snatched the still-running water hose from the shopkeeper. Without pausing, he lifted the end and let the water stream over his left shoulder and down his back.

April saw at once what he intended. Like dousing a burn with cold water, he was minimizing his injury from the acid while helping neutralize its effect. Under the spreading wetness of the water, she could see patches of reddened skin through the tattered holes eaten out of his shirt. She stepped closer, using both hands to sweep the flow of water across the splatters that he hadn't yet reached.

"Don't!" he ordered in hard tones. "You'll burn your hands."

"What does that matter?" she snapped, clutching his shirt at his waist as he tried to step away. Quickly, she forced the spray over the last area where it needed to go, holding the water against his hot skin. The splattering waterfall that drenched her feet made her own minor burns feel so much better that she could only imagine how it must feel to him.

"April," he began in winded tones, then fell abruptly silent. Beneath her hands, she felt him shudder, a hard contraction of muscles that was instantly controlled. At the same time, the tight beading of goose bumps spread over him under his wet shirt. She looked up and was snared by the darkness of his gaze, caught also in the unbearable intimacy of holding her hands against the pebbled yet firm musculature of his back. At the same time, she noted that her hands were shaking with shock.

"What the hell came down here, buddy?" the shop owner demanded from behind them. "What was that stuff?"

It was a moment before Luke answered, then his voice was grim. "Sulfuric acid."

"Whoever threw it got you pretty good. What's the scoop?"

"I wish I knew," Luke muttered. He flung a quick glance at April.

She shook her head. She'd seen few details, only a vague movement from among the crowd of people. The person responsible must have fled as everyone around them scattered.

"Crazy, the things people do these days," the shop owner commented with a wag of his head. "Don't know what the world's coming to. In my day, acid was something we tripped on."

"Yeah."

Luke's agreement was perfunctory, April thought. From the tightness of his features and his penetrating gaze, she could tell he thought the attack was no freak accident, certainly no coincidence. She wanted to contradict him, would have if she could. It wasn't possible.

If he was right, then he'd been burned because of her. That knowledge gave her an almost physical pain, as if her own flesh echoed his suffering. That was one of the drawbacks to having a writer's imagination and empathy; it was difficult not to take the agony of others as her own. It was no more than that, of course, just misplaced identification. Luke's suffering meant nothing to her personally. Of course it didn't.

At the same time, she was ashamed of how much she had resented his showing up in New Orleans. Where would she be now if he hadn't come? She might well have caught that caustic, scarring acid full in the face. She owed him something and she didn't like being indebted to anyone. Least of all did she like being under any obligation to Luke Benedict.

Behind them, a police siren burped a warning. The black and white came to a halt with its lights flashing, and a pair of patrolmen got out. Someone had apparently phoned in a report of the incident on a cell phone.

The official inquiry didn't last long. There were few witnesses since most of those on the scene had melted away, reluctant to get involved. The officer in charge took down the details but was pessimistic about tracing whoever had committed the crime. April had expected no less; still, it was depressing.

The patrolmen offered to run Luke to the hospital emergency room, but the favor was declined. He'd be all right, Luke said. He was heading for home in the morning and would have his family doctor look at the burns. He and April signed the official report, then made their way to his Jeep and drove to the hotel.

As they pulled into the entrance court, April said abruptly, ''I always travel with a first aid kit. If you'll come upstairs, I'll put something on your back.''

A grim smile came and went across his face there in the dim interior of the car. ''Thanks, but you don't have to go to that trouble.''

''It's no trouble, really.''

''Then why the solicitation all at once?''

She looked away from his penetrating gaze. ''I feel so— I don't know. It seems the least I can do.''

He was quiet a moment longer, as if assessing his options or possibly her motives. Then he gave an abrupt nod. ''All right. Why not?''

It had been some time since April had walked into a hotel with a man at night, since the last time she'd checked in with Martin, in fact. She felt conspicuous and a little wary as she crossed the lobby with Luke beside her. That was the trouble with being recognizable, even to a small degree, she thought. Even if nobody was watching, the feeling that they could be was always there. It was worse this evening because she'd practically thrown Luke out of her room the night before.

The clerk at the desk in the rear of the lobby smiled and wished them a pleasant evening but showed no curiosity. Moments later, they were gliding upward in the walnut-paneled elevator. A few

steps down the hall with its rich but subdued car-
peting, and April let herself into the suite. Its heavy
door closed behind them with a solid thud.

Panic moved through April at the sound. What in
the world was she thinking? She'd spent months,
even years, avoiding being alone with Luke, and
now she'd not only allowed him into her room in
the middle of the night but insisted he come in with
her. The attack this evening must have scrambled
her brain.

The best thing to do was to pretend everything
was normal. If he had an ounce of consideration for
her feelings and the situation, he'd do the same.

Turning from him, she removed her small shoulder bag and dropped it on the foyer console, then
walked into the living room area to switch on a
lamp. She went through the suite, then, methodically
flipping switches until every light in the suite
glowed. As she emerged from the dressing room,
Luke was standing in the opening where French
doors divided the bedroom and living room.

"You afraid of the dark?" he asked. "Or is it
me?"

"Neither," she said, her voice crisp in spite of
the heat spreading upward from the neckline of her
suit blouse. "I'd just like to see what I'm doing."

His gaze remained on her features several seconds
longer. Then he reached for the buttons of his shirt,
releasing them without haste. "Right. In that case,
you won't mind if I take a quick shower first."

So much for expecting Luke's help in these circumstances. He meant to make them as trying as
possible. Or was the innuendo in his request all in

her mind? If he expected to upset her, however, he was in for a disappointment.

"Be my guest," she said with a quick wave in the direction of the bathroom. "There's a robe on the back of the door, generic hotel issue, one size fits all."

He thanked her in laconic tones. Seconds later, the bathroom door closed behind him.

April let out her pent-up breath and sank down on the edge of the king-size bed. As she heard the shower running, she jumped up again. She didn't have time to give in to doubts and recriminations. She had to get ready to take care of Luke now that he was here.

She was waiting for him when he stepped from the bathroom. Her gaze flickered over the wet waves of his hair and the droplets that clung to the dark, curling hair on his arms. Her stomach muscles clenched an instant, then she forced herself to relax. "Here, lie down on the bed."

"Whatever you say, ma'am," he drawled, his gaze edged with amusement. He began to shrug one shoulder from the robe, but his features tensed and he froze into stillness with his breath caught in his chest.

"Here, let me," she said, stepping forward.

"No!"

That he flinched away from her disturbed April almost as much as it annoyed her. "Don't be so touchy. I'm not going to hurt you. I wouldn't do that."

"Wouldn't you now?"

She turned sharply away from him, unwilling to

let him see how upset she was by the doubt in his voice. Searching through the first aid kit laid out on the nightstand, she found the bottle of pain medication she always carried. Shaking one of the pills into her hand, she moved to the tray containing the ice bucket. When she'd filled a glass with ice water, she carried it to Luke and thrust it and the pill toward him.

"What's this?"

"Percocet. My doctor prescribed them for the migraines I get now and then."

"I didn't know that." His black gaze was steady as he accepted the medication.

"There are a lot of things you don't know about me." Her lips took on an ironic twist as she recognized the repetition of what he'd said earlier.

He opened his mouth to reply, then closed it again. Shuttering his black gaze with his lashes, he gazed at the pill in his hand. "These things very strong?"

"Not strong enough to affect your driving, if that's what you mean."

He gave a quiet snort that might mean anything. Then he shrugged and popped the Percocet into his mouth, following it with a long swallow of water. April watched him, mesmerized by the movement of the muscles of his strong throat, until she suddenly noticed what she was doing. She turned away then, busying herself with her medical supplies.

When she looked back again, Luke was lying facedown on the bath sheet that she had spread over the mattress. His head was turned away from her and his eyes closed. The bathrobe lay across his lean flanks so he was naked to the waist.

For a scant second, she allowed herself to wonder if he was wearing anything under the robe. It didn't affect her one way or the other, of course. Dismissing the idea with determination, she reached for antibiotic ointment.

His skin was almost hot to the touch. She didn't think it was fever, not yet. Rather, it was his natural body heat, as if the fire of life inside him burned brighter than in most people. It made the tips of her fingers burn yet soothed them at the same time.

The broad expanse of his back was raw and inflamed in an irregular patch across his left shoulder and down the middle of his back. She touched that section lightly, then jerked her hand back as a shiver ran over him. Her voice not quite steady, she said, "Are you sure you shouldn't see a doctor?"

"I'm sure. Just get on with it." His tone bordered on surly.

She caught her bottom lip between her teeth, then squeezed a generous amount of ointment across her fingertips and spread it as gently as possible, barely touching him. He lay perfectly still, with no further sign that he felt her ministrations.

After a moment, she said, "I'm sorry you were hurt because of me."

"What makes you think that?" The towel and soft mattress under his cheek muffled the words.

"It seems more likely than you being the target, doesn't it? Besides, if you hadn't stepped in front of me, I would be the one..."

"Don't even think about it. It didn't happen."

"No, but—"

"Why would anybody want to maim you?"

"How should I know? The same reason they'd want to call the house and harass me, I suppose."

"Call the radio station, you mean?" He turned his head slightly, as if listening closely for her answer.

"What?"

"You said they called your house, but you meant the radio station, didn't you?"

"Yes—yes, of course," she answered with a quick glance at as much of his expression as she could see. It gave nothing away, allowed no clue as to whether he accepted her retrieval of the slip. Finishing with the most serious burn area of his back, she turned her attention to the less tender edges and scattered spots.

Luke was quiet under her ministrations for long seconds. Finally he said, "You think this business could have something to do with what you're writing?"

"My work in progress is a historical," she protested. "What could possibly be the connection?"

"It's still about the Benedict clan."

"What if it is?" She'd thought earlier, when Julianne mentioned her work in progress, that Luke hadn't shown enough curiosity. She might have known it was because he already knew about it.

"There are some who might not like the idea."

The hard undertone of his words was obvious, in part because she'd trained herself to notice such nuances, but also because she'd half expected it. Defensively, she asked, "You, for instance?"

"You could say that. Though I'm not the only one."

Briefly, April wondered if Luke could be behind the threats to her safety. He'd shown up out of the blue just as they escalated, hadn't he? Now he was in New Orleans at the same time she happened to be there. What if his whole purpose was to stop her from writing the book? What if he meant to entice her back into a relationship so he could use his beguiling ways to persuade her to drop the story?

No, that was impossible. He'd shielded her from the acid, hadn't he? Surely that proved he could not be involved. Or did it? With his understanding of women, he might have reasoned that playing the hero, saving her from injury at his own expense, would be the perfect way to redeem himself. But what reason for preventing the book from being written could possibly be worth the pain?

Her voice tight, she said, "You mentioned others. Who else?"

"My grandmother, mainly. But there's also a whole set of backcountry Benedicts who just might form a pickup posse if you show them in a bad light. Or even if they only think you might."

"That's ridiculous."

"Not to Roan. It's his theory."

That put a different light on the subject. She remembered that Benedict family branch he'd mentioned. They'd been a wild bunch back in high school, a tightly knit group who lived deep in the Horseshoe Lake swamplands. They'd looked out for each other in the halls and on the athletic field. If one got in trouble, male or female, all that was required was a high-pitched whistle and suddenly Benedicts with knotted fists and fire in their eyes came out of the woodwork. They excelled at sports, but also had an artistic bent. Most of them could play any musical instrument they picked up, draw anything they saw. One of the quieter boys had become a nature photographer famous on a national level for his swamp studies. Another was a ballad singer with a huge cult following. A girl who had been in April's class at school was a quilt designer with her own line of hand-dyed fabrics and a series of books featuring her elaborate fabric art patterns.

However, there were other cousins who were armored in hidebound ignorance and proud of it. They spat their chewing tobacco on the sidewalks in town, carried hunting rifles in their pickup truck racks, trapped mink, raccoons and nutria in winter, and had been known to wrestle alligators for the fun of it. The words *artistic license* were unlikely to be in their vocabulary.

"I'm not naming names," she said defensively, "only using a little of the background. The Benedicts are a part of the history of the area. Their experiences reflect those of the earliest families to settle Turn-Coupe, only with a bit more color. I certainly don't intend to libel anybody living now."

"They don't know that and they like their privacy. Besides, to their mind there's not a lot of difference between libel and ridicule."

He had a point, as much as she hated to admit it. A frown drew her brows together as she said, "I'll try to avoid either one, but with all the political correctness these days, it's getting harder and harder to find a decent villain for a story!''

"We all have our problems," he answered without noticeable sympathy.

She gave him a dark look, but the effort was lost as his eyes were still closed. Finished with the ointment, she put the top back on it and set it aside, then cut several lengths of bandaging gauze. As she folded these and put them carefully in place, she asked, "How do you know it was sulfuric acid that caused all this damage?"

"Tom, down at the hardware, once sold me a mislabeled bottle of it in the place of the muriatic acid I wanted."

"What would you want that for?"

"The muriatic? It's used to clean bricks. I wanted it to clear the moss from the front steps at Chemin-a-Haut." He opened his eyes. "Why do you ask?"

Pretending distraction as she cut pieces of nylon tape to fasten the bandaging strips, she said, "Just wondering—and thinking about where someone might get sulfuric acid."

"Nothing to it," he answered, twitching a shoulder as he relaxed again. "It's one of the most common chemicals in the world, used for everything from fertilizer and detergent to drugs. It's also the lead acid in storage batteries used in cars. If someone wanted it, they'd only have to pay a visit to the friendly neighborhood junkyard."

"And where did you learn all that?"

"From an encyclopedia when I was trying to figure out what to do with a gallon of it," he snapped. "Lord, April, you can't think—"

"No, of course not," she interrupted as she pressed the last piece of tape in place and stepped back. "There, all done. Now I think I'll take a shower myself so I can put a little ointment on my own blisters."

He turned his head, starting to rise. "You're hurt? But I thought—"

"Don't move!" she warned, but he had already halted as pain cut off his voice. She put a hand lightly on the tense muscles of his arm. "Lie back down a minute until the pill takes effect. The burns I have are nothing, just a couple of spots."

"You're sure?" He searched her face, his own features shadowed with grimness.

"Positive," she answered, and was pleased to feel some of the stiffness leave him. "I'll bring your clothes out here first so you can ease back into them when you feel up to it."

He made no answer, only gave her a close look. April thought she might have overdone the solicitation in contrast to her usual coolness. She turned away and walked briskly into the dressing room with its connecting bath.

Luke's eyes were closed and he had pulled a pillow down under his head when she returned with his shirt and pants. He looked more comfortable than before, as if the pain had eased. It seemed a shame to disturb him to say goodbye, though he'd have to make a move soon in order to take himself to his hotel.

There was something disquietingly sensual about him as he lay sprawled on the bed with his olive-bronze skin in dark contrast to the white bath sheet.

The thick fringe of his lashes made a scimitar shadow across the strong line of his nose. She could see the dark stubble of the beard under his skin, also a small scar in one brow that made it uneven, and the pulse that beat in a sure, steady rhythm in the hollow of his throat. The curves of his mouth hinted at both passion and laughter.

What was she doing? Standing there mooning over Luke Benedict was nearly as dumb as inviting him to her room in the first place. The last thing she needed was for him to open his eyes and catch her at it.

Whipping away from him, she picked up the antibiotic ointment, then searched out her nightgown from her suitcase and moved back toward the bathroom. Once inside, she closed and locked the door.

She decided on a bath instead of a shower and spent several minutes luxuriating in water scented by the bath gel provided by the hotel. Afterward, she went through her ritual of various creams, flossing and brushing, then applied the ointment and a couple of adhesive bandages. She didn't hurry since she wanted to give Luke plenty of time to dress and go. It was perhaps a half hour later when she tied her peach silk bathrobe around her and walked back into the bedroom.

Luke hadn't moved since she'd left him. His chest rose and fell in an even tempo that showed plainly that he was asleep.

Marching to the bed, she put her fingers on his good shoulder and gave him a nudge. "Luke?"

Nothing happened.

"Luke, wake up." She shook him again though

she was reluctant to be too rough for fear of hurting him.

He didn't move. He wasn't going to move. He was out of it, and it was her own fault for passing out medication. She should have let him suffer.

She put her fingers to her mouth as she stared at him, at Luke Benedict sleeping in her bed. A soundless laugh shook her, followed by a wave of weariness. What a thing to happen, yet she couldn't feel surprised. It was exactly the kind of incident that would have bedeviled the heroine of one of her novels.

So, what now?

It was her suite and she was exhausted. Whatever the fallout might be, she would deal with it in the morning. For now, she'd had enough. She was going to bed.

She'd also had enough of being harassed and threatened. On that subject, she'd just taken one of her "bathtub" decisions—the relaxation of bath time being when she saw things most clearly and often had her best ideas. If Luke Benedict had a hand in what was being done to her, she was going to find out. If that meant delving deeper into his family history or spending more time with him, then so be it.

Research was her forte. Putting together bits and pieces from many sources then reaching a conclusion based on logic and informed intuition was what she did for a living. How much different could it be to figure out who was trying to harm her, whether it was Luke or someone else?

There had to be some explanation. It wasn't random harassment; the events of the past few days proved that much. When she had the all-important *why,* then the *who* should be clear. Once that occurred, the person responsible was going to realize she was no helpless victim. She would see to that, no matter what it took.

There was one thing more. If Luke Benedict thought a night spent naked in her bed was going to change anything, he was much mistaken. He would know it, too, before he was another day older. She was also going to see to that detail.

6

As the lights clicked off in the suite, Luke lay perfectly still and allowed himself a few seconds of amazement. He was in; he'd made it. He was spending the night with April. The possibility had hovered in the back of his mind as he set out for New Orleans the day before, but he'd never really expected it to materialize.

Who would have thought it?

Not that he could claim to be sleeping with her exactly. She'd pulled the heavy bedspread from the bed and dragged it with her to the living room sofa. At least he thought that was where she'd gone; he'd check it out when he was sure it was safe to open his eyes.

She'd covered him before she left, though. She'd actually loosened the lightweight blanket on the bed and flung the extra width across him against the air-conditioned chill of the room. What did that mean? Or did it mean anything beyond simple consideration? He didn't care; he was still grateful.

Not that his acid burns were as big a deal as he'd led her to believe. They weren't exactly comfortable, of course, but he'd had worse. To have April hovering over him had just been such a novelty that he couldn't resist playing the wounded soldier. He'd also been curious to see how far her concern would stretch. Now he knew.

He'd expected to be dragged off the big bed and sent on his way when she came out of the bathroom. That he hadn't puzzled him. Gratitude was one thing, but this was something else.

Or was it? Maybe he only wanted to think so. Yes, and maybe gratitude was a poor substitute for what he had in mind. What would she do, he wondered, if he eased off the bed, went and knelt beside the sofa, and…?

He was an idiot to even think about it. He'd gotten this far, hadn't he? The last thing he needed was to scare her away now. With a stifled groan, he wrestled his hormones back under control.

The pain medication she'd given him was stronger than he expected. He could certainly feel its effects. He might be able to fight it off, but there was little need given the hotel's superefficient security. He knew April had flipped the dead bolt on the door and set the heavy safety latch because he'd heard her do it. Still, he'd get up in a few minutes and ease around checking doors and windows, Luke thought. Then he'd allow himself a couple of hours of oblivion.

It was a fine plan and he even followed it up to a point. However, after a second patrol conducted as dawn fingered the edges of the thick, light-blocking window drapes, he dropped into a black hole and didn't come out of it until midmorning.

April was stirring a little, but not really awake. Luke climbed out of bed and dressed with care in the bathroom. He grimaced at the ragged state of his shirt and its lingering sour acid smell. There was nothing he could do about it except wait until the last minute to put it on. He'd rather toss it into the trash, but wasn't about to march half-naked through the Windsor Court's lobby.

While rambling around at loose ends, he discovered a small electric coffeemaker and supplies in the suite's kitchen. He brewed a pot, then carried a cup of it with him as he went to squat beside the sofa.

April Halstead was a sight to behold as she lay sleeping. He'd known that in the old days, from naps on picnics or during the bus trips coming home from late football games. He'd watched entranced then as he was doing now. Her lips looked so smooth and soft, with their generous curves and tucked corners, that the need to test them made him light-headed. The rest of her seemed just as enticing as she lay with one hand flung above her head so he had a stunning view of the tender curves of her breasts under peach silk.

Taking an uneven breath, he glanced away an instant. Then used his free hand to waft the steam from the coffee cup toward her face. After a few seconds, her lashes flickered then lifted.

"'Morning,'" he said with carefully controlled cheerfulness. "How about a peace offering since I took your bed last night?"

She stared at him for long seconds, her gaze soft and vulnerable. Then her lashes swept down. Pulling her bedspread higher around her, she flounced over on the sofa with her back to him. In a voice thickened by sleep, she muttered, "Go away."

Luke gave a wry shake of his head as he lifted the coffee he held to his mouth. Back to square one. He should have known that last night's truce was too good to last.

It was almost checkout time when the two of them finally left the room. While April saw to those formalities, Luke stepped outside to see if their respective vehicles had arrived from valet parking. They had, thanks to an advance call from the suite. After collecting the keys to the Jeep and her Lincoln Mark and passing out tips, he went back inside.

April was just crossing the lobby toward him. She was truly an ice maiden this morning, with every hair in place where it was coiled on top of her head, flawless makeup, and a pantsuit of cool blue silk. Luke had about decided that such perfection was like a mask, something to hide behind. There was no way to know if he was right.

Suddenly a man sitting in the nearby salon rose to his feet and started in her direction. Luke moved swiftly to step between April and this new threat. Holding one hand up in a gesture for her to stop, he turned to face the man.

"April!" the guy called. "I knew you'd show up if I waited long enough. Can you believe they wouldn't give me your room number, even after I told them I was your husband?"

"Ex-husband," she said crisply.

It was Martin Tinsley, the lowlife she'd married in a desperate bid to get out of Turn-Coupe, Luke realized. He'd classified Tinsley in his mind as a smooth operator when he first met him back then and saw no reason to change his opinion now. Of medium height with dark hair and brown eyes, he was a sharp dresser with manicured nails, perfectly trimmed hair, and the kind of slick good looks that bowled over more impressionable females. It was gratifying to Luke to note that April's voice when she spoke to her ex was even chillier than when she talked to him.

"Yeah, all right, ex-husband," Tinsley said with what he apparently thought was an engaging smile, "but that can be changed any time you say the word."

As Tinsley tried to sidestep to get around him, Luke cut him off again. April's ex gave him a dirty look, but Luke shrugged it off. At the same time, he filed away under interesting information the fact that the guy wasn't happy with his divorce.

"What do you want?" April asked impatiently.

"You could act a little happier to see me," Tinsley complained, "seeing that I drove all the way downtown to pay you a visit."

She lifted a brow. "I prefer to wait until I know why you bothered."

The question had also crossed Luke's mind. He wondered, too, what Tinsley had been doing the night before, and if he'd turned up today in the hope that April might be nervous enough to accept his company.

"I saw where you were in town and thought, well, why not?" Tinsley spread his hands in an expansive gesture as if to indicate that he was all hers. Still, his insouciance didn't quite reach his eyes. He appeared to be carefully assessing her reactions, and Luke's.

"I could have saved you the drive if you'd called first," she answered.

"Which is why I didn't. Have you had brunch, or whatever?"

"Luke and I have eaten, yes," April said in clipped tones.

That was a lie, as Luke knew full well. April hadn't touched a bite of the breakfast for two he'd ordered and paid for from his own pocket. At least it proved how little she wanted to linger in Tinsley's company. It also shifted her ex's attention to Luke.

"Benedict here?" The other man's gaze narrowed and he belatedly offered his hand as though April's speaking of him constituted an introduction. "I recognize the family resemblance though I can't say I recalled the first name."

"We met at the wedding." Luke kept his contact with Tinsley brief in spite of the ex-husband's attempt to turn the handshake into a bone-crushing contest. The guy remembered him all right, Luke knew. Denying it was just a part of the game of one-upmanship he seemed to be playing.

"Guess I was a little distracted at the time by my bride," Tinsley said. "I just couldn't see straight for thinking about the wedding night. You know how it is."

The need to knock the guy's head off his shoulders was so strong that Luke gritted his teeth while he fought it. Since it was impossible to reply with his jaws clenched, he didn't bother.

"So, you two are here together?" the former husband continued. "Strange, as I seem to remember that you don't get along all that well."

"We do now," Luke answered.

"We don't," April said at the same time.

Tinsley cocked his head as he tucked a thumb into the waistband of his pants. "So, which is it? Do you or don't you?"

Luke made no immediate answer, but turned toward April with a brow quirked in inquiry. She wouldn't look at him. The expression on her face was remote, as though she wished herself far away from both of them.

If that was the way she wanted to play it, fine. Luke didn't mind carrying the ball. "Things change," he said to Tinsley. "April just happens to need someone around for various and sundry reasons. Now, if you don't mind, we have places to go." Turning toward April, he said, "Are you ready?"

She gave him a brief nod before swinging toward the entrance with him. They began to walk away.

"Hey, wait a minute…" Tinsley broke off what he was about to say as he took a quick step after them. Catching a ragged fold of the back of Luke's shirt in his fist, he exclaimed, "Lord man, what happened to you? Looks as if you've been in a cat fight."

The sneer in the man's voice and its loud tone that drew unwanted attention their way was the last straw for Luke. He turned his head to give Tinsley a steady look. In deadpan tones, he said, "Something like that. Sharp fingernails in the heat of the moment. You know how it is."

Tinsley turned a dusky red and glared as if he'd like to commit murder on the spot. April gasped in outrage. Luke was past caring what either of them thought. He put his hand on April's arm and walked her toward the door without looking back.

She could have balked. She could have given him a piece of her mind the instant they were out the door. Neither happened. Instead, she took the keys Luke handed over and walked to where her vehicle was parked. Luke hesitated a second, then followed her.

"About what happened back in there," he began in some discomfort.

"Nothing happened. Forget it." She opened her car door and slid inside.

"I'd like to, believe me, but it doesn't seem in the cards. Where does Tinsley stand in all this?"

"He doesn't. Just like you."

The glance she gave him held a warning before she turned away to put her key in the ignition. As she reached to close her car door, Luke put a hand on the frame to stop her. "What I'm asking," he said, "is where he stands legally. Is the divorce final? Did you have a will naming him the beneficiary and has it been canceled? What about an insurance policy? In other words, would he benefit in any way if anything happened to you?"

"You make it sound as if you think someone's trying to kill me." The gaze she turned on him was accusing, yet had a shadow of alarm in its depths.

"Somebody's up to something and I don't think they're planning an award for Author of the Year." The endless chime warning of the car's over the open door wore on his nerves. It sounded like a warning for them as well.

"Well, Martin isn't behind it, so you can forget him," she said with precision. "He's too certain he can talk me around to resort to crude scare tactics."

"Would he use them to make you think you need him?"

"I doubt it, since being protective was never his strong suit. On the other hand," she continued, holding his gaze, "that thought had crossed my mind about you."

Luke's chest felt so tight it hurt, but he figured he might as well find out where he stood before this went any farther. "Did it, now? And what did you decide?"

"That anything is possible," she declared in defiance as she tugged on her car door. "Would you please let go so I can leave?"

He didn't budge. "You don't really think I had anything to do with what happened last night?"

"I don't know what I believe," she said a shade desperately. "I don't know you anymore. Sometimes I think I never did."

"I'm the same," he said in quiet certainty. "I've always been the same."

"Well, I'm not! I'm not as stupid and innocent and trusting. Hard muscles, a cocky grin, and my own amorous impulses don't influence me anymore. I don't need protecting by anybody, and I certainly don't need you. Now get out of my way or I'll drive over you and never look back!"

She meant it. Now was definitely not the time to push her. "Yes, ma'am." he said in deadpan agreement as he stepped back and closed the door. "Drive carefully. I'll be right behind you."

"You'd better stick close or all you'll see is dust," she answered as she turned the key.

Luke watched her put the Lincoln in gear and pull out of the hotel's front court. At the same time, the things she'd said echoed in his head.

No, she wasn't the same. Her armor was thick, and the razor-sharp words she used as protective weapons cut deep. She had become a beautiful woman of formidable intelligence and endless layers of protective reserve. Getting involved with her again could be dangerous to his heart as well as his ego.

All the same, he was going to try. He had to try, had to use all his hard-earned experience to entice her back into his arms, even knowing the effort could backfire on him.

So she'd noticed the muscles, had she? He had that much on his side. She had amorous impulses, too. Interesting. Especially if they might be, or could be, directed toward him.

He shook his head as a smile of quiet anticipation tipped one corner of his mouth. "Oh, April, sweetheart," he said softly, "I'll stick close. I'll be so close you'll think I'm your shadow. Every time you look up, I'll be there. Run as fast as you can, but you'll never get away from me. Never."

7

Midnight was gone.

He was a tomcat so had a tendency to roam, especially when April left him alone at Mulberry Point. There was a cat door cut in the back entrance and she always left plenty of food and water out for him, plus had a neighbor look in from time to time. When she returned, he was usually aloof in his annoyance at being left, but never let it keep him from stalking out to meet her as she pulled into the drive.

This time, he didn't come when April called, wasn't in any of his usual haunts such as the old carriage shed that was used as a garage or under the raised floor of the house. Setting his favorite dish on the back porch didn't make him come running. Calling him while she tramped through the woods that crowded one side of the house didn't bring him pouncing from ambush to wind around her legs.

It was possible, of course, that he'd found a new mate during her absence. April had never had the heart to have him neutered, no matter how responsible she knew it to be. His latest romance would last only a short while, no doubt, then he'd be back, battle-scarred, exhausted, and craving sympathy.

She wouldn't worry, or at least not for a couple of days.

Her pet was just an alley cat, a stray she'd found sleeping on the warm hood of her car during her last winter in New Orleans. Martin had hated the idea of a black cat as a pet, which was one reason she'd been so determined to tame and keep the scrawny kitten. She'd fed and groomed Midnight, played with him, told him all her troubles. In return, the cat had given her his single-minded devotion. He lay for hours in the sunny window next to the desk where she worked. When he thought she'd done enough, he often rose and leaped to her desktop, stalked across the piles of papers and books, then sprawled across her computer keyboard.

She missed him.

It was scary, really, how much she worried and fretted. In between bouts of imagining all the things that could have happened to him, she felt deserted and even angry that he hadn't returned. She hadn't realized how much of her emotional life was bound up in that useless cat. The house felt empty without him.

She could settle to nothing, could not get into her book in progress at all. She thought almost constantly about the attempts to get to her and who could be behind them. She had begun her writing career with a lovelorn teens' advice column in her high school paper because she'd always been fascinated by why people did things. She still had a habit of analyzing the attitudes and backgrounds of those she met, noting the way they carried out, and screwed up, their lives. It was doubly frustrating, then, that she could find no motive for what was happening to her now.

She spent a lot of time on the rear gallery of Mulberry Point, sitting at a cast iron table while she stared at the lake that lapped the lawn's edge. It seemed that everyone and everything she cared about left her alone. Her father who'd preferred getting drunk at the local bar to being with his family, then had taken both himself and her mother into the afterworld in a blast of rage and shotgun pellets. Her grandmother who had succumbed to cancer while she was away at college. Luke who had gone from her arms to those of another girl, one who had died because of him.

She'd sent Martin away herself, of course; not that she'd ever really cared. But then being with her self-centered ex-husband had been the next thing to being alone.

Death and loneliness seemed to follow her everywhere. The idea was frightening, but nothing new. Its specter had been with her for years, since well before she had left Turn-Coupe. It wasn't really stronger since she'd returned; it was only the constant reminders of the past that made it seem that way.

Not that she'd given up on Midnight, naturally. He would be back sooner or later. He had to come back.

Her mind drifted often to New Orleans, replaying every scene that had happened there. The last one, when Luke had faced down Martin, nagged at her. Seeing the two men together had reinforced everything she knew about her ex. Compared to Luke, Martin had seemed like a shell of a man, handsome

on the outside but empty within. His smiles and engaging mannerisms had struck her as calculated instead of the natural charm of an outgoing personality. The contrast between the two men had stunned
her so much that she'd hardly noticed what they
were saying to each other.

That was until there at the end, of course. The
very idea of Luke suggesting her fingernails had
ripped his shirt. As if she had so little self-control
that she would do such a thing. On the other hand,
the look on Martin's face had been priceless. She
couldn't help grinning just a little to herself at the
memory—not that she'd forgiven Luke or had any
intention of it. He might have a more solid character
than Martin but he was another man too handsome
for his own good.

The power and heat of Luke's body, not to mention that of his smiles, had not left her unaffected.
He turned her on; it was as simple as that. It was
an interesting if uncomfortable discovery. She'd
thought she was immune, even numb, to that kind
of desire. She couldn't regret the revelation that she
was not, even if she intended to avoid at all costs
the man who'd caused it.

Avoiding thinking about it, however, might be
another thing entirely.

It was a relief to be forced from the house to
participate in Kane and Regina's wedding rehearsal.
That practice went off without a hitch, probably
because Luke wasn't there. Luke, an accomplished
pilot who did his own crop dusting, had flown an
elderly friend of his grandmother's to an appoint-

ment with a heart specialist in Houston. He'd promised to be back in plenty of time for the ceremony,
however, and had been best man so many times that
he had the drill down pat. Regina's young son, Stephan, was drafted to play the part as well as being
ring bearer, and the rehearsal and the dinner afterward proceeded without Luke.

The afternoon of the wedding was hot and bright.
The church parking lot was crowded with cars, as
were the streets surrounding the small Victorian
chapel. Regina was beautiful in champagne silk
heavy with seed pearls and with a Juliet cap on her
flowing auburn hair. Kane was stalwart and handsome in his black tuxedo. Happiness crackled
around them like silent fireworks.

It was touching to see the way they concentrated
on each other during the ceremony, as if no one and
nothing else existed. Their smiles were intense, their
eyes liquid with promise. Watching them made
April's fingers itch for her notepad so she could jot
down descriptions of what love looked like for future reference.

It was as the exchange of rings was being made
that she glanced at Luke. He was concentrating on
his job, but pretended to fumble the bridal ring as
he passed it to Kane. The look Kane gave him held
an amiable threat but Luke's grin in return was un-
repentant.

Nothing was serious to Luke, April thought with
a tight frown. Life was a fine joke, an endless suc-
cession of good times. He worked hard, yes, but he
played harder. He had no ambition, no goals in life
other than farming the land at Chemin-a-Haut and

seeing after his grandmother. He was a throwback to another age. That was a shame because he could have been anything he wanted. She wondered, almost at random, why he hadn't become a lawyer, like Kane, or gone into law enforcement as Roan had done. Why hadn't he tried politics, medicine, business and finance—anything except farming? Was it possible the events of that night thirteen years ago had affected him more than it seemed, after all?

April was so deep in thought that she was startled as the recessional blared forth from the church organ. She hurried to straighten Regina's train as the bride and groom turned to face the congregation. Then April took the arm Luke offered and followed the married couple down the aisle.

"You're looking stunning, as usual," he said with a quick glance at her tea-length dress of pale peach silk.

"So are you," she said with irony. Black tie might have been designed especially to set off the Benedict brand of dark attraction. She could just catch the elusive sandalwood and spice of his aftershave as well. The slight, enticing scent seemed much more likely to encourage females to come closer than the more powerful concoctions favored by most men.

"You know we're supposed to ride together to the reception?" he added. "Seems a limo has been provided for us as well as Kane and his lady, since we're the only attendants other than Regina's Stephan."

"I know." April had her misgivings about it,

though she could see no way out short of being extremely rude.

"Well, don't fall into a depression," Luke advised with a twist to his mobile lips. "It's only a ten-minute drive out to The Haven."

She gave him a straight look. "I know that, too."

"Good. It takes longer than that to seduce a woman, even for me."

There was no time for the scathing reply that rose to her lips. They had emerged on the church steps where the photographer waited. April and Luke stood back while Kane and Regina were immortalized, then they stepped forward to submit to their part of the ordeal. By the time they were finished, the churchyard and its parking lot had cleared and only the two white limos were left waiting.

The chauffeur of the second car held the door for April. Luke stood back until she was seated, then swept her silk skirts out of his way with a practiced hand before joining her. She slipped across the seat as far as it was possible to go. The look he gave her from under his lashes held equal parts of annoyance and resignation.

"I don't bite, I promise. Unless a love nip or two is requested by a lady."

"We should have no problem, then," she said coolly, "since I won't be asking for anything at all."

"Now that's a relief. Demanding women can be so tiring." As the heavy vehicle slid away from the curb behind the first limo holding the bride and groom, Luke slumped down with his long legs stretched out into the open space of the back. He

knitted his fingers over his chest and closed his eyes
with a long sigh.

She could almost believe he was exhausted from
a night of debauchery or, at the very least, a wild
stag party for Kane. The main thing wrong with that
picture was that she knew from Regina he'd only
returned from Houston in the small hours of the
morning. Her voice a little abrupt, she asked, "How
is your grandmother's friend?"

He lifted his lashes. "She's all right—for a can-
tankerous old biddy with more spirit than strength,
one who thinks doctors don't know squat about her
ailments."

"I take it she was more trouble on your flight
yesterday than the women you usually take up with
you?" April's voice was a little warmer as she realized that there was as much affection in his tone
as there was exasperation.

"You take it right. Though what you know about
my flying or my dating habits—"

"Nothing whatsoever except for the little that Regina or Kane mention from time to time. You'll find
this difficult to believe, I'm sure, but I do have other
interests."

"But not amorous interests. Such a waste." He
closed his eyes again.

"You," she said with a curl to her finely molded
lips, "are in no position to judge."

"You saying you go out on the town now and
then? Or are you only admitting to X-rated fantasies?"

"None of your business," she snapped with
something less than originality.

"I could make it my business with a little effort. I wouldn't want you to be too deprived."

She sent him a quick glance. His eyes were closed and he sounded half asleep, as if the discussion were too boring to keep him awake or else he was paying little attention to his own distracted replies. She wondered if the offer he'd just made was a knee-jerk response to any female who appeared in need of male attention, or if he was serious. The impulse to test him hovered in the back of her mind for a full second before she dismissed it. In glacial tones, she said, "Thank you, but I'll pass."

"Not interested, huh? Or is it only that you'd rather be a man's main woman, object of his whole attention and complete adoration?"

"I'm only interested in what's real and true," she answered tightly.

"True love, real love, cherishing and keeping forever, amen, till death do us part?"

"Something like that." She looked away out the window at the stretch of green woodland they were passing where ferns grew under the spreading branches of the hardwoods and vines looped between them like twisted, living ropes.

"Are you sure? Or would you really like the excitement of a wild affair with fast flights and breathless meetings during the afternoon? Come on, admit it. Staid dates won't cut it. You need more."

"Don't be ridiculous," she snapped.

"Am I being ridiculous?" His slow smile curved the sensuous fullness of his mouth. "Don't tell me an affair with no ties or regrets has no appeal?" He opened his eyes suddenly to expose the heat in the depths of his dark gaze.

She tore her gaze away though she could feel the warmth of a flush creeping along her neck. "None at all."

"You're sure?"

"I'm positive," she replied, setting her lips in a straight line.

"You wouldn't succumb, wouldn't let yourself be persuaded? You're sure you would resist to the last inch if I decided to seduce you?"

"You must be joking. You're the last man I'd trust anywhere near me."

His gaze narrowed. "Is that so? Or should I take it as a challenge?"

"It's the unvarnished truth, believe me. But the point is moot since you haven't the least intention of seducing anybody." The words had an irritable sound that she hadn't quite intended, as if her annoyance might stem from his lack of ambition rather than his arrogance.

"Oh, April. You underestimate me. Is it just a habit or deliberate provocation?"

"Call it considered judgment." That had the right tinge of disdain, she thought. Even she winced a little at the sound of it.

He smiled with a slow pleasure that tugged one corner of his lips upward. "It's a challenge then, a bet. I say I can entice you into bed, you say I can't. What we need now is a prize for the winner. I won't make it too hard on you, since I'm easy to please. Shall we say breakfast in bed?"

"Served while in a state of nature, I suppose."

He quirked a brow. "I didn't expect that much of a concession, but if you like that kind of..."

"I don't. Nor do I intend to enter into any kind of stupid bet with you."

"Because you know you'll lose."

The quiet confidence of his smile was infuriating, but she wouldn't be goaded into something she'd regret. The words distant, she answered, "If you say so."

"Chicken," he said softly. "I wonder if you'd fight me right this minute if I decided to steal a kiss? Or would you poker up like a marble-cold statue and let me do my worst?"

She drew back a little, her gaze watchful. "I don't think you want to find out, not with the driver up front."

"Oh, I don't mind Clay—do I buddy?" he called as he switched his gaze to the driver.

The man in the black suit of a chauffeur gave them a quick glance in the mirror followed by a jaunty salute. Seeing it, April felt her throat tighten. "If this is some kind of game, I don't see the payoff. You have no interest in me, and I've none in you. What earthly reason could you have for putting out so much effort?"

"Purest pleasure." His voice was velvety and his gaze slumberous as he let it rest on her lips. With a smooth coiling of muscles, he levered himself upright and eased closer.

"Hardly that. Unless you get your kicks out of a lack of cooperation."

"Who says you won't cooperate?"

"Who do you think?" She retreated slightly as he leaned even nearer.

"Sounds to me as if you mean you accept the bet," he murmured, reaching out to brush her arm with the palm of his hand then smooth the skin in a slow circle.

"No—" she began, then stopped on a sudden catch of breath as a shiver ran over her.

"Oh, I think you did. And do. Or will if you don't want to lose right here and now in a nest of white leather upholstery and pink silk."

"Peach," she corrected, even as she felt her lashes quiver on the verge of closing. The allure of his black gaze was so strong that she couldn't look away.

"Peach," he agreed in a whisper. "Sweet peach-flavored woman. Just a taste can't hurt, can it?"

But it could, and she knew it very well in that part of her mind where instinct stood armed and at bay. She drew a strangled breath as she sought something, anything, to use as a weapon. "Ego," she said, her voice husky. "That's it, isn't it? You need to stroke your ego with one more conquest?"

"The final conquest?" he mused. "Now there's a thought."

"Final?"

"You, my love, are the ultimate." His smile was dulcet. "Roan called you the one who got away and he's not far from wrong."

"How very flattering," she said in dry disparagement.

"Isn't it?"

As he leaned closer still, she put her spread fingers on his chest to hold him back. "You'll have to excuse me, but I don't have time for this game, even if I had the inclination. Don't worry, I'm sure you'll find some other female willing to let you make a fool of them."

He met her gaze a long instant. Something he saw there must have convinced him she wasn't going to play, for he drew back. "Maybe," he replied as he returned to his familiar slouch, "but it won't be the same."

As contrary as it might be, April was pleased to hear that much.

The reception, like Kane's Greek temple of a mansion, The Haven, was only elegant on the surface. Beneath the gloss of antique silver, fine china, lace and rose bowerlike decorations, was a down-home celebration. There was a plethora of good food and drink, great music from a country music band, and a fine company of relatives, friends and neighbors intent on enjoying themselves. In typical Benedict fashion, children of all ages from toddlers to preteens ran and yelled and stuffed their grinning faces. The more staid teenagers courted on the stairs, while the corners were occupied by the elder generation catching up with recent births, deaths, marriages and divorces.

After the cutting of the cake, Kane danced with Regina. The two of them moved together in such harmony, concentrating so completely on each other that it made April's heart ache to see it. The light from the candles on the bride's table gleamed in the ivory silk of Regina's dress and along the fiery strands of her hair. It shone on Kane's face and

warmed his gray eyes until they burned with promise. Love and devotion radiated from them in such
waves that they seemed to shimmer with it. Their
enjoyment of the moment was like a free-running
river so deep and full it carried everything and everybody in its flood.

"I thought for a while there earlier in the summer
that I'd never see this day."

The deep drawl laced with humor came from behind Regina. She turned to smile at Roan who
walked on up to stand at her shoulder. "Because
Kane and Regina were at each other's throats from
the minute she came to town?" she asked. "They
were always right for each other, in spite of it."

"Yes, but it's sometimes a little hard to see that
kind of thing when you're in the middle of a fight.
Sort of like you and Luke."

"Oh, please," she said with a grimace.

"You telling me there's nothing between you?
Hard to believe, when I expect to see the place go
up in flames every time he looks this way."

"He's only outdone because I have better things
to do than fall in with his little dramas."

"Like what? Writing about the family?"

His question carried such disapproval that she
gave him a sharp look. "Don't tell me you're
against it, too?"

"Don't know, since I haven't seen what you're
doing. The question is why you decided on us, and
why now. If it's because we're a part of what you
know and love, that's one thing. If it's to poke a
finger in Luke's eye, that's something else again—
especially if you mean to show us in a bad light."

"All I'm doing is writing a story," she protested. "No deep meaning, no ulterior motives, no personal agenda whatever."

"You're sure?"

His voice was stern, his gaze more than a little judgmental. In some curiosity, she said, "That almost sounds as if you care more about Luke than about the family."

"He's had a lot weighing on him these past few years. Farming isn't the most stress-free occupation in the world, you know, what with constant weather worries, genetically improved bugs and the sky-high cost of equipment. He has a lot of people depending on him, too, not only his grandmother but an elderly aunt or two and a couple of cousins he's putting through college."

"I didn't realize that," she said.

"He doesn't say a lot about it. That's not his way. But if you include the problem of outrunning his demons left over from the wreck all those years ago, it adds up."

"Not to mention juggling his women," she said with a grim smile.

"Luke likes women," Roan agreed. "Young ones, old ones, short, tall, thin, plump—he likes them all. He gets a kick out of how they talk and the way they think, their softness and the way they go about things. Women sense it, and like him in return. It doesn't mean he uses them."

"I never thought it did," she protested.

"Didn't you?" Roan asked, and there was no smile on his stern, rough-edged features.

Perhaps he was right, perhaps she did consider

Luke as an insatiable and indiscriminate user of women. It was easier, and certainly more comfortable, than seeing him as a man seeking an antidote to pain in tender female arms.

In an effort to change what had become a difficult subject, she asked, "What about you? I've been wondering for some time why you have no steady woman. Aren't you interested?"

"I'm not immune, if that's what you mean." He shifted a shoulder. "Truth is, I don't have much time for it."

"But you'll make time when the right woman comes along and holds a gun to your head?"

"Any woman who puts a gun to my head will find herself flat on her back."

She laughed at his instant reaction; she couldn't help it. "Could be that's where she'll want to be, if you're lucky."

A rueful grin lighted the dark gray of his eyes as he answered, "Let's hope so. But a little firearm protection for a woman living alone isn't a bad idea, you know. You might want to think about it. Luke could give you a few lessons in how to handle a pistol or rifle. He's a pretty good marksman."

Such praise from Roan could only mean that Luke qualified as an expert, though it wasn't too unusual in an area where most men were hunters. The skill was hardly a recommendation to her, however, though the sheriff didn't seem to realize that. "I appreciate the thought, but I don't think so," she answered, and turned the conversation in a more comfortable direction.

The reception settled into a familiar pattern.

Kane's grandfather, Mr. Lewis, held a place of honor with his pretty new bride, white-haired Miss Elise, beside him. The elderly gentleman stood up with Regina after she danced the first dance with her groom and the second with her son. Kane led Miss Elise out onto the floor during the slow waltz, circling the floor with her as carefully as if she were made of fragile crystal that might break at a touch.

By tradition, the next dance was reserved for the members of the wedding party. April had forgotten this bit of wedding etiquette until Luke appeared to bow in front of her as yet another slow dance began.

He should have appeared comical as he enacted that bit of pomp and ceremony like some gentleman in tie and tails from a remake of *Gone with the Wind*. Instead, he carried it off with grace and style. April was the one who felt awkward and more than a little conspicuous as she accepted the arm he offered and moved with him to the floor. She'd have refused but couldn't quite bring herself to make that public a rebuff. Consideration for his feelings didn't enter into it. The manners pounded into her as a child were the main factor, but there was also the gossip mill to be taken into account. That kind of display would be enough to keep it in high gear for a week.

In the center of the polished floor created by pushing chairs against the wall and rolling up the antique rugs, Luke turned to April and drew her into his arms. It felt almost dangerous, as if she were doing something she might regret. It had been a long time since she'd been in such intimate contact with a man, but particularly with Luke. That night in his hotel room didn't count. Tending his injuries while he lay flat on his stomach wasn't the same at all. She hadn't been quite so aware, then, of the width of his shoulders, the taut strength of his arms, or the latent power in the way his legs moved against her silk-covered thighs.

"I realize the bow tie I'm wearing is a thing of wonder," he said in amused tones just above her ear, "but do you think you might drag your attention a little higher?"

Her upward glance was instinctive, as was her frown. "I'm glad you think this is so entertaining, because that makes one of us."

The light faded from his dark eyes. "Well, don't let it ruin your evening. It's only a minute or two from your busy schedule."

"Small mercies," she returned automatically, but realized at the same time that she regretted the loss of his good humor. Perhaps because of the atmosphere of glowing happiness created by Kane and Regina, April couldn't quite hold on to her usual irritation. As a small gesture of truce, she asked, "How are the burns on your back?"

"Fine."

"That's good." Both his answer and her comment were meaningless, she knew, but better than nothing. All the same, she wondered how he was healing. As he swung her in a turn, she shifted her grasp on his shoulder slightly, seeking the edge of a possible bandage.

"I said they're fine," he repeated, his voice a little rough.

Her lips tightened as she met his gaze again. She

might have known he would not only notice her small transgression but comment on it. "I know what you said, but it could have been machismo talking."

"I could show you, if you like. Afterward."

She stared at him, drowning in the black gulfs of his eyes while trying to ignore the tingling of her nipples and the drawing sensation in the lower part of her body. At last she said, "Why do you always say things like that? Why, when you know—"

His laugh was wry. "Because I like to see you blush. And maybe I keep hoping you'll take me up on one of my suggestions. I want you, anywhere and any way I can get you, and I always have. I thought you knew that."

"No."

"You knew it once, years ago."

Maybe she had, though what she'd felt for him had been so much wider and deeper yet more nebulous. She had ached with a vast and stunning sweep of emotions from desire to an innocent generosity that urged her to give him whatever he wanted of her. She'd expected to spend a lifetime in his arms and to love and be loved through all the nights and days of that seemingly endless span of years. There'd been nothing in it to correspond to an "I'll show you mine if you'll show me yours" exchange.

"No," she said again quietly.

"Oh, I think you did," he answered, "and still do. Which is why you're afraid that I might be able to seduce you in spite of everything you can do to stop me."

A winded sound left her, part shock, part laughter, part sigh. "You don't give up, do you?"

"Not ever," he answered, his gaze intent. "Never again."

"It's effort for nothing."

He watched her, his gaze moving over her face. Then it centered on her parted lips. Slowly, deliberately, he pulled her closer and set his mouth to hers.

Sweet, smooth, warm, his kiss was so right it was like a well-remembered dream. The pleasure of it seeped through her against her will, destroying her defenses with the inexorable effect of a strong drug. Time and place, music and reason, drifted away to leave only the moment and the man. She wanted to be angry, wanted to push free. Warring against that impulse was the instinct to melt against him, merge with him. The conflict was so disturbing that she made a half-stifled sound of distress.

Luke released her and eased away. She steadied herself, and was glad to discover that only seconds had elapsed rather than the eons it had seemed. Catching at the remnants of her composure, she inquired, "Was that supposed to prove something?"

"Susceptibility," he answered without expression, "though whether yours or mine, I'm not sure."

That was some consolation. It also helped that he didn't appear to realize how much he had disturbed her. "Since it didn't work, there should be no need to repeat it."

"Oh, I wouldn't say that."

In sharp alarm, she asked, "What do you mean?"

"It didn't change how I feel. That being so, I have only one thing to say by way of warning."

She shouldn't ask, didn't want to know, but couldn't seem to prevent the question from springing to her lips. "And that is?"

His smile was rich and easy, a slow curving of his lips that rose to gleam in his eyes. In quiet promise, he said, "Resist me if you can."

8

Mulberry Point sat silent and closed in upon itself in the slanting rays of early morning sunlight when Luke arrived the next morning. The grass along the drive was wet with dew, and so were the edges of the gray slate shingles that topped the massive old house. He should probably wait until the sun dried things off since the moss that accumulated on the shady sides of these old roofs could be as slippery as the path to hell when damp. But April would be up by then. She'd probably order him off the place before he could get his extension ladder off the truck. Once he was actually on the rooftop, however, getting rid of him would be a whole lot harder.

He discovered a big leak over the stairs without much trouble. Tearing the broken shingles off was not exactly a quiet operation, however. He had only pried a couple loose and let them slide down and over the edge to the ground when he heard a hail from below. With a rueful shake of his head, he rose from his haunches and gave a shout in answer.

April appeared a second later, backing up with a hand shading her eyes as she sought his location. She wore a soft-looking nightgown and robe in old-fashioned white cotton. The morning sun outlined her body as a hazy shadow surrounded by a golden nimbus, while her hair gleamed like polished gold. From his high perch, she looked like a fallen angel. Too bad she didn't sound like one.

"What do you think you're doing?" she demanded. "I told you I didn't need help. Anyway, you'll break your stupid neck crawling around up there by yourself!"

"It's my neck." He was too enthralled by the expression of concern for more.

"Well, it's my insurance company that will have to pay the bills. Come down now!"

Luke's brief euphoria evaporated. With a shake of his head, he said, "I might as well finish the job as long as I'm up here."

She stared up at him a long moment without answering, her gaze intent as it moved over him. He let her look, standing loose-limbed and at ease. At the same time, he felt the back of his neck grow hot as he wondered what was going through her head. He was used to a certain amount of female attention but not this kind of searching appraisal, as if she meant to memorize every detail, from his sweat-stained cap to his faded jeans.

Finally, she said, "It isn't going to work, you know. I refuse to feel obligated over something I didn't ask you to do."

Irritation moved over him. "I'm not doing this because I expect anything in return. Old houses appeal to me, okay? They're like fine old ladies. Take care of them, keep them pampered and protected, and they do you proud. Neglect them and they turn into worn-out messes."

"Don't tell me you don't have more than enough to do at Chemin-a-Haut because I won't believe it. But if you want to waste your time, fine. I have better things to do than stand here and argue with you."

She swung away in a swirl of white and marched out of his sight beneath the overhang of the house. A second later, however, she reappeared. With a hand at the neck of her nightgown, she called up at him, "You haven't seen anything of Midnight, have you?"

"That cat of yours? Nope."

"You don't…see anything that looks like it could be him?"

She was asking if he could spot a furry black body better from his high vantage point. Luke gave the front yard a quick once-over, then turned in a slow circle to scan the surrounding area. Facing her again, he said, "Not a sign of him."

She let out the breath she'd been holding. "It was…just a thought." She hesitated, then added, "Thanks."

"No problem," he said with a small salute.

She met his gaze for a moment longer, then put her head down and made for the house again. The front door slammed behind her.

Luke stood where he was, thinking about the lost, almost defenseless look that he'd glimpsed on her face. It reminded him of the night before in that second after he'd kissed her. She'd been so warm and pliant in his arms for a single, mind-blowing second. The feel and taste of her had gone to his head like 150 proof white lightning from some swamp rat's private still. That kind of brew went down smooth and easy, but had a punch like being whaled by the tail of a bull alligator. He hadn't been ready for it and nor, he thought, had April. It was strong medicine; a little went a long way and large doses could be lethal. They were going to have to come to grips with the phenomenon but today was not, apparently, the day. Luke gave a quick, hard shake of his head, then went back to work.

Chemin-a-Haut and Mulberry Point were both from the same general era of building so had similar roof slates. Luke happened to have a supply on hand, bought from a company that stockpiled shingles, lumber, bricks and other architectural pieces saved when old buildings were torn down. He laid these in place, fitting the smooth, gray slates carefully to the adjoining run. It was an easy task for a fine summer morning, or it was when you knew what you were doing. He enjoyed the feel of the sun between his shoulder blades, even if it did make his healing burns itch. The smoothness of the old slates under his hands was also a pleasure, as was the knowledge that what he was doing would keep the interior of the fine old place safe and dry for maybe another hundred years. It was just possible his kids or grandkids would be the ones squatting on this roof one day, taking note of his handiwork and adding their own to it. The thought made him feel good in a way that he couldn't explain if his life depended on it, but kept him at the job all the same.

To do something for April that she couldn't do for herself also pleased him. If there was an obligation between them, it was on his side. He'd been in the wrong all those years ago and knew it well. On the other hand, there was more than one way to get to a woman and he wasn't above using a display of masculine competence in a good cause.

She felt something for him, he was sure. It might be no more than the kind of hot craving they'd shared on a few, too few, summer nights years ago, but he'd settle for that. He'd settle for whatever she had to give him; he wasn't greedy. To make her recognize that something still existed between them had become an obsession, however, one he had to do something about before it drove him nuts. More than that, he needed to regain the trust she'd once given him, to see himself reflected whole and clean, a decent human being, in her eyes.

The tapping of his hammer made a counterpoint to Luke thoughts. When he came to the end of a row, he looked up and discovered that the morning was gone and the job done. He stood and stretched the kinks out of his muscles, then climbed down from the roof. He was hungry enough to eat a small elephant since breakfast had been only coffee and a piece of French bread spread with butter. It didn't look as if April was going to offer to feed him, however, so he'd do without. Going in search of his caulking gun, he started to work on the loose windowpanes that he'd noticed last time he was here.

Sun glare and pulled curtains prevented him from seeing into the house at most of the windows, not that he particularly tried. He grew used to ignoring the rooms beyond the glass until he reached the back of the house. As he set his ladder in place, he noticed a shadowy movement inside. He was outside April's office, he thought, for he could make out the white screen of her computer monitor, the shapes of a desk and other equipment, and the stacked shelves of bookcases. The window itself was closed because of air-conditioning, but he pushed it open with a quick movement, then swung a leg over the wide sill and straddled it for a seat.

"About time you stopped to eat, isn't it?" he asked. "Or are you dieting?"

"Hmm?" Her expression was distracted, almost unfocused, as she stared at her computer. She didn't move from her slouched position with her elbows draped over the arms of her chair and her feet propped on some kind of shelf under her desk.

"I said—"

"I heard you," she interrupted, turning her head abruptly in his direction. "I'm not hungry."

"The creative mind needs sustenance," he said, watching her with fascination. "You should eat something."

She turned her gaze back to the lines on her screen and typed a few words. After a moment, she made a vague gesture in the direction of the door. "There's cheese and peanut butter in the kitchen. Maybe some ham. Make yourself something if you want it."

"I was talking about you."

"I'll get something in a minute." She started typing again, frowning mightily at whatever she was putting down.

Luke watched her a few more seconds, then climbed into the room and padded across the floor. He was tempted to pause and read over her shoulder as he crossed behind her, but figured he'd better not push his luck. He was almost to the hall door, when something he'd seen above her computer desk jarred his attention. He glanced back again.

It was his own face, or rather a collage of pictures of himself. They were pinned to a cork bulletin board, some of them fairly old, some taken a few years back, but several of more recent vintage. Most were snapshots, group pictures with friends and family, but a few were newspaper clippings. The largest shot, however, was a copy of a portrait he'd let Granny May talk him into doing for her last birthday.

April glanced toward him once more, then followed his line of sight. Her blank look grew more stolid as she asked, "What?"

"Nothing." He blinked as he tried to marshal his stunned thoughts. "Just—nothing."

She went back to her work without another word. He turned around and headed into the hall, frowning as he went.

April's refrigerator was fully stocked with easy-to-prepare food, an indication of how she sustained life and limb while she was working. She needed a keeper, he thought, she really did. He slathered mayonnaise on bread, cut thick slices of cheese and wolfed it down with a glass of milk. With his appetite temporarily appeased, he made two more sandwiches and set them on separate paper plates, poured drinks, then headed back toward the office with his load.

April actually smiled at him when he set the food on her desk. She even pushed away from her computer. Reaching for her sandwich, she bit into it as if she were starved.

"Thought you weren't hungry," he commented as he took a seat on a desk corner with his own plate on his knee.

"The sight of food changed my mind."

Her lashes concealed her gaze as she answered, but Luke was satisfied. They ate in silence for a few minutes. Finally, he said, "So, what's with using me for a pinup?"

"Don't flatter yourself. You're just a face and a body I'm using as a stand-in for my hero."

Her answer was so prompt that it was plain she'd been waiting for him to ask. "What do you mean, a stand-in?"

"It helps to have a definite face to describe or use for different expressions, different emotions."

"Why mine?"

She shrugged, though her concentration was still on her sandwich. "Your admirers at the conference elected you. Who am I to fight majority opinion?"

"So, what if your hero was blond?" He didn't really care, but was interested in what she'd say.

"It wouldn't take much imagination to turn you into a blond hunk."

"Yeah? But you must have to think about your hero differently no matter what his coloring might be, right?"

The glance she gave him was jaundiced, as if she saw clearly what he was getting at, but she made no comment.

"I mean, these heroes of yours can't be much like

me—or as you think I am—or they wouldn't be too heroic. You must have quite an imagination.''

''You've no idea,'' she said in dry agreement.

He studied her an instant, but decided to let that one alone. With a slow grin, he asked, ''So, where does this imagination take you when you do the love scenes?''

Hot color flooded into her face. ''I might have known you'd zero in on that subject. I'll have you know romances are about more than sex. They're about courage and commitment and making relationships work. They're—''

''Hold on!'' he protested. ''I'm not putting down what you do, just curious about how you go about it. Mainly, I was wondering how involved you are with the process.''

''I can't explain it, and even if I could I doubt you'd ever understand. Anyway, it's none of your business.''

''Even if I'm the guy in these fantasies?''

''You aren't. At least...''

''I am and I'm not, that it?''

''Exactly,'' she said, her golden gaze even. ''As I told you, you're just a face. The actual hero is only a figment of my imagination.''

''Nobody real, I get it.'' It was a disappointment, but he'd live. As another thought came to him, he narrowed his eyes. ''But maybe he's the way you'd like a man to be?''

''Sure, why not? We all have our dreams.''

Something in her voice, or maybe in her eyes, sent a small ache through his chest. It was disturbing, which in turn reminded him that he had other things to do besides repairs for a woman who didn't appreciate his services. He tossed back the last of his milk and set the glass and his plate aside. As he got to his feet, he said, "Time to move on. I'll check the French door locks on my way out."

"You don't have to—"

"Give it a rest, April," he said, cutting her off with a straight look before he got to his feet and headed toward the hall. At the door, he turned back. "Like being the stand-in for your hero, it doesn't mean a damn thing."

It took longer to shift the contents of the toolbox in his Jeep in order to find antique replacement screws from his pack-rat assortment than it did to fix April's loose locks. While he was at it, he caulked around the French door units upstairs and installed a few lengths of weather stripping. He was putting up his tools and picking up bits and pieces of trash from the floor of the upper balcony when he heard a noise like a rusty hinge squeaking.

He stopped, listening intently. It wasn't mechanical, but was some kind of animal. It came again, and yet again, gathering in volume with each cry. Easing to his feet, he moved to the balcony railing and leaned over to search the tangle of honeysuckle vines and briar roses that edged the wood beyond the old side garden.

Something black and low to the ground caught his attention. It was heading toward the house, yowling in high dudgeon as it came. As it crossed a clearing, a slow grin spread over Luke's face.

Pushing from the railing, he crossed to the nearest French door and opened it to stick his head inside the house. "April," he called. "Can you come out here?"

It was a few seconds before she joined him. As she stepped to his side, she said, "This had better be good, because I was just..."

She trailed off as Midnight squalled again. She whirled away to stare down at the cat, then her eyes met Luke's again as the pupils widened into pools of amazement. She spun around and ran back into the house. He heard her quick steps on the stairs.

A moment later, she emerged below. Luke stayed where he was long enough to watch the delight that shone in her face as the cat sprang from the ground to land in her arms. He picked up his tools then, and went down to join her.

"Look at this," she demanded as she thrust the ragged end of a worn nylon leash toward him. "It's been bitten through, as if someone had Midnight tied up. Who would do a thing like that?"

She was blinking, as if trying to get rid of the tears that welled in her eyes, he thought. He pretended not to see as he said, "Kids who found him roaming around? Another cat lover?"

The look she gave him was scathing. "Oh, come on."

"You'd rather believe it was somebody out to hurt you?" He reached to scratch behind the cat's ears as he waited for her answer.

"I prefer to face facts when they're staring me in the face," she returned, watching as Midnight offered his jaw to be scratched. "Oh, I suppose it could be a coincidence that somebody chose to tie him up now, but he's been roaming around here for over a year without any problem. Doesn't that mean anything to you?''

''It means trouble has a way of piling up on people.''

She made a sound of annoyance. ''Yes, and I suppose you've been working on my door locks because you were in the mood.''

''It just seemed like a sensible precaution.'' He didn't know why he was so reluctant to admit her cat might have been kidnapped, except that he hated the idea of her worrying about it.

She was silent a moment, her gaze still on Midnight who was stretching his neck to allow it to be rubbed, half falling out of April's arms as he tried to push under Luke's hard hand. Abruptly, she said, ''He likes you. Ordinarily, he doesn't care for men.''

''His neck's irritated from the leash, that's all,'' Luke answered.

''Is it?'' she asked, and lifted her questioning gaze to his. ''Or has he gotten used to you? Maybe in the last week or so?''

He should be used to that kind of slap in the face, but somehow he never expected it. What kind of answer he would have made this time, he had no idea. He was saved from the necessity by a passing car.

The vehicle, a sporty compact, slowed as it rounded the big curve where the road from town passed in front of Mulberry Point. The driver's head swiveled as he stared at Luke and April standing there so close together in the front yard. The guy continued to stare, in spite of the bend in the road.

Then as he saw them looking, he snapped his head around and gunned the car. In seconds, he was out of sight.

"Well, of all the..." April began, then stopped. "Who was that?"

"You don't recognize your old boyfriend?" Luke took his hand away from the cat and thrust it into the pocket of his jeans. As she turned a frown in his direction, he added. "Frank Randall?"

"Oh."

It was not a very eloquent comment, considering that Mary Ellen Randall had been Frank's sister. Frank had been a big, burley loner with little to say for himself. He'd joined the air force a couple of months after his sister died. There'd been a couple of weeks during which he and April had hung around together. Luke thought there'd been nothing much to it other than April feeling sorry for Frank, but he'd never been sure. Mary Ellen's brother had shipped out to basic training and that had been that. Now he said, "Frank's been back in town a while, seems to have decided that he didn't want to be a career serviceman after all. You haven't seen him around?"

She shook her head. "Someone, maybe Betsy down at the motel, mentioned that he'd left the service. So, what's he doing now?"

"He's trying to start a guide service for fishing and swamp tours. The trailer he and Mary Ellen were brought up in isn't far off the lake, so he knows the backwaters pretty well."

"A guide service? You think he'll do anything with that?"

"Use it as a fine excuse to fish, hunt or whatever he wants," Luke returned with a crooked smile.

"I might have known you'd make a joke of it," she said, and turned away from him.

Luke hadn't been joking. It seemed as good a time as any to call it a day.

April watched Luke drive off while she rocked Midnight back and forth in her arms like a baby. When he was out of sight, she buried her face in the cat's fur for a long moment, in need of a brand of comfort that she couldn't give a name. Then she sighed and lifted her head. She shouldn't let the man upset her, but how could she help it? He was there every time she looked up. He could get to her in ways no one else had ever tried, much less managed. He made her say things she regretted. He turned her into some kind of harridan full of suspicion, then managed to make her feel guilty for it.

He also made her feel safe while he was around, and that was frightening. She didn't need a man to feel secure, didn't want one. Even now, in the short time that he'd been gone, she felt exposed and vulnerable here outside her house. It was all she could do to force herself to make her way slowly back inside with her cat instead of running for the door and locking it behind her.

Her hand was not quite steady as she smoothed the silkiness of Midnight's coat while she carried him down the hall. She was desperately glad to have him back again. She'd been afraid, so afraid, that he was gone for good, even dead. She hadn't realized how much she cared until she nearly lost him.

It had been all she could do not to let Luke see her cry.

How long had it been since she'd come so close to tears? She was relieved in a way to know that it was possible. That she could still feel something, love something to the point of tears, even if it was only Midnight, was good to know.

In the kitchen, the cat wound in and out around her legs as she opened a can of food for him and raked it into his dish. Watching him eat as if it were his first meal in days, she tightened her lips. Luke hadn't wanted to admit that someone might have taken her pet. Why was that, unless he knew more than he was telling?

She wrapped her arms around her in the air-conditioned chill of the room. It was disorienting to think that about him one moment while she was lusting after his body the next. That was all it was, of course; she wouldn't dignify whatever it was that she'd felt as she stared up at Luke on the roof earlier with a less crass description. It was an automatic response now, she supposed, a natural female re-action to male power and grace so handsomely dis-played against a summer sky. She had sensed the intense current of life that flowed through him and longed to reach out to touch it and be touched by it. It had been a brief impulse, almost like a day-dream. He'd laugh himself silly if he ever knew.

The thought had also flashed through her mind that maybe Julianne was right, maybe it might be possible to allow him back into her life on a purely physical level. Surely she could manage an affair with no attachment, no future to cause complications. All those advantages Julianne had mentioned would be present. She might get over her sensitivity where he was concerned, as well.

She'd almost had a heart attack when she realized he'd seen the photos she had posted above her computer. She shuddered even now, just thinking about it. How she'd managed to pass it off, she wasn't quite sure, but brazening it out had seemed the only way. Luke seemed to accept what she said, but she didn't make the mistake of thinking that was the end of it. No doubt he would bring it up again, and might even try to use it to get to her. The surprise was that he hadn't turned such a damning piece of evidence to his own advantage at once.

Not that anything she'd claimed had been false, of course.

It was odd, but her book had been going well before Luke had interrupted with the news of Midnight's return. Describing him exactly as he'd looked up there on the roof, how the sight of such a man had made her heroine feel, had been the catalyst for a torrent of words. They'd come so fast, in such an endless stream of good, solid sentences that she couldn't keep up with them, couldn't hit the computer keys quickly enough. Even now, she couldn't wait to get back to her story. As soon as Midnight finished, the two of them would go straight to her office.

It was much later when April finally hit the Save key on her keyboard, backed up her day's work on a disk, then turned off her computer. She stretched tiredly, crossing her arms behind her head, then rose from her chair. The long summer evening had given her several more hours of working time. She'd finished a whole chapter, which was nearly twice her average day's work. It felt great. More importantly, it gave her hope that she might finally be coming out of her slump.

The room was dark since she hadn't bothered to turn on a light as darkness fell, working only by the glow of her computer screen. She made for the door with firm steps, since she knew exactly how the room was arranged. Behind her, Midnight leaped down from where he'd been sprawled across her desk and padded along at her heels.

April was into the central hall when she heard the vehicle. It was coming at breakneck speed, its brakes squealing as it rounded the curve beyond her drive. She paused near the parlor doorway as the blinding flash of headlights stabbed through the sidclights around the great entrance door, then traveled across the scenic wallpaper of the hallway. She watched that wild swing even as she reached for the light switch beside the parlor door.

Abruptly there was a cracking report. The glass sidelight next to the door crashed inward with a shudder of its lace curtain and the tinkling rain of glass. A sharp cry scraped April's throat. She dropped to a crouch. Midnight hissed and fled. Tires squealed as rubber peeled away with the vehicle's sudden acceleration.

The streaking headlight beams vanished. The night settled and all was quiet and dark once more.

9

"You called Roan, but didn't call me? You didn't think I might be interested in hearing that somebody was using you for target practice?"

April looked up at that rough question. Luke was walking toward her across the restaurant's back room. "Roan is the sheriff," she answered after a second. "What were you going to do after the fact, anyway? Come hold my hand?"

"If that's what you needed."

She hadn't needed it, but it might have been nice. Though she was not about to tell him that. As she returned to unloading her briefcase onto the conference-size table between them, she said, "What I needed was someone to find out who might have done it."

"And Roan managed that?"

"It was just a drive-by shooting, might even have been an accident."

"An accident." His tone told her exactly what he thought of that idea.

"Probably a stray bullet from some idiot shooting at a highway sign."

"I don't remember any road signs near your house."

"There's one for the curve."

"Too far away and the wrong angle."

"Maybe," she returned in clipped agreement, "but the principle is the same."

"It wasn't a principle that shot at you. Did Roan recover the lead?"

She nodded. "It was in the wall. He seemed to think it came from a .270 Remington."

"The deer rifle of choice for half the men in Tunica Parish." Luke shook his head in disgust. "It figures."

"So Roan said." She closed her briefcase and set it beside her chair, then sat down. "I suppose he told you about the shooting?"

"After I'd heard it from three other people."

"I might have known," she said in dry recognition of the speed and accuracy of the Turn-Coupe grapevine. Since half the people in town were either Benedicts or related to the family, news of accidents and disasters sped from the courthouse and hospital to the far corners of the parish faster than a computer network. "So, what are you doing here?"

"I'm on this committee, too." His smile held grim pleasure, even as he looked away to nod at the other members straggling into the room, taking their seats up and down the long table.

"Since when? You've never shown up for a meeting before." April heard the suspicion in her voice but couldn't help it.

"Since this morning. Betsy always brings in a few strong backs as the festival date rolls around."

Luke's cousin, Betsy North, was the owner of the local motel, and a very likable woman who got things done and took no nonsense from anyone while doing it. She was also chairperson for the River Pirate Revel so Luke's appointment made a weird kind of sense. The coincidence was too much for April's logical mind, however, and the look she gave him said so.

"I swear," he said as he held up his hand in pledge of scout's honor. "I'm also on the kidnapping committee."

"And who's elected this year besides the mayor and sheriff?"

He gave her a wicked grin. "Can't tell, but I promise they won't like it."

"I can imagine."

A feature of the festival was the invasion of Turn-Coupe by gun-toting, knife-wielding pirates. They swarmed from the river two miles away to take over the town for a day as these river rats were said to have done in the early nineteenth century. For twenty-four hours, all law and order was suspended. Town officials were captured and held to ransom to benefit charity. Prominent businesspeople and other citizens were also fair game for the costumed desperadoes, and pretty girls were swept up as prisoners with many a mock ferocious or lustful threat. The theatrics were all in good fun, though things could sometimes get out of hand due to high liquor consumption.

"Are you going with the spirit of things this year, or are you too high-hat for that?" Luke asked, lowering his voice and dropping into the chair across from her as the other committee members talked back and forth around them.

She gave him an incredulous stare. "You want to know if I'll be wearing a costume? And I'm supposed to tell you, knowing you'll be looking for captives? Fat chance!"

"Come on. You can afford to be held hostage."

"It's not the money that worries me," she said shortly.

"What does?" His lips curved in a slow smile as he studied the expression on her face. "Being in my power? Is that it? Hey, you might discover untold advantages."

She didn't much care for the look in his eyes or for the sensation it caused in the pit of her stomach. "Yes, and you might have a surprise or two yourself."

"Can't wait."

His voice was a deep and suggestive purr. He was doing it to rattle her, she knew. The annoying thing was how well it worked. "I'll consider myself warned. You'll have to find me first."

"No problem," he said with velvet promise in his eyes.

She believed him, and she hated that. She made no answer, however. At that moment, Betsy, resplendent in a pantsuit in a bright turquoise-and-purple print that looked striking rather than outrageous on her large form, strode to the head of the table and banged on her iced tea glass with a spoon in a nerve-jarring clatter for attention. The festival committee was directed to go pick up their plate lunches so they could all get to work.

A number of issues needed to be discussed and voted upon. These were taken care of with dispatch under Betsy's able direction. The last item on the agenda was the vending and craft booths that would line the square in front of the courthouse. It occasioned a scintillating discussion of the rival merits of smoked turkey legs, roasted corn in the shuck, and funnel cakes versus pine needle baskets, crocheted doilies and bear statues hacked out with chain saws. With matters settled to everyone's satisfaction, they adjourned.

The mayor, who had shown up at the last minute, collared Luke with a question about the kidnappings. April used that bit of luck to round up her comparison sheets on various drink booths and head for her car. She made it to the parking lot before she heard a call behind her. It was only Betsy, however, and she turned to face her with a silent sigh of relief.

"Where are you off to so fast, hon?" Betsy asked as she came closer. "I wanted to invite you to a little houseboat party as a kickoff for this shindig."

"Oh, I don't know..." April began doubtfully.

"Now don't be that way. It's not going to kill you to have a drink and talk to a few people. You're the only claim to fame this town's got, and the least you can do is let us show you off."

"I didn't know you had a houseboat."

"Not mine, doll. Belongs to a couple of friends from down around Ferriday way. They're bringing it up the Mississippi just for the festival. It'll be anchored at the marina over on the river where the river pirates will be coming in, so they'll have a great view of all the abducting and other shenanigans. I told them I might talk you into coming for their welcoming party, maybe even spending the night on board later. How 'bout it? Come on. Live a little.''

April's mouth curved in a wry smile. "That's the second time today I've been as good as accused of being a stick-in-the-mud.''

"Well, you're not exactly a party girl, now are you? I remember a time when you weren't so stand-offish. You and Luke could always be depended on to be in the thick of things.''

So they could, April thought, but was she really more outgoing back then or had it been Luke's influence? Was she a natural introvert or had she only become one as a part of her vocation and her retreat from all the things she and Luke had enjoyed together?

She really didn't know. In a sudden urge to find out, she said, "Tell your friend I'll be there.''

"That's great! She's a big fan of yours, and will be so excited.''

April only smiled since she never quite knew what to say to that kind of comment. Standing there, she felt a prickling at the back of her neck, as if she were being watched. She glanced around but saw no one except Luke heading toward her and Betsy.

"Excited about what?'' he asked as if he had a perfect right to know.

"April agreeing to the party you thought she should attend,'' Betsy told him in triumph.

"You got her to agree? You're the greatest,'' he said, and gave her a quick hug.

April, watching them, said with an edge in her voice, "Nothing was said about Luke.''

"Oh, didn't I mention he'd be dropping in?" Betsy tipped her head, her glance roguish as she looked from April to the laughing, dark-haired man.

"You know you didn't."

"Sue me," she said in cheerful unconcern. "We'll have a great time, just you wait and see." With a wave of her hand, she strode away in the direction of her car.

Neither April nor Luke spoke as they watched Betsy drive off. Finally, April asked, "Why are you masterminding my life? And when are you going to stop?"

"I don't know that I'd call it masterminding, exactly." Luke rubbed a finger along his jaw in a meditative gesture.

"Does *interfering* strike you as any better? Or maybe *meddling?* What is it with you? What do you want?"

"Do I have to want something?"

"Most people do," she answered, then pressed her lips together as she wished she could take that back.

"Do they?" He paused, then added, "Yes, I can see how they might. All right, then, I'm just as bad. I want you, just you. How's that?"

She turned her head slowly to search his face. "You don't give up, do you? I told you..."

"So resist, already. That's your part, isn't it?"

It was what she had vowed, the traditional role of women. Why, then, was it so unsatisfactory? "Suppose I don't," she said in tight tones. "Where do you think we could possibly go from this hot encounter you seem so set on having?"

"God, April..."

"I asked you a question." He was not, she thought, the most introspective of men. It was entirely possible he'd never thought beyond the bedroom, though she couldn't be sure of that.

He stared at her a second longer, then he nodded. "All right, so I don't know where we'll go. It all depends on how we feel. Or rather, it depends on how you feel since it's usually the lady's call."

"No, it isn't," she said in swift contradiction. "It takes two to make a relationship."

"You're really thinking about this?" he demanded, his eyes searching.

"We're discussing it, aren't we?" She refused to meet his gaze more than an instant.

"Are we? It sounds to me as if you're discussing a clinical experiment."

Maybe he was sharper than she'd imagined, or else it was sheer self-protection to think of him as insensitive. "You'd prefer to just jump in without knowing what it's all about?"

"I'd prefer more heart and less brain power."

"I didn't know hearts came into it at all. I rather thought different anatomical parts altogether were involved."

He laughed, a winded sound, before he asked, "What happened to you, love? When did you get to be such a cynic?"

"Pain turns you that way," she answered shortly. "I don't want to be hurt any more."

"So, what exactly are you suggesting?"

"I don't know that I'm suggesting anything. I'm

only trying to see what I'd be setting myself up for, whether a casual affair or an intense one.''

"And you'd prefer the first." His voice was hard as he made that guess.

She wasn't sure, but she didn't mean to let him know it. "What if I would?''

He was silent as his gaze moved over her face and down the curve of her neck to the quick rise and fall of her breasts under her shirt. Abruptly, he said, "Why? Is it because that's all you're capable of giving? Or only that you think I have nothing else to offer?''

He was definitely more attuned to what was happening than she wanted to consider. "Neither," she answered. "It just isn't worth any greater risk.''

"What would the greatest risk be, sweetheart?'' he asked, his voice tight. "Falling in love maybe? It's a pretty high price to pay, all right, but any game has some risk.''

"So it is just a game to you. I thought so.''

"I don't know that it is, but I do know it's not an experiment.''

She made a small sound that was not quite a laugh. The mix of pain and humor she felt was compounded by something more that she thought might be relief. It seemed she couldn't make up her mind what she wanted from Luke, so why should she be surprised that he was ambivalent? "I'll keep that in mind" she said, "for when my interest becomes something more than academic.''

"April," he began, dissatisfaction hovering in his face as he watched her.

"Never mind. It doesn't matter.''

"It should, even if you were only—testing."

"Yes, well, and maybe it does after all, but I suppose we'll never know."

He didn't answer, but neither did he try to stop her as she turned and walked away.

The next two days limped past with paralyzing slowness. April's short burst of productivity faded and she couldn't get her book going again. Every time she managed to pull a few paragraphs together, some phone call or fax connected with the festival scattered her concentration all to Hades. Midnight didn't help matters, either. He was such a bundle of nerves that he started at every sound and hounded her footsteps as if reluctant to be out of her sight.

When the phone rang yet again late on the second night, she answered with exasperation, expecting it to be Betsy with another crisis. Her adrenaline spiked to record heights as she heard the raspy whisper of the man from the phone-in interview.

"'Evening, honey pot. Are you alone?"

The determination to find out something, anything, that would give her a clue to what was going on congealed inside April. Hanging on to the receiver with a death grip, she demanded, "What do you want? Why are you doing this?"

"Are you sweating, April? Is it running between your breasts? What are you wearing? Is it wet?"

"You're sick, do you know that? You need help. If you can't afford private help, there are public mental health centers that will…"

The response was obscene. Also extremely graphic.

"You just proved my point, I think." April forced the words through her tight throat.

There was no answer. She and the caller waged a war of wills, each waiting for the other to crack, to say something or hang up. April could hear the other person breathing, a short, hard sound as if his lungs were laboring. Somewhere in the distance, she could just make out a swishing noise that might be traffic from a busy street or highway.

After an endless time, there came a sharp click as the call was disconnected. April hung up as well, then put her face into her hands. She sat that way for a long time, feeling the shaking like a rippling vibration that came from inside her and radiated through her body down to her toes.

She couldn't stand this. Something had to be done, and she was the only one who could do it. But where to start was the question. Where?

Her computer was running, a quiet sound she was so used to that normally she didn't hear it. Now it seemed loud. She opened her eyes and lifted her head, staring at the screen. After a moment, she reached for her mouse and clicked the icon for internet connection. She navigated until she discovered the address she wanted. Her shaking stopped.

Next morning, she left the house early. Beside her on the car seat was a piece of computer paper with a small, precisely drawn map. She took the winding roads around the lake at a steady speed, making the turns that led her deeper into the swampland that bordered the water. She hadn't been this way since the days when she and Luke used to go riding on a Sunday afternoon. It would be easy to miss a turning and get lost in the labyrinthine network of dirt-and-gravel tracks that followed no pattern but took the high ground, such as it was, while threading among a series of creeks and branches. These roads were nearly as winding and impenetrable as the swamp itself.

Luke had known the narrow, winding ways, just as he knew the water channels of the swamp. The area had been his backyard playground from the time he could walk; he'd spent much more time learning its intricacies than he had playing with other kids or competing in team sports. Any time anyone failed to make their way out of the back-water, it was Luke who was called in to find them. So far as April knew, he'd always succeeded.

He'd thought it a huge joke, back in the early days, to take her into the farthest depths of the lake where it turned into swamp and threaten to keep her there. She'd known very well that he wouldn't but pretended to believe he might. The forfeit he usually demanded for showing her the way to freedom had been willingly paid, though she often included a refinement or two designed to make him regret his daring. The memory of that horseplay between them brought back a flood of other scenes, other incidents. She pushed them from her mind with determination, directing her considerable concentration to the problem of the moment.

The driveway she was seeking was so overgrown with briers, palmetto and wax myrtle that she almost missed it. She had to back up to make the turn into the dusty track. The house trailer at the end was run-down, with faded paint and a sagging frame. Trash and rusting pieces of cars littered the yard. A skinny cur with glassy eyes came running from the back, barking in warning.

The noise brought a man to the front door. He was tall with a barrel shape but had an air of carrying the weight of the world on his sloping shoulders. The waistband of his shorts showed above his much-washed jeans since he wore no shirt. He didn't call off the dog, but only leaned against the narrow frame and propped one bare foot against his other ankle as he waited for her to get out of her car.

April cut the engine and stepped gingerly into the yard. The dog circled her as she walked forward, but made no move to bite. She stopped halfway between her car and the sagging front steps.

"Hello, Frank," she said in neutral tones.

He stared at her a moment longer, then a slow smile stretched his thin lips. When he spoke his voice was husky, as if he'd just climbed out of bed. "Well, well. If it's not our famous author. Long time no see."

"I'd like to talk to you a few minutes, if you don't mind." The sun was in her eyes so she had to squint up at him. She stepped closer, into the shade thrown by the trailer's bulk. The move brought her close enough to catch the smell of cigarette smoke and stale beer that wafted from the man in the doorway.

"Speak your piece."

His tone wasn't particularly encouraging. His lack of an invitation to come inside was a conspicuous omission, but she didn't mind since it saved her the trouble of refusing. "I don't know if you've heard that I've been having a little trouble."

"Can't say I have. Wouldn't be with Benedict, would it?"

"Why would you say that?"

His bloodshot eyes, so hazel they appeared yellow-green, bored into hers and his jaw with its stubble of beard tightened. "Saw him at your place. He's trouble for any woman."

"Meaning?"

"I shouldn't have to tell you." He snorted in disgust.

"All that was a long time ago. This is now."

"Folks don't change. He used my sister then threw her away. He didn't want her because he was set on having you. He was so set that he didn't give a shit if my El lived or died, didn't lift a finger to save her from burning to death."

"How do you know? You weren't there." It was ridiculous for her to defend Luke, but Frank's rabid accusations brought out that need.

"The evidence, that and what El told me. She was crazy about him, would have done anything for him, she couldn't stand it that he wouldn't even look at her. She called him a million times, went to see him late at night, crawled in through his window to talk with him...or whatever."

"I didn't know all that." She'd been aware that Mary Ellen liked Luke since that would have been hard to miss. That she'd gone to such lengths to get to him was a surprise. April couldn't help but see that being hounded by Mary Ellen was hardly Luke's fault.

"Nobody wanted to tell you he was running around on you. But everybody knows what he's like now. Seems he's made himself a career out of running around, don't it?"

"Has he?"

"Skirt chaser and a half. Gets under most everything he catches, too."

She studied the man in front of her as she weighed the bitter undertone of his voice. "You hate him, don't you?"

"I raised El after our mama ran off and our dad died. She was all I had. She was a good girl, in spite of everything. Why she had to have one of the Bad Benedicts, I don't know, but she didn't deserve to die for it."

"No," April agreed. "But—I have to wonder if maybe you blame me as much as you do Luke."

"Now why would I do that?" he drawled. "You were a town girl, all soft and pretty, always dressed nice. You were never too friendly toward my sister from back in the swamps."

"She was trying to take my boyfriend, if you'll remember. Besides, she didn't like me very much, either."

"Oh, she liked you. Fact is, she tried her best to be just like you so Benedict would want more from her than a roll in the sheets."

"That's not the same thing."

"Guess it ain't at that. Anyway, poor old El never had a chance. You were the one Benedict wanted around on a permanent basis. I saw why, even if I was older. Hell, so did every guy around. But you didn't want anything to do with folks in Turn-Coupe

once Benedict turned out to be such a shit. You
shook the swamp mud off your dainty shoes and
went off to college down in New Orleans. Found
yourself a man there, for what good it did you. Look
at you now, back again and not so different from
when you left.''

Resentment lay beneath the words like slugs under rotting leaves. She'd sat with Frank Randall at
a ball game once after the accident, had let him buy
her a cold drink, but refused to go out with him
afterward. He wasn't the only one whose company
she'd avoided, but he didn't seem to know that.

''I didn't go out a lot after Luke and I broke up,''
she said carefully. ''It was—it just seemed all
wrong.''

''Yeah, he screwed you over good, too, now
didn't he?''

''I don't know about that, but I didn't want to
risk getting burned again.'' The unfortunate phrase
was out of her mouth before she could stop it. She
wasn't surprised to see Frank Randall's face flush
with anger.

''My sister was the one who got burned! You
came out all right, I'd say. You're famous, got your
books and your face in all the stores, making all that
money. Not much wrong with that.''

''It's no substitute for what matters.'' She really
believed that, she thought in some surprise. It wasn't
just words.

''Well, don't come around talking to me about
what's past or any troubles you got now. I'm not
part of your problem, and I sure as hell ain't the

solution. Whatever's going on you'll just have to figure out for yourself.''

Whether it was truth or not, it was all she was going to get from of him. ''Yes,'' she answered quietly, ''I'll see if I can't do that.''

10

On opening day of the festival, the general malaise that had hung over April for weeks extended itself to what she was going to wear. She couldn't decide which way to go, whether casual or costume. Few of those attending would be in fancy dress other than the festival organizers. Many of the women would have on the kind of sloppy T-shirts and cutoff jeans that made an ordinary sundress look like haute couture.

She didn't even know why she was worrying except she sometimes felt she was held to a different standard. She was expected to look romantic, whatever that might mean, or else like a successful writer. Staring at the choices she had laid out, a gingham halter top and skirt, or a Victorian era dress and petticoats that she'd worn a couple of times for special parties at romance conventions, she wondered why she cared. Luke was the only one who might actually say anything, and his opinion hardly mattered. No, of course it didn't, so she might as well wear what she liked. The swish of long skirts around her ankles made her feel graceful and feminine, and she enjoyed that as a change from her eternal jeans or shorts. With a defiant toss of her head, she reached for the costume. If she put it on, it would have nothing whatsoever to do with not wanting to be a stick-in-the-mud.

The different reaction she got from men when she wore her petticoats was always a secret amazement. They gave way, stepping back as if afraid they might step on her skirts or get them dirty. Their faces softened and they had a tendency to stare, looking her up and down with a bemused expression that hovered between appreciation and intrigue. She was offered places to sit or help in getting around obstacles or through doors, and was positively not allowed to lift anything heavier than the hem of her skirt. Her patent helplessness, as annoying as it might be on occasion, seemed to bring out the gallant side of the men she came across. She'd thought more than once that the women of past centuries might have been onto something modern females were missing.

A crowd had already gathered at the river's edge when she reached the dock near the boat marina. The sun was hot and bright, though a light breeze blowing off the water tempered the heat. A couple of sheriff's deputies were parking cars in orderly rows on the long stretch of paving that bordered the river, and several tailgate parties were already underway with music blasting from boom boxes and tops popping on beer cans. Quite a few older couples had brought their lawn chairs and were sitting in comfort in the beds of their pickups, with drinks in their hands, hats on their heads, and faces shiny with sunscreen. People were in high spirits.

A number of houseboats sat in the marina slips,

from ancient, listing tubs to those that qualified as yachts. Most were familiar from visits April had made to the River Park nearby, but one stood out as a new addition. It was a sleek, blue-trimmed white vessel that featured a hull designed for the open sea, a flying bridge, large expanses of glass, and chrome-railed decks that were set with two tables topped by gaily striped umbrellas. She was fairly sure this was the party boat, even before she saw Luke's cousin Betsy standing at the stern.

April's progress toward the dock was slow. She was stopped with questions about her books, both what she had coming out next and her work in progress. She also answered queries about how she liked living on the lake, comments on how glad they had been to see a hometown person take possession of Mulberry Point when the big old house had gone up for sale, and how happy they were to have her back. She was warmed by the obvious goodwill, but also reminded of how much of a recluse she had become since she'd seen so few of these people in the year since her return.

The instant she stepped on the houseboat, Betsy hailed her and waved her toward the rear deck and the people sitting around the glass-topped tables. "Here she is, our local celebrity! April has written—how many books is it, now, hon? Nineteen? Twenty?" Hardly pausing for an answer, she rattled off introductions to a state senator and his wife, a doctor from Baton Rouge with his teenage daughter, a pair of engineers who were married to each other, the artist-wife of the boat's owner, and their host himself. The doctor pulled out a chair for her, the boat's owner pushed a glass of champagne into her hand, and within seconds April was a part of the group.

They were an interesting bunch, with decided opinions and a witty way of expressing them. That they had known each other for some time was plain, and April soon realized they had all traveled upriver together, with the exception of Betsy. It was pleasant to sit back and listen to them while letting the breeze from the river finger her hair and watching the sun shift with a sequin glitter across the rippling water.

She sighed unconsciously as she felt herself relaxing. With almost guilty pleasure, she realized she had nothing to do and nothing she should be doing, except sitting here enjoying the gentle movement of the boat on the water. It was the same sensation she'd had in New Orleans. Added together, she thought the two instances were an indicator of the stress she was under, had been under for some time. She really needed to do something about that, and would as soon as she finished her current contract, as soon as she discovered who was harassing her, as soon as she found someone to share the burden of her many responsibilities....

Where had that thought come from?

She didn't mean it. The last thing she needed was anyone in her life.

She was temporarily out of the conversational flow as the group around the table discussed a Florida golf tournament. Rising to her feet, she moved to the rail, staring upriver. The boat's end slip position gave it a superb view of the curve of the waterway where the pirate flotilla would soon heave into view. It shouldn't be too long now. Most of the crowd was gathering just past the marina, in the open grassy area of the park opposite the stretch of open dock where the dastardly villains would make their landing.

"What's matter, hon? Not in the mood to party?"

April summoned a smile for Betsy before she turned her head. "Nothing's the matter. I suppose I'm just waiting for things to get started, like everybody else. I was…thinking about Kane and Regina. Has anyone heard from them?"

"Are you kidding? Turn-Coupe is the last thing on their minds. We'll be lucky if we get a coherent word out of either one of them for a year—or until they make a baby, whichever comes first."

"Oh, Betsy," April said on a laugh.

"You think I'm joking? You shouldn't. You know Kane—and his Regina. Those two were any more wrapped up in each other, they'd require surgery to get them apart."

"Must be nice." It was the usual dry comment suited to such situations, April told herself. It didn't mean anything. Still, as her level of discomfort rose, she quickly added, "There's something I've been wanting to ask you, if you don't mind."

"I won't know if I do or not until you lay it on me," the other woman said cheerfully.

"It's about the Benedicts. Luke doesn't want me writing about the family history, but all he gave me was some vague excuse about his grandmother not liking it. Do you have any idea what it's all about?"

Betsy lifted a shoulder. "Beats me. I mean, you

weren't intending to turn our little town into another
Peyton Place or make us out to be Southern igno-
ramuses like characters from *God's Little Acre,*
were you?''

''Hardly,'' she said with a smile. ''Though now
you mention it...''

''I know, I know. All towns have their types, as
the guy said in *Fiddler on the Roof.* But you know
what I mean.''

April sobered. ''Too well. But my South isn't like
that, just as the people I know aren't like that.''

''So what did you want to do that's put the fat in
the fire?''

''Mainly the story of Luke's Native American ancestress who guided the first Benedicts into what's
now Tunica Parish. She must have been quite a
woman to go off into the wilderness with four men,
brothers who were a few steps in front of the law.
She married one of them and helped start a dynasty,
but very little factual information exists about her.
She apparently left her Native American name behind, was baptized and took a Christian name before
she was married. Yet one story I came across said
that when she died her people came and took her
away to be buried on their tribal lands.''

''Yeah? I never knew that, and she'd be my great-
great-however-many-grandmother, too. But you
want to be careful how you dig around in that bone
pile, dear heart.''

April gave her a direct look of inquiry.

''There was a branch of my late husband's family
always claimed to have Indian blood, too—''

''Native American,'' April corrected with a grin.

"Yeah, right. Well, a lot of folks around here had ancestors who ran in the woods, so to speak. So one of my husband's cousins decided to look into the situation. It seems the oil and gas revenues paid to the tribes in Louisiana, not to mention the government benefits, have been pretty substantial for a couple of decades. Now they're into this land-based gambling casino business, so it's higher still. Anybody who can prove they have an eighth—or maybe it's a sixteenth—Native American blood in their veins can share the wealth, pick up a monthly check. Some families pull in six figures. You can see cause to head straight for the courthouse and start checking out the family connections, yes?"

"So, where's the problem?"

Betsy gave a slow wag of her head. "It's in the records, sugar. My husband's cousin found out something she hadn't planned on. Seems her ancestors weren't here to wave old Columbus ashore. They came on slave ships instead."

"Oops."

"Exactly."

April saw what Betsy was trying to say. There might be parts of the world where such a revelation would be as commonplace and mildly interesting as discovering Native American heritage. Louisiana was not one of them, though interracial relationships were growing more common every year. That Betsy didn't seem particularly upset about it was laudable, but it was her husband's bloodline in question, and the two had never had children. It might be different if it were her own.

"Do you really think the Benedicts might have the same situation?" April asked.

"Who knows? But a lot of these older ladies like Luke's Granny May are nervous about it, since their generation is the one that agonizes most about the whole thing. They'd rather not stir up something that could rear up and bite them. They'd rather nobody else did, either."

"I can certainly see that, but…"

"But what?"

"How far do you think they might go to prevent it?"

"Good question," Betsy said with a shake of her head. "Wish I knew the answer."

Their attention was caught just then by a commotion running through the crowd onshore. It gathered in volume. Everyone was craning and staring upriver. A group of young boys were pointing and yelling as they teetered on the dock's edge. Abruptly, a single voice rang out.

"Here they come!"

The shout was repeated along the riverbank, a loud, clear warning that the festivities were about to begin. April shielded her eyes against the sun's glare with one hand as she gazed toward the wide bend where river pirates should appear. The heat haze and glitter off the water made visibility uncertain, though she thought she saw shapes dancing over the waves.

Suddenly the flatboat carrying the ferocious crew surged into view with its single sail bellied and straining. On it came, plowing the water as it bore down on them. A carefully camouflaged motor powered the large raft, though the gang onboard made a mighty show of poling their craft shoreward. The tall mast that centered the flatboat sported a black flag above its sail.

A tall figure stood beside the mast. Dressed in a loose white shirt that billowed in the wind, leather knee breeches, stocking cap, and wide belt with a knife and a pistol thrust into it, he had one booted foot propped on a crate and a fierce grin on his face. It was Luke, looking raffish and untamed, and more handsome than he had any right in such a ridiculous get up.

He turned his head and his gaze met hers over the expanse of water separating them. Then it flickered down to her petticoats that flapped in a froth of white around her ankles. With his expression registering something near approval, he shifted upright and tipped her a brief, one-fingered salute. No doubt he was glad to have company in the costumed misery, she thought as she returned his gesture with a quick wave.

The flatboat rocked on the river waves, coming closer. One of the men next to Luke, perhaps Tom Watkin's son from down at the feed and seed store, leaned to say something to him. Luke glanced toward the houseboat again, his gaze moving over the other guests who had joined April and Betsy at the rail. He answered whatever comment had been made then laughed, a sound of rich merriment that echoed across the water.

Abruptly, a stunning thought struck April. Luke knew exactly where she was and what she was wearing. He had arranged for her to be on the houseboat so he could be certain where to find her when the pirate abductions began.

She had been set up.

The flatboat rode nearer, pushing a rolling wave of yellow-brown water before it. People streamed toward the far end of the dock where it would land. The crowd had thickened since the last time April looked. Still more were coming, jumping out of their vehicles as they saw they were about to miss the climactic moment.

April waited until the pirate flatboat slowed, easing toward the dock platform. As those onshore rushed forward in the usual mock attempt to repel the invaders, she stepped away from the rail, then waited until she was sure a fair-size group of laughing, shoving teenagers were between her and the flatboat. At the same time, she made a hurried explanation to Betsy. Luke's cousin began to protest, but April didn't listen. Lifting her skirts in both hands, she spun around and headed for the prow of the boat. At the gangway, she leaped to the catwalk, then hurried along it to the dock. There, she blended with the flow of people. Instead of joining them, however, she moved against the flow of revelers, away from the landing.

Half walking, half running, she skimmed around family groups and dodged couples. She had to get away before Luke saw where she was going, needed to make it to where she'd parked her car if she was going to foil his plans for her. That he'd head straight for where she'd been standing, she didn't doubt for a moment. He'd think it great fun to display her as his prisoner during the triumphant march into Turn-Coupe. He might still manage to kidnap her at some point during the festival, but she was going to make it a lot harder for him than he expected.

Shouts, grunts, and a few halfhearted yells sounded from behind her. Glancing back, she could see the top of Luke's capped head in the middle of the melee of citizens and pirates as he and his crew fought their sham battle in order to land. April was halfway across the parking lot when she heard the full-throated cry of victory that signaled the successful pirate invasion for another year.

Hard on that sound came a deeper roar that erupted in a thunderous explosion. The ground shook. April was buffeted by a wave of hot air that sent her stumbling, falling. Pain spiked into her knees and hands as she caught herself. For a stunned instant she was still, locked in a deafened silence. Then she inhaled sharply and her ears cleared in a rush of noise.

Shrill screams rasped on the hot air. She swung around to look back.

People were crawling and running in all directions. Pieces of wood and metal hailed down around them, rattling and splashing as they hit pavement, wood dock and water. Flames roared heavenward, chasing the black skirts of a mushrooming cloud of smoke. Several people were in the river, struggling toward shore, though one or two floated without moving. Where the houseboat had sat was a shattered and fiery hulk.

April struggled to her feet, jerking her petticoats out of the way as she started forward. At the same time, she saw Luke running toward the burning craft. He dodged people, shoved gaping onlookers out of his way. As he reached what was left of the houseboat, he didn't stop but hurtled forward in a fast but shallow dive. He surfaced almost at once, then with his arms flashing wetly with every stroke, he cleaved his way past burning patches of gas and oil and through a rain of ash and fiery debris. Curling smoke spread over the water to wreath his dark head as he arrowed toward a splashing survivor.

April lost sight of him as the gathering crowd obscured her view. Then Roan was there on the catwalk in front of the hulk. He gave orders in a staccato stream, adding a few curt gestures as he directed his deputies. Order began to emerge from the chaos. The crowd was controlled, sent back out of danger. Luke's cousin didn't wait to see it, but shed hat and boots and hit the water to help with the rescue of survivors.

The next few minutes were filled with sirens and flashing lights as fire trucks, emergency rescue crews and ambulances arrived. Personnel went to work in a carefully orchestrated sequence. The silent and awed revelers stood around in quiet groups, watching with strained expressions and talking among themselves as those who'd been blown into the water from boat or dock were brought ashore. Among the first, April saw, was Betsy North. She was pale and shaking, but had a wry quip for the technicians who lifted her onto a gurney.

Speculation ran like wildfire through the muttering assembly. Some theories centered on the engine compartment located aft as the source of the explosion, but most leaned toward a leak in one of the propane tanks carried by most houseboats. Mention was made of cigarettes and trapped gas fumes, though with little foundation. That it might be something more than an accident didn't seem to be part of the equation.

April wasn't so certain. She knew no one had been smoking, knew there had been no smell of the usual odor-causing chemicals that were added to scentless propane gas. She was beginning to feel as though she were in an action-adventure movie where something desperate happened every time she turned around. It was surreal, as if she had stepped from the quiet, semi-intellectual country life she had made for herself into a nightmare. She couldn't help wondering if she was supposed to have been one of the people pulled from the water and sent away in an ambulance, one of those who might be pronounced dead on arrival at the hospital.

Again and again, Luke swam and dove and brought limp, half-alive bodies to the shore. He was like an automaton programmed for rescue, unflagging, endlessly searching the rippling river surface for yet another person, determined, apparently, that none should be overlooked. Finally, April saw Roan swim out to meet him, saw him catch Luke's arm, give him a shake, and point toward the river's edge. Luke turned in that direction, staring at April where she stood on the outer edge of the crowd. Then he gave a single hard nod.

The two men turned as one then, and swam with slow, tired strokes to the dock. They lifted themselves to the jutting catwalk with lithe strength

while water fell from their clothes in shining torrents that were painted bloodred by the reflections
of flames. Roan twisted around and perched on the
edge for a moment with his head down and his chest
heaving. Luke rose to his feet at once and stalked
along the dock leaving a wet footprint with every
step.

He was coming toward April.

She felt an insane impulse to run. It was impossible. She couldn't move, couldn't decide how to
act for the morass of her thoughts. Luke had been
searching for her in the water. He'd plowed the
rocking river waves like a machine because he'd
thought she was lost in them, hurt, dying, even
drowned. Whether to save her or only to prove that
she was gone, he had expended heart-wrenching effort, battled spreading oil, gas fumes, fire and
smoke.

He had lost his jaunty stocking cap and his hair
was slicked to his head. His once white shirt was
stained a dirty brown streaked with oily black. It
molded to his body to show every ridged muscle,
every wrenching breath. His leather breeches were
so water-soaked they were glutinous. His lashes
were stuck together in spikes and his eyes were
bloodshot. A smear of blood streaked one high
cheekbone. His clenched fists swung at his sides.

For a long moment, she thought he meant to walk
up and take hold of her, though whether in embrace
or punishment was impossible to say. Just before he
reached arm's length, she wrenched her muscles under enough control to take a hasty step backward.

He stopped. A visible shudder ran over him. In

low, even intensity, he said, "I thought you were dead."

The spectators nearest to them began to edge away. Those walking past gave them a wide berth, though several curious looks were cast in their direction. In the settling quiet, April could hear Luke's hard breathing, and her own. She could feel the pump of the blood through her veins and the thudding of her heart.

"I changed my mind about staying onboard," she said with care. "I thought—I thought it would make me too easy to find."

"Easy?"

He spoke the word as if he'd never heard it before. She moistened her lips as she answered, "For you. To kidnap me."

"Yes," he said, his eyes behind their shield of lashes dark with anguish, "but I didn't know. And so I pictured you drowning in a shroud of petticoats, burned beyond all recognition...."

"Don't," she said in sharp repudiation. He had pictured her burned as Mary Ellen had been, dying as she had died, in agony that he was helpless to prevent. For an instant, April felt empathic understanding of his pain and helplessness wash through her with stunning force.

"Anything was likely, and I thought of it all," he continued relentlessly. "It was not a fun few minutes I spent until I saw you standing here all dry and clean and whole. And when I did, I wanted to—"

He stopped, closed his lips tightly across his

teeth. Water droplets from his clothing made soft plopping sounds as they hit the ground.

"You wanted to what?" She lifted her chin, meeting his gaze with valiant effort.

"Do desperate things to you, not all of them suitable for public viewing." He wiped a hand over his face, rubbing at the water that oozed from his hair and along his taut jawline.

"I don't think that would have helped matters."

"Neither do I, but it might have helped my feelings. It still might." He bit the words off as he reached to close the fingers of one wet, oily hand around her upper arm. His fingers pressed into her skin in a hold just short of painful. Glancing around, he centered his gaze on her car and started to walk toward it, pulling her with him.

"What are you doing?" she asked. "This isn't—"

"I'm taking you home—or rather, you're taking me to Chemin-a-Haut. I need to shower and change before I can get on with this."

The glance she threw at his set face as she fell into step beside him did nothing to reassure her. "Oh. I thought..."

"That I was kidnapping you, after all? You're right, I am," he said, his voice grim as he stared straight ahead.

She could fight him or she could go quietly. Crossing him in his present mood seemed like a bad strategy. She would have to accept her capture with as good a grace as she could manage and consider it a reasonable contribution to soothing Luke's ill humor as well as to charity.

He was moving so fast that it was hard to keep up with him, at least with any dignity. She reached to lift her skirts with her free hand to keep from tripping on them. Her voice a little breathless, she asked, "You got everyone from the houseboat out?"

"I think so. I counted eleven in all."

"Was anyone—? That is, were there any fatalities?"

He shook his head. "Couple of broken bones, some burns, maybe internal injuries. Everyone should be all right. They were lucky."

"I was luckier,' she murmured, almost to herself. Then she added, "I saw Betsy. She seemed okay."

"Could be in shock, just not feeling the pain. They'll know more when they get her to the hospital."

She agreed. At the same time, she glanced at the cut on his cheekbone that was dripping blood onto his shirt collar. She wondered if he felt it, but knew it was pointless to ask. She'd learned that much in New Orleans.

He put her into her car then walked around and crawled inside. She'd left her key in the ignition, a common habit in Turn-Coupe where car theft was not exactly a growth industry. Luke turned it to start the Lincoln and they pulled out of the parking lot, heading toward town on the main road that would take them through it then on out to the lake.

"You don't think you should stay and help Roan?"

"He has it under control."

She hesitated, then said anyway, "We could wait to see if they're going to cancel the whole festival."

"They won't," Luke said with a shake of his head. "Too many out-of-town visitors and vendors who need to recoup investments. Disappoint them and they may not come back next year."

His comments were perfectly civil, but his voice was grim and he didn't bother to look at her. There was a closed-in set to his features, as if his mind was elsewhere. An odd pain formed around April's heart. In that moment, she'd have given anything to see his familiar grin or look of cocky insouciance.

A glimmering of suspicion slid into her mind. What if he wasn't taking her to be held for charitable ransom? What if he really meant to carry her off somewhere for his own purposes? He could do it, nothing easier. Even if she kicked and screamed and called for help, no one would come. They would think it was all a part of the festival ritual.

She felt chilled in spite of the summer heat inside the car. Then she gave a tiny shake of her head. That couldn't happen, no way.

Could it?

11

How in hell was he going to get April onto his boat?

Luke frowned over that all-important question while he took a fast shower then skimmed into jeans and a T-shirt. He'd like to throw her over his shoulder and carry her, but the situation called for a little more finesse than that. He didn't want to start out on an extended stay in the swamp with her ready to scratch his eyes out the minute he let down his guard.

She was going with him, however, no matter how hard she fought. It was the only way he could be certain of where she was and what she was doing.

He'd died a thousand times there in the river while he searched for her. He wasn't going through that again any time soon. The years since Mary Ellen's death had been haunted by the things he hadn't done, hadn't been able to do because he'd failed to look ahead. This time he'd make sure that if he had to live with regrets they'd be for things he damn well *had* done.

April was standing in the front parlor when he came down the stairs. Her attention was on the portrait that hung over the white marble mantel. The expression on her face was pensive as she studied it, her concentration so total she apparently failed to hear his approach. She looked so right there in her long dress with her hair spilling down her back that he stopped in the doorway, reluctant to disturb her and spoil the illusion. She was more attuned to his whereabouts than he'd thought, however, for she spoke over her shoulder after a moment.

"This is your grandmother as a bride, isn't it? She was beautiful."

"Still is, in her way," he agreed as he came forward. "It's in the bone structure so it doesn't go away. You'll be the same when you're her age."

She sent him a quick look without comment as if she suspected some motive behind the compliment. It was annoying, mainly because she was right.

After a moment, she changed the subject, saying, "I didn't see her at the pirate landing today."

"She doesn't think much of the festival, says she has better things to do than waste time with play-acting or looking at arts and crafts that have more to do with making money than with either art or craft."

"A woman after my own heart."

"I always thought the two of you would get along again, the way you did when you were a kid, if you had a chance to really know each other." He kept his face straight to hide his brief amusement. Granny May had thought April was too dreamy and impractical as a teenager and that he spent too much time mooning over her. April had resented the fact that he discussed her with his grandmother. Both thought the other had too much influence. Neither was right.

"Possibly," April answered as she turned away. "Are you ready to go?"

"Not yet."

She stopped and her gaze flicked over him, as if to check that he was decently dressed. As she lifted it to his face once more, wariness hovered in its depths. "People will be wondering what became of you," she said in tentative tones.

She was right, or would be if he hadn't made a couple of calls while he was upstairs. "I have a proposition for you to think about first."

"Such as?"

"We could skip the rest of the day, maybe take the pontoon boat and a picnic out on the lake. It would give you a chance to smooth out the kinks and forget your close call. We might even extend it to a couple of days, if you wanted."

She tilted her head. "I don't want. Anyway, our bypassing the main day of the festival won't do much for the bottom line of the charity Turn-Coupe is honoring this year."

"Certain things take precedence. Your safety is one of them."

"My safety? And how is a day on the lake going to aid that?"

"It should keep you out of harm's way until Roan has a chance to look into the explosion," he answered in the most reasonable tone he could manage.

"But it won't help me discover what's going on.

I promised myself I'd figure that out for my own peace of mind. It's more important now than ever.''

Luke felt his scalp crawl. "It's more dangerous now than ever, you mean.''

"You don't know that. The explosion was probably an accident. Even if it wasn't, that doesn't mean it had anything to do with me.''

"Tell yourself that if it makes you feel better,'' he said. "I don't buy it.''

"I'm supposed to believe that someone blew up a covey of strangers just to get to me? How would he know I was even on the boat?''

"Betsy never could keep a secret. Half the town was waiting to see me board the craft and carry you off over my shoulder.''

"But that makes me responsible for what happened and I—'' She stopped abruptly and swung away from him as her voice caught in her throat.

"It does nothing of the kind,'' he said in sharp contradiction. "But if you go haring off trying to find out who's behind it, and somebody gets caught in the crossfire, you will be at fault.''

"Then I'm surprised you care to be anywhere around me since I'm so dangerous to know.''

"I can take care of myself,'' he said evenly.

The look she sent him over her shoulder was waspish. "I'm sure that will be a great satisfaction to me when I'm crying over your grave.''

"Would you? Cry over my grave, that is?'' It might be stupid to ask, but he couldn't help it.

"Don't joke about such a thing!'' She shuddered visibly as she looked away.

No doubt it was his own fault that she took everything he said as a joke, he thought darkly. Bracing an arm across the doorway, he said, "If it bothers you that much, you can always cooperate for my sake."

Her head snapped around again as she demanded, "Why are you so determined to talk me into this? What is it to you?"

It was a good question. Luke wished he had an answer. If he had any sense, he'd stop talking and cart her off whether she wanted to go or not. Was he hesitating because he was afraid of what she might think of him? She could hardly see him in any worse light. Or maybe it was something to do with his self-righteous disapproval when Kane had carried Regina into the swamp earlier in the summer. He'd been pretty snide toward Kane about that. Luke himself had no use for violence against women and was reluctant to take on even its appearance, much less the actuality. The cases were different, but had enough surface similarity to make him uncomfortable. Granny May always said that those who judged others often wound up in the same fix themselves, and she had a nasty habit of being right.

Yes, and it just might be that he was leery of laying hands on April for fear he couldn't make himself let go again. Or that the price in pain of freeing her would be more than he could afford to pay. On the other hand, letting something happen to her could cost everything he had, everything that was in him.

He was damned if he did and damned if he didn't. In that case, he might as well please himself. The

problem, then, could be making sure he didn't
please himself too much.

Without bothering to answer her question, Luke
swung away from her and walked toward the
kitchen at the back of the house. There, he pulled
open the refrigerator and began taking out meat and
cheese, lettuce, fruit and an assortment of juices.
When April followed him and stood watching with
her arms folded across her chest, he ignored her.
Turning to the bread box, he took out a fresh loaf
of French bread.

"I told you," she said with emphasis, "that I'm
not interested in a picnic."

"I know." He brought the picnic basket from the
pantry and began to pack things inside.

"In fact, I'm leaving. If you want me to drive
you back to wherever you left your Jeep, you'd better come on now."

"I don't think so," he answered, weighing the
merits of dill or bread-and-butter pickles, then toss-
ing both jars into the basket.

"Fine. I'll see you around."

As she whirled around and began to walk away,
he called after her, "Aren't you forgetting something?"

"I doubt it," she answered without looking back.

"I have your car keys."

She stopped, turned in a slow half circle. "I'll
thank you to hand them over."

"Can't do that." He gathered an armload of
canned goods and dumped them into the basket,
tossed in some paper towels, then added several
more items from the refrigerator.

"I mean it, Luke."

The basket was full. He covered it with a handy tea towel before he turned back to her. Crossing his arms over his chest as he leaned against the cabinet, he gave her a slow smile. "Want to wrestle me for them?"

"I'm in no mood for games."

"Maybe you should be. You work too hard, take everything way too seriously."

"Nearly getting blown up is a serious business," she said shortly.

"But it didn't happen. You're alive and you're here. You have the choice of relaxing a while or heading back into town where everyone will be talking about the explosion and how it happened and what you know about it. Of course, if you enjoy being in the public eye and answering prying semi-dumb questions, I guess that's all right."

She glanced away an instant. When she looked back, her gaze was stony. "You are the most..." She stopped, took a deep breath. "All right, so we'll picnic. But I warn you—I can't stay long. I have work to do this evening."

It was a major victory, but one he couldn't acknowledge by so much as the twitch of an eyelid for fear she'd go back on her decision. He nodded his understanding, if not his acceptance, then tipped his head toward the refrigerator. "Could you get the ice and that bottle of Chardonnay on the top shelf? I've got my hands full."

The rig he kept for outings of the kind he had in mind was no seagoing monster like the craft that had blown up, but it wasn't half-bad. A thirty-two-foot pontoon boat with a 120 horsepower outboard, it had an enclosed fiberglass cabin for weather protection. Though not really designed for extended living, it afforded reasonable comfort for twelve or more people for a few hours, or decent overnight accommodations for two for a few days — or longer if provisions were replenished. Twin cushioned benches on the front deck could be made down into two single beds or a double. Otherwise a portable table could be set up between them for dining al fresco.

Inside the cabin were all the comforts of home, including a tiny galley with hot and cold running water, three-burner stove, sink, gas-powered refrigerator, and built-in dinette booth. A shower and toilet were located in the back. Sliding glass doors at each end of the cabin allowed the air to blow through and gave access to the rear deck as well as the front.

An aluminum dinghy with a ten horsepower outboard was tied to the rear of the pontoon boat. This gave added convenience and maneuverability, since there were many places in the swamp where a craft as large as the pontoon boat couldn't reach. For day trips or just messing around on the water, the setup couldn't be beat.

If April was impressed, she managed to hide it. She didn't appear nervous of stepping onboard, however, which had been a question in Luke's mind after her experience earlier. Moving aft ahead of him, she helped him stow away their provisions then took a seat on one of the front benches nearby while he fired up the outboard and settled it into a rum-

bling purr. He could have asked her to step back
out on the pier to shove them off, but he preferred
to do it himself. A moment after he sprang back
onboard again, he put the motor in gear and they
headed toward open water.

As they left the dock, Luke saw April staring at
Chemin-a-Haut, at the weathered gazebo near the
water's edge, the sloping lawn with its green velvet
sheen in the slanting summer sun, and the big old
two-story mansion that sat foursquare and solid with
its back gallery overlooking the lake. He wondered
what she was thinking as she gazed so pensively at
its West Indies roof line, massive columns and shut-
tered coolness, if she was thinking how she might
have been its mistress or only comparing it to Mulberry Point in her mind.

He'd never know for sure without asking. And
asking was the last thing he'd ever do.

There was a swimsuit or two and a couple of
extra T-shirts and shorts stored with the rough bed-
ding under the bench where she sat. Luke thought
of suggesting she change for comfort's sake, but
couldn't bring himself to do it. Something about her
old-fashioned dress and how it clung to the curves
of her breasts and the slender turn of her waist fired
his senses. So did the way the wind ruffled the hem
of her skirt across her ankles and flipped it up to
show her lace-edged petticoats. She was a walking
invitation to exploration, even as her manner for-
bade all thought of it. It gave him such pained pleasure to look at her that he wasn't about to deprive
himself of it.

A great blue heron, squawking in protest at being

disturbed in his fishing, lifted from the shallows beyond the house. April turned her head to follow its
water-skimming flight. The wind of their passage
stirred her hair that she wore free and loose between
her shoulder blades and the sun slanted across her
face. Her lashes flickered down an instant while her
chest rose and fell with a long, deep breath.

Abruptly, as if she felt his stare, she opened her
eyes and looked back at him. He shifted in his seat
as he realized he'd been caught but didn't look
away. She held his regard while the trace of a smile
banished the strain from her eyes, replacing it with
tenuous accord. She reached up to catch a strand of
hair that was fluttering across her mouth. Holding it
back, she lifted her voice above the roar of the boat
motor. "This may not have been such a bad idea,
after all!"

Guilt hit Luke like a hard jab to the solar plexus.
For a single second, he considered whipping the
boat into a wide turn and taking her back to land.
That, or telling her the truth.

He did neither. Instead, he revved the engine to
a faster pitch and sent the pontoon boat flying toward the channel that would funnel them into the
backwaters of the swamps where no one could track
them, no one could find them—unless he wanted to
be found.

This was the right thing he was doing; he knew
it. April wasn't going to like it, but he'd deal with
that when the time came. Meanwhile, he had a couple of peaceful hours, give or take, ahead of him.
He'd make what he could of them.

A few minutes later, he left the channel, took a

few turns, and nosed into an old slough known by the unromantic name of Sand Dump. He chose the place, named for a peculiar mound of sand at the water's edge that might or might not be an old Indian mound, in part because of its distance off the main boat track but mainly for the deep shade cast by the cypress trees that enclosed it. The water was a dark brownish green from the tannic acid that dripped from the trees, and so still it appeared glassy in the still heat of the day. Turtles slid from a log at their approach. The fishy smell common to such places reached out to them.

Luke selected a small cypress, squinted at the branches for any roosting snakes, then headed toward it. He cut the engine and let the boat glide with its own momentum as he went forward with a rope. Snagging the tree trunk in an expert move, he tied up. One of the aluminum pontoons bumped their makeshift stanchion with a soft, hollow boom, then everything was quiet.

Actually, it seemed far too quiet to Luke. He moved back to the console and slid a George Winston tape into the player. As its mellow strains drifted on the air, he began setting up the outside table at the front of the boat where any stray breeze could reach them. Behind him, April rose and stretched, then lifted her seat cushion to take out the picnic basket he'd stowed underneath. He made an abortive move to stop her, but it was too late.

"Good grief," she exclaimed as she hefted the basket. "You have enough food in here for an army."

Improvising rapidly, he said, "Nothing like having a choice. Besides, I can leave the extra onboard for emergencies.''

''Such as when you get lost?'' she inquired, her tone dry.

She had him there, since the last time he'd failed to find his way home was when he was eleven years old. Still, he didn't give up. ''You never know when a motor will quit on you.''

''Or you'll run out of gas?''

The suggestion was saccharine sweet. He'd pulled that stunt on her back in the good old days. The slow paddle back to Chemin-a-Haut under a summer moon, with frequent pauses for kisses to keep his strength up, had been something else. It was one of his favorite memories, in spite of the mosquitoes that had nearly eaten the two of them alive.

He gave her a crooked grin as he answered, ''That, too.''

She let it go, maybe because she didn't want to open that can of catfish bait. Regardless, the sharp glint of suspicion remained in her eyes.

Lunch wasn't fancy, but it was filling. It seemed a nervous truce had been declared between them. Though they weren't exactly at ease, they still talked in a desultory fashion. A major topic was the explosion. He grilled her about it in as offhand a manner as he could manage, trying to see if there was anything at all she'd heard or seen that rang any bells. So far as he could tell, there was nothing—no warning, no hint of trouble.

After they finished their sandwiches, he reached for a mango to peel for them both. He glanced at her a couple of times as he wielded the knife, his gaze lingering on the almost transparent skin under her eyes. He said after a moment, ''You aren't sleeping much, are you?''

''What makes you say that?''

''Shadows,'' he said, describing a small semicircle with his knife blade.

She lifted a brow, a challenge in the movement. ''I do some of my best work at night.''

He considered giving that remark the salacious comment it deserved, but decided against it as he saw expectation flood her face. With supreme self-control, he settled for a disbelieving grunt.

''It's true!''

''And I suppose all the other junk that's been happening doesn't disturb your sleep at all.'' His gaze was sardonic as he offered her a mango slice on the tip of his blade.

Her only answer was a moody shrug, but she didn't refuse the fruit.

''So, maybe you should take a little nap.''

''We don't have time.''

''We'll take time, if it's what you want.'' He met her gaze, his own steady.

She seemed to consider it, then gave a quick shake of her head. ''I don't think so.''

Luke didn't push the point, but neither did he forget it.

Yellow jackets and flies, attracted by mango nectar and other goodies, began to buzz around the table. He and April cleared things away and rinsed their sticky hands. Afterward, Luke sat in a comfortable sprawl on the bench across from April with his long legs crossed at the ankles. He drank the last of his apple juice and flipped the bottle into the trash can, then stretched hugely. A trickle of sweat between his shoulder blades set off a round of itching in that area. He rubbed against the seat a little, but the smooth vinyl wasn't a lot of help. Turning a hopeful gaze on April, he said, "I don't suppose I could talk you into scratching my back?"

"You must be joking."

The look she gave him was not only incredulous but also a potent reminder of the tasteless comment he'd made to her ex-husband in New Orleans. He ignored it as he said in plaintive explanation, "It's the scabs from the acid burns. They're driving me nuts."

Her eyes widened a fraction, then she shook her head. "The deeper places must still be sore. I might hurt you."

"I'll risk it," he said as he rose to his feet and stripped his T-shirt off over his head. Crossing in a single stride to the bench where she sat, he lay down on his stomach and calmly settled his head in her lap with his cheek resting on her thigh.

She smelled of cotton and roses and clean woman, an aphrodisiac so heart-stoppingly potent that he closed his eyes to absorb it. At the same time, he draped a long arm across her knees. The swift rise of strained heat in his lower body was not exactly unexpected, but considerably more virulent than normal. He thought without humor that it was a good thing he was lying facedown.

He didn't relax, but kept his guard in place since he expected to be thrown off at any second. April made no move in that direction, but only sat as if too surprised to react. Then she relaxed by hesitant degrees that he could feel under his head. Putting a tentative hand on his back, she smoothed up and down his spine, brushing away the perspiration so it evaporated. Then she began to rake gently with her nails at the healing scabs in that region.

Luke was in heaven; that was all there was to it. The sensations that ran over him were so exquisite that it was all he could do not to groan in sheer bliss. He was also amazed at April's instinctive understanding about exactly where his back itched. Purest gratification made a prickle of gooseflesh spread across his shoulders. At least, he told himself that was the cause.

The boat rocked gently on breeze-pushed waves, squeaking a little against the tree that held it. Gentle musical strains poured from the stereo. The sun shone down, shimmering on the water in a hard brightness that he could see even behind his closed eyelids. A fly hummed in a sleepy circle, around and around. The soothing touch on his back moved in a ceaseless rhythm for some time. Then it slowed. Stopped.

Luke raised his head a cautious fraction. April was sitting with her arm braced on the bench's back and her head propped on her palm. Her eyes were closed and her breasts, so near his face, rose and fell in a telltale way.

He forced reluctant muscles to move enough to lift his upper body off her lap then rise to his feet. She opened sleep-drugged eyes as he hovered over her, but didn't protest as he eased her to a reclining position. A sigh lifted her bodice and she reached to drag her long skirts up to midthigh for coolness. Then she was quiet again.

Luke slid her low-heeled sandals off her feet and set them quietly on the floor. Then he backed away, clenching his hands as he fought the impulse to touch the skin she'd bared, to push her skirts higher and press his lips to the raw scrapes on her knees that were doubtless a souvenir of the morning. In the back of his mind was a glimmer of just how dangerous this idea of his might become to his sanity.

It couldn't be helped. What was done, was done. He wouldn't go back now, even if he could. As he felt the opposite bench behind his calves, he sat down abruptly. Then he lay down with striated patience and closed his eyes.

He was dreaming. In the gray mists of half-acknowledged fancy, April hovered over him. Her hair fell forward around his face, caressing his cheeks. Her lips smiled. Her eyes shone with promise and excitement. Her hands smoothed over his naked shoulders, pulling him closer, closer....

"Wake up, damn you, Luke! We have to go back. It's almost dark." She was shaking him, yelling in his face.

Blinking into wakefulness, he saw that she was right. The sun was almost down, its last rays streaking the water with russet and rose. Dusk was gathering under the cypress trees. He couldn't remember when he'd slept so soundly in the middle of the day, or at any other time for that matter. April wasn't the only one who had been burning the midnight oil, but it was more than that. He'd known she was near. He'd been content for the first time in long years.

"Yeah, all right," he said, putting a firm hand on her arm, pushing her away before he did something he might regret. "We're gone."

They were, too, in record time, zooming out of the slough and heading like an arrow through the baffle of trees and along the winding paths that would take them away from the main channel. He shoved the control into high gear, kicking up a frothing wake that spread in rolling waves to the far, back reaches of the lake and on into the deepest depths of the swamp. With his eyes narrowed against the wind, he watched for stumps and logs and cypress knees, swerving to avoid all obstacles as he charted a course that not many could recognize, much less duplicate.

He failed to reckon on the fact that April had been there before.

She had been sitting with her face turned into the wind, staring almost unseeingly at the water, the trees, and the darkening sky. An abrupt frown drew her brows together. She swung her head to stare around her, following the line of sight of the channel he was following. She whipped around toward him again, then called above the boat's roar, "You're going the wrong way!"

He made no answer nor did he slacken his speed.

"Luke!"

He turned his head to meet her eyes. "We aren't going to Chemin-a-Haut!"

"We have to," she shouted. "I have to get home."

He didn't answer, but only faced forward again and sent the pontoon boat skimming straight for the swamp's darkest heart.

12

April stared at Luke while alarm skittered through her. Where could he be taking her if not home? There was nothing this way except swampy wilderness reaching to the Mississippi River's natural levee. He must have gone crazy.

She couldn't keep screaming at him across the space between them, however, especially if he was not going to answer her. She gathered her skirts and slid from her seat, keeping low in the fast-moving boat. Going to one knee beside him at the console, she put her hand on the corded muscles of his arm.

"Where are you going? What are you doing?"

"You'll see," he said, and closed his lips tightly together again.

She hated that macho phrase, as if she had no reason for concern or was too emotional to know the worst in advance. "If this is a joke, it isn't funny. Turn around. Now."

He made no answer. The boat swerved, jostling her against him as he swung to avoid some floating log or underwater snag.

"Why are you doing this?" she demanded, pushing free of him as she righted herself. "What's got into you?"

"I'm seeing to it that you're safe. If you won't take care of yourself, then I'll have to do it for you."

"I don't need you to take care of me," she declared as her temper rose.

"You can do it yourself, I suppose. The way you did this morning." Derision underlined the words.

"Nothing happened to me."

"By the grace of God and your lucky stars."

"Anyway, you're going to kill us both going so fast!"

He glanced at her then and slackened the speed a notch. That was all.

"Take me home, Luke," she commanded. "Take me home *now!*"

No answer.

"I mean it. Take me home or—"

"Or what?" he interrupted, his voice hard. "I'll be sorry? I am already, but that doesn't change a thing. We aren't going home, so just sit back down and enjoy the ride."

He was kidnapping her, he really was. It wasn't playacting, had nothing to do with charity. They were threading their way deeper and deeper into the swamp. At some point, he'd stop. And then what?

She couldn't imagine, didn't want to imagine. Pushing away from him, she resumed her seat. Still, she couldn't take her gaze from him, couldn't stop measuring his tall form, his taut features, and his hard, competent hands on the boat's wheel. She couldn't prevent herself from comparing their relative strengths, his against her own, and wondering what it would take to stop him.

She wasn't sure anything would.

It was not a comfortable conclusion. Wrapping her arms around her waist, she turned her face into the warm evening wind and stared straight ahead. She didn't look at Luke again.

Gray twilight was spreading over the water when they finally nosed into a narrow channel half-choked by cypress knees and floating mats of lavender water hyacinths. They rounded a bend and emerged into a quiet pool ringed by moss-hung cypresses and with more water hyacinths and yellow water lilies nearly obscuring the water's surface, growing so thick they appeared solid enough to stand on. Luke cut the engine and they slid in among the undulating plants with the boat's aluminum pontoons pushing them aside, forcing entry. Then as their forward progress stopped, the greenery closed in around them like a living boat slip.

Luke snapped off the radio, perhaps to conserve battery power. Then he removed the ignition key and pocketed it. He dropped a front anchor then headed toward the rear to let down another. As he stepped past her, she drew her feet up onto the seat and clasped her arms around her knees. He gave her a narrow glance but said nothing.

April stared around at their new place of concealment. It was perhaps fifty feet across and edged with marshy growth and trees even thicker than where they had tied up earlier. A pair of egrets perched on a dead snag a short distance away, their plumage glinting white in the last vestiges of daylight. Pale orange flies of some kind swarmed over a section of water lilies, and a long, muddy brown shape against the bank farther on was either a rotting log or an alligator patiently waiting for a meal. The place was dank and uninviting. It was also deserted, totally deserted except for the two of them.

Luke returned to the front of the boat and took out a propane-fueled two-burner grill that he set up in its special niche near the forward railing. He fired it up, then threw a pat of butter into an ancient skillet and set it on a burner. While it was heating, he peeled and sliced a small onion, then broke several eggs into a bowl and beat them with milk and seasoning. He glanced at her now and then as he worked, but she refused to meet his gaze.

That avoidance seemed to annoy him. As he poured the egg mixture into the sizzling skillet, he said, "If I'd known you were going to sulk, I'd have brought along company."

"I'm surprised you didn't anyway," she returned in cool hauteur. "From habit."

"You know nothing at all about my habits."

"And want to know less!"

He gave a hard laugh. "Afraid you'll find them too appealing? You could always chalk it up to research."

"No, thank you. But if we're going to talk about appeal, I should point out that I didn't kidnap you."

"Well, if you think I brought you out here to make love to you, you can forget it. I could have done that in greater comfort at Chemin-a-Haut."

"You relieve my mind," she said, her glance scathing.

"I thought I might."

"I don't care a rat's left ear what you thought! I

want to go home. I need to work. I need a bath and more comfortable clothes. I need to feed Midnight!''

''Your damned cat will survive. And so will you.'' He attended to his omelet, lifting the edges to allow the center egg mixture to run to the bottom, then adding sliced onion and a handful of cheese.

''Thank you for the kind consideration,'' she returned acidly. ''But if you think that solves the problem, you're more of a Neanderthal than I suspected.''

''If you think your opinion of me is going to change the situation, you're more of a prima donna than I knew.''

She hated that title, even if she did apply it to herself when trying to stop worrying about her precious words and just get them on paper. ''What I think is that you're going to have a lot of explaining to do if and when we do leave here. I sincerely doubt, for instance, that Roan gave his approval to this business.''

''Now you've got my nerves jangling like pocket change.''

''If I press charges for kidnapping,'' she said pointedly, ''you may need all your pocket change to pay a good lawyer.''

''You're going to get up before God and everybody and say I forced you to come with me?''

''Enticed me,'' she corrected.

''I'm sure the countryside will be fascinated by all the intimate details,'' he continued as if she hadn't spoken. ''If they aren't, you can make up something thrillingly sexy. Or if you can't, maybe I can.''

''You wouldn't.''

He flipped his omelet over then looked up. ''Try me.''

He would indeed, she thought, and enjoy doing it. He'd always been a little over the top, but common sense and decency had acted as brakes back when they were younger. How was it that he'd ceased to care about those things? When had what he thought and wanted become more important than anyone else's needs or feelings?

It was plain that getting angry wasn't going to help. In fact, arguing with him only seemed to make him worse. What she needed was a reason to return that would be to his advantage, something that might even accomplish whatever goal he had in mind.

Persuasion was obviously her best course. A quick review of her options showed plainly that there were serious obstacles to any alternative.

She might manage to get her hands on the boat key, but it would take some doing. Even with it in hand, using it would be nearly impossible while Luke remained onboard to stop her.

She could swim to shore, but the swamp that surrounded them was a morass of marsh grass and unstable mud cut by water channels nearly impossible to navigate on foot. Alligators, poisonous water moccasins, and bog holes of mud and quicksand were added dangers, not to mention the swarms of mosquitoes that would make every step a living hell. On top of all that was the risk of losing her way.

There was the dinghy attached to the rear. Its motor required no key, but would need time to get running and set in motion. Once she was underway, she would probably be able to retrace their route among the many branching channels they'd taken, but again, she might not. It would be embarrassing, not to mention dangerous, to escape only to get herself lost. Still that was a risk she might have to take.

"Ready to eat?" Luke asked, his eyes hooded as he neatly divided the omelet and slid the halves onto a pair of disposable plates.

"I'm not hungry." She really wasn't, though the combined smells of butter, eggs and onion were interesting, and the omelet appeared beautifully browned.

"Fine." He dumped the extra portion back onto his plate. Turning to the ice chest, he took out a bottle of wine and filled a plastic glass. With the wine and a chunk of French bread in hand, he sat down to his dinner.

If she didn't eat now, she'd have to resort to something cold later. Besides, a glass of wine sounded wonderful after the day just passed.

"Oh, all right," she said, as she swung her feet off the bench and turned around to the center table. She pulled the discarded plate toward her, then found a fork and reached to spear her share of the omelet.

In a blur of movement, Luke dropped the bread in his left hand and caught her wrist. "No, you don't. You weren't hungry. Now it's mine."

He was making a point, she thought. She could

cooperate or accept the consequences. It was not one she much needed to have driven home.

In tones gone suddenly flat, she said, "Don't push it, Benedict. You've won for now, but there will be another time."

He held her gaze, his own clear and assessing. Then slow and unreliable joy dawned in his eyes and spread to curl around his mouth. "A challenge," he said softly, "or rather, another one. Now that's more like it."

His grip on her arm was firm but not hurtful. The warmth of it seeped into her skin, radiating through her until she felt hot and breathless. She refused to acknowledge it, however, much less succumb to it, as she replied, "You may not think so before this is over."

"We'll see, won't we? But I suppose it's only fair to let you keep your strength up." Releasing her, he allowed her to take her part of the omelet. "Will you have wine? Or are you afraid of losing your head?"

"My head," she said, unsmiling, "won't be affected."

He picked up the bottle to pour. "No?"

"No."

"How about a test?" he said as he filled her glass.

It was her turn to be satiric. "With one bottle of wine?"

"Who said that there was only one? The others just aren't cold."

She might have known. "If getting your women

drunk is the usual practice, it's no wonder your reputation is so lurid.''

He put the cork back in the wine. ''Actually, I prefer *my women* not to be too anesthetized. It doesn't do much for my rep if they can't remember the details.''

''You can be sure I won't be enhancing your precious rep since my limit is one glass. I'm well aware that women's bodies absorb alcohol at a faster rate than men's.''

''I offer you the perfect excuse and you won't take it,'' he complained as he picked up the plastic glass and handed it to her. ''Make up your mind, sweetheart. Do you want to, or don't you?''

''How can you think my mind isn't made up, for pity's sake!''

''For a start, those leading questions you asked the other day in town.''

''I was just curious. Though I should have known you'd turn it into something it wasn't.''

He broke the French bread with his long fingers, then popped a loose piece into his mouth and chewed. Finally, he asked, ''Is that what I'm doing?''

''You know very well...'' She stopped, took a deep breath. ''Anyway, you said a few minutes ago that sex isn't why you brought me out here.''

''What if I said I lied? Would you be more resigned?'' There was a glint of some suppressed emotion in his eyes.

Her heart kicked into a faster rhythm. She didn't know how to answer even if he meant it, which she was by no means certain he did. Instead, she asked,

"Wouldn't it have been simpler just to say you'd changed your mind?"

"Probably. But where's the fun in that?"

"Everything doesn't have to be fun," she answered in irritation.

"No," he said smiling straight into her eyes, "but making love works a lot better that way."

She had walked right into the verbal pitfall. She snapped, "You should know!"

"So should you. Or wasn't that your experience?"

"We'll leave my experience out of this, thank you." She put down her wine and picked up her fork.

"I'd like to, believe me, but I think it's there whether we want it or not. Good or bad, everybody takes their past to bed with them."

"Deep, Benedict. But we aren't going to bed."

"Too bad," he said, and saluted her with his wineglass.

Instead of answering, she cut off a forkful of the omelet and put it into her mouth. It was good, but she'd expected nothing else since Luke was good at most things. She wondered almost at random if he was better at making love now, better at making it fun. As if it mattered.

Strange, but she wasn't sure whether to be relieved or disappointed that he'd accepted her decision. She did know that she was confused. If she accepted at face value his claim that he wanted to keep her safe, then she had to assume he had something more in mind than a brief expression of gratitude for the protective maneuver. What did he expect to gain if not a night or two of passionate recompense?

Not money, surely. She couldn't imagine him doing anything so sleazy, for one thing. More than that, he worked hard at farming and had never shown the least interest in wealth above the minimum required for reasonable comfort. He was fit and healthy with none of the classic symptoms of someone with a drug habit that called for regular infusions of easy cash. What on earth was he doing then?

She could absolve him of more tender motives, she thought. He had been attracted to her years ago, but that was all. If it had been more then he would never have invited Mary Ellen into his car that night. He might have a lingering interest for old time's sake, since they'd been friends before they were lovers. That and a strong busybody instinct was most likely what had brought him to her door the day she'd taken that weird call on the air. If there was more to it, she didn't know it.

She had no idea what he wanted, then, but whatever it was, he wasn't getting it. She would not be coerced any more than she would stand for being protected against her will. She was a grown woman of reasonable intelligence, one well able to decide the level of danger she could stand. She didn't need Luke Benedict to run interference for her.

It crossed her mind that she was being cynical and possibly unfair. If so, it was because he had made her that way, or at least had begun the process. Since he didn't see fit to explain his actions, she had to take them as she saw them. Whatever misjudgment he might suffer because of it was on his own head.

They finished their meal in silence. As Luke began to pick up their dishes and carry them into the cabin, April rose to help him. The tiny galley hadn't been designed with two people in mind, however. As she put her wineglass in the sink, he stepped behind her to return the butter to the refrigerator. The front of his jeans brushed across her hips. She moved away at once and he muttered an apology. A moment later, she picked up the French bread and turned to put it in the waxed paper wrapper lying on the cabinet. He reached at the same time for the damp cloth that lay beside it and her forehead bumped his shoulder.

He shot out a hand to steady her, then used his grip to turn her toward the rear of the boat. ''Let me take care of this, okay? There's a couple of T-shirts and some shorts under the seat over there if you'd like to change. I can't guarantee the fit, but at least they're clean.''

It seemed like a sensible suggestion, especially since she was feeling a little dizzy. It was, of course, the bump between the eyes affecting her, and not the close proximity to a hard male body in close-fitting jeans.

The T-shirt she found was one of Luke's, as were the shorts. Both had a slight mustiness in their folds from being stored but smelled mostly of laundry soap. The shirt reached past her hips and she had to tighten the string belt of the shorts, but the outfit promised sleeping comfort and a bit more maneuverability than had her dress.

Her hair was a mass of tangles from blowing in the wind. As she raked her fingers through it, she stood on tiptoe and looked out the tiny window of the small shower cum toilet where she'd changed. She could see into the dinghy that was tied to the stern of the pontoon boat. A long-handled paddle lay in the bottom.

She had once known how to paddle a light boat as well as run an outboard, though it had been some time since she'd tried either. If she could just slip out the back doors and over the side without being caught, she could make a silent exit from their lagoonlike anchorage by paddling, then use the motor only after she was far enough away that Luke wouldn't hear. The best time to try it would be later in the night, however, well after he was asleep.

By the time she emerged with her rolled dress and petticoats under her arm, Luke had finished clearing the galley and was in the process of lowering the inside table to convert the dinette booth into a bed. A quick grin came and went across his lips as his gaze lingered on the way the T-shirt hung around her, draping over the small hills of her breasts, but he made no comment.

"You can sleep here," he said easily. "I'll take the bench outside with the dive-bombing mosquitoes."

"That's very noble of you," she said. It was also very convenient. Too convenient?

"That's me, noble to the core," he answered. "You don't have to turn in now, if you don't want. There's a collection of books and magazines that

Regina and first one and then another left on board, or I could beat you in a few hands of cards.''

''What, no television?'' she mocked, though she seldom turned on the set at Mulberry Point.

''Hard as it may be, you'll have to make do without.''

''Some host you are,'' she groused for the sake of form, then added a second later, ''I think I'll read awhile.''

''Fine.'' He threw a couple of pillows onto the quilt he had spread over the padded surface of the dinette cushions. Then he stooped to pull a farming magazine from a stack in the bench storage. Sitting on the bed, he rested his shoulders against the high back of the dinette's booth.

He meant to use the light that glowed over the converted bed for his reading since it was the only convenient source of illumination in the small cabin. April thought she could hardly object to that. She thumbed through the stored books, noting three or four of her own titles. Selecting a mystery novel she hadn't read, she joined Luke under the single light, but on the opposite end of the bed.

It was hot and muggy, still an occasional breath of air drifted through the screens of the open windows and doors. Silence hung in the cabin, broken only by the turning of pages or occasional rasp as one of them cleared their throat. After a time, however, a mosquito that had found its way inside whined around their ears. Luke dispatched it. Quiet reigned again.

It wasn't really silent, however. There was a veritable concert of night sounds coming from the surrounding swamp. Insects sang in a rising, falling cacophony. Bullfrogs croaked from various compass points like a cast of egotistical and competitive operatic tenors. Somewhere in the distance, a bull alligator roared out his need for a mate.

Once, a higher-pitched squawk sounded. April looked up. Without raising his gaze from his magazine, Luke identified the source with a single, laconic word: "Crane."

That he'd noticed her startled interest was an indication, she thought, of how closely attuned he was to her movements. The knowledge didn't help her feelings.

It was a short time later that she glanced his way and discovered he was staring at her knees. She frowned at them herself before she said, "What?"

"You should put something on those scrapes. Or I could do it for you."

"Oh. I found the antibiotic cream in the bathroom while I was changing. But the cut on your face..."

"I took care of it when I showered earlier."

How self-sufficient they were, she realized, which was good under the circumstances. April nodded and went back to her reading.

Maybe the nap Luke had taken during the afternoon kept him from being sleepy, and maybe it was just that he was a night person and used to late hours. Whichever, it soon became obvious that she wasn't going to outlast him. Her eyes were burning and the pillow she was leaning on had an enticingly comfortable feel to it. She gave up, finally, and closed her book. Smothering a yawn, she said, "I think that's it for me."

"Sure." Luke rose from the bed in a single smooth movement. Stepping to the front doorway, he slid open the screen and exited to the dark forward deck. Just before he closed the screen behind him, he said a quiet good-night.

April answered just as softly, even as a line appeared between her brows. She was inside, and he was outside. There was nothing between her and the dinghy except the back screen door. Soon, Luke would be asleep. Somehow, it seemed too easy.

The boat rocked, exaggerating Luke's movements, as he took a rolled sleeping bag and a flat sheet from the bench storage, shook them out, then spread them over the deck bench. Watching him through the screen, April realized she would have to move with care when the time came in order to keep from telegraphing her own movements. That train of thought was abruptly derailed as she saw his hands go to the waistband of his jeans. The sound of a sliding zipper was like a buzz saw. In simple reflex action, she reached and clicked off the light above her head.

He was still visible in silhouette, however, outlined by the lake surface beyond that reflected the light of the stars. She should look away, she thought, as her eyes adjusted to the dimness. Instead, she watched intently as he shucked his jeans, then dragged his T-shirt off over his head.

He paused an instant to turn the shirt right side out. The silvery light of the night outlined the muscled ridges of his back and legs and highlighted the contrast between his natural copper-bronze coloring and the white of his briefs. It glinted in the darkness of his hair and left interestingly shaped shadows here and there. An odd feeling, half artistic appreciation, half yearning, shifted through her. Luke really was a magnificent man. If only his character were a match for his looks, how easy it would be to…

No, she wouldn't think like that, couldn't for her own peace of mind. There was no profit in it since he had never had that kind of integrity and was unlikely to change at this late date. Turning over with a flounce, April shut her eyes and kept them that way until the front of the boat was absolutely still.

An hour and a half, or perhaps more, passed with excruciating slowness. To keep awake, April went over the last scene in her book, considering possible additions and changes. Exhausting that, she began to plan the next. She had an entire chapter and part of another mapped out before she finally heard a soft sound between heavy breathing and a snore from beyond the front screen. Lifting her head, she waited until it came again.

Asleep, finally. Thank heaven.

She eased upright and slowly swung her feet to the floor. Luke's long body was a shadowy shape under the sheet that protected him from mosquito bites. Her gaze fastened to that white length, she stood up then moved step by slow step toward the back of the boat.

As she reached for the rear screen door, her fingertips brushed the wire mesh with a faint scraping noise. Luke's breathing changed. He shifted from his back to his side, but didn't wake. Though she stood for endless ages hoping to hear his snores begin again, they didn't come.

She couldn't wait forever. With a silent imprecation, she tried the screen again, rolling it open in minute increments and wincing at every slight grating on its track. When it was back far enough, she glanced toward Luke again. He hadn't moved. She slid around the screen door, leaving it open behind her because it would be too nerve-racking to try to shut it again.

The aluminum dinghy bobbed quietly at the end of its line. The water around it appeared black and murky, as if it were semicongealed sludge. She stepped to the railing and climbed over it rather than risk opening the gate. Then she skimmed down the rear swimmer's ladder. On the bottom rung, she caught the dinghy's line and towed the light craft toward her. Carefully, then, one foot at the time, she let herself down into the lighter boat. It was a balancing act in the dark to transfer her full weight from one craft to the other without making the pontoon boat rock, but she managed it with a quick, controlled movement. Jerking loose the slipknot that held it fast, she pushed off and sank quickly onto the front seat.

She was clear. She was free. Exultation coursed through her veins. There was no time to savor it, however. Keeping low, she shifted to the center seat and felt around on the floor for the paddle she'd noticed earlier. She got a firm grip on it, then leaned over the side to dip it in the water.

Abruptly, the water surface broke and something wet and monstrous surged up from its glassy black lower reaches. It reached up in an arc of splattering, glittering droplets to catch the boat paddle. It pulled, and April plummeted forward. She gave a gasping cry as she hit the water.

Her shoulder crashed into something slick yet warm and firm. Hard bands closed around her, squeezing tight. She gulped air, trying to scream. Then she was dragged down into the thick, dark depths of the lake.

13

Long legs twined around hers. She was pressed against a hard form in full body contact. A familiar form, long remembered, recently felt.

Luke. It was Luke.

Rage exploded in April's brain. She brought her hands up, shoving, kicking out by sheer instinct. The man who held her twisted in a strong defensive movement. Then he thrust upward with her still clamped in his arms. They surfaced in a violent rush and splattering spray of water. She pushed free enough to catch the side of the dinghy. Clinging for a instant, she dragged air into her lungs and wiped wet, plastering strands of hair from her eyes. Then she faced him.

He looked like a water god, wet, slick, naked from the waist up and with a small water lily pad draped over one ear and a larger one lying on his shoulder. Powerful, omnipotent, intriguing in his perfect meshing with his watery element, he had no right to be so at ease or to grin at her with such a flash of white teeth.

"What in hell do you think you're doing?" she demanded. "You almost drowned me!"

"Not even close," he said in mocking correction

as he treaded water beside her, "though it did cross my mind. It was such a dumb thing to do, you know, trying to steal off in the middle of the night."

"I...don't know what you're talking about."

"No, I'm sure," he said, unperturbed. "It did occur to me that maybe you were taking a bath. The least I could do, in that case, was bring you the soap."

"That's the most ridicu— Where is it then?" She didn't believe him for a minute. Since he'd introduced that element of farce, however, she might as well follow his lead.

"Over there." He nodded a few feet to his right even as he reached to pick the water lily pad from his shoulder and hold it up by its slimy stem. "You wash my back and I'll wash yours."

He was telling the truth. A blob of white in the dimness, the bar of soap floated on a buoyant dish of some kind. For a single instant, she hovered, confused. Was he really being helpful, or only giving her an out, a way to save face by glossing over the fact that she'd been caught trying to escape him? Was he hoping she'd take it so he needn't deal with her tantrum over his tactics? Or was he offering a playful romp in the water that might lead to other things? With Luke, it might be any of these. Or something else entirely.

"Who," she asked astringently, "is going to wash the alligators and water moccasins that decide to join us?"

"You forgot the loggerhead turtles and lunker catfish. But I'll hold them and you can do the honors—if any self-respecting critter is within a mile after the racket we've made.''

It might be true that the area wildlife was as nervous as she was, but somehow that didn't help. On the other hand, a quick wash to remove the fishy smell of the lake water could be a wise move. Which meant that he was extremely thoughtful, very practical, or so certain he had the upper hand that he could enjoy a private joke at her expense.

Reaching for the soap, she said through set teeth, ''You can wash your own back.''

His chuckle, rich and deep with acknowledgment, echoed across the water. It startled a heron from its roost on a dead tree so it sprang into flight. It flapped with wind-sweeping beats of its wings, rising above the line of trees until it was a black and graceful shape against the moon that was just climbing above them.

The sight touched something raw inside April that caused her throat to tighten. Pausing with the soap in her hand, she said in sudden stark determination, ''You can't keep me here.''

''Oh, I think I can,'' Luke answered as he sobered a fraction. ''And I will. You can fight it, if that's what you want. Or you can relax and enjoy it. The choice is yours.''

''Some choice.'' She didn't bother to hide her weariness.

''Better than dying,'' he returned.

That was certainly true, but she was by no means sure it was that simple. She stared at him a moment longer, then lowered her lashes and began to rub the soap over her arms.

Lather floated around the pontoon boat in all directions, mingling with the lily pads and mats of water hyacinths, by the time they finished bathing and climbed back on board again. The clothes April had on were sopping wet, and Luke handed her another T-shirt and pair of shorts through the door of the bathroom before she stripped. Since she had no more underwear, she was forced to do without. Her nakedness under the loose-fitting clothes made her feel both vulnerable and wicked. Finding a comb in the medicine cabinet above the small corner lavatory, she carried both it and her wet things with her as she stepped into the cabin again.

Luke had changed into shorts also and raked his wet hair into windrows with his fingers. He rose from the edge of her bed and took the wet clothes from her. As he walked out onto the front deck to hang them over the railing beside his own, he said over his shoulder, "Much more of this and we'll both have to go naked."

"Which would bother you no end, I know," she replied as she begin to drag the comb through her hair.

"It might."

She glanced at him, but he had his back to her as he draped her bra over the railing with casual competence, as if he did such things every day. Maybe he did, but the sight annoyed her all the same. "Don't tell me none of the legions of females you know have played Adam and Eve with you like this."

"Adam and Eve?" he queried as he came back inside and closed the screen. "I don't think their idea of fun runs to fantasies, or their imaginations. Unlike some people's.''

"I didn't say I liked fantasies.'' She kept her head down so the fall of her hair could conceal the warm color she could feel in her face.

"No, but it's almost a given, isn't it?''

"Nothing is a given,'' she returned. "You don't understand me and never will, so don't try to guess how I think or especially how I feel.''

"Oh, I'd never presume that far,'' he said in a mocking drawl. "Your secrets are safe.''

She should have been reassured, but wasn't. As she met his eyes, something bright and intent rose in their black depths that sent alarm zinging along her nerves. She caught a hank of wet hair and plied the comb on the ends as if the tangles that snarled it were personal enemies.

"Here, give me that,'' he said gruffly as he leaned to pluck the comb from her hand. Seating himself on the bed again, he scooted back, then caught her wrist and tugged her toward the space between his spread thighs. She resisted an instant, but was really too tired and strung out to fight him. In any case, she told herself as she turned her back and fitted herself into the opening provided, she needed to save her strength for more important battles.

He gathered her hair with gentle hands and arranged it across her shoulders. Working with care from the ends up, he untangled the snarls and knots until the comb glided along the long strands without hindrance.

Having her hair brushed or combed had always been soporific for April. One of her most certain memories of her mother involved the two of them at bedtime, as her mother brushed her hair and told her how pretty and shiny it was before braiding it for the night. Under the steady movement of Luke's hands, she could feel the tension draining from her body. The temptation to lean back against him grew so great that she had to stiffen her spine and brace a hand on his knee to keep upright.

The muscle of his thigh flexed under her palm. His hands stilled for a moment. Then he drew her hair into a long skein and draped it forward over her shoulder. As it spilled across her right breast, she turned her head slightly in inquiry. At the same moment, he circled her waist with his arm to draw her closer against him, then he brushed the back of her neck with his warm lips.

"Luke—" Her voice caught as a small shiver ran down her back.

"Shhh," he said, feathering the rash of goose bumps on her skin with his warm breath.

"What are you doing?"

"Experimenting," he said, and kissed the bumps of her spine in a slow, questing descent.

"Why? You said..."

"I told you I lied," he interrupted. "Or rather, I've changed my mind. I've decided I want to know all about you, every single secret. Especially the fantasies."

"I don't have any," she said, trying to ignore the insidious tightening of her nipples, the small voice in her head that said give up, give in, and enjoy.

"Then we'll make some up," he answered.

She had known being alone with Luke would be

dangerous. That was why she'd fought so hard against succumbing to his sweet reason and laughing blandishments. Even more dangerous was her reaction to him. Was it pure chemical attraction, the half-legendary bliss of young love remembered over the years, or could it be the meeting of soul mates, no matter how ill-matched? She didn't know, but something about him stirred her as no other man ever had or would. It had been that way years ago and was true still.

Moistening her lips, she asked, "That's what this is all about? Bringing me here?"

His hesitation was so slight she almost missed it. "It could be. Probably is, after all."

"You still want to seduce me."

"I want whatever you can give me," he murmured against her ear. "Where we go from there may depend on what I can give you."

"It wasn't necessary to go to these lengths." Was she grasping at straws by assigning that reason to him? She didn't know, couldn't think coherently for the brush of his hand across her breast, the way he slowly enclosed the soft globe in the trap of his fingers. The firmness of his body against her was an insistent argument for surrender. It had been so long since she had felt a man's arms around her. So long.

"Wasn't it?" he asked softly, his warm breath feathering her skin.

She didn't answer, couldn't find the words. She could fight him, but her own needs and impulses were more formidable foes. Besides, he had appealed to her imagination. Against its well-exercised power she had no real defense, and wasn't sure she wanted any.

She tilted her head back, letting it rest against his shoulder. He cupped her chin, lifting her face so she met his wide-open gaze. They held the contact for a stark instant then she lowered her lashes in automatic shielding. Her attention clung to the chiseled shape of his mouth until his face blotted out her vision, then she closed her eyes.

His mouth was warm and sweet, flavored faintly with wine. She allowed him entrance with grace and hunger and, once he accepted the entree, was neither stingy nor too aggressive. They had eons of time and something in his manner, touch and taste assured her he meant to use it. He was no longer a wildly eager teenager. He'd learned balance, control and the value of anticipation.

Still their hearts beat higher with each caress, every slowly bared inch of skin and daring exploration. Rampant and aloof by turns, they tested the limits of faith, of trust and of endurance. Their sweat-gilded bodies gleamed in the light, shivered in the moist heat as they hovered so near perfect convulsion that they frowned in their pleasure.

He was her pirate king, daring in his demands and with an edge of roughness. Or maybe her water god, Neptune rising in splendor from the deep to claim her, mind and body. At the same time, he was still Luke, her young lover, young stud, wild and dramatic and misunderstood, with tenderness under his sullen bravado and pain behind his existential despair.

Nothing mattered, nothing was allowed to impinge on the delicate unfolding of the senses. Nothing marred their superheightened awareness of life and death and all the fine acts of creation that lay between. Connected, tenderly violent yet inviolate, they held each other, held past and future and the glory that unified it all. Until its magic bloomed in their hearts and minds with the silent splendor that illuminated, for a single instant, the answer to life's most elusive riddle.

Afterward, they lay sprawled in naked semiconsciousness and a lingering embrace while their breathing slowed. They slept with the light breeze off the lake cooling their flesh and that brief fever of the heart. But sometime in the night they roused enough to separate, to pull up a sheet to cover themselves, protect themselves.

"Where the hell is April?"

The question, with its undertone of steel, came at Luke before he could get the dinghy tied up at Chemin-a-Haut. It was Roan who asked it from where he stood on the dock with his feet spread and his hand resting suspiciously near the butt of his pistol. Luke didn't blame his cousin for his anger or his concern; he could remember feeling both when he'd discovered that Kane had made off with Regina. He just hadn't expected to have to account for his actions before he got his story straight in his head.

In laconic tones, he answered finally, "Somewhere safe."

"Such as?"

"You don't need to know."

"Wrong."

"I don't think so," Luke told him patiently. "That's the whole point—nobody needs to know."

There was no relenting in Roan's face. "Does she want to be there?"

"What makes you think anything else?"

"Eyewitnesses who saw you hauling her away from the scene of the explosion." His cousin's eyes were as bright and hard as the badge on his shirt pocket.

"Let's say she's getting used to the idea." At least Luke hoped she was, after the night before. Fighting with her all day and making love to her all night didn't seem like a very workable program.

"You'd better hope she's delirious about it when I see her. If she isn't, if you've finally gone too far, your ass is mine."

"Look," Luke began, his eyes narrowing as he felt the stir of possessive anger.

"Don't blow up at me, bucko, because I'm not in the mood," Roan overrode him. "I've got weirdos shooting off guns, boats exploding, and an unhappy mayor breathing down my neck because his big yearly festival fell all to pieces and both his number one river pirate and his celebrity guest failed to show. I've got newspaper people wanting to know about our local crime wave and April's exhusband breathing down my neck because she's nowhere to be found and no one, not even her agent, knows where she went. I've got—or did have—my stupid cousin missing, too, and had to worry that he'd got himself shot or blown up or drowned. Or that he'd done something really stupid like kidnapping April, a federal offense that just may bring swarms of uptight idiots in button-downs crawling all over me. You're lucky you're still standing, cuz. Give me any trouble and you won't be.''

The worry under that spate of harried annoyance was balm on Luke's own wrath. A slow grin mounted to his lips. In lilting tones, he asked, "So, what if I did take her?''

Kane ignored that for the blatant provocation it was. "Since you're here, and in such a jolly mood, I think I'll let you deal with the ex. You can field the next call from a pushy woman named Cazenave, too. After I have your word that April is safe, sound and unmolested.''

"My word is good enough? Amazing," Luke commented. If Roan wanted to take that as an assurance of April's well-being it would be all to the good, but he had other things on his mind. "Why is Tinsley in such a dither? He's supposed to be history.''

"Maybe April's the love of his life and he's still hoping. Maybe she's his meal ticket and he's hungry. And maybe he's just a decent guy worrying about a woman who was once important to him. How the hell do I know?''

"You could have asked.''

"You do it, if you're so interested. I had other things on my mind. Such as what reason you might have for disappearing with her.''

"You didn't know I had her, so how—?''

"She was last seen leaving the river dock in your company, like I said, and her car is sitting in front of your house. And I know how you think.''

"You should have known, too, that I'd be back to tell somebody what's going on. You were at the top of that list, though it's nice of you to save me the trouble of going by your office."

"I didn't much feel like waiting. Besides, I had to bring your Jeep back here." Roan paused, then added, "You sure you know what you're doing?"

"I'm sure it's necessary." There were certain methods Luke wasn't so certain about any more, but it was too late to agonize over them.

"You may have faith in your precious swamp to cover your tracks, but don't push it too far. It's water and mud and trees, not your private compound."

"Thanks for the advice," Luke countered with exaggerated courtesy. "I'll try to remember."

They watched each other, gray eyes clashing with black, there on the damp wood dock, while the rising sun used scissors of light to cut the lake mist into gray streamers. A breeze rustled the leaves of the live oak overhead and brought the drifting scent of cape jasmine from the shrub border near the house. Somewhere, a rooster crowed, the sound traveling across the water.

Finally, Roan nodded. "Don't forget to go by your grandmother's, too. She's another one who's been driving me to drink."

"That'll be the day," Luke said.

"Yeah," Roan answered, unsmiling.

Luke drove Roan back to his office in town since he needed the Jeep that his cousin had delivered. Afterward, he stopped by his grandmother's place. Granny May was much happier to see him than his cousin had been. Feeding him buttered biscuits and fig preserves washed down by chicory-spiked coffee so strong it was a serious threat to stomach lining, she sat bright-eyed and straight-backed at the table. She accepted his heartfelt compliments as her due, but he knew she enjoyed watching him eat as much as he enjoyed the food.

She questioned him about the explosion, gave him a rundown on the injuries of the survivors, and brought him up-to-date on the public remarks and private sentiments of the festival committee. However, she was not at all pleased to discover that he'd made off with their neighbor the writer.

"You did what?" she screeched, pushing her bifocals up on her nose so she could glare at him through the correct half. "Have you gone *totally* mad?"

Blandly slathering a biscuit with jewel-like preserves, he said, "You don't think it's a good idea?" He popped the biscuit into his mouth.

"Your being alone for hours on end with a woman who writes love scenes for a living? She'll have you in her bed before dark."

Luke choked as a biscuit crumb went down the wrong way. Coughing, gasping for breath, he protested, "She writes them, she doesn't live them."

"Oh, God," his grandmother moaned. "She's got you already."

He grabbed his coffee and took a swallow. "I thought it was the other way around."

"No, no, it doesn't work like that, not once you fall. You think you can change her mind, get her to stop putting our family in her book. Instead, she'll worm all the juicy details out of you."

"But I don't know any juicy details."

"You just think you don't." She gave a weary shake of gray head.

"Even if I did, I wouldn't tell her anything damaging."

"Oh, you won't even notice. She's like a spider enticing you into her web. She'll smile and tease and play with you until she gets what she wants from you. Then she'll eat you alive."

The idea conjured up images he definitely didn't want to share with his granny. "You don't give me much credit."

"With anyone else, any of your other women, I would. This one's different. She's more than a pretty face. She's smart. She knows people—how they think and what makes them act as they do."

"Why, Granny May," he mocked, "if I didn't know better, I'd think you'd been reading her books."

"So I have—though I skip all those parts that are about—well, you know."

"You mean sex?"

"Take that smirk off your face, young man! You may think you invented procreation, but it was around long before you were born, let me tell you. I just don't need to read detailed descriptions to enjoy a book."

"Oh, you enjoyed April's book, did you?"

"She's a good writer, but that's beside the point."

"What is the point? That April knows what love between and man and a woman is all about or that she dwells on it?"

"She uses it to explain what her men and women are all about, how they are deep inside where most books never look, to show how they feel and think when they're at their weakest."

"Or strongest," Luke said, unable to stop teasing her in spite of his fascination with how she saw April's writing.

"Well, yes. But those things are private. They cut too close to the bone. I don't want to know what a man thinks about when he's holding a woman, don't want to read how being kissed feels because it makes me remember—"

"What?" he asked softly as he watched the color come and go in his grandmother's face.

"Your grandfather, and how I used to get all— Never mind! The point is that she's dangerous."

"To me, you mean. Maybe I'd better read some of her books to protect myself."

"No, no, you don't want to do that!"

He lifted a brow at her vehement tone. "Now, why not?

"Because her voice is in them, her words flowing as if she's reading, or maybe singing, to you. It leads you on page after page until you forget the time or what you're supposed to be doing. She makes up this world and pulls you into it bit by bit until you feel like you know her people, can see them walking around, hear them talking. And you want to know them, wish you could know them, but never can, so it's a cheat."

"But they're always there between the book's covers, aren't they? Anyway, it's what storytellers have always done, create imaginary people, imaginary worlds.''

Her face crumpled. ''You're taking her part against me. She has you already, and she hasn't had time to even get started on you.''

''Don't fret,'' he said with as much patience as he could muster. ''April Halstead doesn't want or need me, and hasn't tried to get a thing from me. I took her away from here, remember. She didn't take me.''

''More fool you!'' Her eyes filled. ''She'll hurt you, my honey Luke. She will, without half trying, because she doesn't know what you're really like.''

''It's just for a few days.''

''A few days too long. She'll hurt us all, and she won't care as long as she has her story. She lives in those stories of hers. She's there on every page, all the things she thinks and feels and knows. Too much of her is in those stories of hers, I think. She's exposed for all to see. I don't know how she stands it. But she doesn't have time for anything real. She just—couldn't.''

It was a fascinating theory, he thought. He was really going to have to check it out.

The couple of hours Luke intended to use taking care of business at Chemin-a-Haut turned into half a day. It was midafternoon before he could wind things up and head over to Mulberry Point. He parked the Jeep in back to keep from attracting attention. Getting into the house was no problem; he simply used the key taken from the small handbag he'd found in April's car.

He had given a lot of thought to the things she

would need while on the boat. As he gathered them and stacked them in the upper hall, he checked off a mental list. The stack grew bigger and bigger. He eyed it with jaundiced consideration for the size of the dinghy, but he didn't stop.

He was standing with his hands on his hips, contemplating the printer for her computer, when he heard a metallic squeak from the direction of the kitchen. A few seconds later, Midnight padded into view. The cat paused as he saw Luke, then streaked from the room. Luke shrugged and forgot him.

It was maybe five minutes later when a car pulled up outside. Stepping out of the office, Luke glided down the hall and into the parlor. At one of the front windows, he carefully lifted the drape and lace sheer to look out.

It was Martin Tinsley. He was dressed like a male model in an ad for golf clubs as he climbed from a green Jag and sauntered toward the house. Removing thirties-style round sunglasses and tucking them into his shirt pocket, he glanced around with an elaborately casual air. He mounted the front steps and started across the porch floor before Luke lost sight of him. Then his footsteps stopped.

Luke stepped back a little, frowning as he listened. Then the screen that covered the front window closest to the door creaked. A grim smile settled over his mouth. He eased over to that window and put his back to the wall next to it. Then he folded his arms and waited.

Tinsley had one leg over the windowsill and was reaching inside for purchase when Luke grabbed his shirt collar. A hard yank, and April's ex plunged headfirst into the room. Luke was upon him in a second, kicking him flat, putting a knee in his back and twisting a wrist into an extremely uncomfortable angle between his shoulder blades. Tinsley howled and began to curse.

"What are you doing here?" Luke growled.

The man he was holding down squirmed, fighting for a furious second, before he stopped abruptly. Breathing hard, with his hundred-dollar haircut in disorder and his red face against the hardwood floor, he answered, "I could...ask you...the same thing."

"I doubt our answers would match. Talk to me. Unless you want a broken arm."

"No! I thought—I hoped I might find something to show where April is, a message on her answering machine, a note, an E-mail post. I don't know, just...something."

That was almost incoherent enough to be the truth. Exerting more pressure on the arm he held, he asked, "You can access her E-mail? You know her password?"

Tinsley grunted. "I had a few guesses at her password to try, that's all!"

"I doubt the lady would appreciate your screwing around with her computer, even in such a good cause. Me, now, I've got doubts your cause is worth a damn."

"I don't know what you're talking about."

"I'm wondering what else is on her computer that you might want," Luke answered impatiently. "A manuscript, maybe? Or could it be a list of payments—especially royalty payments due?"

"I'm just worried about her. That's no crime, is it?"

"You don't strike me as the worrying kind."

"Same to you," Tinsley gasped.

He was probably right, Luke thought, but he'd get no prize for it. He studied the sweat that streaked the face of the man on the floor and dampened the expensive knit of his shirt. "What are you hanging around April for in the first place? It's supposed to be over between you two."

"It's never over. Don't you know that?"

Luke's grip tightened an instant before he forced himself to relax. No doubt he should have felt fellow sympathy, but that was the last thing on his mind. "So, are you trying to make sure she needs you? Is that it?"

"What?"

"Or have you figured out some other way to make a profit off her?"

"You don't know a damn thing about it."

"Don't be too sure, pal," Luke said, the anger in his voice slicing like a whetted sword. "I know that you worked less than ten months out of the years you were married to April. You not only took a settlement big enough to choke a mule during the divorce proceedings, but also had the nerve to ask for alimony—and might have collected if the judge hadn't decided you were able-bodied enough to work. I also know that you were ass-high in credit card debt before you married her, and have piled up the bills again since the divorce."

"How'd you find out? You have me investigated?'' Martin Tinsley lay rigid as he waited for the answer.

''Let's just say I'm interested, have been for a long time. And I have a cousin with access to information.''

''You want her, don't you? And you actually think she'll trust you enough to let you get close to her again? That's funny, or would be if you'd ever heard what she had to say about you.''

April had spoken to her ex about him? Somehow that possibility had never crossed Luke's mind. He didn't like it. He also didn't like the fact that Tinsley thought he knew and understood her better. ''My wants and prospects aren't the question here,'' he said, the words so discordant they clanged together in his own head like badly strung wind chimes. ''We were talking about you. There are names for men who live on women, none of them too pretty. If you don't leave April alone, you won't be too pretty, either. And that's a promise.''

As Luke spoke, he caught a movement from the corners of his eyes. It was at the hall door. Turning his head quickly, he saw Midnight hovering there with his back in a bow and his hair standing out in a disturbed ruff that made him look ten pounds heavier. The cat was staring at Tinsley with malevolent eyes.

The other man ignored the cat. ''You can't be speaking for April. She wouldn't allow that.''

''I wouldn't dream of it,'' Luke answered. ''I'm speaking for me. I don't like you, Tinsley. April's cat doesn't like you, either, a valuable second opinion. You've had the only warning you're going to get. Remember it.''

He released the man in a sudden, open-handed gesture, then stepped back. Tinsley got slowly to his feet, brushing at his clothes, smoothing his hair. He turned toward the hallway with stiff movements and walked through it to open the front door. Turning back a moment, he said, ''This isn't the end of it.''

''No,'' Luke said in quiet acceptance. ''I think it may be the beginning.''

14

April knelt on the deck in front of Luke's multi-tiered fishing tackle box and surveyed the contents. Baits of every color in the rainbow lay in precise order in the top trays, each one in its appointed slot. There were top water baits of all kinds, from silvery streamlined plastic fish to those that resembled nothing so much as some kind of space worm. There were spinners and chuggers used for bass at different times of the year, and also the jigs that were attractive to crappie. Spools of plastic line, small containers of sinkers, hooks, and swivels were lined up in the bottom of the box, along with pliers, pocket and filet knives, and a dozen other fishing essentials.

The most interesting items, however, at least from April's point of view, were the foldout trays of unique, collectible lures. Dating back at least sixty years, they nearly qualified as antiques. Many of them were irreplaceable.

Luke loved to fish. Apparently he valued these older baits. She hoped he loved them, hoped they were treasures saved from his boyhood. They easily could be, she thought, since she remembered seeing baits like them in her grandfather's tackle box when she'd gone fishing with him as a child. That made them perfect.

She picked up a blue-and-red lure with a flirty rubber tail like a grass skirt and lettering on the side that identified it as a Hawaiian Wiggler. She hefted it a couple of times while a grim smile curled her lips. Taking care to avoid its dangling hooks, she stood up then threw the bait as far as she could. It arched high, shining in the sun, before landing in the water with a satisfyingly final plop. April gave a decisive nod, then knelt in front of the tackle box again.

She'd teach Luke Benedict to kidnap her, make love to her and then abandon her. That was exactly what he'd done, as hard as it was to believe.

He was gone. She was alone on the boat. How long he'd been gone, she didn't know. Nor did she know where he'd gone, when he'd be back, or even *if* he'd be back. He'd left no note, but simply sneaked off while she was sleeping. He had also taken the spark plugs from the pontoon boat's big motor, making it impossible to start. She was stranded on this floating prison.

She was so mad she couldn't see straight. The anger sizzled in her veins as it had all day. She couldn't remember the last time she'd been so consumed with emotion of any kind. Unless she counted the night before, of course. But thinking about that only made her more angry.

She selected a bait known as a Paw-Paw and sailed it into the lake. How dare he laugh and tease and swear he was taking her away to protect her, then go off and leave her alone? What gave him the right?

A Pico Perch followed the Paw-Paw, splashing between two lily pads to sink out of sight. Luke Benedict was a low-down, conniving liar, and the very scum of the earth.

As she picked up a so-called Lucky 13, one of its hooks snagged her finger, leaving a long scratch behind. There was nothing lucky for her about the stupid piece of tackle. But there would be nothing for Luke, either, not any more. The lure hit the water and sank from the weight of its hooks, dropping down to be buried in the deep, soft mud of the bottom. It served him right. He'd taken away her freedom of movement and ability to fend for herself. She'd taken away a few of his prized possessions in return.

The scratch stung, and she put her finger in her mouth to soothe it as she dropped back to sit on her heels. What a fool she'd been for almost believing Luke, almost trusting him. She was even more of an idiot for plunging into intimacy with him the night before. She didn't know what had come over her; it had been ages since she'd acted so impulsively. She'd thought she was past such sophomoric weakness. To discover that she wasn't upset her as much as everything else combined.

The strident buzz of a boat motor brought her head up. It sounded familiar. She couldn't be sure it was Luke, but it was coming fast and heading in her direction. She leaned to slam the lid of the tackle box closed and push it back into place beside fishing rod and reel. She didn't want to advertise what she'd done, but would rather let him come upon it when he least expected it. One unwelcome surprise deserved another.

It was indeed Luke in the boat. He slid into view around the curve with the slanting rays of the westward-leaning sun making a gold nimbus around him. He sat at ease, controlling the boat with one hand. It seemed he was in his natural place, at one with the low-lying craft, the dark and shining water he traveled upon, and the swamp around him. He came into the backwater anchorage as if on a homing instinct, and she could see that he was grinning as he saw her waiting on the deck.

The very sight of him made her furious all over again. She moved to the back deck where the dinghy had been tied up before, and stood with her hands on her hips. She didn't wait for him to stop, but flung her accusation at him as soon as she thought it could be heard above the slowing hum of the motor.

"You don't even snore, do you!"

Wariness replaced the pleasure in his face. "Not that I know of."

"You tricked me, pretending to be asleep last night," she continued, aggrieved as well as angry. "You expected me to try something and encouraged me to go for it early so you could stop me with a minimum of effort."

He switched off the motor and moved to the front of the boat to secure it. "I don't know as I'd put it that way, exactly."

"But it's what you did, isn't it?" The point was one of many she'd worked out during the long day alone. Realizing how thoroughly she had been hoodwinked had not improved her temper.

"Did I?"

"You certainly never made a sound for the rest of the night."

His smile was wry as he finished his job and straightened to his full height. "I couldn't risk you getting lost back in here, now could I?"

"Oh, right," she answered in heavy sarcasm. "Or take the chance that I might press charges!"

"Would you do that? Now?"

His dark eyes held teasing promise and something more that made her suddenly aware of the hot sun beating down on her head, the stillness that surrounded them and their isolation. Clutching her anger like a talisman, April answered, "I certainly should!"

He sobered a fraction. "Did you think I might not come back? Is that what this is about?"

"Not at all. I knew you wouldn't leave your boat." He was only half right. The rest of the question had been just when he'd return, and if he'd expect her to be gone, conveniently lost in the swamps, after all.

"I had more to come back for than a boat," he said, his voice dropping to a sultry note.

That might have been gratifying if she could believe it, but she wasn't ready to do that. She wasn't, even if the look in his eyes was a strong reminder of just why she'd succumbed to his practiced lovemaking.

She was saved from finding an answer by a movement near Luke's feet. Something black and furry oozed from under the dinghy's triangular forward seat and stretched, then looked up at her in expectation.

"Midnight!" she cried. "Oh, I can't believe it." She glanced at Luke again. "Where did you find him? How did you ever manage to get here with him?"

"I paid a visit to Mulberry Point. He seemed happy to have company, and didn't object too much to going for a ride." Luke stooped and lifted the tomcat in one large hand so he hung like a limp fake fur rug as he was passed up to her. "I swear the dumb cat knew where he was headed. He got right in the boat."

"That makes him a smart cat instead of dumb, doesn't it, boy," she murmured to Midnight as she cuddled her pet and accepted his ecstatic chin rub of greeting.

Luke watched her for a second, then shook his head in amazement. "Don't you want to know what else I've brought?"

She spared him a brief stare. "I can see that you stocked up for a long stay."

"I brought your computer—well, your laptop, anyway."

"That'll be good for all of half a day's work before the battery quits."

"More than that with the generator that's on board," he informed her. "But I also threw in paper and pens and whatever else I came across that looked like notes."

That got her attention. Voice cool, she asked, "You went through my desk?"

"I raked off the top of it—literally. But I didn't have time to read much if that's what's worrying you."

If he'd brought everything that was scattered in helter-skelter fashion over her desktop, then she should have most of what she needed to work. And if he was telling the truth, and had managed not to look over what he picked up, she could almost feel in charity with him again. Which had nothing to do, of course, with the way his jeans molded and stretched over his lean flanks as he unloaded the dinghy, hoisting box after box to the deck of the pontoon boat. Nor did the fact that she was relieved to see him, grateful to know that he hadn't left for good, have any bearing.

"In that case," she said at last, "I suppose I'll have to admit that you're very considerate, as kidnappers go."

He paused with a grocery bag in each hand to give her a pained look. "Is that all?"

"All?"

"No promise of fervent thanks at a later time? No kiss hello? No welcome home and invitation to...come onaboard?"

"No come-on of any kind," she said crisply, keeping her attention on scratching behind Midnight's ears. "If you're thinking about last night, that was a mistake."

"If it was," he said with precision as he set the grocery bags down and reached for more, "you made it."

She turned her head sharply. "What does that mean?"

"We had a bet. You lost."

"You didn't play fair. I don't think this qualifies." She made a vague gesture to indicate the boat.

"Sure you do, you're just afraid. That's all right, April love, but you're going to have to make up your mind what you want, sooner or later. In the meantime, I have another game plan. You've heard it before, but I can give it to you again, short and sweet."

It wasn't necessary. It was there in the set of his shoulders, the curve of his lips and the uncomfortably intent look in his eyes. Most of all, it lingered in her mind, echoing in the deep cadences of challenge from that day at the wedding reception: *Resist me if you can.*

She leaned to put Midnight down, then picked up a box with something sticking out of it that looked suspiciously like the hem of her silk nightgown. "I'm not afraid of anything," she said, "least of all you and your threats."

"Good," he replied in quiet satisfaction. "That's good."

April pretended not to hear that as she walked away with her burden. He'd think twice about how good it was when he discovered his precious baits were at the bottom of the lake.

She and Luke stowed everything away, since it was both something to do and necessary if they were to have room to move around in their cramped quarters. Afterward, they had a light snack when they discovered that they'd both skipped lunch. The sun was going down by the time they finished. Luke

got out his tackle box and began to rummage
through it.

April watched him from inside the cabin, standing
back in the gathering shadows as she waited for the
explosion. It didn't come. Apparently, he hadn't noticed the missing tackle. As she saw him tie on a
shiny new spinner, fastening it to his line with a fast
and dexterous sailor's knot before moving to the
front rail with his rod and reel, she almost wished
she'd dumped his entire tackle box overboard.

She thought she should try to work; she no longer
had an excuse to avoid it and awareness of her
looming deadline was like a sore spot at the top of
her brain. She couldn't make herself do it, however.
It was possible she had been more tired than she
knew, because all she really wanted to do was nap.
That wasn't the effect of the night before, either, for
she'd slept until the middle of the morning.

Carrying her glass of iced tea with her, she settled
on the outside bench with her back braced against
the driver's console beside it and her legs stretched
out on the seat. From that vantage point, she had a
good view of Luke as he stood casting for bass at
the boat's prow. Midnight joined her for a few
minutes, until Luke reeled in a three-pound bass.
The cat jumped down then and went to investigate,
after which he took up a post atop the closed charcoal grill to watch the action.

She was almost sorry Luke had brought her writing equipment to her. Though she'd chafed about it
earlier in the day, there'd been peace in knowing
she couldn't do it. Now it nagged at her, a constant
irritant.

Perhaps she could give herself this evening off, however, if she vowed to start early in the morning. She wouldn't think about it, then. She'd let work go while she simply enjoyed the gradual cooling of the evening. The coolness was relative, of course, a mere eighty-five degrees in contrast to the burning ninety-five degrees of noon.

The evening was sultry with humidity as well. The breeze over the water had failed. The lake surface around them was as still as a mirror except where fish rose to feed with lazy slapping sounds, or the occasional bubble of swamp gas broke the surface in a concentric circle. The heavy boat barely moved. An elusive fragrance, perhaps from the water lilies, or maybe from ripening fruit back in the woods, drifted on the heavy air. Cicadas in the trees along the shoreline sang. Frogs and crickets joined the chorus. Now and then, the booming of far-off thunder came from the southwest.

Joining the sounds, an almost natural addition, was the intermittent whine and splash as Luke plied his rod and reel. His concentration was total, his face smooth with contentment in the evening light. He seemed oblivious of her presence so she was able to watch him without feeling self-conscious about it. He fished as he did most things, she thought, with competence and a graceful economy of motion. At the same time, he made it look easy.

Without thinking about it, she began to notice details of the picture he made as he stood at the end of the boat. Descriptive phrases for what she saw began to rise in her mind with no conscious effort on her part, emerging as naturally as the fish coming to the surface of the lake.

The light of the day's end painted shadows under the ridges of his cheekbones. It tinted the white of his T-shirt with purple and gold, and gilded the sweat that glazed his skin until he had the look of a bronze statue. Infinite patience overlaid the concentration in his face. The calm certainty that was an integral part...

April got up and moved into the cabin, returning a moment later with a yellow legal pad and her favorite fountain pen. Maybe she would work just a little, after all.

"What the hell?"

That sharp exclamation jerked April from a succinct phrase describing the reaction of the hero of her book to the heroine's treachery. She looked up to see Luke squatting before his tackle box with a frown meshing his brows over his nose. He was staring at the empty slots in one of the middle trays.

Show time.

"Missing something?" she asked with innocence suffusing her voice.

"Yeah. Several somethings." He gave her a brief glance. Then he looked again as he registered the expression on her face. "I suppose you wouldn't know anything about it?"

"I would, as a matter of fact."

"You took my baits?"

"I don't know that I'd put it that way, exactly." She shifted slightly on her seat.

"How would you put it?"

"I liberated them, since I couldn't liberate myself. If you're really lucky, you might find one next time you go swimming.''

He came to his feet with a slow uncoiling of hard thigh muscles. ''Are you saying you threw my baits overboard?''

She lifted a brow, though it was sheer bravado. ''They belonged to my dad.''

''You should have thought of that before you dragged me out here.''

''I can't believe you did it.'' He shook his head, a slow movement of amazement as he put his hands on his hips.

''Believe it,'' she returned with a lift of her chin. ''What did you think? That you could do whatever you like and I'd take it? It doesn't work that way!''

''I was only—''

''So you say. But you can't make decisions for me and expect me to go along just because you think it's best.''

He watched her a long moment. ''I never expected you to be underhanded about it.''

''Didn't you? When you sneaked out of here at dawn without a word or a decent goodbye? What else did you leave me?''

''Is that what this is about? That I didn't wake you up to tell you I was going?''

''It's about lack of choice. It's about you being high-handed and tight-lipped and all the other macho idiocies that keep me from having a say in my own fate. It's about—''

She stopped as her voice failed her. Turning her head, she looked away from him out over the water.

"April," he began with a quick stride in her direction.

"No," she said as she faced him again. "You took something from me that I valued, my free will. I took something not quite so hard to replace—a few pieces of antique tackle. We're still not even, but at least we're a little closer to it."

He gave a slow shake of his head. "I don't think so."

"What do you mean?"

"What you took was pieces of memories of fishing trips with my dad before he died. That's added to all the hopes for the future that I used to have way back when. Things like that aren't replaceable at all."

Her voice not quite steady, she said, "I had hopes, too. And dreams."

"Did you?" There was a minute adjustment of the planes of his face before he inclined his head. "Maybe we're even after all."

He picked up his rod and reel, then went back to his fishing. After a moment, April retreated into her writing once more. By dark, she'd filled three pages and Luke had caught two more bass. While he cleaned and filleted the fish, she mixed the cornmeal coating that would go on them, and peeled and sliced potatoes. He fried the fish and potatoes in the peanut oil on the outside burner that was part of the charcoal grill, while she chopped cabbage and carrots for cole slaw, then made hush puppy batter. They worked as a team, with little discussion of the various tasks or who would do them, perhaps because the division of labor was traditional and they both knew exactly what was required.

April could have let Luke do all the work himself. She was there under protest, after all, and having fish for dinner was his idea. Her sense of fairness wouldn't allow it. They both needed to eat, and her help speeded the process. Anyway, she'd made her point and saw no need to hammer it into the ground.

The thunder had faded away to an occasional far-off thud, but heat lightning flickered on the horizon, playing among the clouds at treetop level. It made a fascinating show to watch while they ate, even if the bright light they'd left on in order to watch for fish bones toned it down. Later, after the galley was cleared, they turned off the lights and took their iced tea out onto the dark front deck, the better to see the weather show.

Talk between them was sporadic. The smell of hot oil, fried cornmeal and onions from the hush puppies lingered on the air. The night seemed to crowd around the boat though, at the same time, an expectant feeling permeated the dense, muggy atmosphere. April thought it was the effect of the ozone released by the distant lightning, or perhaps the stillness of the night creatures as they hovered, waiting to see if it would rain. Now and then a frog croaked out an inquiry, but that was all.

April glanced once or twice at the man beside her, and also at the long bench on which they sat. The padded plastic had started out as his bed the night before. Where would he expect to sleep tonight? Would he brave the lightning that threatened or was he counting on sharing her bed in the cabin? His comment earlier made the latter seem likely, but there was no way to be sure.

Should she wait to see if he was going to make a move in that direction, or do the charitable thing and invite him inside? Did she want to continue where they'd left off, or should she force him to make the first move then see how she felt about it?

Make up your mind, he'd said, but it wasn't that simple. She felt somehow that she'd succumbed too easily to his blandishments. She'd allowed herself to be influenced by propinquity and wayward emotionalism instead of making a rational decision. Having done that, it seemed illogical to maintain her distance now. Still, she wasn't sure she wanted to continue.

A particularly vivid lightning flash disturbed Midnight who had been performing his evening toilette while sprawled on the carpet in front of April and Luke. The cat stared toward the night sky a fixed instant, then rose with a maltreated air and sprang up between them.

As a familiar smell wafted from the animal to April's nose, she frowned across at Luke. "Have you been feeding him raw fish?"

"He was hungry," he said in lazy answer. "Anyway, I made sure it had no bones."

"It's bad for him!"

"A vicious tale put out by the pet food industry to deprive cats of their natural food—or it's only true if the fish bits are left lying around long enough to attract flies." He reached out to scratch along the cat's chin. "Isn't that right, Midnight, old boy?"

April's pet eyed Luke a moment, then he deserted

her to climb onto his lap. The cat settled down along one jeans-clad thigh and began kneading Luke's knee with his extended paws.

"Maybe, maybe not," April said, then added, "I thought you didn't like cats."

"I don't—especially when they use me for a scratching post!" He reached out and removed a paw with its claws extended. "Damn it all, cat, stop that."

"It's a sign of favor," April said, hiding a smile.

"You sure it's not jealousy because I'm here with his mistress? Or maybe bloody revenge for bringing him along?" When Midnight retracted his natural weapons, Luke released the paw again.

April wasn't sure of the answer, but didn't intend to admit it. "More likely it's cupboard affection. Next time maybe you'll leave his feeding to me."

"You can have the honors," Luke said, wincing as Midnight dug in again. "By the time he gets through I'm going to need first aid. Or will after I take a bedtime dip."

She glanced at the dark water and disturbed sky. "You're going to bathe in the lake again? I thought you brought more fresh water today."

"Only another fifteen or twenty gallons. That won't go far if we both shower all the time. You can have that privilege as well as the cat feeding. The lake is fine for me."

"For me, too, if we need to conserve water," she answered.

He didn't object, which she took to be a sign of agreement. Neither moved, however, but returned to their contemplation of the heavenly fireworks that lit the underbellies of the dark clouds filling the night sky. April drank a swallow of her tea, and the tinkle of the ice against the sweat-coated glass seemed loud in the strained quiet.

She contemplated several subjects for conversation, but could settle on nothing that seemed natural—if there was such a thing under present circumstances. The silence grew steadily more uncomfortable. She was about to opt for something totally mundane like books or swamp creature movies, when Luke spoke.

"I'll bed down out here, in case you're wondering."

"Why?" She hadn't meant to ask; the word just popped out.

He turned his head where it rested on the back of the bench as he sat slouched down with his legs stretched out before him. "What do you mean, why?"

"Is it out of consideration? Or did I do something to turn you off? Is it a trick, maybe? Or some kind of test?"

"Lord, April," he said on a cross between a laugh and a groan. "You think too much."

"And maybe you don't think enough." She looked away in annoyance.

"It isn't an intellectual exercise. You have to go with how you feel."

"I've tried that before, and look what it got me."

"What's that?" Wary curiosity was in his voice.

She crossed her arms over her chest as she said, "A failed first love, a disaster of a marriage, and a waning career as a romance author."

"I don't know about all that," he said judiciously. "Could be it's the exact opposite, it all came about from going with brain power instead of instinct."

"That's a nice clear answer, isn't it?" she inquired as she turned back to him again. "If you're such an expert, then what is it you *feel* now that made you decide to sleep out in the weather again?"

He gave a slow shrug. "I don't know that I can put it into words. Or that I want to try."

She filtered through the sound of his voice for clues, but found none. "That's no answer."

"All right," he said after a taut moment, "I guess I feel that I took advantage of the situation I created here, okay? I rushed you into something you maybe weren't ready to accept. It seems like a good idea to back off a little and regroup while you catch your breath."

"That's very—"

"Dumb?" he supplied as she paused.

"Generous," she said in correction. "Understanding, even."

"Don't get carried away. I haven't given up."

His dry tone carried a welcome touch of humor. "I didn't think you had."

"Fine," he said evenly as he removed Midnight and set him on the bench. "As long as we know where we stand."

April had nothing to say in reply. It was just as well, since Luke didn't wait to hear it. He got to his feet and walked to the railing where he kicked off his deck shoes and stripped away his shirt and jeans. He stepped over the railing, then, and hit the water in a fast, clean dive. It was a long time before he surfaced, so long, in fact, that April got to her feet to search the dark, shimmering surface with a wide, strained gaze. A sigh left her when he finally bobbed up with his head as wet and sleek as a turtle's.

Luke turned toward the boat with a splashing swirl, slicking his hair out of his eyes with one hand as he treaded water. Raising his voice across the gently undulating waves, he called, "Throw me the soap, will you? Or bring it."

April thought there was just the barest hint of a dare in the request. She wasn't fool enough to answer it, however, not this time. Fetching the soap, she stood hefting it in her hand, strongly tempted to heave it at his head. The risk of it being lost was too great, however, and she wasn't entirely sure there was another bar on board other than the extra sliver in the bathroom that she meant to use. Taking careful aim, she lobbed the soap to him and watched him snatch it out of the air. Then she turned and went into the cabin.

It was sometime later, well after she'd had a quick wash while clinging to the swimming ladder then gone to bed, that she felt the boat rock as Luke came back onboard. She wasn't too surprised at the delay, since at her last sight of him, he'd been swimming strongly toward the bottleneck entrance and the open lake as if he meant to seek the lightning. That hadn't boded very well for his mood, she thought, but it could have dissipated some of his extra energy. The question was whether it had gotten rid of enough.

She tensed, waiting, but he didn't come inside.

By slow degrees, she relaxed again. Sleep wouldn't come, however. She lay staring at the window above her bed, watching the intermittent glimmers of lightning and listening to the booming of distant thunder. The last, she thought, sounded like an irregular throb in the heartbeat of the earth.

Immediately she wondered if that rather purplish gem of expression was worth the effort of getting up to scribble it on paper. It didn't seem likely.

Was the lightning coming closer, getting brighter? She monitored its progress, staring wide-eyed into the night. If it was, it would be more dangerous to someone sleeping on an open deck. It was selfish of her to leave Luke alone out there, exposed to the elements. She really should tell him to come inside. But what would he think? No doubt, the obvious. Was that what she wanted?

Make up your mind....

It was so hot, without a hint of breeze. The air felt disturbed with the roiling of the elements. She was so restless. There was no comfortable position to be found on the firm plastic foam mattress of the makeshift bed that was so different from her soft one at Mulberry Point. The warm weight of Midnight lying across the end of it didn't help matters, either. Her short silk gown felt too restricting as well, too tight around the hips and across her breasts. It was as if her skin couldn't breathe. She was half inclined to strip naked so she could feel the little air movement there was available.

It was the weather; that was all. Her feverish chafing had nothing to do with the man outside. Nothing whatever.

To lie to Luke was one thing, a perfectly under-
standable self-protective gesture. Lying to herself
was something else again. She wouldn't be half so
disturbed, she knew, if she was alone on the boat.
She might as well admit it and be done with it.

Make up your mind...

April kicked the sheet away from her in such violent irritation that Midnight meowed in protest and
jumped to the floor. She pushed a hand under her
neck, sweeping her hair from beneath her and across
the pillow for coolness. With tight-lipped concentration, she closed her eyes. Firmly, she routed from
her mind the flickering scenes from the night before:
two bodies damply entwined, a symphony of
touches and tastes, glorious striving.

Sleep, she had to get to sleep. Seeking the stillness of progressive relaxation, she breathed deep
once, twice, three times, then began the mental
chant that would encourage her body to release tension beginning from her toes and spreading upward.
She got as far as her knees before her mind wan-
dered and she found herself staring at the flickers of
light beyond the windows again.

Abruptly, she sat up, swung her feet off the bed
and stood. She moved to the door, slid the screen
aside.

Luke roused instantly at the noise, pushing himself to one elbow so smoothly that it was obvious
he hadn't been asleep. The outline of his body was
plain against the white sheet on which he lay, as
was the gull's wing shape of his briefs. That last,
she thought with sudden conviction, was a conces-

sion to her supposed modesty. He was the kind of man who would normally sleep naked.

The boat rocked gently. Its anchor rope squeaked, then stopped. Long moments passed while neither of them spoke. April hadn't planned anything to say, could think of no light comment to suit the occasion, no sophisticated way to introduce what was on her mind. Her brain was empty of everything, in fact, except fretted impulse.

Lightning blinked again. The blue-white glow touched Luke with silver, plated the straight set of his shoulders, the streamlined musculature of his arms and legs. It glinted in his hair, but left the hollows of his eyes in impenetrable shadow.

"What is it?"

His voice, husky, yet resonant, reached out to her, reached into her to add to the aching fullness in the lower part of her body. Boldly, baldly, she answered him. "My mind is made up. Come inside."

15

"I thought you'd never ask," Luke said, then controlled a grimace at the banal phrase and the truth it both revealed and concealed. He'd been so certain she wouldn't ask that he'd deliberately exhausted himself, swimming until his breath came in labored gasps, his arms were leaden weights, and he could hardly pull himself back onto the boat. It hadn't done a lot to lower his flood-stage testosterone level, but might now benefit his self-control.

Giving April a chance for second thoughts was not in the cards. He slid off the bench and stalked toward her. At the door, he swooped down to put an arm under her knees and one behind her back, then lift her against his chest. Easing through the doorway, he shoved the screen shut with his foot.

He hesitated at the bedside, almost afraid to go farther. In any case, her silky excuse for a nightgown with firm flesh beneath it was such an acute bodily enjoyment that he barely suppressed a groan of pleasure. With legs spread for balance, he swayed in a delirium of doubt and half-crazed longing. Finally, he said, "This *is* what you meant?"

"If it's what you want," she whispered.

"You know it is, but I have to be sure I'm not going too far."

She lifted a hand to his lips, brushed their sensitive surfaces with her fingertips as she murmured with a smile in her voice, "You think too much. But if it will help matters, I promise to tell you when to stop."

It was enough.

He talked too much, too, whispered compliments and bits of stupidity that signified nothing except the boundless nature of his satisfaction. Also requests and questions of location, placement and degree. He was quiet with wonder, however, as he scaled the peaks of her breasts with the awe of a lowland swamp boy investigating his first mountains, delved into warm hollows with the caution of an explorer in dangerous territory. He had all the time in God's creation, and he used it to gather a thousand sensations and impressions, a precious hoarding against the time when there might be no more.

April was silent, this writer who used words as her stock in trade. He thought, from observations going back years, that they sometimes got damned up inside her, unable to emerge, when they mattered most. So he pried gently at the mental barrier holding them, teasing, taunting until she joined him in his paean to anticipation.

She was so sensitive. A brush of breath or lips could make her shiver in overextended pleasure. Too refined, or too empathetic to use her nails in the recklessness of her need, she still held him with desperate hands, showed him unerringly what she needed. To provide it gave him more joy than anything that he'd ever known.

She was all grace and caring, an exquisitely polite lady of firm grasp, generous inclinations, and reciprocal notions. She was silk and velvet and sweet-scented wonder. She was perfect glory. Burying himself in her tender depths until he could feel her heartbeat mesh with his own was the completion for which he'd been born, the solace he had searched for through eons of useless time. Sending them both spinning into silver-streaked darkness was his only purpose, the reward for every good thing he had ever done, every well-intentioned effort he'd ever made. It was his natural place. The fusing with the other half of himself that made him whole.

Afterward, holding her and staring blindly into the dark, he cursed in silent rage the Fates that had taken years of loving April away from him in a single, careless night. And he was afraid, so afraid that he might have to be satisfied with no more than a taste of her sweet promise when once he might have had it all.

The sun in Luke's face woke him. Turning away from the dazzling brightness, he yawned, and inhaled the soul-pleasing smells of brewing coffee and bacon frying, with a faint undertone of well-crumpled sheets. A slow smile spread over his face and he stretched with his arms above his head until his bones creaked.

His elbow touched something warm and furry. It was not what he might have hoped for, certainly not what he would have preferred, since April was already up.

The damned cat.

Luke opened a jaundiced eye and turned his head. He was practically nose to nose with the critter. It wasn't enough to spoil his mood, however. In an excess of good humor, he slid a hand under the feline and lifted him up to dangle above him. Midnight was so big and so boneless that his back feet rested on Luke's chest. He made a sleepy cat noise of inquiry.

"Good morning to you, too, friend. Where were you when your mistress deserted us, huh? The least you could have done was wake me up before she could get clean away."

"Meow," Midnight replied.

"Well, yes, I know you had a disturbed night, and I'm sorry, but you'll have to make allowances for the commotion since I'm sure she does the same for you now and then."

The cat meowed again right on cue.

"Not lately, huh? Your three-day escapade as somebody's unwilling guest not only cut into your fun time but also got you shut up at night? Too bad, but you know she's only doing the best she can by you. It's not so bad, considering her limited understanding of male—"

"Ego?" April supplied from the doorway.

He turned his head to give her a slow smile. "Needs, I was going to say."

"My understanding in that area," she said with an intriguing tilt of her lips, "is improving by leaps and bounds. Breakfast is ready."

"So am I." The hunger in his voice had nothing to do with bacon or coffee.

She lifted a brow as she studied his face. "Really?"

"Really."

"It's your payoff breakfast."

"My what?"

"For our bet?"

The stupid challenge, she meant, and the suggestion that she must make breakfast for him if she succumbed. He shook his head. "Forget it."

She unfastened the tie of the short robe she wore as she moved toward him, letting it fall open to reveal her nakedness underneath it. Taking the cat from him, she deposited the beast on the floor. She lifted a knee to straddle Luke's torso, then settled slowly onto the firmness at the apex of his thighs. "Some people," she complained, "are just impossible to please."

"Aren't we, though," he said in husky appreciation as he reached for her.

"Meow," Midnight said.

It was infernally hot as the morning advanced. Luke worked on the outboard motor, restoring the spark plugs he'd removed the day before, cleaning and fine-tuning it, then topping it off with gas. While he was at it, he checked the lines as well. The job helped pass the time and he figured it was best to be prepared in case they had to move fast and on short notice.

Afterward, he did a little cleaning on the front deck, sweeping off trash and leaves, wiping the ever present spider webs from the railings, and straightening around the grill where he'd fried fish the night before. Feeling hot and grimy when he was done, he went for a swim in the cutoff jeans that was all he had on. When he crawled back onboard, he didn't bother to change, but let his makeshift swimsuit dry on him for the coolness.

April, he was happy to see, had also pared down to essentials in shorts and a tank top without a bra. She let him putter around the boat by himself, however, while she stuck to mental effort by concentrating on her writing. At first, she used her laptop, but seemed to tire of squinting at the screen in the bright outdoor light. She soon switched to a real ink pen and spiral notebook. The only time she moved over the next several hours was to follow the shade from the rear deck to the front with the changing direction of the sun. Luke left her alone as much as possible.

He did search out the sunscreen and take it to her at midmorning. He'd have liked to be invited to put it on for her, but took it like a man when no such request was forthcoming. It didn't seem like a good idea to push his luck too far.

His reward came in the afternoon when a rain shower rumbled through and drove them both into the cabin. He and April made love while the warm rain thrummed overhead and the moisture-laden wind swept through the screens to cool their overheated bodies. Replete, they napped, waking only when the sun came out and raised the inside temperature so high that a swim was blessed relief.

In late evening, Luke cast for bass again, with Midnight watching from nearby in tail-twitching interest. As Luke cleaned the fish, he sneaked the cat a few more tidbits when he thought April wasn't looking. If she did notice, she didn't comment. He thought that maybe she didn't mind as much as she'd pretended, after all.

The result of the feeding, however, was that the cat became his shadow. Of course, the few quick scratches between the ears and nonsensical conversation he gave the beast off and on all day may have played a part as well. Luke couldn't help it. The poor animal was at loose ends with nothing to do on the boat beyond eat and sleep, and scant attention from his rightful owner in her involvement with her work. He wasn't developing a sneaking liking for him or anything like that, or so Luke told himself. He just knew how Midnight felt.

About dark, when his hunger pangs got too bad to ignore, he asked the cat, "What do you suppose Miss April would like for supper?"

Midnight sat down and considered the problem, finally uttering a tentative meow.

"Fish? An excellent suggestion, Monsieur Chat. We just happen to have a nice bass this evening. Now, with your knowledge of the lady, would you say she'd prefer it fried again or baked?"

Midnight turned his head and yawned.

"True," Luke agreed, frowning. "It really is too hot to light the oven, not to mention too much trouble. But the same holds true for frying, you know."

April, looking up from where she sat on the far end of the bench and smiled over at them as she said, "How about grilled?"

"Did you hear that, Midnight, old boy?" Luke exclaimed. "She spoke. She honored us with three whole words. And a brilliant suggestion, too, I might add. I knew we were keeping her around for some reason.''

"Meow.''

"Well, yes, I see what you mean. And I'll admit her attention is pretty intense at such times. But we spend so little time in bed that...''

"You,'' April interrupted, ''are asking for it.''

"Better than begging, don't you think?'' Luke tried to look pathetic but was afraid he made a poor job of it.

She closed her notebook and put it down, then placed her pen carefully on top. "I'll make the salad,'' she said, ''so it doesn't take so long to get from the fish course to your...just desserts.''

That day set the pattern for the next two. It was an easy time. Luke was content, for the most part, to live in the moment. At stray moments, he let himself forget that there was a point to this idyll, that someone, somewhere might be trying to find them, might be intent on harming April. Still he was alert to every unusual noise, kept a wary eye out for distant boat traffic that might veer in their direction. He scanned the tree line of the shore around them for movement, however unlikely that was. It was instinct as much as caution. Not many knew of this small cul-de-sac, and fewer still could find it except by accident.

It was while organizing the cabin late in the afternoon of the third day that he came across one of April's novels. Remembering his inclination to check out her stories, he picked it up and stood turning it in his hands. The cover was a brilliant blue-green metallic embossed with copper lettering that curled around a man and woman clasped in a suggestive but unlikely pose. A shade lurid, maybe, but eye-catching. The back copy sounded interesting, something about an ex-CIA agent and an independent female.

Luke took the book out onto the shady back deck and stretched out on the bench seat, making himself comfortable. He flipped the pages back and forth, reading a bit here, a bit there, and finally whistling in soft comment. Turning to the front, then, he settled into the story.

It was maybe an hour later that April came down from where she'd been working on the roof of the cabin that doubled as a sundeck. She started inside then stopped, staring hard at him where he lay with the book propped on his chest and Midnight stretched out along the wide seat back just above his head.

After a moment, she said, "You must really be bored."

"Nope," he answered with the briefest of grins, his attention still on the page.

"I never pictured you as much of a reader."

That rankled briefly for some reason. "Now you know different."

"Surely there's something else more your style here somewhere," she added, her voice taking on a strained note.

"And what would that be, do you think?" he asked with a lifted brow as he gave her his full attention. "A hot rod magazine or just *Playboy*?"

"I didn't mean—"

"Yes, you did."

She flushed and glanced down at her bare feet. "No, really. What I had in mind was more along the lines of *Louisiana Conservationist* magazine or an action thriller."

She'd come uncomfortably close to pegging him. She really was a smart lady, something he was growing more and more aware of the deeper he got into her story. Watching her mental processes unfold on the page had made him aware that there was usually a secondary reason behind most of what her characters said and did. He wondered if there was something going on in her mind at the moment other than an interest in his reading habits.

"What's the matter?" he asked. "Everybody else reads your books. Why should it bother you that I'm at it now?"

"I don't know, it just does," she said, lifting her chin. "Maybe it's because of why you're doing it."

"And that is?" He kept his gaze steady.

"You tell me," she returned. "I just doubt it's because you loved fairy tales as a child or happen to think that romance is a great panacea for what ails the human race. I can't imagine you're really involved in a story where the woman always wins, or that affirms love as a life-giving power and the direct antidote to the male urge to kill."

"Romance was invented by men," Luke said deliberately.

"They didn't invent it," she contradicted him. "They just wrote about it at a time when most women lacked the knowledge or the time to put words on paper."

"Maybe, but nothing and no one is more romantic than your average sixteen-year-old boy in love for the first time."

"Too bad they grow out of it, then! Maybe men should relearn what it means to be romantic instead of getting together to practice drum beating and primal howls."

"They don't grow out of it," he said evenly. "The romance just gets beaten down by all the jeers and rejections. They don't have to learn again, but only to remember."

"Are you saying—" She stopped, her breath coming so quickly that her chest rose and fell as if she'd been running.

Luke didn't answer. If she wanted to take the comment personally, it was all right with him.

She gave him a look of disgust and turned away. Then she paused and looked back, calling, "Here, Midnight, come on, boy."

Midnight turned his head to look at her and flipped his tail, but didn't budge. It seemed fitting. After all, Luke thought, he was a male, too.

April spun on her heel and stalked into the cabin. Luke looked after her for long seconds, then he sighed as he muttered to his good buddy, Midnight, "Guess this means no nap time today."

Luke finished the book just after dinner. For long moments, he sat staring into space, thinking. Then he got up and went to find another April Halstead romance.

It was unbelievable how caught up he got in the worlds April constructed sentence by sentence. The color and warmth of her vision led him on, her plots

intrigued him, and he felt as if he were exploring
the far edges of her personality as he followed the
thought processes of her female characters. Her
guys seemed a bit glorified, but then he wasn't paying too much attention to them other than as stand-
ins for his own involvement in the story. Maybe
that's why it was such a body blow when it finally
hit him.

He was the hero.

Or the hero was him, he, however you wanted to
put it. He was in April's books. She hadn't just used
him as a physical model for her men as she'd led
him to think. She had put the very essence of him
into her pages.

No wonder she'd been nervous about his reading
material.

To be sure he wasn't hallucinating, Luke gathered
all three novels onboard the boat and scanned their
pages. He found bits of description, pieces of business such as how the guy moved and spoke, his
habits, his mannerisms, his good qualities—and his
faults.

The hero really was based on him.

She hadn't used him just one time, nor was it a
recent idea. The three books were older titles published long before she returned to Turn-Coupe, and
he was the hero of all three. What was more, April
had caught him so well that it made the hair rise on
the back of his neck. She had put him under a mi-
croscope and dissected him, exposing his heart and
his thought patterns for the entire world to see.

Yet it wasn't really him, either, Luke saw after a
moment. He'd never been that strong, that good-

looking or sharply intelligent. He'd never in his life had that much flowery stuff to say.

Nor, to his knowledge, had he ever been that fantastic in bed.

After all the buildup, he had to wonder if April hadn't been disappointed. Of course, the love scenes could have been taken from her relationship with Tinsley—now there was a happy thought. But if that was it, Luke couldn't imagine why the two of them had ever split up.

Yes, and now he thought of it, there was that day in New Orleans when April and her writer friends had teased him unmercifully about being the heroic type. God, but she must have been giggling up her sleeve.

And the photos tacked to the bulletin board behind her computer? They hadn't been there by accident or because he was a handy face and form. The collection wasn't of recent vintage, either, something he should have realized at the time. No, she must have used them as reminders, inspiration, or whatever for years. That meant she was probably still using him, might even now be scribbling out some scene that made him look like a horse's behind or else had him in bed with her heroine doing who knows what. Or even doing exactly what he'd done the night before.

That certainly accounted for the measuring looks he'd gotten from her in the past few days.

If he was the hero, though, who was the heroine? Did she use herself? Had she been going to bed with him in her mind for years on end while he'd never had a clue?

Yes, and did everyone in Turn-Coupe—Betsy, Regina, Granny May and the other women who read her books so religiously—know that she used him? Had they recognized it ages ago, when they read her first books, and never told him?

Luke put the books back in the cabinet where he'd found them and left the cabin for the dark front deck. Standing with his hands braced on the railing, he scowled as he slowly came to grips with the whole idea. He had to decide what it meant—if it meant anything beyond the fact that he was a certain type, someone April knew fairly well and didn't mind exploiting.

The easiest thing would be to ask her, but he wasn't sure he wanted to do that. For one thing, the truth might be hard to come by. For another, he probably wouldn't like it when he heard it. Then there was something else stirring in his mind, a half-formed impulse he couldn't quite grasp.

Then he had it.

What if April secretly longed for the hero she had created for herself? What if this ideal man was what it would take to really get to her? What if he turned himself into that man insofar as it was physically and mentally possible?

It was a tall order.

"What do you think, Midnight?" he asked the cat who had followed him outside. "Do I have a prayer in hell of it working?"

Midnight walked over, wound around his legs, then sat down on Luke's foot and began to purr. Luke took it for encouragement.

He didn't go back inside, but braved the mosquitoes to sleep on the deck. The atmosphere between him and April was still strained the next morning, so he kept to the front end of the boat along with the third novel he'd retrieved for a textbook. She retreated to the cabin roof once more with her pen and notebook. They both came close to sunstroke as the day wore on and the sun's angle shifted, being too stubborn to occupy the same small section of shade at the same time.

It was late afternoon when Luke heard the buzzing. It was like a far-off chain saw in operation or else a radio-controlled model plane. He listened hard while the adrenaline rush of his warning instinct began to pour into his veins.

The sound was increasing and coming fast. It was no model plane but a real one. Now he could pinpoint not only the source but the make, model and engine ratio as well. It would have been a crime if he couldn't since he dusted crops with a similar model five days out of seven most summers, should be flying his Cessna now, on this windless evening as the sun went down. This one was coming fast and keeping low, almost skimming the treetops as it closed in on their hiding place.

Luke rolled off the bench where he lay and came erect in a single movement. Waving at April up top, he shouted, "Get down here. Come on!"

She stood up, staring down at him with a look on her face that said she'd been miles away and thought maybe he'd gone crazy while she wasn't looking. "What is it?"

"A plane. They could be looking for you. Get down here now!"

She glanced at the sky as comprehension bloomed across her features. Then she whirled away from him, heading toward the ladder on the rear deck.

It was a good move. Luke heard the thud of her footsteps overhead as he flung himself into and through the cabin, then ripped open the sliding screen door at the back. As he emerged on the back deck, the aerial buzz was becoming a roar. April was at the top of the ladder, but they had run out of time. As he reached the bottom rung, he yelled, "Jump!"

Her face was pale, her eyes huge. Her notebook was tucked into her tank top for he could see its outline. She didn't hesitate this time, but grabbed the ladder's top rail with one hand and sprang down feet first.

Luke caught her at the waist, clamping her to him even as he staggered and recovered. Then he dived for the cabin, half dragging, half pushing her inside.

The sound of the plane was deafening. Its shadow swept over the boat first as it bore down from the southwest. Then it went by overhead in a rush of air that swayed the surrounding trees like a hurricane, shivered the top of the water, and made the boat rock against its anchor ropes.

"Midnight!" April screamed above the racket. "Where?"

But the cat, no fool, had streaked through the front door, tail high and ears flat against his head. He was inside with them where it was safe.

Or where it had been safe. Until now.

16

A tremor ran over April as she stood in the hard circle of Luke's arms and listened to the receding racket of the plane. The clutch of her fingers made white dents in the muscles of his upper arms. Despite the heat of the day, the warmth from his bare chest was welcome. She felt cold from the inside out.

"Who was it?" she asked when she could force the words past her cold lips.

His voice compressed, Luke said, "I didn't get a look at him."

"Neither did I." She forced herself to release her grip, then brushed at the half moon marks made by her nails in his skin. Before she could step away, the sound of the airplane changed. With a quick upward glance, she added, "He's coming back."

"So it seems. I think…"

"What?"

"That whoever is at the controls will expect to see somebody onboard instead of a deserted-looking boat. With the commotion he made, most people would be outside taking a look."

"You think he'll expect to see you." It was a statement, though a tentative one.

He set her from him, began to move toward the door. "If he's checking this far back in the swamp then he must have a reason. He could know I'm missing from Chemin-a-Haut, could even have identified the boat as mine."

She had reached the same logical, if unwelcome, conclusion. The plane was coming closer. Something had to be decided. "You're sure?"

"No, but what else is there? Especially if I want a better look?"

The time for discussion was fast running out. The words tight, she said, "Be careful."

He gaze turned opaque for an instant. "I'll do that," he answered, then turned and ducked out onto the front deck.

April watched as his movements slowed to the saunter of a man with time on his hands. He was good, she had to admit that. He tipped his face toward the sky and thrust his hands into the back pockets of his jeans, rocking back on his heels like the most gape-mouthed hayseed.

"Don't overdo it," she called, anxiety putting a snap in the warning.

The only sign that he heard her above the roar of the oncoming plane was the quick twist of his lips.

Briefly, April pictured the explosion she'd have had to endure from Martin if she had dared to criticize one of his more macho exploits. Her ex-husband was not a man to see humor in chancy situations. But then, he wasn't the kind to willingly step into danger in the first place, either.

She was thinking, analyzing, as protection from the fear that ballooned inside her as the plane noise overrode all other sound once more. The staunch yet jaunty way Luke faced it tugged at her heart. The need to yell at him to come back, to grab him and pull him under cover again, was like an ache inside her. She clenched her hands into fists. She couldn't stand it, she couldn't.

What if whoever was in the plane had a gun? What if they dropped some kind of explosive to blow up the pontoon boat? What if they came in low enough to let a swimmer bail out, harpoon gun in hand like some stupid action-adventure movie? What if...

The plane streaked above the boat. Luke pivoted to keep it in sight, squinting into the last rays of the sun as he watched it bank north and disappear. The rumble of its engine faded into stillness.

April closed her eyes, inhaled and let it out again. Overactive imagination, that was her problem. It was an occupational hazard.

When she was sure the coast was clear she walked out to join Luke. He had moved to the prow of the boat, staring to the north with his arms crossed over his chest. As she stopped beside him, he gave her a brief glance before he asked, "Know anybody who flies a plane?"

"Other than you, no. But anybody can hire a pilot."

He gave a nod of agreement.

When he didn't speak again, she asked, "You don't think it could be a coincidence, the plane coming in so low?"

"I'd love to believe it."

His features were taut, with little in them to re-assure her. "But you don't."

He made no answer, but she needed none.

Midnight came out to join them then, winding around their legs and leaning against the ankles of first one and then the other in fine impartiality. It seemed that he sensed their disturbance, though that might be foolishness and his only real concern was his evening ration of fish.

With her gaze on the cat, April said, "You told me yourself that Roan figured out I was with you because we were seen leaving the festival together. What will happen if whoever was in the plane de-cides to come back by water to check out the same possibility?"

"The chance of them being able to find their way back in here isn't that great. Unless..."

"Unless they find a guide," she supplied. "Someone who knows the swamp as well as you."

"Not many do."

The claim carried certainty without a shred of ar-rogance. Still, it didn't have enough conviction to suit April. "You know someone who might?"

"It's possible, if he saw the boat from the air or was shown an aerial shot."

She would remain as sanguine as he seemed if it killed her. In even tones, she asked, "Anyone I know?"

"Frank."

Frank Randall, who carried a grudge against Luke and might not mind doing him a disservice. The man who blamed them both for his sister's death.

The possibility had been there all along. Reinforcement for her own suspicions was not something she was overjoyed to receive. "He doesn't have to be involved," she said. "And if it's someone else, if he's approached strictly for his ability as a guide, he may not take the job."

"Or he could jump at the chance."

She didn't like the grim note in his voice. "Just in case, then..."

He turned his head to meet her gaze, his own hard with purpose. "Right. We move the boat as soon as it's dark."

That was what they did, raising the anchors in swirling torrents of mud and easing out into the lake again at turtle speed and without running lights. April sat at the front railing and acted as lookout, straining her eyes in the light of a three-quarter moon and calling back warnings about sand spits, stumps and floating logs. After what seemed long hours, they reached a small meandering ribbon of water half-choked with marshy growth and overhung with trees. As Luke drove the boat into it, the pontoons scraped grittily over saw grass and water hyacinths while low-hanging limbs scratched along the cabin roof. They plowed along for perhaps a quarter mile, until they were well screened from the lake, then he shoved the big, unwieldy craft under and into the dense overhang of a big, leaning pin oak. As the dragging tree branches halted their forward progress, he cut the big outboard motor.

In the silence that descended, they could hear the creaking and rustling as displaced tree limbs eased back into place. April, standing near the console where she had retreated as they slid under the natural cover, let out the breath she'd been holding. Luke rose from behind the wheel, then moved to flip on a couple of battery-operated lights. Raking a hand through his hair to dislodge a couple of dead leaves and a white streak of spider web, he said, "We should be fairly hard to spot in here. I'll add to the camouflage in the morning."

"I hope there isn't much damage to your boat." The words were stilted, she realized, and not precisely what she wanted to say. "I mean, I'm grateful that you risked wrecking it because of me, and sorry if it got scratched."

"I bought the thing to be useful. If it gets a little beat up, hell, that's life. I can't think of a more worthwhile cause."

It was difficult to stay mad at a man who not only felt that way, but was protecting her at his own risk. He made her feel safe, and that was miraculous. More than that, he had in some strange fashion freed her creative drive so words poured from the end of her pen as if from an artesian well. Or maybe it wasn't so strange. He had always been a wellspring for her art, a source of inspiration for the edgy yet tender heroes she created. The physical rapport they had shared only renewed that while adding another, more vibrant, dimension.

She was back; she was a writer again. That was something else she owed him.

As disturbing as he could be, then, and as distracting, she was fiercely glad to be there with him. Perhaps because of his example as well as his rock steady confidence, she was able to push her fears aside and exist in the moment. In the less fraught days just passed it had occurred to her that however much she resented being tricked into this seclusion with him, it had not been a bad thing.

Amazing, but it could not be denied.

Whether she would feel that way when the episode was over, she had no idea. What would come from the development between her and Luke was equally unknown. For now and until this was over, she wanted to be with him, wanted him, needed him.

Their being at odds today had been disturbing and not so productive. There was more to it than that, but what exactly was something she didn't care to question too closely. If part of her reluctance was the problem of why he was willing to risk so much for her sake, it was something else she didn't want to examine. And perhaps couldn't afford to probe as long as they were so isolated together. All she knew was that she wanted things back the way they had been between them in the quickest and easiest possible way.

"Are we going to anchor or just tie up?" she asked, though she was fairly sure of the answer.

"Tie up, just a couple of lines to keep us from swinging into the open if a wind comes up."

"Tell me where you want the lines and I'll give you a hand. It's been a long day, and unless you have a better idea, I'm ready to turn in."

The look he turned on her held close consideration. "You go ahead. I can get the lines."

"Then I'll make down the bed. I—if you don't mind, would you sleep inside? It bothers me, having the cabin all alone while you're out here with the snakes and bugs."

"Not nearly as much," he said with the ghost of a smile, "as it bothers me."

"That's good, then." She wasn't totally sure he understood what she was trying to say, but at least she'd have the chance of making it clearer later.

"No, *chère*," he said, his voice rich and deep, "it's fantastic."

She should have known he wouldn't need to have it spelled out in one-syllable words.

He came to her shortly afterward smelling of night freshness and a faint, wild hint of the lake from his bath. There was something different about him, she thought, as he settled beside her and reached to draw her close. He still whispered and cajoled with enjoyment threading through the words, but his touch was more commanding, his caress more lingering yet less tentative. He seemed to sense what she wanted, guess what she needed before she knew herself. His concentration was absolute, and directed toward the goal of her fulfillment to the exclusion of all else. He reached it, expanded it with skill and fortitude until her every nerve ending was sensitized almost beyond bearing, singing with the need to feel his weight against her, to have him deep inside her. In answer to the direction of her clinging hands, he slid into place.

It was a rampaging ride, an endless sounding of such power that she responded with stunning force. He was everything she'd ever imagined in a lover, skilled, inventive, tireless, cherishing. Still, when he was finally quiescent, lying with her held close against him, she stared with wide eyes into the darkness while she smoothed her palm over the hard planes of his shoulder as if to soothe him, soothe them both.

They slept late. The huge tree that sheltered them also filtered the morning sun, giving them a deeper shade than before so the heat was held at bay a little longer. When April woke at last, nestled against Luke in spoon fashion, she was reluctant to move. She didn't want to disturb the man who held her, but also, for the first time in days, didn't feel like getting up to work. She just wanted to lie there, to simply be, secure in the moment. There was such rightness in it, as if she were where she belonged.

Not that it meant anything special, of course. It was all a matter of chemical attraction and physical compatibility. These things had little to do with love. They were transient while love was permanent. She'd learned that lesson long ago.

All right, then, her attraction to Luke had endured in spite of everything that lay between them. That didn't prove a thing, didn't mean it was love. It couldn't be. How could she possibly love someone she couldn't trust?

Or could she trust him after all? Wasn't it, just possibly, a bit illogical to depend on someone to keep her safe while refusing to accept him into her heart?

Julianne had been right. He was nothing like her father. He never had been, which was why she had turned to him all those years ago. Her father had been morose and cynical and self-involved. He had loved her, yes, but he'd cared more for his pride. She could see that now with clarity she'd had trouble managing while she was a teenager.

She could also see Luke far more clearly. She did have faith that he would protect her. In spite of the way he had lured her onto the boat and kept her there, she could no longer consider that he was involved in what was happening to her. She had tried to feel that way in self-protection, perhaps, but had known for some time that it was almost impossible.

No, he could not be so diabolical as to pretend to rescue her from a danger he had created himself. Besides, he had been too caring, too patient and practical in his concern for her comfort. He had nothing to gain by such an elaborate ploy; he'd made no promises, asked nothing of her. The intimacy that had developed between them was incidental, not the result of anything he'd done. Anyway, no sane man would concoct such an elaborate hoax for that kind of reward.

Would he?

She eased away from Luke and turned over, then propped herself on one elbow. His face was relaxed in sleep so he looked younger, less cynical, though there was nothing boyish about his dark stubble of beard. Laughter lines bracketed his mouth, however, and made fanlike rays at the corners of his eyes. His lashes were so thick they meshed together. The firm curves of his mouth were pure sensual temptation and the perfectly molded contours of his ears gave her an almost irresistible urge to tickle him awake.

"Well," he said in sleep-drugged sultriness, "what are you waiting for?"

"Not a thing," she said on a low laugh of delight.

And didn't.

Much later, she took her pen and notebook out

onto the front deck once more and settled on the bench with her feet tucked under her in yoga fashion. Though she was in no real mood to work this morning, she'd discovered long ago that inspiration was a lot more likely to come around if she was ready for it. In an attempt to get started, she did a little automatic writing, just jotting down whatever ran through her head, letting her thoughts flow in black ink onto the page. Sometimes, that was all it took.

Luke disturbed her concentration, however. He was hacking off the low-hanging branches of the oak that were scratching against the fiberglass of the cabin walls and roof. These branches he tied to the rails as additional camouflage. When he finished that task, he brought out a large olive green net that he spread out on the cabin roof and draped over the exposed rear deck. Standing on the roof, he stretched up to snag a high branch to use as a tent-like support for it. Holding its leafy end under one arm, he fastened a rope to the net's grommets and, in turn, knotted the rope around the branch. Then he released both.

The branch sprang back into place with a snap that shook the tree. April looked up at the sound. At that moment, something long and gray-black dislodged from the tree branch above her. It fell heavily. It landed across her lap in a twisting coil of long muscle.

Snake!

April yelled. Her notebook flew in one direction and her pen in another. She surged to her feet, dumping the water moccasin on the carpet. The snake landed with a thump and whipped to its belly. It hissed, mouth wide open to show the cotton-white lining of its throat. In the same instant, April sprang away, stumbling against the rail.

Movement flashed above her as Luke leaped from the cabin roof. He landed on the balls of his feet, balancing as he countered the violent rock of the boat. His eyes were hard, and the ax he'd used earlier was in his hand.

The snake struck. Luke swung. The snake's head sprang free, cleaved from its body in a single clean stroke. Immediately, Luke moved forward and batted the remains over the side. Then he swung to face April.

She flung herself at him, her body shaking convulsively as she held tight. He closed her in the circle of his arms and rocked her like a child.

"You're all right? It didn't bite you?"

She moved her head in a jerky negative.

"You're sure. I didn't think there was time, but—"

"No—no, I'm sure. I'm just…"

"You're shook. Anybody would be. The damn thing must have been lying along a limb above you. I didn't see it. I'm sorry I—"

"You couldn't help it." She cut across that hurried explanation with its undercurrent of self-blame.

"I'd have had to inject you with antivenin, and I wouldn't have liked that at all. And we're so far back in here that by the time we got you to a hospital you would still have been mighty sick."

"It didn't happen. I'm fine." She lifted her head

to give him a look that was somewhat steadier. "Could you really have done that, used antivenin?"

He shrugged a little, his brown gaze serious. "It goes with the territory."

"Amazing." She smiled. "My hero."

His face changed abruptly, losing all expression. Then he flushed so thoroughly that even his ears turned red. He stepped away from her, saying with awkward humor, "See that you remember it."

It was a creditable attempt at recovery, still she saw through it as plainly as if he'd accused her. Her secret was out. Luke had discovered what she'd done, what she had been doing for years. He knew that he was the prototype for her heroes. He knew, and he wasn't happy about it.

He was turning away, getting ready to go back to what he'd been doing before the snake intervened. She took a quick step after him to put a hand on his arm. "Wait."

"What?" He paused, his manner polite but not encouraging.

She couldn't do it, couldn't bring it all out into the open right now. She couldn't confess while they were stuck here together on this boat. His anger and withdrawal would be intolerable if there was no way for them to get away from each other.

She moistened her lips, searching for something, anything, to say instead. "I—wouldn't you like to stop for a while, maybe have something cold to drink?"

He met her gaze for a long, considering moment, then his eyes warmed a fraction. "Don't want me dropping any more snakes into your paradise, that it?''

''Maybe. And maybe I just feel like company.''

He tilted his head. ''That's a switch.''

''A lot of things have changed,'' she replied, holding his eyes with an effort.

He was silent while a warm puff of breeze like a lover's sigh stole through the leaves above them and sunspots fell around their feet in shapes like ancient, irregular gold coins. Then he gave a short nod. ''You make the drinks while I finish up top. Then we'll talk.''

''Talk?'' she asked. ''What about?''

He studied her a long second before he turned away. Over his shoulder, he said, ''Later,''

April felt the muscles of her stomach tighten. It didn't sound good.

17

Luke had the best of intentions, but he wasn't sure where or how to start. He'd been silent so long about what happened that night thirteen years ago that he couldn't seem to find a way to open the subject. The whole point of bringing it up had more to do with April than with himself, however, and that seemed the best approach, maybe the only approach.

"About Frank Randall," he said finally as he sat thumbing the condensation from the side of his glass of iced pineapple juice. "If he's behind all this, it isn't because he has anything against you. He's been threatening to get even with me for years. Looks as if he's finally figured how to go about it."

"Through me, you mean."

April had never been slow on the uptake, he thought in reluctant admiration. "Frank never thought I was sorry enough for what happened to his sister. Maybe he thinks I need another woman on my conscience."

"Another— Good grief, Luke! Is that supposed to make me feel better? To be told he has no hard feelings toward me, but wants to kill me anyway?"

"I'm not sure how it should make you feel, but I thought you ought to know the reason."

Her clear golden gaze was intent on his face as she replied, "Yes, well, that's an easy one."

"There's a little more to it than you might imagine."

"Meaning?" She waited.

He was quiet, his gaze on a great blue heron that stalked minnows along the water's edge a short distance away. Turning back to her at last, he said, "You never asked me about the night Mary Ellen died. Why was that?"

"I didn't have to. Frank told me."

"Exactly. Frank told you. But what did he say?"

She lifted a shoulder. "What does it matter? His sister was with you. You'd both been drinking. There was a wreck. You lived and she didn't."

"God, April, you and I were the next thing to engaged. We had talked about where and how we were going to live together, what we'd do with our lives and how many kids we wanted. We had a future."

"We were supposed to have a future," she corrected.

"You were the one who decided we didn't."

"After you proved it wouldn't work!"

"I was in an accident. I could have been killed. But you didn't even want to see me, didn't want to know from my own mouth what happened." The old pain was in his voice, but he couldn't avoid that. The things he was saying had festered inside him for years. He might as well get it all out while he was at it.

''You left me at my front door and went off drinking and joyriding with Mary Ellen Randall,'' she answered in low distress. ''What more was there to say?''

''You might have wondered if I'd really been drinking. Or if there had been any *joy* in it for me.''

Her lips twisted and she refused to meet his gaze. ''Don't be any more crude than you can help.''

''There you go again!'' he said, thudding a fist down on the padded bench between them. ''You're judging me without a hearing, condemning me on the word of a man who may be doing his dead level best to kill us both.''

''I don't—''

''Or just maybe,'' he added, ''you're putting me in the same category as your dad.''

''We'll leave my parents out of this, if you don't mind,'' she said, her lips in a hard line as she faced him.

''I'd love to, but they're part of it because they are part of you. Your father shot your mother in a drunken rage at the end of a quarrel over another man. But the truth is that he was accusing her of what he did regularly himself. In fact, it all began because someone told your mother he'd been seen parked out beside the lake with another woman.''

''That's not so!'' she cried.

''It is,'' he insisted. ''It's all in the case file. A neighbor who heard part of the quarrel told the police. You were there. You knew it back then, so you should recognize the truth now. Somehow, you got it into your head that I was like him, maybe because we looked something alike. You never did trust me, and when I was caught in similar circumstances, you immediately assumed the worst. You still do.''

''No, you're wrong,'' she insisted, but the words were hardly more than a whisper and the look in her eyes was haunted.

Luke gave a stubborn shake of his head. ''It's the truth.''

She glanced from him for long seconds. Finally, she said, ''He almost shot me, too, my dad. He put the pistol to my head and held it there forever. He was shaking. My mother was— There was blood everywhere, so much blood. I was crying so hard I couldn't say a word.'' April set the palm of her hand on her bare thigh, rubbing hard. ''I don't know why he changed his mind.''

''Because you were his little girl and he loved you,'' Luke answered in low reassurance as he reached to cover her cold fingers with his own.

''He said I was like my mother, all sweet and innocent when I was little but I'd grow up to be false and hard-hearted and—''

''Don't,'' he said.

''And tainted,'' she finished.

Luke cursed the dead man to himself before he said, ''The man your mother was supposed to have been seeing on the side was a lawyer. She was seeing him, all right, but about a divorce. Rumor was that he waived his legal fees for attractive women. That may or may not have been true, but your mother's best friend said there was nothing between them. It's likely your mother was exactly like you back then. In other words, completely innocent.''

A small sound left her that was neither exclamation, sob, nor sigh, but something akin to them all. "You make it seem so simple. But there's no way to be that certain about something that happened so long ago."

"I told you, I saw the file. Roan showed it to me. The lawyer your mother was seeing made a statement, as did a couple of neighbors. Your father's statement was there, too, the few words he spoke before he…"

"Before he died of a self-inflicted gunshot wound to the head," she said.

"And grief," Luke added. "The one thing he said over and over was how sorry he was for what he'd done, how much he wished that he could undo it."

"Oh, dear God," she whispered with tears rising in her eyes.

"It hurts, I know," he said, his voice low. "I'm sorry."

"No." She took a deep breath. "I never knew that part, how he felt afterward. I only remember him standing over me saying those things, then the shot. At first I thought that I was— But he'd turned the gun on himself."

"You were only five." Luke felt so helpless. He wanted to reach out and dry her tears, but didn't quite dare.

"A lifetime ago, yet it seems like only yesterday." She wiped the wetness from under her eyes as if she'd noticed his attention centered there. "But we were talking about Frank, weren't we? What reason would he have to lie to me?"

She meant to distract him from her problems,

Luke thought. He was reluctant to let it go at that, but there were still things that needed to be said. "Why? Revenge, in part. To take whatever happiness I had in exchange for what I'd taken from him. Maybe even to put the blame on somebody, anybody, other than himself."

"You make it sound so personal."

"It was," he answered in grim certainty. "It still is."

She turned toward him on the bench, her gaze searching his face. After a moment, she said simply, "All right. Maybe I didn't ask when I should have. Tell me now."

Luke felt his heart swell in his chest. It was all he could do to breathe, much less talk, yet he had to make her understand. This might be the only chance he'd ever get.

"Mary Ellen was my age," he finally began, "which made her a couple of years older than you, a big difference in high school. You may not remember a lot about her, but she was a brown mouse of a girl until she turned fifteen. Then she went over the top—fifties bleached hair, Dracula nail polish, dressed like Fredrick's of Hollywood. The guys were gaga over her, some of them. Of course it was the wrong kind of attention. She turned wild, slipping out at night, showing up in the wrong places, drinking, collecting scalps."

"If by that you mean she crawled into the back seat with any boy who asked, and some who never got around to it," April interjected. "I do remember that part. And if you're looking for a nice way to say she used to chase you, I remember that, too."

"You were jealous," he said, too amazed by the discovery to be more diplomatic.

"I was not! I felt sorry for her, in a way. She was so obvious, and had so little pride. Besides, even Frank admitted she was after you."

"She didn't make saying no too easy. The only thing she understood was a downright refusal, yet she had so few defenses. It's hard to get away from something like that without hurting somebody."

"Something you had a hard time dealing with," she said with a faint twist to her lips.

"Maybe. She seemed so desperate, always reaching out for closeness but never having enough, never quite expecting anything real, as if she didn't deserve it. She was afraid of Frank, too. She used to try to hide from him, and was always making people swear not to tell him where she was. It didn't work. He usually found her."

"Frank was overprotective, is that it?"

Luke hesitated. "I don't think any of us gave it much thought at the time. Their folks were dead and there was some aunt who'd lived with them for years, and belonged to one of the fundamental church groups. Part of Mary Ellen's wildness was rebellion against years of never being allowed to wear makeup or jeans and that sort of thing. But looking back, I think there was something else going on, something not quite right between her and her brother."

"Are you trying to say there was something— unnatural about Frank's attitude?"

"You got it. The way she acted that last night,

some of the things she said, suggested it. Not that we'll ever know for sure.''

April gave a slow shake of her head. ''I can't believe it. Poor Mary Ellen.''

''It happens.''

''Yes,'' April said quietly. ''But what about that last night? How did she wind up with you after you took me home?''

''I passed through town on the way back out to Chemin-a-Haut. When I got to the hangout near the courthouse, I noticed Roan and Kane there with some of the gang, so I stopped. I left my hot rod running while I walked over to tell the guys something—what, I don't remember, though it seemed important at the time. I noticed Mary Ellen with the rest of the crowd, but didn't think much about it. While we were standing there, I heard my car door slam. Mary Ellen had climbed in and was sitting behind the wheel.''

A startled expression appeared in April's eyes. ''You mean she— Never mind. Don't let me interrupt.''

Luke was grateful for her forbearance since he'd as soon say what had to be said while he still had the courage. ''She was upset. She'd had a few beers and wasn't making much sense, though I gathered that she and Frank had been fighting. She chose my car because it was handy, but also because she thought I might protect her from him. At first, I tried to talk to her. Kane and Roan left me to it and headed for home. After a few minutes, Mary Ellen looked past me and said Frank was coming after her. She yelled at me to come on if I wanted my car back. I barely made it through the open window before she took off like a missile."

"Was Frank chasing her?" April asked with a frown.

Luke was tempted to lie. He just couldn't do it. Getting it right this time was too important. "If he was, I never saw him. Nobody was behind us. Before we were two miles down the road, I realized she meant to kill us both."

"She—but why?"

"What she said was that if I was too good to sleep with her, then maybe I was good enough to die with her."

"You hadn't slept with her?" Her brief glance was strained and a little skeptical.

"Lord, April. You were the first and only girl I'd been with like that back then. Couldn't you tell?"

"How was I supposed to do that when you were the only boy I'd ever gone out with, much less slept with? But I always assumed the two of you were doing something besides riding that night."

"So did everyone else," he said bitterly. "Afterward, it seemed that since I had the name, I might as well enjoy it."

April apparently didn't care to follow that lead. She said instead, "So, Mary Ellen was driving when you left town. When did you take the wheel?"

"I didn't."

"Frank said—"

"Frank wasn't there so how was he supposed to know? But everyone else believed him. Even you."

"Because it made sense. You always drove fast and your car was a hot rod, as you said. It was the next summer that you and Kane and Roan went on the NASCAR circuit.''

''That doesn't make me reckless. Or suicidal.''

''But Mary Ellen was?''

Luke couldn't tell whether April believed a word he was saying or thought he was lying through his teeth. It didn't matter. He'd come this far, so might as well go all the way to the end. In answer to her question, he said, ''It's hard to be sure, now. Sometimes I think it was a suicide mission, and other times I believe she was just crazy wild, hurting inside and mad at the world because of it so she didn't really care what happened. She drove like a maniac, topping hills in the middle of the road, flying around blind curves on the wrong side, taking scary chances. She wanted to see how fast she could go, I think, and how far she could stretch her luck. It was as if there was something she needed to outrun. I don't know, maybe it was her demons.''

''Demons,'' April repeated, her gaze unfocused.

''That's Roan's word for problems caused by past mistakes,'' he said. ''We all have them. They may come in different shapes and sizes, but they're there.''

''Yes. So, Mary Ellen's caught up with her?''

He tipped his head in agreement. ''She rounded a curve and met a church van. I thought she meant to hit it head-on. At the last second, she swerved. We went off the road, rolled over. I was thrown clear since I was looking for a chance to take the wheel and hadn't fastened my seat belt. Mary Ellen was still inside when the car hit a tree and exploded in flames. I got to her, could touch her hand, but she was trapped with her legs pinned in the wreck-age. I couldn't get her out, though I tried. God, how I tried. But the fire was so hot, and she was scream-ing. Sometimes, I still hear—''

''Don't!'' April said sharply. ''Just—don't. Try not to think about it any more.''

''No,'' he said, and repressed a shudder as he exhaled in slow release from the old nightmare.

April was quiet a moment, then she said abruptly, ''All this time, I thought you were driving that night. You never spoke up to correct that impres-sion, at least not that I heard.''

''You weren't interested in anything I had to say. If you assumed the worst, what did I care what any-one else thought? And why should they believe me if you, who knew me best, was so sure I had as good as killed Mary Ellen? There was also no way to talk about it without bringing Frank into it along with all the ugly things I suspected. I was your typ-ical inarticulate half-grown redneck boy who barely knew what incest was, much less how to describe that kind of relationship.''

''So, you let yourself be blamed.''

''Why not? I had this stupid, quixotic idea that I should have been able to save her. Added to that was a feeling that I would be maligning someone who could no longer defend herself. Enough had been done to Mary Ellen.''

April was quiet for long moments then she shook her head. ''Honorable, after all,'' she said quietly. ''I'm sorry. I should never have said what I did at dinner that night in New Orleans.''

He tried for a careless shrug, though it felt as if

a tight rope around his chest had been loosened. ''Don't worry about it. Nothing I've done since has exactly polished the image. Anyway, I was confused and a little shell-shocked back then, in the day or so after the wreck, not thinking heroically or even very straight. By the time I realized the damage caused by keeping quiet, it was too late to correct it. I'd have sounded as if I were making excuses or lying to avoid the blame. So I just—let it go.''

A considering quiet fell. Then April inhaled and let it out in a soundless sigh. Voice compressed, she asked, ''So, you really think Mary Ellen died because of Frank?''

''As I said, she never put it in so many words. It may have been nothing more than a case of an overbearing brother with fundamentalist ideas about a woman's place. But something was there, something was driving her.''

''It might explain the weird phone calls if Frank had some kind of sexual hang-up,'' she suggested.

''The thought had occurred to me.''

''But I really don't see why he should target me now, after all these years.''

He was ready for that one. ''My theory, for what it's worth, goes something like this. Frank may have seen us together at Chemin-a-Haut for the Memorial Day party back earlier in the summer, and could have heard that Regina was playing matchmaker by making you maid of honor at her wedding.''

''She was?''

''You didn't notice? Where was your head? She and Kane are so damned happy they want everybody in on the act.''

"All right, but I still don't get the connection."

"Frank knew you were important to me and always had been. Maybe it looked like we were getting involved again now that you're back in town."

"In other words, he wanted to deprive you of any possible association with me as he was deprived of his sister. Even if there had to be a permanent removal."

"Something like that."

She stared into her juice a moment. When she looked up, her gaze was clear. "Very plausible, a neat theory, in fact. It certainly gets you off the hook."

"What's that supposed to mean?" He tried to control the surge of anger he felt for her apparent doubt. In spite of everything.

"It doesn't address the fact that you don't want me writing about your family."

"Lord, April, I don't care what you write. It's Granny May who doesn't want you poking around in our history and stirring up a stink."

"I don't stir up stinks!"

She looked, he thought briefly, as exasperated as he felt. Why the devil was it that they could never be together more than five minutes without some argument flaring up between them? He raked a hand through his hair before he said, "Surely you don't suspect my grandmother of making obscene phone calls?"

"No, but someone could have done it for her."

"Me, you mean."

"The one to the radio show was made from a cell phone. You were in your truck at the time."

"Come on, April. You'd recognize my voice."

"Would I? In that situation?"

He flung up his hands. "Right. Thanks a lot, but I hope I have more imagination than that creep."

She turned tomato red. He'd have given a lot to know which memory of the past few days and nights might have set off that reaction.

She said finally, "I had about decided you did, also you weren't such of a pervert."

"I'm glad to hear it." He was, too, and intensely glad that she could admit to that much. Her vacillating might be a self-protective instinct. He hoped so, since it might be a sign of how much the truth mattered to her.

"Which?"

"Both," he answered without missing a beat. "Though it would help my feelings if you'd also admit I might feel a tad remorseful about trying to blow Cousin Betsy to kingdom come."

"Maybe a little," she allowed. "After all, she's family."

It was time for a change of subject, before he said too much. He let a few seconds pass then said, "Speaking of the clan, what about this book of yours? For instance, what if you discovered some juicy scandal involving the Benedicts? Can you honestly say you wouldn't be tempted to use it?"

"Being tempted is one thing, but writing a story that might hurt someone is something else entirely," she protested. "I would never use anything that wasn't common knowledge, never construct an episode in such a way that anyone was held up to ridicule."

"No?"

"No! Publishers frown on libel suits, you know. More than that, it would make me too uncomfortable to know I'd harmed someone, especially a nice old lady like Granny May. I mean, she showed me how to find four-leaf clovers and make clover bloom chains. She used to make gingerbread men for us, for Pete's sake!"

Luke could feel the amused twist of his lips and didn't even try to stop it. In quiet approval, he said, "So she did."

"We had our differences. I think she felt we were too young to be so serious, but that's all in the past. Why would she think I'd try to hurt her now?"

"The girl I knew wouldn't have," he said with care. "The woman I know now might, for all I can tell. As you said yourself, you're not the same — we're not the same."

She looked away. "I haven't changed that much."

What did that mean, he wondered? That she still felt the same as she had back then? That everything between them was, or could be, as it had been before? He'd like to think so, but was afraid to risk it. At the same time, he thought the fact that they were still talking, and even able to joke a little, must mean that she believed at least a portion of what he'd told her. Trying to stick to the subject, he asked, "What are you writing about the Benedicts, then? What's all the secrecy?"

"There isn't any. I just don't like talking about a story in progress because it takes away some of the excitement. If I reveal too much, I may lose interest in putting it on paper."

"I guess that makes sense," he allowed, "but it would help if I could give Granny May some idea of what you have in mind."

April drank the rest of her pineapple juice. Instead of answering then, she gave him a glance from under her lashes. "You mentioned a juicy scandal. Is there one to be discovered?"

"Anything's possible. Lord knows, the closets at Chemin-a-Haut have their share of skeletons." He wanted to be honest, since he thought the question was in the nature of a test, to see if he'd level with her since he was asking her to level with him.

"But...?" she suggested.

"But keeping to ourselves is too much of a family tradition to permit straying far, so the kind of thing Granny May has in mind seems unlikely."

"And that would be?" April tilted her head inquiringly.

Here it came. With a deep breath, he said, "A little friendly miscegenation?"

She looked amused. "Really, Luke, your family tree is a matter of public record. Half a dozen cousins have compiled genealogical records and left copies on file at the Tunica Parish Library. It's all there, documented back to the Doomsday Book in England and far into the Celtic mists of Scotland. The only deviation I found was the Native American branch represented by your great-great-great-great-grandmother. And that's my story."

"You're only using Granny Adochia?"

"I promise. It's enough, don't you think? Most people think of New Orleans and the French and Spanish colonial settlement when they think of Louisiana history. Few seem to realize that settlement of the north central part of the state took place less than 150 years ago and parallels the opening of the west—the same patterns of immigration, same kinds of people, and much the same Indian problems and frontier mentality.''

''And that's it?''

A rueful smile came and went across her face, possibly for his dismissal of her history lesson. ''Isn't that enough, this powerful attraction between your handsome ancestor and his Indian maiden, excuse me, Native American maiden?''

''I'm not sensitive about it,'' he said obligingly.

''A good thing, too. But where was I?''

''Talking about my handsome ancestor, the one I look so amazingly like it's hard to tell us apart.''

She gave him a quelling look. ''Anyway, I'm intrigued by what would make a woman of such a different culture leave her people, accept a new religion and a new baptismal name, and follow a strange man into the wilderness to make a home.''

''Other than love?'' he suggested.

''Other than love.'' The agreement was without inflection.

''Trust. Caring. The need to be with him? It's happened untold times over the centuries.''

''Agreed,'' she said with a nod, ''which says a great deal about the courage of women.''

''In the case of my ancestress, I prefer to think it says more about what a great guy my grandpa must have been.''

''And you take after him in personality as well as looks, I suppose.''

''How'd you ever guess?'' The look he gave her was as sultry as it was teasing.

Color rose to her hairline, but this time she didn't look away. The time was fast approaching, he suspected, when she might well call him on his smart remarks. She might even admit that she had put him in her books. What would he do then?

He'd decide later. For now, a diversion would come in handy. "As long as we're talking family suspicions, what about Tinsley?"

"Martin? What about him?"

"I know you said once that he was too slick and certain of his charm to resort to scare tactics, but he's not exactly a disinterested party here. In fact, in a contest against Frank for villain of the year, he'd get my vote."

"You accused me of jealousy just now, didn't you? I'd say that almost sounded like the same thing."

"That's only because it is," he explained with a great show of magnanimity. "The guy took you away from Turn-Coupe for years, had much more of your time to himself than he ever deserved. If he's terrorizing you now in the hope of making you fly back into his arms, it will be my personal pleasure to kick the smarmy son of a—to kick the creep from hell to breakfast."

"A consummation devoutly to be wished," she said with dry emphasis.

He lifted a brow. "You really feel that way?"

"I do," she answered. "But I still don't think he's capable of the dedication to pull it off."

"No?"

"Not even to my money," she said with a sigh.

"I'm not so sure about that. He seemed pretty interested in New Orleans."

''Yes, you were there.'' She gave him a look under her brows.

''Meaning?''

''Dog in a manger.''

''I never did get that parable,'' he complained. ''The dog might not have wanted to eat the hay, but why should he give up his nice warm bed?''

''Luke!''

He tried to look virtuous. ''What did I say?''

She threw the ice cubes at him. Catching a couple of them, he weighed them in his hand while he gave her a considering look centered primarily on the scooped neck of her tank top. Then he set his glass on the deck, reached for her hand holding her glass and disposed of it as well.

''Luke, wait,'' she said, moistening her lips as she flashed a glance from his face to the ice cubes in his hand, then back again.

''Oh, I don't think so,'' he drawled. ''There was something just now about consummations to be wished, I believe? I happen to have one in mind.''

''You wouldn't.'' She paused. ''Would you?''

She tried to pull away from him, but it was a halfhearted effort that he conquered without half trying. ''I think maybe I would, pervert that I am.''

''I didn't mean it. I told you I didn't think that!''

''But I think you do,'' he said as he transferred his hand to her waist in a quick movement and drew her across his lap, at the same time slipping his hand with the ice cubes under the hem of her top.

She caught her breath as the ice touched her, and a rash of goose bumps rippled under his fingers. They had little to do with being cold, however, or so he hoped.

Her voice barely above a whisper, she said, "You're a fiend."

"I know," he said sympathetically, even as he slid the fast-melting ice along the valley between her breasts then up the gentle mounds on either side.

"A monster." She was no longer struggling. Instead, she trailed a hand to the back of his neck and drew his head down closer to her mouth.

"Yes." He brushed her lips with his, feathered the edges with his tongue. At the same time, he circled the taut nipples of her breasts with the ice, then began a slow track downward, sliding, skating the cube in a wet track toward the elastic waistband of her shorts. He slipped his hand underneath.

She caught her breath for a half-strangled instant. Then she placed a small kiss, quickly, at first one corner of his mouth and then the other before promising, "You'll pay for this."

"I hope so," he whispered, and flattened his palm, ice nestled in its hollow, against the fluttering surface of her abdomen.

A soft sound, half exclamation, half moan, lifted her chest. He caught her closer and took her mouth in a plundering kiss as an answering shiver ran over his own skin. With easy strength, he pulled her with him as he sank down on the bench. She lifted her legs to the plastic surface, lying against his long length. Carefully, thoroughly, he cooled her, until she writhed against his hand. The blood pounded in his heart, throbbed in the veins of his legs, and pooled with shuddering force at the juncture of his thighs.

Silence caught them, then, broken only by the soft applause of the leaves above them, the calls of birds, and the ceaseless lap of water against the boat as it rocked slowly, endlessly, in the breeze. The ice was soon gone, lost in the rising heat between their bodies.

They removed damp clothes with more haste than finesse. The warm tree shadows caressed their skins, made feathery patterns across them that danced as they moved. There was no one to see their hot, hot joining. No one to watch their rhythmic dance of life.

Completion swept in on them like a summer storm, a thunderous upheaval of nature. Luke caught April to him, stunned and glorified by the moment. He stared down at her, at her face flushed with pleasure, the damp tendrils of her hair that framed it, her parted lips.

"Don't close your eyes," he said in both whispered command and breathless entreaty. "Look at me."

Her lashes swept upward. Dazed, golden and deeply tender, her gaze met his. She saw him. Him, and not some fantasy fictional hero larger than life and as false. She saw Luke Benedict, just a man, with more than his share of a man's faults.

Certain that she knew who was making love to her, he let himself slip over the edge. He carried her with him into the turbulence of the hurricane, flying straight and sure for its windswept center. Then he surrendered and let it take them.

18

April lay among the tangled sheets of the made-down bed and watched the day brighten beyond the screen door. No matter how hard she listened, she could hear no sound of a splashing bath or swim, no treads out on deck as Luke checked their mooring ropes, no soft whir of a line zinging from a reel as he cast for early-morning bass. Everything was quiet, too quiet.

Luke was gone. She was alone again.

She knew why he'd left in the night, or thought she did. He wanted, as much as possible, to avoid being seen coming and going. Still, she wished that he'd discussed the trip with her. She didn't like being on the boat without him. It felt too deserted. She had a sense of being unprotected, vulnerable to whatever or whoever might happen by.

He'd gone for water and fresh food, she knew, but she suspected that wasn't all. No doubt he wanted to find out if anything had changed, if it was all right for them to emerge from hiding. Somehow, she wished he wasn't quite so anxious to get back to civilization. She wasn't, not any more.

It had occurred to her, when she first opened her eyes, that she could get used to this kind of swamp idyll. To be away from the distractions of phones and faxes, E-mail and endless obligations gave her a wonderful sense of freedom. She could almost feel the kinks in her neck and shoulders relaxing and the creative center of her brain expanding. At least, she could as long as Luke was near, on guard. She didn't like it at all without him.

How had she come to this in such a short time? It wasn't supposed to be this way. She couldn't afford to let dependence on Luke become a habit. What would she do when this was over and she went back to normal life at Mulberry Point? Nothing had been said to indicate that their intimacy would carry over to dry land. For all she knew, Luke might view these few days as nothing more than a convenient release from tension, or else a limited association to resolve the issue of her past rejection. He wasn't used to being tied down to one woman, not Luke-de-la-Nuit.

And what was their lovemaking to her? She scouted around that question in her mind, not quite daring to grapple with it. It was difficult enough to get used to the idea that she'd been wrong about Luke and Mary Ellen. To decide where she wanted to go from there was almost impossible.

She heard the helicopter perhaps ten minutes later. She raised her head as she recognized the dull, whipping sound, as if the blades were beating the warm, moisture-laden air like cake batter. It sounded as if it were hovering low, barely above water level. She reared up on her knees, trying to catch sight of it through the window, but the dense foliage of the tree above the boat was in the way. Midnight, at the

foot of the bed, came up on all fours and leaped for
the floor in a single, fluid motion. He streaked to
the darkened bathroom cubicle where the door hung
open, and disappeared inside.

The helicopter passed over perhaps a quarter mile
away. It was close enough to scare the birds into
flight, but not so near that whoever was in it was
likely to spot the boat under its cover. As the noise
of its rotary blades faded into the distance, April
scrambled out of bed and reached for her clothes.

The helicopter returned three times. Once, it flew
within a hundred yards while the air of its passing
swayed the trees and flattened the water's surface.
If its pilot saw anything, however, he gave no sign.
Shortly after noon, he made a final pass and didn't
come back. The quiet afterward seemed unnatural,
almost ominous.

It didn't last long. Two hours later, about the time
April's nerves had calmed enough to allow her to
think about working, she heard a boat. It swept past
some distance out on the lake with its motor whining at a distinctive speedboat pitch. A few minutes
later, it returned from the other direction. Like a
persistent mosquito, it zipped up and down as if
quartering the lake, coming closer and closer to the
opening of the narrow waterway where the pontoon
boat was secreted.

The noise set April's teeth on edge. It annoyed
Midnight, too, so that he hunched on the front deck
with the tip of his tail jerking as regularly as a met-
ronome.

She tried to tell herself the boat rider was a fisherman, or maybe some guy with a new toy that he

had to try out by running it up and down the lake as fast as possible. She assured herself it was a coincidence that he'd shown up so soon after the helicopter incident. She tried to convince herself that the pontoon boat was so well hidden no one could ever find it, so whoever was in the smaller craft was only chasing himself in circles. All the time she was thinking these things, she also wondered when Luke would return, and what would happen if the nut riding up and down saw and recognized him.

Was it possible that was what he was waiting for, to catch Luke before he could reach her? The idea made her feel sick with horror. She wished she had some way to warn him—or to stop him from coming back at all.

Oh, but surely Luke wouldn't be caught in that kind of trap. After the flyover by the spotter plane, he wouldn't come directly to the pontoon boat, but would check out the area with an advance pass or two. If he saw anything at all suspicious out there beyond where she was hidden, he'd steer clear.

That was, of course, if he returned at all. What if Luke had known the sharks would be circling today? What if that was the reason he'd left? It might well be that he'd got what he wanted from her, and was now satisfied to leave her to whatever fate had in store.

No, she wouldn't think like that. There was no good reason, no reason at all.

Still, she had so little idea of what he felt toward her or what he wanted from her. There was only his word for what he was doing there with her or for what had taken place years ago. It was hard to imagine a future based on such meager beginnings.

She wanted to, however; she wanted it too much. It was so important to her, in fact, that she could settle to nothing. She couldn't work, couldn't read or research, couldn't sit still for more than a few seconds. Instead, she paced up and down the boat while frowning over the difference between words like *hope, trust* and *faith*—and also listening, always listening.

Her vigil was rewarded as the sun disappeared below the horizon and the summer twilight began to lay streamers of transparent lavender hues across the water. It was the time of day when shadows grew long and concealing, and the dimming light made vision most uncertain. There was no movement on the meandering waterway, she saw no boat, no outline of a man, yet she was sure she could just catch the dip and swirl of the boat paddle among the quiet splashes of feeding fish.

Gladness rose inside her to swell her chest and warm her heart. The triumph that went with it was equally fierce. She moved to the rail and listened intently while straining to see.

There he was, easing quietly along the near shoreline. It was Luke, it really was, bending and straightening, his muscles flexing and stretching with his steady rhythm. He was less than fifty feet away. As he looked up and saw her, he lifted a hand. Then he bent lower, dug deeper, to send the dinghy surging toward her. He was almost home. He was coming home, to her.

The shot rang out from the opposite bank. It made

a cracking boom that echoed over the water and away through the trees. The thudding impact of the bullet was perfectly audible, as was the choked sound that Luke made as it hit him in the side. He arched as if struck by a knife between the ribs. Then he toppled over the side of the dinghy and hit the water. The force of his fall splayed water around him like a fountain, sending ripples racing toward where April stood.

She gave a gasping cry. A second later, she was over the side in a fast dive. She surfaced and looked wildly around. Spotting the long shape of the boat, she lunged toward it, swimming with hard, purposeful strokes.

Luke wasn't there. He was nowhere near where he'd gone into the lake, nowhere in sight. She made a grab for the dinghy's aluminum gunwale and hung on, gasping for breath as she searched the water's surface. He must have been so badly injured that he'd sunk like flatiron. Dragging air into her lungs, she plunged deep into the murky water.

Something caught her arm, gripping in a hard hold. She shied away instinctively, trying to fight free as it threatened her buoyancy. It did no good. She was propelled upward. Her head broke the water in the shadow of the dinghy, then she was pulled quickly to the lee side, away from the other bank.

"What the hell are you trying to do?" Luke demanded in a furious whisper.

She knew who had her, knew the glide of his body along hers, the feel of his skin and touch of his hands. The knowledge that he was alive, rather than drowning in front of her, sent reaction zinging

along her nerves. Added to it was the instant response to his anger. "I'm trying to save your stupid
life," she answered with in a furious whisper.
"Where did you go?"

"Where any sane person would, out of the line
of fire! But never mind. Get your backside in this
boat and get out of here, now!"

"Are you crazy?" she demanded, searching the
lean lines of his face that were so near as they tread
water together. "You were hit, I saw it. I'm not
going anywhere."

"I'm fine. Anyway, it's not me they want. Come
on, I'll give you a boost."

He wasn't fine. She could see the red swirl of
blood in the water near his side, see its pink stain
on his white T-shirt. "You're hurt. Let me—"

"Damn it all, April," he exploded with desperation in the darkness of his eyes.

"Damn you, Luke Benedict! You—you got out
of the line of fire, but you want me in it?"

"Whoever is out there saw you dive in—hell, the
whole world saw you! I'm betting they don't want
you dead, at least for a while. If you take the boat,
you'll have a chance. Stay here, and you're trapped.
There's no way to get the pontoon boat out before
they get to us. If they get their hands on you, then
I can't—" He stopped, folded his lips in a tight line.

Luke meant that looking out for her would ham-
per his ability to fight. She saw his point, but still
she hesitated. Where was the gunman now? Was he
maneuvering for another shot? Could he be slogging
his way back to wherever the boat he'd come in

was stashed? Or was he sending someone to get them like a hunter retrieving a downed duck?

"You'll still be here," she whispered. "Alone."

"But not without a defense or two. Now get in the damned boat before we both get killed!"

He reached to circle her waist with a long arm, getting ready to hoist her up and over the gunwale that bobbed above their heads. She could fight him, but was by no means sure it would do any good, and the struggle might take more of his strength than he could afford to lose. More than that, he was right; she was the one they were after. Luke was only in danger because of her. If she took the dinghy, she might be able to draw whoever was out there away so he could get to the first aid kit on board the pontoon boat and perhaps to a weapon. At least it would give him a chance.

"All right," she said in low reluctance. "I'll go. But what if I can't find my way back?"

"Don't come back. Go to Turn-Coupe, to Roan."

"And if I get lost trying to do that?"

"I'll find you. This is my swamp. It can hide you from most, but not from me. No matter where you are, I'll find you."

She believed him, believed in the clear purpose in his eyes as he gazed into hers there in the fading purple-gray light. The moment stretched. The water lapped at their chins and pushed them gently against each other. It made small slapping noises against the dinghy that mingled with the tried sound of their breathing.

Then a boat motor roared into life not far away.

Luke's lips thinned as he glanced toward the racket. "They're coming. You have to go. Now."

"Yes," she whispered.

Still, he watched her for a moment longer, as if he would imprint her features in his mind for all time. Then his face twisted as if in pain. Abruptly, he reached to clasp the back of her head and drag her close for a fast, hard kiss.

April returned it, putting all her fear and hope into it, and her love. Then he freed her, pushed her toward the dinghy. She grabbed the cool aluminum above her and kicked hard as she hoisted herself upward. Luke pushed from below. As she jack-knifed into the bottom of the boat, he let his hand trail down her leg and along the bend of her knee. It was a last caress.

"The motor should crank at the first try," he called, his voice no more than a ghost of sound as it drifted to her. "Yank hard, then give it all it's got. Head straight out of here until you reach the channel, then turn west. And don't look back."

His last words were almost lost as the motor exploded into life. Still they repeated themselves in her brain like a litany.

Don't look back. Don't look back. Don't turn to see if he can keep his head above water. Don't watch to make sure he reaches the pontoon boat. Don't check to see if someone is going after him. Don't snatch a last glimpse in case you never see him again.

The instructions were impossible to follow. She had to look as she gunned the motor and sent the dinghy in a turn that sprayed water in a wide arc.

She searched the dancing waves with burning eyes for a last, lingering view of the man she owed so much, the man who had taught her to love. The man she had loved when she was a wise teenager and had never truly stopped loving in all the foolish years since.

He wasn't where she'd left him. His swamp had taken him, hidden him, may even have swallowed him.

A second later, she rounded the small channel's bend and the pontoon boat and wake-rippled cul-de-sac were lost to view. Tears rimmed April's lashes. They spilled over, streaming backward across her cheekbones. She let them come as she hurled the dinghy forward, sent it speeding along the narrow path of water.

The outboard purred as she gripped the combination tiller and throttle. Her wet clothing flapped, splattering droplets of swamp water around her. Ahead of her, she saw a small alligator near the bank sink out of sight at her approach. The enclosing swampland sang its evening song but, though she listened hard, she could hear nothing else. There was no other boat nearby except her own, she thought, though it was impossible to be sure.

Pain and remorse rode with her, but beneath them was slow-growing rage. She'd never thought it would turn out like this, had never expected Luke to be hurt again. She couldn't believe it had happened, and for what? The petty machinations of an individual who had to be sick, or worse? She couldn't stand it. Somehow, some way, she was go-

ing to get to the bottom of it. But first she had to
get to Roan.

Rounding a curve, she saw the wide mouth of the
waterway where it opened into a branching channel.
Beyond it lay a strip of sundown-streaked sky. Silhouetted against the light was a heavy fiberglass
bass boat with the shapes of two men in it. As she
appeared, it roared into life. Then it jerked into motion, churning foam, leading a wide white arrow of
fast-moving wake, as it skimmed forward.

The bass boat was bearing down on her. April
held her course. With her hand steady on the tiller,
she zeroed in on the other craft and headed straight
for it.

One of the men reached into the bottom of the
other boat and came up with a rifle. He nestled it
into his shoulder. The other man yelled and leaned
to shove the barrel skyward. Words were exchanged, then the rifle was set back down where it
came from.

April sped on, coming closer and closer. She narrowed her eyes, trying to make out faces. The two
looked nearly alike in camouflage shirts and pants
that gave them a thick body shape, and with iden-
tical caps pulled low over their eyes. In their same-
ness, they were featureless, impersonal, as stolid as
soldiers.

She was going to hit them. Their boat was not
only heavier, but also wider and more stable in the
water. If they did collide, the dinghy would nose-
dive, might drag her under. She could be crushed
against the other boat.

She didn't care.

The lips of the man at the larger boat's console moved in a curse. He spun the wheel hard right. The fishing boat swerved. April shot past then hit the first rolling wave of its wake.

The dinghy bounced high. She grabbed the side as it came down in the following trough with a bone-cracking thud, then shot up again as it ran into the second wave. The crash as she bottomed again drove her to her knees. She felt the sting of a cut. At the same time, she tasted blood and knew she'd bitten the inside of her mouth.

Then she was dancing over the minor ripples with the double roar of both outboard motors in her ears and the rush of wind in her face. Ahead of her was a baffle of cypress trees. She put her head down and sent the dinghy flying for the widest opening between them.

Behind her, the other boat was turning, crossing the furrows of her lighter wake. The men in it had seen her, knew who she was. They were preparing to chase her down.

Hard exultation swept through April. She could do this, could draw the pursuit away from Luke. She would get away from them, then make it to Roan to bring him back. Nothing was going to stop her. Nothing.

The other boat straightened and raced after her. The thunder of its motor was throttled down now, however. The big fiberglass craft might be more powerful and faster, but these advantages couldn't be used among the trees and curving channels. The dinghy was smaller and more maneuverable, could go places, cut through outlets, where the other boat couldn't. She kept well in front as she zigzagged in and out, taking first one branching waterway and then another, always seeking the widest path. On she sped as the minutes passed.

She tried to remember the way Luke had come. That big dead cypress towering ahead was one she was sure she'd seen before. The rusted metal advertising sign nailed to a stump looked familiar as well, as did the line of plastic milk jugs hanging from a limb that was a fisherman's trotline swept from its moorings during some storm. If she kept heading toward the lightest section of the horizon as best she could make it out through the trees, she should be heading west toward Turn-Coupe.

But the sky was darkening, the night closing in. Everything was beginning to look the same. The speed she was traveling was dangerous in the failing light. It would be easy, too easy, to tear the bottom from the dinghy on a submerged snag or unseen stump. Worse than that, she couldn't search for open water through the trees.

Perhaps ten minutes later, she realized she had lost her sense of direction. She had no idea if the channel she was following led to the lake proper or only deeper into the morass of sloughs and canals cut through the swamp long ago by loggers. It seemed wider than the others, but she thought she should have reached open water by now. Surely Luke hadn't come this far?

He might have, easily, might have backtracked, gone in circles, anything. He'd been trying to confuse her, she knew. It seemed he'd made a good job of it.

As she swung around yet another curve, she saw a fork in channel. Which way, left or right? She had to decide.

She swung left. That way looked familiar. She hoped it wasn't because she was traveling in circles, prayed that it was because she was getting back into an area she had once known in the old days when she'd roamed the lake with Luke.

I'll find you.

The words he had spoken hovered in her mind. They steadied her nerves, comforted her as she watched the waterway narrow. Then she sped along a wide bend, came out into a lily-pad covered pool.

The way she'd turned should have been familiar since she had been there just days before. She had returned to the place where Luke had first anchored the pontoon boat.

April groaned and threw the dinghy into a turn. It was too late, however, and she knew it. The other boat was closing in behind her. Her pursuers were at the bottleneck where the channel and the pool met. They blocked her way. She eased off the gas, letting the dinghy idle in a slow circle through the rocking water hyacinths and lily pads as she tried to think.

The man in the front of the other boat had his rifle lying across his lap. He leaned forward and flipped a switch with a click that came sharp and clear across the water. A spotlight beam flashed across the waves. Its white glare shone full in her face, blinding her. Then a shot exploded. The whining hiss of it crossed in front of her boat then ricocheted off the water and into the crowding ranks of cypress tress.

"Stay where you are! We're coming in. Don't make any trouble and you won't get hurt."

The shouted order came across the water in rough, hard-edged tones amplified by some type of bullhorn. The threat it carried was real. She could go quietly or else.

That voice, flattened and distorted by the water, sounded familiar. It was the voice on the phone.

19

The shanty appeared out of the darkness after what seemed like hours. It squatted at the edge of the lake; a low rectangle thrown together from mixed scraps of raw lumber weathered to mildew gray. The screened porch on the front was so close to the lake that its sagging door opened directly onto the short, rickety catwalk to the dock. No lights shone from any of the house windows. There was no sign of power lines or roads. By all appearances, the place was a primitive camp used only for fishing or hunting and with access solely by water.

Dismay crowded April's chest as she stared at it. The only people who would have much knowledge of the camp were those who used it. Whatever her captors had in mind, it was unlikely they would be interrupted.

She still hadn't seen their faces. The spotlight had been kept in her eyes while the dinghy was attached to the back of the other boat by a mooring rope. Then she'd been towed across the lake like a defeated Cleopatra being hauled into Rome, though with less audience or fanfare. In fact, no had seen them that she could tell. They had steered clear of the main channel, making their way by circuitous back routes with unerring certainty.

Because of that expertise, she could guess the identity of one of the men who had chased her down. There was only one person who fit the job description: hunter, fisherman, gun-toting redneck—delusional maniac.

Frank Randall. It had to be. Anyway, she thought she recognized his sloping shoulders and burly body. In all likelihood, then, this fishing camp was his choice. If it was supposed to be the headquarters for his guide service, she didn't think much of his chances of success.

What did he want with her? What could he want? She could guess, but she wasn't anxious to find out if she was right.

As the two boats came alongside the dock, Frank sprang from the heavier craft and secured it. The other man centered his rifle on April's chest, indicating with a jerk of his head that she should step up onto the dock. When she complied, he moved in behind her. He prodded her with the barrel of his weapon, urging her toward the porch. She walked lightly along the catwalk's rattling boards in her bare feet while Frank skirted both her and her captor and went on ahead. The screen door shrieked on its spring hinges as he opened it, then slammed shut behind the three of them as they crossed the porch and entered the house.

The dark interior smelled of moldy upholstery, rancid bacon grease and sweat. There was also another odor she couldn't quite place. Frank moved deeper into the front room, a drifting shadow that stopped at a shape that appeared to be a table. He picked up something that glinted in the moonlight through the window. Then there came a scratching sound, like a match being struck.

Coal oil, the strange smell was coal oil lamp fuel. She focused on that bit of information while the match he held flared red and gold and lamplight bloomed in the small, dirty room. Then she gathered her courage, and lifted her gaze to stare across the burning flame at Mary Ellen Randall's brother.

His eyes were wide and opaque. If he felt any regret, any doubt about what he was doing, no sign of it showed on his face. He replaced the lamp globe he had removed, shook out the match and tossed it to the tabletop. Then he turned away.

His easy dismissal sent anger through her like a lightning flash. "Why are you doing this?" she demanded. "What have I ever done to you?"

"Nothing," he answered as he turned back with deliberation. "Nothing except high-hat my sister, brush her off as if she were nobody."

"I barely knew her!"

"And didn't want to know her any better," he answered in grating contempt.

It was true, she hadn't. But it wasn't because she thought she was better than Mary Ellen as Frank was suggesting. Mary Ellen hadn't cared for books or ideas or bits of esoteric knowledge, and April had only the most fleeting interest in makeup, clothes and celebrity magazines. Besides, there had been that other problem.

"Your sister wanted Luke," April said. "We could never have agreed on that."

"My sister was a fool," Frank said, his lips twisting with contempt.

April frowned. "But if you think that..."

"You aren't here because of him, April Halstead," broke in a voice behind her. "You're here because of what you did to me."

April stiffened. She turned slowly to stare at the angular figure, the face that had such a masculine cast in its unflattering collection of features, the bulbous hazel eyes and colorless mouth.

"Muriel," she said in a stunned whisper.

The other woman gave a barking laugh. "For somebody who thinks she's so smart, it took you long enough."

It was true. Muriel had been in the service. Muriel had a grudge against her of long standing. Muriel was frustrated and unbalanced, and ready to lash out at the person she blamed for her failures.

Still, it wasn't easy to accept. She had to, however. Muriel still held her rifle and her camouflage pants were muddy to the knees, as if she'd been wading in the swamp.

April, staring at that last telltale evidence, felt her face harden. "You shot Luke."

"He was in my way."

"For what? What do you want with me? For heaven's sake, Muriel, you trashed my book. Wasn't that enough?"

"A fat lot of good that did when it made the bestseller lists anyway! Besides, other people thought it was good, the stupid cows, and kept saying so and saying so. It was too much to bear when my work was just as well written and meaningful. But would you help me bring it to people's notice? Oh, no! You didn't want the competition. You couldn't stand that somebody else might take the limelight away from you. You wanted it all.''

''Your book was—'' April stopped abruptly as she realized telling Muriel hard truths about her story while she pointed a gun at April's breastbone was hardly wise.

''My book was wonderful, a masterpiece!'' Muriel declared with a brightly feral gleam in her eyes.

It had been grandiose, rather, and so derivative it hovered perilously close to plagiarism. There had been at least three phrases that April had recognized as coming directly from her own work, and several others with the familiar style of different authors she knew well. The urge to point out these faults was so strong that she had to struggle with herself to conquer it. ''Your book,'' she said finally, ''had a few problems.''

''It was perfect!''

One of the great mysteries of writing, April thought, was that the person closest to a work was least able to see its defects. ''I'm sorry,'' she said, ''but we have an honest difference of opinion. I didn't set out to harm you in any way, and would have been happy to help if I had thought—''

''Liar! You're a lying bitch,'' Muriel declared, with spittle collecting at the corners of her dry lips. ''You've never done anything for anybody.''

''That's not true.''

"You're selfish and egotistical and so sure of yourself that it was ridiculously easy to make a fool of you. But I've got you now, and you're going to write me a bestseller to make up for the one you took away. You're going to finish your work in progress and turn it over to me."

"I don't think so," April said with steel in her voice.

"You'll do it or you'll starve. Or maybe I'll find some other way to change your mind. Maybe I'll let Frank, here, help me. You're not his sister, but could be he'd like to pretend for a little while."

"Shut up, Potts!" Frank growled from behind April. There was angry recoil in his voice, but also a desperate self-loathing that didn't sound good. It didn't sound good at all.

April lifted her chin as she held Muriel's gaze. "You can't keep me here that long. Even if you could, I don't know how you can expect me to turn out decent work."

"It won't be that long. For the rest, what's the big deal? You can write anywhere."

April laughed; she couldn't help it. "It takes more than just putting words on paper. You need concentration and emotional involvement, and the less stress, the better. Besides, I don't have the manuscript. And I don't see a computer here anywhere."

"No problem," Muriel replied with grim satisfaction. "I broke into your office and printed out a nice clean copy from your hard drive. And longhand will do just fine for the rest. I can always transcribe it later."

"You've been in my house, in my computer

files?'' It was difficult to say which felt like the greater violation. The idea of either was enough to make her shake with rage.

Muriel took off her cap and tossed it aside, then ran bony fingers through her thin blond hair. ''Piece of cake,'' she said with offhand satisfaction. ''That old house of yours is like a sieve. And we use the same word processor.''

''I've added a great deal to the story in the past few days. You don't have that.''

''So, that's what you've been up to out in the damned swamp. I thought you were getting it on with your nighttime Luke. Doesn't matter. Frank can go get the extra pages.''

She had an answer for everything, April saw, but she had one last card to play. ''You'll never get away with it. My writing style is distinctive. Anyone who knows my books will recognize it. Even a judge will be able to see it, I think, if I show him the original story proposal and my research notes.''

''So, I'll rewrite a few sentences here and there. Problem solved,'' Muriel said with a hard glitter in her eyes. ''But I don't think you'll be going to court.''

The only way April might fail to lay claim to her work was if she wasn't around to prove her authorship. That meant Muriel didn't intend for her to live long after she typed ''The End'' on the manuscript.

Muriel Potts would benefit from all her hard work. Muriel would claim her story about Luke's family. Muriel would benefit from the exploitation of his history, the intimate family story of the man she'd shot. April couldn't stand it. It was all wrong, a desecration of monumental proportion.

As these thoughts struck April one by one, she felt a major shift inside her. Suddenly she understood why Granny May objected so strenuously to her using the Benedict family history. The sense of trespass must be far stronger in someone who'd been a part of the family so many long years.

She, April Halstead, would never be a Benedict. And that was something she wanted now with such anguished longing that she felt sick with it. Strange, but she might never have realized either Granny May's position or her own desires if she hadn't been forced out of her seclusion and self-absorption by Muriel Potts. Now that she knew, it was too late.

Too late to tell Luke how much he'd meant to her long ago. Too late to let him know how constantly he'd been in her thoughts all these long years, how he had lived with her so vividly in her fantasies that she'd turned him into the dream lover of millions of women. Too late to apologize for letting her fears convince her of his guilt in Mary Ellen's death. Too late to tell him she believed in him now, or that she loved him and always had, always would. Too late to let him know that he was right in his suspicions, and he'd always been her hero.

It was also too late to discover if he'd felt anything for her in the days they'd just spent together except protective concern based on the past and simple sexual appetite.

She really couldn't stand it.

"Nothing else to say?" Muriel asked, her thin lips curling. "That's smart, but then you've always been that, haven't you? Fine. In the meantime, I think I'll have the famous romance author cook me dinner while Frank goes and gets my manuscript.''

"You want it now?" Frank asked, putting his hands on his hips.

"Now!" Muriel snapped as she turned to him. "I want her butt in a chair working by good daylight in the morning. She can get on faster if she picks up where she left off.''

His face set, he said, "I don't think going back there is a good idea.''

"I'm not paying you to think, buster! I'm paying you to do whatever the hell I say. Get our ass back out there and don't come back without every scrap of paper she had on that boat. You got that?''

His only answer was a grunt. Stalking into the back of the two-room shack, he returned a moment later with a second rifle. With it hanging from his hand like a part of his body, he slammed out through the screen door with a force that made the walls shudder. His booted heels sounded on the dock. There was a silence during which April thought he was probably detaching the dinghy from the big fishing boat. Then the heavier craft rumbled into life and sped away.

"You do know how to cook, don't you?''

April's concentration on what was happening outside was so strong that she started at that snide question. Glancing around, she saw that the table where the lamp sat was part of a rudimentary kitchen that took up one corner of the front room. A cheap metal cabinet holding a sink could just be made out in the dim lamplight, along with what looked like a woodstove.

"On that?" She nodded at the ancient contraption of pig iron and corroded nickel.

"Why not?"

"It will take forever for the thing to get hot enough to cook. By the time it does, this place will be like an oven."

"So?"

Forcing April to do her bidding was plainly more important to Muriel than logic or comfort. Not that it mattered, April told herself. It wasn't as if she had anything else to do, or would be able to sleep if she were ever allowed to go to bed. This way, Muriel could be lulled into thinking that she was going to accept her situation. There would be other, more important, battles to be fought.

With an attempt at a negligent shrug, she asked, "So, what do you want to eat?"

The menu they settled on wasn't exactly gourmet fare. The hardest part was building a fire in the old stove. Kindling and newspaper had been stacked beside it, however, along with sticks of stove wood. In a short time, the makeshift meal of canned meat, canned beans and potatoes steamed with onion was cooking. As an added bonus, the heat of the stove finished drying April's shorts and tank top as well as the long, tangled skein of her hair.

As she stood over the stove, turning slabs of meat with a three-tined fork, she thought of all the things that had happened to her in the past week and more. Glancing at Muriel, who had moved to lounge at the table with a beer in front of her that she'd taken from an ice chest, she said, ''Was that really you on the phone during my interview. Or did Frank—''

''Frank? That wuss?'' Muriel leaned back in her chair and hooked a thumb in one pants pocket. ''Lord, he's such a redneck that he blushes whenever he thinks of talking to a woman, much less saying dirty things to her in public. Of course I did it, dummy, with the help of modern electronics. The deal for the phone that changes women's voices to men's was a Christmas present from my mom, bless her heart. Just like I hadn't learned enough about protection in the service to send most would-be burglars or attempted rapists to the hospital—or the morgue.''

''Is that how you know Frank, from the service?''

''Think you're smart, don't you? Yeah, we ran across each other in a beer garden in Germany, would you believe. My ears perked up when I heard he was from the place listed in your books as your hometown. I was a big fan about then, you know, wanted to know all about you. Ain't that a laugh?''

''So, he told you—''

''He was drunk. He spilled a lot of things that came in handy when I decided to make my move. You might say I couldn't have done it without him and his grudge against Benedict.''

''But you're the one who threw the acid at Luke?''

''And made off with your cat, shot up your house and all the rest. Frank wasn't in it until later. You were the one who was supposed to have your face all scarred like a freak, though. Benedict just got in the way.''

"I should have guessed, since it happened in your territory."

"I was too smart to leave you any clues. Anyway, you might not be here if your Luke hadn't been around that weekend. It was after I missed that I decided to get you but good." Muriel took a swig of her beer. "Well, and after I heard somebody sniggering about how you'd paid me back for that review."

"I see. Tit for tat." She also saw that the other woman had more than her share of ego, something that might come in handy.

"Yeah. You sent my career and my life down the toilet, so I'm returning the favor."

April gave a slow shake of her head. "I failed to endorse your book, that's all. It was one person's opinion, not a wholesale attempt to ruin you."

"Oh, cut the crap, will you? When you refused to endorse my book, my publisher turned down my next. My live-in boyfriend found out about that and figured my writing wasn't going to be the cash cow he'd hoped, so he skipped a week before the wedding. I had dreams, plans for babies, a family. Instead, I went from being a bride-to-be to a reject overnight, from a Wanna-be to a Has Been without stopping off at being a Somebody. Now I'm back doing shitty little reviews and teaching writing classes. And you're surprised that I'm pissed?"

For the first time, April understood the bitter disappointment etched in Muriel's face, sensed the pain behind the pseudomasculine bravado. April had always known that being a romance author wasn't all glamour and magic, that it had more frustrations and sorrows than rewards and a failure rate that made becoming a professional football player look like a shoo-in. She'd shed her own tears at times, but hadn't been around too often for those of others. Like most successful authors, she tended to stick with her own kind at professional gatherings. It wasn't because she wanted to be exclusive but simply because she was more comfortable around people who understood the pressures of the game, and because so many beginners wanted things from her that she couldn't give and still hold on to her own creativity or integrity.

"I'm sorry," she said abruptly. "I didn't realize."

"No, you wouldn't, would you? You're too busy being a superstar, too wrapped up in your stories and—oh, never mind." Muriel drank more of her beer, maybe to dissolve the sudden tightness that sounded in her voice.

Frowning, April tried again. "I mean it. I really am sorry. I know it's hard—"

"You don't know diddly."

"What makes you think so?" she returned in a spurt of anger. "I wasn't born a romance author, you know. We all have to start somewhere. I've had my rejections and story ideas that didn't work. I've had publishers who dropped the ball on promotion or didn't do what they promised. I've felt that I can't write another word or another page, or that everything I've gained has been only because of luck. I've had agents and editors and publishers talk as if what I do or have done doesn't count, that it was all their big plans and promotions or deals or whatever that put me where I am, and so I should be grateful that they allow me to—'' April stopped herself, as Muriel had done, afraid her voice would break if she went on.

''Right, but it's all worked out for you, hasn't it?''

''So far,'' April agreed, blindly turning meat with her fork. ''But there's no guarantee that it always will.''

''Which doesn't mean that you'd do a damned thing different for me if you had it to do over again.''

That much was true. She wouldn't lie and say that Muriel's book was good when it had been terrible. She couldn't use the name she'd worked so hard to build to endorse a title that might make readers buy a book they thought would be great but she knew wasn't worth the money. More than that, she knew in her more upbeat moments that a lot more was required to reach the top besides luck and publisher support. It also took talent, craftsmanship, a willingness to work long, hard hours, and the ability to look beyond the first idea that came along for that fresh and unique slant. Plus something more than could only be described as heart: you had to feel it or it didn't work.

Muriel laughed with a mirthless sound, as April remained silent. ''That's what I thought.''

''Why can't you do something else,'' she asked. ''Why does it have to be romance writing?''

''You can say that?'' Muriel answered with a pitying shake of her head. ''Why can't you do something else? Why do you write?''

"I write for the stories that are like carrying whole other worlds around in my head. I write for the flow of words that run through my brain like a song with flow and rhythm and sudden high notes of meaning that thrill me, if no one else. I write for the joy."

"That's it," the other woman said with a slow nod. "Yeah. Only now I can't have that any more because of you. Which puts us right back where we started."

So it did. April turned the meat and potatoes and said no more.

Muriel was a professional. She kept her rifle near her right hand, and was aware of every move April made. She watched her as she ate, stayed close while she washed the dishes, and followed her out the back door of the rear bedroom when they both visited the outdoor toilet. Afterward, she handcuffed April's wrist to the frame of the sagging bed in the back room, then lay down on the other side of the mattress. She slept in light catnaps, but jerked awake every time April moved.

April couldn't sleep. The mattress was lumpy and sour smelling, she needed a bath, a comb to rake the tangles from her hair, and something to sleep in besides her clothes. The handcuff cut off her circulation so her fingers felt numb. It was hot and stuffy in the shanty compared to the pontoon boat, and the tin roof overhead snapped and popped as it released the broiling heat of the day.

After a while, the moon rose, shining through the dirty window in one wall. In the ambient glow,

April stared around the room at the unfinished walls with faded shirts and jackets hung on nails. She noted the complete absence of pictures or any effort to decorate that declared the place a male strong-hold, and studied the back door that lead to the toilet. She let her gaze linger on the rifle Muriel had leaned in the corner on her side of the bed, then shivered a little as she looked away again.

Something else stood there next to the rifle. At first April thought it was a mop or broom, but then decided it was another weapon, a deer rifle. It made sense if the place was used for hunting.

Exhausting the possibilities of the room, she lay still while her mind moved in endless circles. She thought of Luke, wondering if he was all right, where he was, and what he might be doing. All the things they had said and done played over and over in her mind along with everything she maybe should have said or should have done. She considered her work and what it meant to her, both what she was writing and what Muriel wanted from her, and also a thousand other things.

Somewhere in the midnight hours, she came to a decision. She'd rather die, she thought, than let Muriel steal her ideas or profit from her hard labor.

She wanted very much to live, however, to have all the pleasure, and yes, the pain, that being alive might bring. She was tired of being a recluse, of hiding from responsibility to others and from her own needs and feelings. No matter what happened, she'd seen the last of that pose. She meant not merely to live, but to be wholly, vividly alive, and to know it.

Before that could happen, she must get away from Muriel. She required transportation: a boat and a supply of gas. She needed to reach Roan and convince him to take her back to Luke. She had to see if he was okay, to talk to him and discover if they had a future.

It was essential that she have a plan.

The idea came to her in the early hours of morning, not long after she heard the bass boat as Frank returned with her notebook. Those pages, along with her work in progress, were key to the whole thing. That was what she would use.

It would require a sacrifice. She hated it, felt the pain already from just the thought. It couldn't be helped. She had her priorities straight now; she knew what was important in a way she never had before. Besides, there was no other way.

Would Muriel fall for it? April didn't know. She'd have to wait and see.

The next day passed slowly while April waited for her chance. She spent it being as quiet and polite as her temper and her pride would allow and hoping that would feed Muriel's ego and lull her into carelessness. It wasn't easy. Muriel not only dragged her from bed before dawn but laughed at her request for a change of clothes, forced her to cook breakfast, then sat her down with pen in hand and refused to let her eat or drink unless she wrote a page every hour.

April kept her head down to hide the rage inside her. She worked, too, scribbling something, anything, for hour after hour. It didn't matter what she put on paper because Muriel made no effort to read it after the first page or two. Precisely because April wasn't trying, wasn't editing her thoughts, however, the sentences came in a steady and nicely coherent progression. She thought she needed to take a lesson from that.

At first, her attention was diverted whenever she heard a boat motor out on the lake. She listened as long as it was in hearing distance, waiting to see if it was Luke coming to find her. Then she noticed Muriel watching her with narrow eyes and a small, chill smile on her mouth. After that, April kept her interest to herself.

Sweat rolled off April during the hot afternoon, dripping from the ends of her hair and dampening the paper under her hand and wrist. Flies tormented her, sticky houseflies that buzzed around her head and walked along her arms with germ-laden feet, also stinging deerflies that found her bare legs under the table. These were joined by mosquitoes, blood-thirsty little dive-bombers that whined around her head as if to tell her secrets before they chose a spot on her exposed skin to have their afternoon snack. The insects came in droves through the rusty and torn screens over the windows that, like the doors at front and rear, were thrown wide-open to catch the least hint of a lake breeze. But there was none, just the relentless, scalding heat and white-hot glare of the sun.

The sun went down like dropping the old-fashioned roller curtain of a minstrel show. As the light went with it, April closed her notebook with the pages she'd done for the day and stacked it neatly on top of the printed copy of the manuscript that Muriel had taken from Mulberry Point. Rising from her chair, she stretched the kink out of her back with her eyes squeezed shut and her arms above her head.

"What do you think you're doing?" Muriel inquired with a whip edge to her tone from where she sat in the doorway, fanning herself with her cap bill.

"It's too dark to see. I thought..."

"You don't think here, got that? I tell you what to do and you jump."

April clenched her jaws to keep the sharp retort at the end of her tongue from escaping. Between the heat, the uncertainty and Muriel's harassment, she wasn't sure how long she could hold on without exploding. It was possible, however, that she might use Muriel's petty vengeance to achieve what she intended.

Lifting her hair off the back of her neck, April sought for a complaining whine as she said, "It's just so hot, too hot to work, almost too hot to breathe. I hope you don't expect me to cook anything tonight, because there's just no way. I'd rather die than light that stupid stove."

"That can be arranged," Muriel said, putting a hand on the rifle over her lap and caressing the smooth, wooden butt.

"Oh, come on, Muriel!" April wailed. "Have a heart."

"Steak and fries, I got me a yen for steak and fries. Hey, Frank, don't you want some steak and fries?"

Frank only grunted from where he lay on the floor of the porch with his cap over his face, rifle propped against the porch screen beside him, and a row of empty beer bottles nearby.

April resisted an impulse to stamp her foot like some virginal heroine in an old-fashioned romance from the fifties. That would, she felt, be carrying the act a bit too far. Spinning away in a show of pique, she huffed over her shoulder, "I can't believe you! I think you enjoy watching me suffer."

"I can't say I exactly hate it." The other woman's drawl was flat.

With another resentful glance, April reached for the lamp on the table and lit it. The flare of orange-red light, dim as it might be, made it appear darker outside than it really was. That was something she'd have to watch.

She turned to the cookstove and jerked open the wood box door. Muttering under her breath, she proceeded to lay a fire with newspaper and pine kindling and a few pieces of split wood. Flames were soon roaring up the chimney.

She was in no rush to put the steaks on, which was natural enough since the stove needed to get hot. She found a heavy iron skillet and scoured it out, then dried it over the slowly building heat of the stove. After taking the steaks from the ice chest, she made a marinade from salad dressing and let the meat sit in it. She could have peeled the potatoes while she was waiting, but that would have speeded up the process which was the last thing she needed. Instead, she puttered around, washing dishes and wiping cabinets like a busy little housewife. When she felt it would be too obvious to delay any longer, she heated bacon drippings left over from the morning, then laid the steaks in the pan. As they began to sizzle, she turned them carefully, taking pains to see they browned uniformly.

She was so hot from hovering over the stove that she felt light-headed with it. It didn't matter. Exhilaration hummed in her veins along with grim anticipation. She used the poker to stir the fire to greater heat, then added two more sticks of oak to it.

"You got it smelling good around here," Frank said, lifting his head and raising his cap brim to stare at her through the door. "But a man could starve to death before you get supper on the table, the way you're going."

"I like things just so." April gave him what she hoped was a nervous-looking smile, then surveyed the dimming light beyond the screen. It would be at least another quarter hour before good dark. She needed a distraction, she thought, at least a small one.

Getting out the potatoes, she rinsed them in a pan of water. As she took up her knife to start peeling, she glanced toward Frank. "I've been thinking about Mary Ellen. Luke had a few things to say about her the other day."

"Don't want to talk about it." Frank retreated beneath his cap again.

"No? Don't you want to hear his side of it, or at least know what he said about your sister's last night?"

"Won't change a thing."

"That's not true, you know. It might not change the facts, but it could change how you feel about them. That's something, at least." When he said nothing in return, she continued, "He's sorry, you know. Sorry that she died, sorry that he couldn't give her whatever it was she wanted from him. Most of all, he's sorry that he couldn't save her."

"Yeah, so am I. So what?"

"He said she didn't take her own life. Oh, she was talking about it, maybe even had the impulse, but a lot of teenagers do that. For some it means something, for others, nothing. Your sister tried to avoid the wreck that killed her. She swerved off the road to keep from hitting that busload of kids coming home from a church revival meeting. It was an accident, that's all. Just an accident." She thought Frank was staring at her, but this time she busied herself slicing potato rounds into French fries instead of meeting his gaze.

"He said that, did he?" Frank asked.

"Yes, he did." Actually, she'd embroidered a little on what Luke had said, but had kept to the spirit of it. She thought the circumstances warranted the white lie.

Frank snorted. "She'd still be alive if she hadn't gone with him."

"Maybe. But he didn't force her into his car, you know. She invited herself because she was upset. Could be the blame lies with whoever caused her to feel that way that night."

"Me, you mean."

"If you're the one who made her cry."

He stared at her a long moment. Then he said deliberately, "It's too late. Things have gone too far."

Did he mean it was too late for Mary Ellen? Too late for Luke? Or was he telling her it was too late to change what would happen to her? From the steely look in his eyes, it could have been any of them—or all. From the corner of her eye, she saw Muriel was watching their byplay with an unreadable expression on her face.

Tilting her chin, April said in quiet challenge, "Is it? Is it, really?"

Frank didn't answer. A curl of smoke rose from the steak pan. April looked down hastily to see that they were browning too fast.

She turned one piece of meat to check its doneness, then transferred it from the skillet to a plate. When she'd taken up the other, she added cooking oil and let it heat while she finished with the potatoes. As she dropped the fries into the hot oil, the sound of the hissing, crackling grease filled the quiet then died down again.

April watched the fries with one eye while keeping the other on the deepening night. She might prolong things a little more by browning slices of bread in the leftover bacon grease, but she thought Muriel might become suspicious at such a cholesterol-laden treat. Anyway, she thought that she'd drawn her meal preparation out long enough.

She took up the fries as they browned and put them on a plate, then she turned to set it on the table. In a show of making room for them to eat, she picked up the pile of manuscript with her notebook on top, cradling both in the crook of her arm while she shifted the lamp more to the center. She served the steaks onto plates then, and put them and eating forks in front of three chairs.

As she worked, she let her gaze linger on the window that opened behind the table, measuring its height with her eyes one last time, checking its rusted screen that barely hung in the frame. Yes, she had wasted enough time.

At the stove once more, she took a folded rag and used it as a pot holder to open the firebox of the stove as if to tend it one last time before closing the damper. At the sudden draft, heat and a few sparks boiled up toward the dirty ceiling overhead.

"I've decided something, Muriel," she said conversationally as she set the folded rag aside.

"Whoop-de-do." Muriel got to her feet with her gaze on the plates of food. Behind her, Frank began to lever himself from the floor to an upright position.

"I don't think I'm going to let you have my book." Taking her manuscript and notebook in both hands, she bent the pages nearly double.

Muriel barely looked at her. "You've got nothing to say about it. Wha––!"

April might have laughed at the woman's look of jaw-dropped horror, and would have if she'd had the time. But she didn't.

She was too busy shoving her unfinished book into the red-hot maw of the cookstove fire.

20

Muriel screamed and lunged toward the stove. Dropping her rifle, she snatched up the poker and rammed it into the firebox door. The scattered sheaves of pages inside crackled and flamed. Bits of burning paper and ash flew into the air as she raked a few sheets of flaming manuscript out onto the floor and began to stamp at them with her booted foot.

April didn't wait to see more. Whirling toward the window behind the table, she took three running steps then threw herself at the rusty screen. The rotted wooden frame burst outward. She tumbled over the sill and into the dark beyond.

Stinging pain lanced through her shoulder as she hit the ground. She ignored it as she rolled, then scrambled upright. Behind her, she heard Frank yelling and Muriel cursing. A large shadow crossed the window opening she'd just vacated, looming across it. April put her head down and ran.

Tree limbs snatched at her. Brambles clawed her legs and bit into her bare feet. Her heart pounded in her chest and her breath burned in her throat. Behind her, a shot rang out. She stifled a cry and ducked automatically. Two more shots blasted. She heard their bullets cutting through the tree leaves above her.

Frank was shooting at the noise she was making, April thought. Either that or he didn't intend to hit her. She halted abruptly and stood trying to decide which it was while also catching her breath. Glancing over her shoulder, she saw him jump down from the window. He was silhouetted for a second by the light of the lamp glow from inside the shack, then he moved off in her direction. He swung his head from side to side as he searched the darkness.

He didn't seem too sure of where she was, she thought. It seemed best to go with that idea, since the alternative could get her killed. Easing away a few steps, she pivoted sixty degrees from the direction she'd been heading. Then she took off again, circling toward the rear of the shack with as much stealth as she could manage. Thankfully, Frank didn't deviate from his path.

She had escaped, but now what? The shack was just off the main body of the lake, she was fairly sure, which meant that the land directly behind it was less swampy. The direction of the sun during the day indicated that Turn-Coupe should still be to the west. It was at least twelve or fifteen miles to the main road through deep woods cut by countless little creeks and branches that all looked the same. A few dirt-and-gravel roads wound around the lake, but she might or might not cross one. Chances were high that she'd get lost before she'd gone a mile.

The best escape route was by water, then, using the boat at the dock. However, that was exactly what Frank and Muriel would expect her to try. The slam of the screen door at the front of the house was a strong indicator that the ex-romance writer was even now moving to cut off access.

What was she going to do? April thought frantically. Run? Hide? Swim for it?

Running was out, period. She had no faith in hiding, waiting to be found, even if there had been decent cover. She swam well enough but had scant chance of reaching safety before she was chased down by boat. So, what was left?

If this was one of her romance novels, and her heroine had just saved herself so handily, it would be time for the hero to come charging up to complete the rescue and deal with the villains. It didn't seem likely to happen. Nothing moved out on the lake and there was not a whisper of an outboard motor's roar. April had no one to depend on except herself.

Regardless, she had once written a scene with an escaping heroine who had doubled back like a vixen with the hounds after her, going to ground, so to speak, in the cave where she'd been held. Yes, and hadn't she found herself a weapon...?

A weapon. There had been an extra rifle in the shanty's back bedroom.

Was it still there? If she could reach it, would she have the nerve to use it? She'd never fired a gun in spite of all Luke's attempts to teach her years ago. She knew the theory from those days and from researching action scenes for her books, but that was all. She despised the heft and polished smoothness of firearms, hated their deadly purpose. They were connected in her mind with loss and change, with blood and terror and the horror of seeing her father lying sprawled in death across her mother's body. She wasn't sure she could bring herself to touch the rifle, much less load and fire it.

Was her aversion as strong as her need to live? It looked as if she might have to find out. Whatever she did, she needed to make up her mind and go for it. Time was running out.

April closed her eyes and squeezed them tight. Then she jerked into motion once more, heading back toward the house.

As she reached the rear wall, she flattened against it. Foot by foot, she eased closer to the back door-steps of the bedroom. This was her best chance. At the south side of the house, one end of the catwalk had steps leading to the dock and the screen porch entrance, but the screen door would screech like a night owl if she tried to open it. Muriel was still in front guarding the dock. She thought Frank was still on the north side of the house, searching the edge of the woods where it touched the lakeshore. She just hoped he stayed there.

The back door had been open for air before, and it still stood open. Silent as a cat, April eased up the steps and slipped into the bedroom.

The lamp still burned in the kitchen. Its light fell in a dim triangle through the connecting doorway. April stood listening, but could hear no movement from the other room. The smell of burning paper was strong in the air, and she felt a brief pang for her vanished words, lost time and effort. Then she banished it from her mind as she glanced toward where the firearm leaned in the corner.

It was as she'd thought, a hunting rifle. She reached for it, then curled her fingers into a fist. The reluctance she felt was much like reaching out to pick up a snake. The barrel of the weapon looked just as dark and deadly.

Then from the front of the house, Muriel shouted out. "April! Where are you?"

April grabbed the rifle, lifting it by the barrel and swinging it under one arm. It was a 30.06 automatic, well balanced and not too hefty. Stacked beside it were several boxes of ammunition of different caliber. She sorted quickly through them, found the right one. Dumping the shells on the bed, she loaded the rifle's clip, snapped it back in place with shaking fingers, and stuffed the remaining ammo into the pocket of her shorts.

"April! Come out here! You can't hide from us!" The yell was punctuated by a fusillade of shots.

She froze in place with her breath caught in her throat and the rifle held in front of her like a shield. Then she realized Muriel couldn't know where she was or she'd be tearing back into the shack. No doubt she thought April was hiding in the woods and hoped to flush her out.

Muriel might get more than she bargained for, April thought in grim resolve as she breathed again. The woman had shot Luke, had cornered and humiliated her and forced her to destroy something important to her. Now she was standing between her and the freedom to discover what had happened to the man she loved.

Strange, but the firearm she held no longer felt like a threat. It was, instead, a source of empowerment, the means to help her get what she needed. She tucked it under her left arm in a loose hold. Then she set her lips in a straight line and moved toward the door.

Seconds later, she was outside again. Moving soundlessly, she left the back step and started toward the south corner. As she approached the turn, she stopped, took a quick look, then drew back again.

The portion of the dock she'd been able to see was clear, but the screen porch prevented a full view. Nothing had moved in the general vicinity that she could tell, still she hesitated. She wasn't exactly anxious to fire on a human being unless it was absolutely necessary. She frowned and held her breath as she tried to locate Muriel and Frank by sound.

From somewhere in the distance came a ripping buzz, as if someone had fired up a Jet Ski. A rumbling echo followed it, as if several fast boats had been cranked up and were idling around each other. It reminded April of the noise made by the teenagers from the more ritzy lake houses as they faced off for night races down the main channel. The far-off sound only emphasized the quiet around her.

No hum of electricity came from inside the shack, no traffic noises intruded or sirens wailed. There wasn't even the racket of a barking dog. The lake lapped against the pilings of the dock. A breeze fluttered the tops of the trees. Other than that, there was only the mating chorale of insect multitudes.

Then from the other side of the house, she caught a quiet curse, as if someone had stumbled or run into a briar vine in the dark. Frank and Muriel must have given up on the lakefront and were working their way through the woods behind the house. If April didn't move, they might catch sight of her. Tightening her grip on the rifle, she stepped around the corner.

Muriel was less than four feet away. She let out a squawk and started to bring up her weapon. April didn't pause, didn't think. In a sudden rush of white-hot fury, she stepped forward, doubled her fist, and struck straight and hard for the woman's midsection.

Muriel sucked air in a wheezing gasp. She clamped a hand to her belly as she brought the barrel of her rifle around in an awkward swing. April ducked, then came up from her crouch with a punch aimed at Muriel's nose.

It struck true. April felt flesh and bone give under her knuckles. Pain raced up her arm to her elbow. As Muriel howled and stumbled back to land on the seat of her pants, April stepped clear. Then she sprinted for the dock and the dinghy that lay tied up at its end.

It was the snick of the safety catch being released that warned her. Before she'd fully registered the sound she was diving, rolling toward the near end of the dock. The first shot tore up ground where she'd been, the second splintered a piling, and the third kicked mud and water into her hair as she scuttled behind the protection of the wooden staging.

The rage that exploded inside her obliterated thought. It wiped away fear and doubt and the last vestige of rattled nerves. Her every instinct quieted to a deadly calm. She saw nothing, heard nothing,

except the firing of Muriel's rifle and the red streaks
that marked her position. Stretched out behind the
flimsy barricade of the dock, April brought her own
rifle to bear.

It was as if the years disappeared and she was
with Luke once more, a healthy teenager in shorts
and a ponytail lying beside a lanky, hard-muscled
boy. She could almost hear his careful instruction:
*Snug the rifle butt into your shoulder. Bring the
crosshairs into alignment. Don't jerk the trigger but
squeeze evenly.*

It worked. The 30.06 bucked and Muriel
screeched, then scrabbled for the cover of the house.
April sent another shot flying after her to encourage
her to stay hidden.

Then Frank was yelling and Muriel shouting
back. Within seconds, it seemed, April was under
fire from a new angle. The shots were high, kicking
up water behind her, but she kept her head down,
covering it with her arm. As they stopped and the
echoes traveled away through the trees, she waited
until she thought there might be a target. Then she
bobbed up, sent two fast shots toward the north
house wall where Frank stood, and dropped back
down again.

She hadn't hit anything and she knew it. She'd
been in too much of a hurry, been too afraid that
Frank's aim was steadier and better than Muriel's
had been. In the sudden quiet, she thrust her hand
into her pocket for shells and began to reload. Even
as she chambered a shell, shoved more into the clip,
and snapped it in place again, her brain raced. Her
chances didn't look good. She was outnumbered and

outgunned. All Frank and Muriel had to do was co-ordinate their fire, pin her down then close in and finish her off. She could give them a little trouble, but her cover was scant and her ammunition limited, so it was just a matter of time. Unless, of course, she killed one or both of them.

Could she? She wasn't sure. So far, she'd been intent on doing damage, not taking their lives. She thought desperation and the blessed numbness of her adrenaline high might combine to overcome her reluctance, but she wasn't sure. There was only one way to tell.

Dear God, how had she come to this? What had she done that she was forced to fight for her life in the mud against a crazy woman and a burned-out drunk? She was a writer, not ex-service personnel like Muriel. She hated killing roaches and flies, much less anything warm-blooded. Fast-moving action scenes on paper were one thing, but living them was another kettle of fish altogether.

Damn Luke Benedict for getting himself shot, and damn him for not being here when she needed him. But she wasn't going to cry over it. She wasn't. No. What she was going to do was make Muriel Potts and Frank Randall extremely sorry that they'd mistaken her quiet life-style and polite manners for weakness, or that they had ever tangled with a woman who plotted convoluted stories with sneaky endings for a living.

She'd be damned if she was going to die before she told Luke Benedict to his face that she loved him.

I'll find you.

He'd said that, and he'd meant it, she knew it with every shred of her heart's fiber and every beat it made. If he had not followed through, it was because it wasn't possible. That was all right. Though there was nothing she'd like more this minute than to have him there beside her with his arms around her, it didn't have to be that way. If he couldn't find her, then she would make her way back to him. She would do it because she must. She would do it if it was the very last thing she accomplished on this earth. She'd do it because she knew he loved her even if he never said it.

There was no time like now.

She sprang up in a rush of mud and water and poured a couple of fast shots toward first one corner of the house and then the other. Hard on them, she hit the water, splashing toward where the dinghy was tied, swimming as the water deepened. She had a few seconds, a precious few, for she'd heard Muriel's invective, seen Frank duck behind the house. If they would only stay down a minute longer...

The explosion of rifle fire and crack of shattering wood was muffled by the water around her ears as she dog-paddled with one arm and tried to hold the 30.06 above water with the other. She couldn't look to see, wouldn't think about, what the other two were doing. All her energy and concentration was centered on reaching the aluminum dinghy.

It loomed above her sooner than she expected. The rifle made a dull clatter as she heaved it inside. She clung a moment to the back of the motor, gathering her strength and her courage. Then the dull thud of a bullet striking metal sent her swirling around to the far side. Hand over hand, she made for the front and the line that held the bobbing craft. It was tied in a slipknot, as it had been tied the night when she'd tried this before, so short a time ago, yet so long.

She jerked the knot loose, shoved the shallow fishing boat away from the dock. Then she clung to the rope as it pulled her into the lake with its momentum. She wasn't sure she had the strength to lift herself over the side, or the nerve left to try. Even if she did, she feared she'd be picked off the instant she showed her head above the gunwale, long before she could get the motor started.

She couldn't do it. She wasn't going to make it.

Abruptly the world shook with a thunderous roar. White light blossomed, spreading, pushing back the night and taking all color and sight with it. She felt no pain, no wrenching agony of separation. One moment she was alone, struggling in the water. The next she was encompassed by warm closeness, buoyed up in sheltering arms. She floated, comforted and at peace, locked in the eternal shelter she had needed all her days without knowing it, sought all her life and never found. And peace settled over her, touching her soul, except for one small, desolate corner where regret lived that she had not reached Luke, after all.

Luke, her only hero ever. Her whole life long.

"You can let go of the line. I've got you now."

That low-voiced growl came from beside her ear. Luke...

She started so violently that she wrenched away from him, went under. She swallowed a large portion of the lake and came up coughing, clinging helplessly to a hard and intimately familiar shoulder. Luke grinned into her face, supporting her, while beyond him loomed the shape of an airboat, and beyond it a police boat with spotlights on each end whose powerful beams illuminated the water and raked the shanty with their white glare.

Roan was there, holding his weapon on Frank and Muriel who stood exposed in the spotlight's brilliance with their hands above their heads. Farther out, other boats circled slowly, rocking in the water with their spotlights trained on the house and the men in them standing at the ready with rifles in their hands. It was the Benedict clan, she thought, the backcountry Benedicts who always came with balled fists and fire in their eyes when one of their number sent out a call.

Gladness bubbled up from deep inside her on a choke of laughter. Her voice half strangled, she cried, "You found me!"

"Sure, sweetheart," Luke drawled with bright eyes and bone-deep Benedict confidence. "Didn't I say I would?"

April had no answer for that just then. It was a little while later, after she had been lifted into the airboat and an ancient beach towel smelling strongly of insect repellent and fish draped around her, that she spoke in simple wonder. "How? How did you ever manage it?"

"Process of elimination," Luke said, turning his attention to her from where he'd been keeping a close eye on Roan and the others as they disarmed Frank and Muriel.

"Meaning?"

"Frank almost had to be in on it. Regardless of spotter aircraft, it took someone who knew the lake to locate us. Roan checked out his trailer but he wasn't around. He got on to Clay—our limo driver who's the nature photographer, you know? Clay remembered that Frank had joined the hunting club that uses this place. There were several other possibilities, though, so I called in the clan to check them out. We settled on here when we saw the smoke from the stovepipe."

"I can see that must have taken a while."

"Actually, we pinpointed this place early this morning, but were afraid to storm it for fear of what might happen to you. The idea was for me to come in nice and quiet after midnight, to check the situation and find a way to get you out. That plan was scrapped the minute the shooting started."

"I—wasn't sure I could afford to wait."

He smiled at that. "You did fine. I guess you really didn't need us."

"Don't say that! I'd gone about as far as I could go." He meant that she hadn't needed him, she thought, and that wasn't true at all. She put her hand on his chest, willing him to believe her. Her fingers touched a familiar thickness under his T-shirt that wasn't warm flesh. In quick concern, she said, "You were really hurt. I was so afraid—how did you get to town?"

"The pontoon boat is equipped with a radio distress signal, and I had Roan primed to monitor it. He zipped out to pick me up."

"Because it would have taken too long to cut the

pontoon boat free of its camouflage and drive it in yourself. And I suppose the hole in you was just a scratch.'' The censure in her voice came from caring, but she wasn't sure he knew that.

"More or less," he said with the lift of a shoulder, "but it needed patching before I could get into gear."

"And now you've doused it in the lake. You'll be lucky if it doesn't get infected."

He rested his fingertips on her thigh where a long red weal stood out against her light tan. "Since you've got more cuts and scratches than the law allows, I could say the same about you."

"Yes, well," she said, looking past his shoulder, "I had to get away from Muriel. She wasn't—isn't really..."

"Sane?" he suggested, his voice grim.

"I suppose. What will happen to her, do you think?"

"Nothing good. Roan and Kane will see to that. As for Frank, that's another story."

"I don't think his heart was in this, not really. He's a marksman and a hunter. He should have killed me a couple of times but didn't."

"You can put in a good word for him," Luke said evenly, "if that's what you want."

She looked down at her hands where she clutched the edge of the towel. "I don't know. I feel sorry for him, in spite of everything. He's lived a long time with what he did to Mary Ellen. He'll never escape it any more than she could."

"No," Luke answered as he looked away.

April discovered that she would rather Luke

didn't spend too much time brooding over Mary Ellen. It was not a nice feeling to realize that she could
be jealous of a girl long dead. She said abruptly,
"Muriel wanted my book, wanted to publish it as
hers. I burned it."

"The story about the Benedict family?" he asked
with a quick frown. Then his features cleared. "You
still have it on your computer hard drive at Mulberry Point. You can always print it again."

She shook her head. "I don't think I want to."

"But you worked so hard on it."

It felt good to know that he realized the labor that
went into it. "I know, but it doesn't feel right any
more. Besides, I have another idea. What do you
think about a series of books with Southern gentlemen heroes, wonderful backcountry men who all
live in wonderful old houses that sit on a lake with
a swamp behind it, men who can do anything, and
will—for the right reason."

"April," he began.

"I think this may be something for a movie. I can
see it now. As the credits roll, some female soloist
will be singing the song about this guy always being
her hero. Wouldn't that be great?"

"Just great," he said deliberately.

"You don't like it?" she asked, her gaze innocent.

"Depends."

"On what?"

"Where you do your research. And who you do
it with."

She pursed her lips. "That last sentence wasn't
very grammatical."

"Neither is what I'm likely to say if you put too much about us in these books."

"Would I do that?" She gave him a long glance from under her lashes.

"In a heartbeat. You're not to be trusted."

She slid her fingertips higher up his chest, then circled his neck and clasped them behind it. "I don't know why not," she said in low sincerity. "I trust you."

He drew back a little to search her face, his own gaze dark. "Do you really?"

"Yes, I do," she answered. Then she took a deep breath before adding, "But I love you more. It may seem a little strange, but I've loved you a lot longer."

"April, you..." He stopped, then began again. "You wouldn't say that just because you..."

She lifted a brow. "What? Feel like rewarding you because you found me so—heroically?"

"Something like that."

His gaze was vulnerable; she saw that clearly. She also saw something else, that he needed to be told in words just how she felt. With a slow smile, she said, "I might. Because you are my hero, you know. You always have been, and always will be."

"I'm just a man with all kinds of faults and failures. You don't want to go making the mistake of thinking I'm some kind of fantasy man."

"Oh, I don't think I'll do that," she said with a slow shake of her head. "Fantasy is fine, lovely in fact, but I'm no more likely to mistake you for that kind of hero than the women who read my books mistake the fantasy adventures I write for real life.

I want you, the man who fries fish for me and brings water so I can take a bath. The one who makes me laugh and tries so hard to keep quiet so I can write that he drives me nuts. I want the man who lets himself be eaten alive by mosquitoes so I can have the best bed, and who—''

''I get the picture,'' he said gruffly.

''Yes, but do you like it?''

''I love it,'' he answered as he pulled her close. ''Just as I love you, *love* you, and have all these long, damned years when I thought I'd never hold you or have you or hear you say my name or see you smile at me, just for me. All I want is to love you and keep you safe and do all the things that will make you happy to be with me....''

She caught his strong face in her hands and kissed him. She did it in part to stop the flow of words that had such echoes of pain and loneliness behind them, but also because she couldn't stand not to have that close contact, the nearest thing to blending that she could manage in such a public place.

It was some moments later that she noticed something soft rubbing her ankle, something that had nothing to do with the man who held her unless he'd developed a third hand. At the same time, she heard a plaintive sound, a soft mewling that hadn't, surely, come from her own throat. Releasing herself reluctantly, she glanced down at her feet.

''Midnight!'' she cried in quiet wonder. ''Oh, Luke, you brought him with you. I can't believe it.''

''I didn't bring him. The damned cat brought himself.''

''I'm sure,'' she said with a dry look as she

reached to smooth her hand over her pet's head and down his back.

Midnight accepted her caress as his due, preening under it for a moment, rubbing his chin along her hand. Then he ducked away and leaped to her lap. He didn't pause, but clambered up to Luke's shoulder where he coiled around his neck and licked a drop of water that was clinging to his ear.

April made a sound between laughter and amazement. "Well, of all the — you've stolen my cat!"

"No way." Luke winced away from the cat's rough tongue at his ear lobe, but made no effort to dislodge Midnight.

"I guess you know this means you have to take both of us?"

Luke paused, gave her a steady look. "Really?"

She nodded while brightness shone in her eyes.

"Okay," he said, "I guess I can handle that. You probably won't eat much more than a cat."

"I meant the cat comes with me, not the other way around!" she said, bumping his forehead with her own by way of punishment.

His smile was slow and easy and a glory to see. "I know," he said in rich promise. "And I think it just may work out if you'll lick my other ear."

"If I'll *what?*"

"You heard me," he said, and lifted a brow.

She tilted her head and lowered her lashes. "Careful, or you might start more than you can finish."

"Oh," Luke said, grinning as he pulled both cat and woman close, "I doubt there's much danger of that."

___Author Note___

In keeping with a tradition begun in the first book of the Turn-Coupe series, *Kane,* included below is a recipe for the red beans and rice dish mentioned in *Luke.* This old Cajun favorite was often served on Monday, or wash day, since it could be quickly thrown together and left to simmer without close attention.

The version given is the one I use, though there are as many recipes for red beans and rice as there are cooks in Louisiana. What usually happens is that the contents are adjusted according to the likes and dislikes of the family or to the ingredients in the cook's kitchen. If you'd like to cook Louisiana style, just take this recipe as a starting point and add your own touch!

Red Beans & Rice

1 lb red kidney beans
1 lb smoked ham, cubed
2 cloves garlic, minced
1 tsp Italian seasoning
1 medium bell pepper, chopped
1 medium onion, chopped

1 stalk celery, chopped
1 small, whole hot pepper, minced
(or ¹/₄ cup red pepper)

Wash beans and place in a heavy, 4 qt sauce pot. Add ham and cover with water. Add garlic, bell pepper, onion, celery, hot pepper, and Italian seasoning. Simmer 3 to 4 hours, until beans are tender and bean soup is thick. Adjust salt to taste. Add an extra pinch of Italian seasoning, and serve immediately over cooked rice.

Many cooks in Louisiana use the electric Hitachi rice pot to cook their long grain rice for this and other rice dishes. I've used one for years, but recently began to steam my rice, Chinese style, in an electric steamer. Regardless of how you go about it, the idea is to produce tender rice with every grain separate. The cooking method used by old-fashioned cooks like Granny May is:

Cajun Rice

4 cups water
2 cups rice
1 tsp salt
1 tbsp butter

In a heavy sauce pot with a tightly-fitting lid, bring water to a rolling boil. Add rice, salt and butter. Stir quickly with a fork, and place lid on pot. Simmer on low heat for 30 minutes *without removing the lid*. Fluff with a fork. Let sit, covered, until ready to serve.

I hope you enjoy this taste of my home state, and *Luke*.

Warmest regards,

Jennifer Blake
http://www.jenniferblake.com